SNOWBOUND IN HIS BILLION-DOLLAR BED

KALI ANTHONY

DESERT PRINCE'S DEFIANT BRIDE

JULIEANNE HOWELLS

This book is produced from independently certified FSC™ paper
to ensure responsible forest management.

For more information visit www.harpercollins.co.uk/green

MILLS & BOON

First Published in Great Britain 2022
by Mills & Boon, an imprint of HarperCollins*Publishers* Ltd,
1 London Bridge Street, London, SE1 9GF

www.harpercollins.co.uk

HarperCollins*Publishers*
1st Floor, Watermarque Building,
Ringsend Road, Dublin 4, Ireland

Snowbound in His Billion-Dollar Bed © 2022 Kali Anthony

Desert Prince's Defiant Bride © 2022 Julieanne Howells

ISBN: 978-0-263-30068-0

SNOWBOUND IN HIS BILLION-DOLLAR BED

KALI ANTHONY

MILLS & BOON

To my darling aunt and godmother Joanie,
who gave me my first craft book on writing romance
and told me to follow my dreams.
They really did come true.

CHAPTER ONE

'You don't know what you're talking about, Moretti.'

The man on the other end of the phone sounded full of bravado, but it was all an act. Stefano was conscious of every nuance in the voice. The heightened tone, the subtle tremor. And it was right that this worthless member of Lasserno's upper echelons should worry. Yet another thief of the country's treasures Stefano was intent on rooting out.

He settled back into the antique leather chair, which creaked underneath him. They all started out like this—with denial. And so far they'd all told the truth in the end. Liars. Every one of them. All about to fall from grace with a thud unless they gave him what he wanted.

He knew all about falls from grace. The landing was an uncompromising one. Stefano Moretti, Count of Varno, former private secretary to Lasserno's Prince Alessio Arcuri, had died on a hill of good intentions months ago. What had risen from those ashes was a man with a coal-dark heart, harder than black diamonds.

'My proper title is *Your Excellency*, but I'll ignore the slight.'

It reminded Stefano that word of his fall was now more than a speculative whisper. Those who'd sought to cut him down were emboldened.

He let out a long, steadying breath. There was no time

for this introspection. He had a job to do. Self-appointed, but an important role nonetheless. One that would protect his siblings, even though he might never be forgiven and would certainly never forgive himself for what he'd done.

Betrayal had no sweetener. Secretly reporting your monarch's private movements to the press tended to be a deal-breaker—particularly when you were said monarch's private secretary, most trusted confidant and best friend.

It didn't matter that his motives had been altruistic. The press had been grossly unfair to Alessio when he'd taken the throne after his father's abdication. It had caused fear and instability in Lasserno, which had already been suffering from the former Prince's excesses. All Stefano had suggested was using the press for good as success- fully as Alessio's father had done for nefarious means. When Alessio had shunned the idea Stefano had taken matters into his own hands. Leaks about Alessio's pri- vate visit to Lasserno's Children's Hospital had been care- fully dropped.

But what Stefano hadn't figured on was losing con- trol of the beast. The press hadn't been satisfied with the scant crumbs he'd scattered for them and had scrabbled for more.

As good as his motives had been, he'd faced up to the consequences. Alessio had almost lost Hannah, his one- time portrait artist and now beloved Princess, because of Stefano's actions. It had ended well, with a marriage during Stefano's exile and a little prince or princess on the way soon. But, whilst there didn't appear to be any long-term harm, he accepted the need to pay a penance, possibly for as long as he lived...

'Let me refresh your memory on what I'm after.' Ste- fano stopped trying for a conciliatory tone and injected every shred of contempt he could find into each word. 'A diamond. Ten carats. Formerly from the Arcuri parure. Does that sound familiar? I've no doubt you'll remember, since Signor Giannotti reports that someone of your *exact* description tried selling it to him a week ago. As questionable as that man's honesty might be, he knows his gems. When he realised the stone came from the Crown Jewels, he called me immediately.'

Silence.

They all fell silent when they realised how far his reach still went. He had eyes everywhere and he wouldn't fail in this mission. His brother and sister relied on his success.

The Moretti family was inextricably linked to the Crown—a centuries-old obligation. One he'd blighted by his actions. He didn't want his siblings shackled to that now poisoned chalice. They should be able to leave Lasserno and find their own future. He'd promised them that freedom and he wouldn't deviate. Because his fall from grace could not stay secret indefinitely, and the country would see them as guilty by association. Already the rumours had reached their ears, impacting on their prospects. They'd reported being snubbed by some. Now he'd completed his degree in horticulture, Gino's employer was taking too long to provide a letter of endorsement to assure an introduction at Kew, where his brother dreamed of a role. Emilia's final months in teaching and early childhood seemed to be mired in an inordinate amount of paperwork, with no-one having the inclination to finalise it so she could take up a hoped-for placement overseas.

When his job was complete, he'd ask for his siblings to be released from the link to the royal family which would always hold him. Then they could do as they wished—he wouldn't allow his taint to spread over them like a slick of oil. He'd redeem the Moretti family name for their sakes. Stefano considered himself irredeemable.

'You think you're so clever,' rasped the disembodied voice on the other end of the line, 'but no one believes the palace's fairy-tale that you're on a sabbatical to restore your family castle.'

This was the official version. An innocuous press release to explain why Stefano was no longer seen in his role as Alessio's private secretary, when once he had always been at the Prince's side. A final act of grace from his former best friend and employer.

It was more than Stefano deserved for his betrayal.

'I don't care what people believe,' he said with disdain, when all he wanted to do was rage.

Stefano quelled that desire, doused the burn threatening to ignite and roar into life inside him. *Patience.* This was only the first part of his plan to free his siblings. He wouldn't be distracted from the task of recovering the precious gems Alessio's father had given away like meaningless trinkets in the months before his abdication.

His second task, however, was proving far more difficult. Some might say unachievable…

'The many artisans clamouring to work on Castello Varno's restoration would say otherwise.'

Often the biggest lies were hidden behind small truths.

His work for Alessio had kept him in the capital, and his siblings hadn't paid much attention to the state of the castle. Gino and Emilia were tangled up in their own dreams of the future he'd promised them when he'd taken on the role of their protector as a teenager, since his parents had had little interest in the younger children.

Even though they knew he would always take their calls, his brother had thought him far too busy to worry about some stones crumbling from the ramparts in the unused reaches of their home. Likewise, his sister hadn't thought about the maintenance of the central heating, which seemed irrelevant in a mild summer, but critical when winter arrived in force.

Perhaps he should have shared with them what it truly took to run the castle. Being head of the family since his father's death four years earlier, he viewed their ancestral home as his personal responsibility. And, whilst he might have disgraced the Moretti name, he would not let the castle which had dominated the mountains of this northern province of Lasserno for five hundred years fall into ruin. He was still the Count, even if he no longer deserved the title.

'A pretty little bird tells me you have your own problems,' the other man said, as if trying to regain some of the ground rapidly sliding away from him.

The words found their mark, straight and true.

Stefano shut his eyes. *Celine.* What was one more arrow of pain embedded in his heart when he'd already taken so many? She must be the one to have started the rumours because Alessio would say nothing, of that Stefano had no doubt.

When he'd taken the honourable route and resigned from his position, he'd believed Celine would understand. They'd been together for five years, engaged for three, and were planning a future—a dynastic marriage of their own.

A member of Lasserno's aristocracy, Celine had professed her love for him soon after they'd begun dating. Smiled with apparent joy when he'd proposed. They'd planned to wed after Alessio was crowned... Yet their break-up had followed fast on the heels of Stefano's resignation and return to Varno. He couldn't forget her final words, now a poisonous and constant voice in his ear.

'You're nothing, Stefano, if you're not working for the Prince.'

All those years she'd whispered that he was better than the role of private secretary. That he should ask Alessio for something of greater prestige, as if his centuries-old title as the Count of Varno wasn't enough. He hadn't cared at the time, since helping his friend navigate the abdication and the financial mire into which his father had plunged Lasserno had been vital work.

Yet Celine had been right. The moment he stood on unstable ground the vultures had circled, fighting to fill the void with their refusal to take his phone calls, their quiet disdain not only of him but of his brother and sister, who didn't deserve similar contempt.

The brutal ache of realisation burrowed deep. One of the few people he'd thought he could trust had not kept his devastating secret. But, as he well knew, information was currency, and news of his downfall would be more fodder for the aristocratic rumour mill. Celine was only protecting herself from being tarnished by association, making herself queen of the gossip circle at his expense. Anyhow, he had no cause to expect anything else, since he'd betrayed his best friend. In that act he'd shown that no one could really be trusted—most of all himself.

Celine had been right to walk away on her towering heels, without a backward glance. He was not worthy of forgiveness. Disgraced. Untrustworthy. What good was he to anyone now? She'd made that brutally clear. In those final moments of their relationship any hope and all expectation of how his life would play out in front of him had withered and died.

Stefano gripped his phone till the edges cut into his fingers. Whilst his problems were entirely self-inflicted, he didn't have to lie down and allow himself to be kicked.

'You shouldn't listen to pretty little birds. They may sing a lovely song, but all they're doing is distracting you from the raptor in the clouds above. I sharpen my talons each night. Don't think you'll escape my grip when I clasp you tight.'

When he was successful, his mission would allow him to walk into the royal palace with his head held high, rather than slither back on his belly like the snake he'd become. He had nothing left to him but the merest splinter of pride, and he would *not* lose that as well.

'You have no evidence bar the words of a known criminal.'

'I have CCTV,' Stefano replied. 'I have Signor Giannotti's signed statement. I have enough.'

A choking kind of sound was all that came down the line, followed by a few more moments of silence.

'His Highness *gave* it to me.'

Ah. The whining. Lies first…bargaining second. The pattern was familiar and sickening. Anger tended to come third, and Stefano was spoiling for a fight.

'The former Prince may have given it to you. The current Prince wants it back. You had no right to keep it. That diamond is the country's, not yours.'

Which wasn't entirely true. Being the principality's absolute monarch meant the Prince or Princess could do anything they pleased.

Cold like a block of glacial ice settled in Stefano's gut. So long as Gino and Emilia were protected, he would take whatever came his way. He tried not to think of what his future might hold…of the unopened letters in his desk from the palace and the calls he'd ignored. Not yet. Because they signalled nothing good. His attentions must be fixed on the task at hand. He wanted no more pleading. Weasel words sickened him. People should own their actions and make reparation before seeking forgiveness. Nothing else was acceptable.

'Here's what will happen,' he said. 'You'll return the diamond to the palace and all will be forgiven.'

Stefano was in no place to make that promise, but so be it. He didn't care so long as it got him what he wanted.

'If you don't, I will storm down upon you like an avalanche from the mountains and you *will* be crushed in my wake. Nothing will remain, I promise you.'

'It…it may take some time.'

There it was. The capitulation. These people were weak. If you stripped the meat from all of them you'd barely have enough bones to make one spine. At least his family's centuries-old role as Shield of the Crown was still good for something other than the burden it imposed. He should have made more of it. Fought Alessio for what he believed was right rather than let it go and make the fateful decision to go to the press.

But he could indulge in disgust at his personal failings sometime later, when this job was done.

'Since I'm a generous man, I'll give you two days. Only remember. My eyes are everywhere. There is not a jeweller, pawnbroker, thief or fence in Europe who doesn't know about the missing stones and all are looking for them at my request. Two days.'

He disconnected. Tossed his mobile on the desk, where it landed with a clatter on the burnished wood. Talking to these thieves and fools left him in need of a shower. He might be soiled by his personal actions, but he'd never be as grubby as them, stealing the nation's heritage.

Stefano stood and walked to the window, staring out at the last of the melting snow. Spring was overdue, and winter not keen to relinquish her grip this year. Luckily he'd sent any remaining staff back to their homes a few days earlier, with the weather reports and a glowering sky hinting that more snow was on its way. The castle's aged heating, not coping of late, left most of the building's rooms with an unforgiving chill. There was no point in his staff being trapped in the cold too.

They'd worried about him, being alone here, but he'd only opened few rooms since his return, and he'd assured them he was perfectly capable of looking after himself.

Anyhow, it didn't matter if the unseasonal mountain weather cut him off from the rest of Lasserno. He'd been cut off from the country ever since that fateful day he'd announced his betrayal to Alessio and handed in his resignation, returning to Castello Varno, where he hadn't set foot for three years. Still, though his current work wasn't officially sanctioned, he'd continue until he was done. Stefano wasn't about to allow his brother and sister to suffer any more for his sins.

Time spent gazing out of the window wouldn't solve those problems. Stefano returned to his well-worn chair, his computer. He glanced at the half-full bottle of grappa sitting on the desk in front of him. Many like it had kept him company over the long, cold winter here. A shot of that would keep him warm for the next few hours as he worked. He grabbed a glass. Poured a solid measure into it. He took a hefty gulp which wouldn't have done justice to a finer blend, but this local version was more moonshine than anything else.

The burn of it heated him from the inside out, fortifying him for the long night of work ahead. Stefano needed to spend some time on the second part of his plan to ensure that his brother and sister were protected. An almost impossible task, yet one which would yield the greatest reward for his siblings.

'If you can find the Heart of Lasserno I'll give you anything you want.'

A promise from a prince to a friend.

Back then, with an arrogance which should have sounded a warning of his future failings, Stefano had joked about being made Prime Minister. He and Alessio had both been younger and less world-weary then, trying to make their mark. What better way than finding the Heart of Lasserno—their country's coronation ring— lost since it had been handed over to a foreign soldier for protection in the desperate dying days of World War II?

If he recovered the jewels, and if he found the ring, it would cement his position once more. He'd be able to walk back into the palace, his family's reputation safe and assured, and respond to whatever command his monarch might make with some pride left.

But there he'd hit a wall built by time.

Stefano opened the document his investigator had

emailed to him. Read it. No matter how much money he burned trying to find that Australian soldier, all he had was an unlikely amalgam of a name. Art Cacciatore. A man who'd ceased to exist—if he'd ever existed at all.

Stefano glanced at the half-empty glass on his desk. Tempting as it was to drown his sorrows, now was a time for work. He'd drink the castle's cellar dry in celebration when his job was done.

The investigator's report held no further joy for him so he left his desk. Approached an armchair near the fire crackling in a marble fireplace, readying himself for the seemingly endless chore of trawling through dusty boxes of family records for any useful information. The weight of the task, the exhaustion, the self-recrimination—all threatened to crush him. But this was not about his feelings. He wasn't in the practice of granting sympathy for self-inflicted wounds.

As he sat down, a distant chime rang out. The doorbell? Perhaps the local village mechanic and handyman, Bruno, had finally decided to risk the weather and come to assess the castle's heating, as he'd promised to do for the past week.

Stefano rose and left his office, rubbing his arms against the bracing temperature away from the fire. He made his way to the entrance hall past rooms shut down when his mother had left to live in an apartment in Lasserno's capital after his father had died. The whole place looked as unlived-in as it had since he'd returned here all those months ago in self-imposed exile.

The bell chimed again. Loud, strident this time, as if someone had leaned on it.

'Sí, sí. Sto arrivando!'

He reached the entrance foyer, undid the ancient locks, which groaned in icy protest, and hauled the front door open to a blast of frigid air.

Not Bruno.

On the steps stood a woman doing her best to mimic a pale blue meringue in an oversized puffy jacket, zipped up high. A thick scarf wound round her neck, covering her chin. On her head was jammed a woollen hat, replete with polar bear patterns and pom-poms. Strands of golden hair had escaped from its confines, drifting round her face. Even though she was wrapped up tight against the icy breeze her cheeks had taken on a windblown pink and her nose glowed a cute rose-red. She gripped a solid-looking rectangular case in one gloved hand, and the rickety handle of a battered wheelie bag in another.

A traveller. Who now offered him a faltering smile from her generously proportioned mouth which lit the whole of her and turned 'ordinary' into something luminous.

A distraction.

He would have no distractions—not here. No angelic visions with pale skin, honey eyes and cherry lips. Whilst other castles in Europe were open to the public, his family had resolutely refused to share this most private of spaces. Barely any photographs of the treasures here existed in the public domain. Once he'd thought it a waste. Now he saw it as a blessing—one which he would not have disturbed.

'Niente turisti,' he said, perhaps a little emphatically.

Those honey eyes widened and she took a step back, her mouth opening in a perfectly drawn *O* accompanied by what sounded like a squeak…like a little mouse in his doorway. Except her eyes were not the eyes of a mouse. They flashed tiger-gold.

'C-Count Moretti? Your Excellency? I don't speak Italian. *Non parlo It—*'

'No tourists,' he repeated, in English now, given his initial oversight. The words rasped out of him and he cleared his throat. It had been so long he'd almost forgotten how to engage in polite conversation. Not that he felt particularly polite in this moment. The internet and guidebooks, if anyone still used them, were quite clear. 'The castle does not take tourists.'

Her shoulders drooped, and then she seemed to collect herself. Straightened. 'I'm not a tourist. I'm Lucille Jamieson.'

She said the words in a broad accent that was neither English nor North American, as if she had every expectation that he knew who she was.

'You're not from here.'

'No, I'm Australian. But—'

'Then you *are* a tourist and you have travelled a long way for nothing.'

'I'm working in Salzburg right now, so only about fourteen hours' drive away, and—'

'Not from Lasserno—ergo, a tourist.'

He crossed his arms. Her golden gaze followed the move and a pleasant warmth seemed to glow in his chest, a balm against the cold outside. Clearly the grappa was finally doing its job. He might even be able to remove his sweater soon.

He ran his finger around the neck. Its wool was suddenly overheating him, even in the bitter breeze.

The woman—*Lucille*—bit into her plump bottom lip. That warm glow inside him ignited and caught fire. Those perfect white teeth were torturing her delicate flesh. He saw how it blanched a pale rose, then flushed into something darker. It must sting, what she was doing... How he'd like to soothe it for her...

'I sent a letter. Since you don't have a public email... which is very old school and kind of like my grandfather was...but I suppose you do live in a castle.'

His head spun at the tumble of words spilling from her unchecked, but he understood one of them loud and clear. Had she said he was like her *grandfather*? Something about that comparison punctured an ego he hadn't realised he still possessed. Stefano couldn't understand the sensation at all. She looked young and, sure, at thirty-one he might be a little bit older. But why did it matter to him?

He didn't dwell on it. She wouldn't be here long enough for him to need to, or care.

'I have received no letter, Signorina Jamieson.' Though a small stack of mail, including some official and ignored pieces of correspondence from the palace, *did* sit in a drawer of his desk. He was waiting for an opportune time to open them, because pieces of correspondence like that never contained good news... 'You must leave. There's a *pensione* in the village where you can stay.'

A flurry of snow fell behind her, soft and white. The narrow roads here would soon become treacherous for anyone inexperienced in driving on them.

He'd loved snow as a child, until he'd realised the danger when you didn't pay careful attention. If he hadn't found Emilia that dark night long ago, when she'd run away to catch a last glimpse of their mother in her fairytale gown on the way to yet another ball, he'd have lost his younger sister for ever...

That was the moment he decided that if his parents weren't going to care for his siblings, he had to.

'I'm booked in there, but there's been some mix-up and they aren't ready for me. The owner told me to go sightseeing for a while, and drive towards the castle since they knew I was looking to come here...eventually.'

Her mouth began to tremble now, but her eyes remained clear and warm. No hint of tears. He'd know if there were. Celine had given him enough whenever she hadn't got her own way for him to recognise the early signs. Signorina Jamieson's shoulders had slumped again, like a plant wilting for lack of water. Then her gaze drifted behind him with a look almost like pain. Her eyes wide with longing.

'Please. M-my car b-broke down. I've w-walked a l-long way and it's s-started s-snowing.'

Her teeth were chattering. This woman, Lucille Jamieson, was cold, and he knew how dangerous hypothermia was if it set in. He gritted his teeth, a curdle of dissatisfaction stewing in his gut. No matter how little he wanted this stranger in his home, he couldn't send her away with no transport. He had no choice.

Stefano stepped back and gestured behind him, beckoning her in. 'The broken-down car should have been where you *started* our conversation.'

She stood seemingly frozen on the doorstep, framed as a bright, vibrant splash against the grey and white world behind her. Her eyes widened, her gaze slowly tracking down his body. All of him tightened at her thorough perusal.

'Y-you confuse me,' she said.

'There is no confusing my invitation. Come in.'

The inertia that had gripped her slowly lifted and she half wheeled, half dragged her bag over the threshold. She hadn't moved far when it listed to one side and the wheel fell off with an undignified clatter on the mosaic floor. She looked at it, and let out a noise almost like a whimper.

That small, defeated sound tugged at something inside of him he'd thought long dead. A shred of empathy.

He sighed. Reached out his hand. 'Let me take that.'

Then at least he could get her in front of the fire and start to thaw her out. Her lips had taken on an alarming bluish tinge, almost the same frigid colour of her travesty of a jacket. Not that he had been staring at her lips again. It was normal concern, that was all.

In response, she dropped the handle of the wheelie bag, but clutched the other case tight to her body as if it held the Crown Jewels. 'Thank you. I'll carry this one.'

He shrugged, shut the door on the rapidly plummeting temperature behind them and grabbed her bulging suitcase. Whilst he considered himself strong enough—he was spending more time than usual in his gym of late, when he couldn't sleep—even he could tell this luggage required an excess baggage warning.

'*Dio*, what do you keep in here?'

'Oh, you know...' She shrugged. Her windblown cheeks darkened, her gaze darting around the space. 'Crucifix. Garlic. Wooden stakes.'

Stefano tensed. He dropped the bag back to the floor, where it landed with an impressive thud. 'You're carrying *what*?'

She gave a trilling kind of laugh which sounded as musical as it did nervous.

Who *was* this woman? Someone who wrote him letters and drove to his castle in an impending snowstorm. He might almost be concerned, except standing here, in this vast entrance hall, Lucille Jamieson didn't appear to pose any threat. She simply looked sad and somehow...*crushed*.

He was overcome by the inexplicable need to hunt down and conquer whatever had wounded her.

'Look, I've driven a long number of hours straight to get here. Now I'm in a creepy castle with a man who's a count. Tell me this doesn't sound *exactly* like a horror movie.'

'You were making a joke. Of course.' Stefano relaxed a fraction. After a few days alone his imagination seemed to be running as wild as hers. 'But the castle is not *creepy*.'

He took umbrage at the assertion. *Uncompromising* might be one description. *Imposing* an even better word.

Signorina Jamieson's gaze darted around the expansive entrance hall, with its forbidding paintings of former Counts covering the walls.

'Those pictures are all of judgemental-looking people wearing black. I'd describe the vibe as...*funereal*.' Her voice was almost a whisper, and she bit into her lip again, which thankfully had some colour returning to it.

'My father said it was a statement of intent to any who entered.'

'Well, it doesn't exactly scream *warm welcome*.'

Her eyes were big and wide. Every part of her appeared stiff and tense, especially the way she still clutched her remaining case to her, as if in self-protection.

'I can't promise there aren't more pictures of my disapproving ancestors throughout my home, but I *can* promise I'm no creature of the night. You're welcome here.' The lie about her being welcome slipped easily enough from his tongue. He had no desire to terrify a stranded woman. 'Please follow me.'

'Thank you.'

'*Prego.* Lasserno's hospitality is renowned. I intend to uphold those traditions.'

Now he needed to make a decent attempt at showing her some of the hospitality he professed to have. Stefano headed through the entrance hall towards the living area. The heated prickling at the back of his neck told him the woman was close on his heels.

After a few minutes of walking through the cold, deserted halls, he opened the door to a room which had been the playroom of his childhood. When Stefano had relocated from the capital and begun full-time residence at the castle, he'd taken over the space and moved some of the more comfortable furniture inside. The memories here, at least, were fond ones. Of spending time with his siblings even though they'd been younger and at the time it had seemed like an imposition, being left to care for them with a neglectful nanny.

The rest of the castle was meant as a showcase for his family's might and power in the province of Varno. Designed to impress, inspire awe. In this room, where he'd spent so much of his time, he always felt as if he'd come home.

He deposited Signorina Jamieson's weighty bag inside the door, walked to the fire and carefully placed more fuel on the low-burning coals. Prodded it until the flames blazed brighter.

The woman in question stood at the entrance to the room as if she was taking it all in, then she raked off her hat. A spill of strawberry blonde tresses fell about her shoulders, unruly and golden. She looked as if she'd recently been tumbled into bed with her mussed-up hair and her rosy cheeks...

But his role here was not harbouring illicit thoughts about stray tourists. And it didn't seem she had similar opinions about him. She didn't pay much attention to him at all, instead hesitating, then looking down at her mud-splattered footwear.

A frown crinkled her brow. 'I'm sorry. My boots really are a mess. I should have taken them off.'

Everything about her seemed uncertain. Tentative. Even her comments about spooky castles and counts and horror movies. Was she afraid? He'd never frightened a woman—ever. On the contrary, once he'd known how to be gentle and kind. How to exhibit care. His official designation—Shield of the Crown—meant he was a protector. As little as he wanted her here, that instinct was ingrained. He'd try to put her at ease until he could safely have her collected and returned to the village.

'There's no need for an apology. You can take off your boots in a moment. Please sit.'

The way she swayed on her feet made him believe she might fall over, and he had no desire to catch a swooning female. To clasp that soft, curved weight in his arms. To feel the way her head might nestle in the crook of his shoulder, her breath feathering his neck as he carried her to the couch...

No. They were things he wished to avoid, even though the thought made him delectably warm. Or perhaps it was merely the fire. That must be it, since he was still crouched close, tending the flames.

She finally made her way to the couch nearest to the fireplace, resting the black case she still held gently beside her, settling it into the cushions, ensuring it was steady. Then she tugged at her laces and kicked off her boots. Her feet were encased in woolly blue socks with a polar bear pattern that matched her hat. She pointed her toes in the direction of the fire and wiggled them.

Then she pulled the gloves from her hands, exposing slender fingers, and flexed them, before digging the thumb of her right hand deep into her left palm. Something about her seemed too fragile and soft. A strange contrast in this place where the past months had been all too hard. He wondered what had brought her here…what made her seem as if a part of her carried a mortal wound.

Stefano grabbed the fluffy blanket that his housekeeper had insisted would add an ambience to the room, for reasons which he found inexplicable, and held it out to her.

She took it and wrapped it round herself. 'Why is it still so cold in here?'

'The heating's been unpredictable. I'm waiting for Bruno, the local mechanic, to come and repair it.'

'He's the man I was talking to at the *pensione*. Who suggested that I come here.'

Of that, Stefano had no doubt. Bruno's wife ran the *pensione*. Bruno would have thought it a great joke, sending someone Stefano's way. Especially a young tourist who claimed not to be a tourist.

She leaned forward again, stretching her hands towards the fire now. He couldn't help but witness the small tremor running through her fingers.

'Ugh, I hate winter.'

Stefano had an intense desire to apologise, as if he were personally responsible for Lasserno's unseasonal cold snap. He ignored it. 'I'll call Bruno and ask him to tow your car. Come and collect you and return you to the *pensione*.'

'The car's a rental.' She stared into the crackling fire, the light of it flickering golden across her pale face. 'I guess I need to talk to the company.'

'If you give me their name, Bruno will deal with them. If they give him any problems, they can deal with me.'

She withdrew her arms from in front of her and wrapped them round her waist, then turned to him and smiled. It was as if a hundred candles had been lit in the room, the brightness of her in this moment. The crinkles at the corners of her eyes. The way her beautiful mouth turned upwards, showing white teeth.

She was looking at him as if he were the solution to her every problem. But he was *not* that man. He never would be again. And yet the faith she showed in that fleeting, perfect moment made the blackened heart he'd thought had ceased to beat, stutter to life again.

'My grandfather was right about Lasserno's hospitality.'

'He travelled here?'

'That's what I tried to say in my letter. He was a navigator in World War II, on the run after his plane came down. He crossed the border from Italy to Lasserno. I—I believe your family might have taken him in till he could get back to his squadron?'

Stefano stilled. It was as if with her earlier smile the universe might have smiled down on him as well. But it was then that he noticed how drawn she appeared. A bluish tint under her eyes giving them a bruised quality. He shouldn't press. He should give her a hot drink and food, in the greatest of Lasserno's traditions. But it was as if every solution to his problems might rest in this one exhausted traveller, and he needed answers now. They would inform his next move.

'What was his name?' Stefano tried not to appear too eager. 'We kept some records, but many were lost when the enemy occupied our castle. Our country tried neutrality and was still drawn in.'

'Arthur Hunter. His friends used to call him Art. Did your family ever mention him?'

'That isn't a name that immediately comes to mind.'

Hunter… Hunter… His great-grandfather had written of a man, never forgetting promises made of taking a precious treasure to safety through the underground as the enemy were beating down the castle's door.

Could it be this easy? Stefano didn't know of an Arthur Hunter, but the English translation of *cacciatore* was "hunter". In the war, with language barriers, perhaps he had been given a name which was easily understood. Or perhaps he'd used the name as a joke, trying to hide himself all along.

But one thing was certain. Lucille Jamieson would not be returning to the *pensione* in the village. No. She would be staying here until he had the answers he sought.

CHAPTER TWO

Lucy tried to get comfortable in the astonishing room, with its silk-lined walls, golden accents and frescoes on the ceiling. Even though the couch cushions were plush and deep, easy enough to sink into and never want to leave, it was hard to feel at ease with the Count of Varno… *looming.*

He was a man who looked as if he belonged in a gothic movie. Days-old stubble that on anyone else might have looked unkempt but on this man, added to his *film noir* appeal. He was tall, imposing, with a shock of thick black hair. Eyes so dark and piercing it was as if they had no pupils as he stared at her in an unblinking kind of way. *Glowered* at her, really. And, whilst she might have been frozen to the marrow, one look like that from him and she went up in flames.

When he'd first opened the door of this castle which rose ominously out of the mountainside, her instincts had told her to run. Slabs of gloomy grey stone… Turrets spearing from the solid base… Windows like the Count's dark judgemental eyes, piercing the sides of the structure.

But those instincts had let her down so poorly in recent months that she hadn't trusted them. So she'd kept on standing there, weak with exhaustion and the recognition that she was going nowhere on foot in the snow.

She liked to think she could be sensible about some

things, even if the thought of walking into a castle that really did look like it belonged in a horror film had filled her with dread. But the truth was she had nowhere else to go. Her life in Salzburg, imploding. Australia, no haven either. Lasserno held answers to questions she didn't want to ask, but was being forced to, nonetheless.

Her grandfather had filled her head with stories of the kindness of the country's people to him during the war. It was a place he'd been over three-quarters of a century before and had never forgotten, although in his final days his memories had been fractured and consumed with guilt. He'd become obsessed by his culpability for some unnamed sin, which had been upsetting to both her and her mother, trying to comfort him without knowing the reason for his distress.

Still, she hoped his fond recollections of Lasserno had meant something, as all she craved right now was a bit of kindness. It was why she'd thrown everything she could fit into a single suitcase, turned her back on her life, and fled.

She closed her eyes, trying to shut out the thoughts that filled her head of those last days in Austria. Walking into her flat a little earlier than normal, finding her boyfriend, Viktor—

'My apologies, Signorina Jamieson. You've travelled a long way and must be tired.'

That voice of his stroked over her skin, all midnight and black velvet. She shivered—and not from the cold. All she wanted to do was lean back in the seat and listen to him speak. Bask in the rich allure of his voice and let it wash over her like water from a hot bath. But, as tempting as that seemed, it was all just fantasy, at a time when she'd been forced to swallow a hefty dose of reality.

Sadly, reality was overrated.

She opened her eyes again.

'Thank you, Count Moretti. Or is it Your Excellency?

I tried researching the correct form of address on the internet and I don't want to get it wrong.'

'There is no need for titles, *signorina*. Please call me Stefano.'

'Oh… Okay… And you can call me Lucy.'

Calling him by his first name seemed too intimate—as if some essential barrier between them had become shaky, turning into a kind of crumbling foundation that she really wanted to shore up with every bit of scaffolding she could find. But demanding more formality would be rude, and she hoped that here, in this castle, she might get the answers she searched for. Because it was that quest which now kept her glued to the seat.

That, and exhaustion. She was pretty sure her legs wouldn't move now, after walking as far as she had uphill, since the rental car she could ill afford had given an undignified lurch, a bang, and promptly died.

The corner of the Count's mouth hitched in a kind of smile, and the panic that had been churning around her stomach settled into something less like a hive of bees and more like a kaleidoscope of butterflies.

'Lucy.'

Her name sounded wonderful when said by him. Special. Important in a way that had been lost to her years ago.

'What else did you research on the internet?'

She'd researched *him*. She wasn't a complete flake—even if this ill-fated and underprepared trip suggested otherwise. Any limited English language press showed Stefano Moretti in the background of photographs, behind Lasserno's Prince. Always looking sharp in dark sunglasses. More like a bodyguard than the private secretary those same press reports said was his job when he wasn't restoring his own castle.

The Count of Varno's official-looking website had plenty of information about his illustrious history and the Moretti family's proud links to the Crown, as if anything else about them was meaningless. The photograph of him there was a formal study in an exquisitely tailored suit. Tamed black hair. Shaved jaw sharp enough to cut glass. Undoubtedly a handsome man, yet the bland image was almost like a photo of a waxwork dummy.

This man in front of her was something more. Not restrained, perfectly pressed and two-dimensional, but bristling and alive, with the look of someone untamed. Almost feral.

A man she was now staring at, with the firelight flickering over his imposing form, making him appear like the king of the underworld, lording it over his minions...

But she really needed to stop these fevered kinds of fantasies. He was just a man. She was just a woman.

Somehow that realisation just made it worse.

And she still hadn't answered his question.

The Count of Varno—*Stefano*—raised one perfect black eyebrow. He stared at her cold and hard for a few moments and she wanted to blurt out all her secrets then and there. *Everything.*

But if she started it could take a while. A *long* while. She had no idea how he'd respond, given some of those secrets involved his family. Until she could figure out what his reaction might be, silence was her best friend.

'Oh, you know... Lasserno. The history of the Varno province.' *You.* But she didn't say that. She simply shrugged and hoped that covered the rest.

'I hope you will find Lasserno worthy of the visit.'

She hoped so too. Everything about her life lay in tatters around her. She needed answers—and they started in a family past she hadn't dwelled on much since her school days, when she'd had to write an essay on someone heroic and had written about her grandfather.

Lucy swallowed down the knot in her throat. Blinked away the sting in her eyes. She'd loved her granddad, and she missed him, wished she could ask him the truth about his history. But he'd passed away after a long life months earlier, and his death had left questions she had no answers to.

She wasn't sure now whether he was the hero she'd always thought him or the villain in a bigger tale. She hoped for the former, but the evidence suggested otherwise. It hurt almost worse than Viktor's betrayal, because Lucy was in desperate need of at least one man in her life to *stay* a good man when the rest had let her down.

'I'm sure your country will live up to its expectations.' Or at least she prayed it would.

Their eyes locked and somehow she forgot about the bone-deep cold that she'd thought would never leave her. Her cheating ex… The uncertainty of her position at work… How everything about her life that she'd thought solid had proved its foundation to be unstable…

There really was only her and him and the fire that cracked and popped in the huge marble fireplace beside her.

Then he blinked, broke the moment. Looked out of the window to the steady fall of snow outside. Whatever had passed between them was lost but she'd felt it—those fleeting seconds when all her focus had been on the present and not on what had gone before or might come next.

If only she could live in that blissful 'now' for ever. But her recent past was a mess and her impending future was bearing down on her with the terror and fury of a bear roaring out of the woods. She only hoped that she could put the broken pieces of her life back together.

'I'm forgetting myself,' he said, his voice a rough burr over her skin. 'Would you like a hot drink? Something to eat?'

'Please…' She'd eaten little in the past twenty-four hours, snatching food at service centres on the long drive from Salzburg to Lasserno. She really hadn't had the stomach for anything other than her escape.

'I've sent my staff back to their homes, given the snow warnings. And, whilst I can vouch for my beverage-making skills, the food will be simple.'

They were alone here? She tried not to think about it.

Surely he'd call the man in the village and get him to collect her? Then she'd arrange an appropriate time to talk—one when she'd look less waif and more like the capable woman she usually was, wearing the only nice dress she'd packed. Not muddy and unkempt…a damsel in distress needing rescue.

This was not the way her journey to the mountains of Lasserno was supposed to begin after she'd fled her home of the past twelve months. At twenty-four, she'd forged a career as one of the youngest orchestra leaders of the day. A girl from Down Under making it big as principal violinist in Europe… She should be proud of her achievements… But her life had unceremoniously unravelled before her and all she'd been able to do was watch in horror as it had careened out of control.

Yet again the sting of tears threatened. But these weren't tears of sadness—they were tears of anger. She blinked them away. There was no chance of her cheating jerk of an ex, Viktor, being granted any more tears. Not. A. Single. One. She couldn't have known that he'd also been spreading rumours to orchestra management about her niggling strain injury, which had led to the suggestion that she take some time away 'to consider her future'. Then her parents' relationship had finally fallen apart after one too many of her father's outrages. And now Lucy couldn't shake the sensation that every part of her life was a fraud.

No. Those thoughts weren't intruding again. The only fraud here was the travesty of the car she'd really not been able to afford to rent, so had found the cheapest option. Paying to keep her mother afloat after she'd finally left Lucy's dad, paying even more for solicitors so her father wouldn't steal everything her mother had built from her own career, had stripped Lucy financially. Lucy had become embroiled as well, with her father's solicitors saying the violin she played should form part of the financial pool in the wash-up of her parents' failed marriage. They'd claimed her mother had never given ownership of the centuries-old violin to Lucy, instead only loaning it to her.

And, to top it all off, she might be stuck here in a large, spooky castle with a man she didn't know. A man who still looked at her as if she was an unwelcome oddity dropped on his doorstep.

'I should ask… Do you have any likes, dislikes, allergies?'

That shred of thoughtfulness almost undid her. No one had thought of her much at all in the past months of what had turned into a bitter Austrian winter.

She shook her head. 'I don't eat brains or tripe.'

Stefano raised an eyebrow. She wanted to bury her head in her hands. She had no idea what caused her to ramble like this in front of him. It would be no surprise if he sent her back out into the snow.

Lucy tried to sound like someone who had control over her life and a working social filter. She even gave him what she hoped was a thankful smile. 'Whatever you have will be wonderful.'

He nodded and walked to the door. She could stare unabashed now at his broad shoulders, lovingly covered by the dark navy woollen sweater. At the glorious vee of his torso which spoke of consistent effort and strength. She really had no time for men with all the focus on her career. If asked, she'd say she was generally attracted to less hard-looking males, but in Stefano, Lucy was coming to realise the allure of testosterone-fuelled magnificence. Because 'magnificent' was the only adjective that really suited this man. He was almost dizzying with it.

The door shut behind him with the soft click of well-oiled hinges and she turned to the solid case beside her, designed to protect the precious contents within, which she always kept close.

Her violin.

She'd worried about it in the rapidly chilling weather. The instrument needed to be kept warm, like her. Treated with all the care such centuries-old wood deserved.

With her mother's own performing career in a string ensemble long ended, her mum had given Lucy the violin. The violin's history was almost as precious as the instrument itself, because it had saved her grandfather's life during the Second World War. He'd disguised his true identity as part of a downed allied flight crew by hiding as a violinist, playing in a band. No one had questioned the entertainers, and he'd travelled to safety with an instrument that was supposed to have been a reward for some heroic deeds—or so the family story had gone.

All lies.

This violin that she credited with her success was *far* more than an old and valuable piece of her family's tapestry. Everyone who knew anything about music commented on what an uncommon instrument it was, with its magnificent tone. Her grandfather had claimed it was a reproduction, no matter what the worn label inside might say. Still valuable because of its age and the expertise with which it had been made, was the only reason her father was trying to get his greedy hands on it. He'd ultimately stolen everything else of value from his family—why not this as well?

It was only when her mum had finally begun cleaning out Lucy's grandfather's house after his death, going through the diaries and papers packed tight into an old suitcase under the bed, that she'd discovered that what Lucy held in her hands at each concert, and played with love as an extension of her body and soul, was no copy. It was real.

A Stradivarius.

Lucy unclipped the travelling case with trembling fingers to check, but the violin lay safe and undamaged on the black velvet inside. After her mother's call, she'd been almost afraid to touch the instrument again. And even more terrifying than the knowledge that this violin was almost priceless was the reality that her grandfather hadn't been given it, but that it had been...*taken.*

Lucy had brought copies of certain diary entries with her—what her mother had managed to go through so far in her grief. Neat script written in wartime, when her grandfather had feared he wouldn't make it. Mention of some woman, Betty, was all wound up with talk of his time in Lasserno and then on the run. Parts, almost a coded chronicle for his family if he didn't survive, or that was what she thought.

It was as if by reading it she was learning something new about the gentle, caring man she'd talked with for hours about life and love. Whom she'd written to as she'd travelled overseas because he'd loved her postcards and letters. She'd adored him as a role model and a good man, because her father had always failed them. Although now she recognised that the family had been given a sanitised version of his past before. The diaries told a story that was far darker and murkier. Of love, desperation and theft in wartime.

The violin is Lasserno's heart, not mine...

One thing seemed plain. Her grandfather had been given something priceless to protect by a family—most likely Stefano's family—and had kept it for his own. Fleeing with it to save himself.

Lucy knew the pain of having precious family items stolen. Her father had taken a gold necklace his mother had given her and pawned it one day, to put a bet on the horses. He'd sworn Lucy to secrecy over that loss. Lucy had witnessed her mum's pain on being unable to find her own mother's engagement ring, never confronting Lucy's father over taking it to pay off some debt. But they were mere trinkets when compared to a Stradivarius. The loss of an heirloom so precious would have hurt a family deeply.

Now her father was trying to take the violin too.

It was yet another reason she'd come to Lasserno after her life had imploded. The solicitor she was paying so much for had said her father would have a hard time proving the violin hadn't been properly gifted to Lucy. But if her mother couldn't get any mention of it struck out of the divorce proceedings, Lucy knew the true value of the instrument would be revealed. Her father's solicitors had already asked for a valuation.

She'd been assailed by twin dreads: losing her violin in a court battle and having it sold to some investor, or losing it to the family from whom it might have been taken over three-quarters of a century before.

She couldn't live with the suspicion that her violin might not have been given willingly, being stolen instead. Her father's lack of honesty had taught her the true importance of that moral quality. She'd never be like him. And this castle and Stefano Moretti might hold the truth that her Stradivarius hadn't been handed over as a generous symbol of thanks but was actually the spoils of war.

It wasn't hers to keep. It might never have been.

She didn't know what she'd do if that was the truth, because the most important parts of her professional career had been spent playing it. Losing her violin would be like losing part of herself. She may as well cut off her arm. Was it too much to ask that the person she might have to relinquish it to would be someone who deserved it? Who'd value it as she did?

The door opened and Stefano walked in, carrying a

tray. Any dark thoughts were swept away by the glorious smell of something sweet and chocolatey filling the room. Her mouth watered. Stefano placed the tray on the table, and handed her a cup filled with thick, dark hot chocolate. He'd pushed back the sleeves of his sweater, exposing strong, muscular forearms. The pianist in her orchestra had forearms like that, from hours of practice. They'd never really appealed—or so she'd thought. This man's, though, with the tanned skin and all the dark hair... She could sit and contemplate their wonders for hours.

But illicit musings about her reluctant host weren't going to get her anywhere. The hot chocolate, however... She clutched the cup in her hands, letting it warm her. Took a hefty sip of its creamy sweetness. Eyed the delicious-looking plate of food—a small selection of meats, cheese, bread.

She sighed with happiness. 'Thank you.'

'Prego.' Stefano sat in an armchair beside the glowing fire. 'But I have some unfortunate news.'

He leaned back, one foot slung casually over his knee, a picture of masculinity. Nothing about him looked as if he was about to impart anything unfortunate. He appeared almost smug, with one eyebrow raised and the barest curve of his lips.

'I've called Bruno, who tells me the snow has set in and it won't be safe to retrieve your car...or you.'

Her heart raced—or that could just be all the sugar in her steaming drink. 'For how long?'

He shrugged. 'A few days. The roads are unpredictable when it snows. You'll have to stay here until they're passable. Black ice makes conditions treacherous.'

Stay in the castle. With the Count and no other people.

Tightness banded her chest, making it hard to breathe. She reached up and unzipped her puffer jacket a little, trying to get some air. 'I knew there were good reasons I hated winter.'

'I'm sorry. Bruno will have his snow plough out soon enough, but for now we're at the mercy of the weather.'

'It's not your fault,' she said. Though even in casual clothes the man in front of her looked so commanding that she was surprised he couldn't control the weather's whims with a flick of his hand. 'Back in Australia I thought snow sounded romantic, you know? All pristine, white and soft-looking. I couldn't wait to see it in real life, rather than in photographs.'

But the reality was all too different from her blissful fantasies of spending time in front of roaring fires, drinking hot chocolate, like she was now, and toasting marshmallows. The pervasive grey of it had sunk under her skin and sapped all happiness. Ever since the day she'd come home to their tiny Salzburg flat and found Viktor stoking the home fires with someone else. Even more humiliating, the woman was a viola player from the orchestra.

And if that wasn't the last nail in the coffin of her own personal *annus horribilis*, it was the fact that Viktor now sat in the lead violinist's chair instead of her. She had to wonder whether their relationship had meant anything to him at all. When she'd been pouring out her secret fears and insecurities to a man she believed she could trust, had he simply been mining them so he could undermine *her* and steal the concert leader's position she'd worked so hard for?

'I take it you weren't born somewhere cold?' Stefano said, pulling her back to the present with that smooth, deep voice. As sweet and tempting as the luscious drink in her mug.

'I'm a child of the subtropics. Snow's a disappointment. Cold and wet. Highly overrated.'

The corners of his lips tugged upwards the tiniest of fractions, but Lucy wouldn't call it a smile.

'What possessed a woman from Australia who hates winter to live somewhere it snows?'

She shrugged. 'Work.' It had been the opportunity of a lifetime. One that had now slipped through her cramped and injured hands. 'I'm a member of an orchestra. Principal violinist.'

Although it wasn't as if she could really play much right now, needing time to recover from the injury which had been quietly plaguing her. Fodder for the nasty rumours which now saw her here, on enforced leave to 'consider her future'.

Stefano cocked his head. In the gloomy afternoon light his eyes showed no colour, just intense dark focus, all fixed on her. 'I'm patron of Lasserno's Symphony Orchestra. You're young for such a huge responsibility.'

Something about those words sparked a simmering coal of anger inside her—one she'd been carrying for weeks. Since discovering that her violin might not be hers, since her father had tried to claim it in the divorce, since realising Viktor's treachery.

Viktor had given her guidance on her playing. She'd appreciated it in the beginning. He was older, brilliant in his own right, and she'd wanted to be perfect, always striving for more. He used to tell her that she hadn't lived enough, that because of her youth she'd lacked nuance. That if she didn't practise harder, and more, she'd fail.

Lucy had tried not to let his observations eat at her confidence and self-belief, but she recognised now that this was what he'd been trying to do. She wondered, in retrospect, whether their relationship had any truth to it, or whether he'd always had his eyes fixed on her principal violinist's role.

'At twenty-four, I'm not the youngest who's ever been principal violinist. And my position comes through hard work. Dedication. Determination. You're reported to have taken on the role of Prince Arcuri's private secretary when you were around my age. Was that too young for such a huge responsibility?'

His whole body stiffened. A look crossed his face and he almost flinched, as if in pain.

'All the members of my family commence service with the Crown when our monarch requests it. As for you… My words weren't meant as a criticism. I've no doubt of your determination, since you've walked here in this weather with your bags, one of which weighs enough to sink a boat. I assume that's your violin?'

He nodded to the case sitting next to her on the couch. She nodded too, and reached out to place her hand protectively on the travelling case.

'Yes, it's always with me.' She'd left her other violins, those she used for practice, stored with the orchestra. This one would remain by her side—especially now.

'I'd like to hear you play.'

Her heart jumped, pounding at her ribs. Once, she'd loved playing for anyone who asked. The joy of it…the way the music sang through her. Now it was as if the pain in her hands was a punishment—a sign of being *weak*. Her confidence in all things had been shattered.

She stretched her left hand again. It had suffered during the kilometres upon kilometres when she'd clutched the steering wheel in a strangling grip.

Lucy tried to ignore the stiffness plaguing her hand, reached out and grabbed some bread, cheese, meat. Made herself an open sandwich.

She wondered if she'd ever really play again. Whether she'd want to—whether the passion remained to make her strive for greatness and perfection when everything seemed so broken. Though in not playing, she was only half a person. Since the age of five, she'd rarely been without a violin in her hands. Lucy didn't know who she was without it.

'Maybe later,' she said. 'It's been a long drive.'

She couldn't admit her injury to him—not when she hoped to impress rather than disappoint the man who held the future of her violin in his hands. Her inability to play had left her bruised and vulnerable, as if an essential part of her had been lost.

But that was a thought for another day. The food was too tempting, and her stomach grumbled, so she took a welcome bite of her sandwich. She savoured the explosion of flavour in her mouth, the spice of the meat, the creamy saltiness of the cheese. She closed her eyes and almost moaned in delight at the combination.

'Ooh, this is *delicious.*'

All the while she had a prickling sensation at the back of her neck, as if she was being watched. She knew that Stefano was looking at her—that was normal, they were in the room together. This was something more. As if she was being studied. Not that it was an unpleasant sensation—rather a blistering awareness of something *more*. Like being drizzled with syrup and…licked.

The shock of that thought zapped through her like an electric current.

Lucy opened her eyes and Stefano leaned forward, forearms on his knees, hands clasped in front of him, long fingers, perfect nails. Firelight flickered in the depths of his dark eyes. There was the merest of frowns on his face. She pressed back into the couch, her heart kicking up its thready rhythm again. It should scare her, but she wasn't sure fear was what her rapid heartbeat was trying to tell her.

She couldn't sit there any longer without saying something. 'What? Have I got food on my chin?'

It was as if the words shook him out of a kind of trance. He leapt from his seat, and she was forced to look up at his imposing frame.

'Forgive me. I'm being a poor host. It's been too long since anyone's stayed here. You've had a harrowing day and must be exhausted.'

'Thank you. That's—'

'I'm sure you'd like to use the facilities and rest. I'll prepare your room.'

Then he stalked out through the door, and she once again watched him go. Wondering what on earth she'd done wrong.

CHAPTER THREE

STEFANO KNEW HOW to be a gracious host. He'd held countless parties and soirees, allowing him to navigate polite
society, and had once been able to slip into the role as if
it was another of his bespoke suits. Yet nothing about him
felt gracious or polite tonight.

He sat at the vast table in his ancestral home's dining
room. A place where he'd not eaten for years, preferring
the castle kitchen or his suite for his meals. The memories here were of lonely dinners, where children had most
definitely been seen and not heard—decorative items to
be brought out and cooed over, once bathed and polished,
then kissed on the forehead and tucked into bed.

His parents had often left them to the nanny and taken
themselves to the capital, where they'd stay for weeks.
Only occasional phone calls to check on his schooling
had reminded him that he had parents at all. Court in-
trigue and maintaining their position in society had been
their preferred and natural environment. Children were
a necessity to maintain the family line, and so long as
they appeared to be following their lessons and behaving it was enough.

He had never been viewed as an individual by them,
but as a means to ensure his family's power. His father
had been a remote and imposing figure, whose lessons
had been all about duty and not disgracing the family

name. And his mother's last words to him, when rumours of Stefano's fall had reached her ears, had told him all he needed to know about where her thoughts lay.

'It's a blessing your father isn't alive to see you now.'

But those weren't the thoughts driving his dark mood tonight. He'd sat in his study after taking Lucy to her room. Engaged his investigator to cease his efforts in chasing a ghost and turn his attentions instead to Lucy and her family. Then he'd heard it, drifting through the lonely castle halls. The sweet sound of a violin. Not a tune, as such, but the heavenly swell of a few perfect notes.

He'd forgotten how much he missed music, here in his mountain exile. His patronage of Lasserno's orchestra had never been an obligation for him, but a true labour of love—much to Celine's disdain, because she didn't enjoy classical music.

Rather than concentrating on his task of retrieving the Crown Jewels, he'd spent too many hours straining to hear more of the pure, single notes Lucy played. He'd re-searched her achievements. She had strings of awards and accomplishments. And then there were the videos... No sight of the windblown waif who'd arrived unannounced and unwelcome on his threshold, but a glimpse of per-fection, with polished skin and smoothed strawberry gold hair. Lucy played like a celestial being. With her face a study of emotional pain mixed with joy, she looked like an angel about to fall.

Stefano craved to be the man who caught her.

But he had no right to these fruitless desires. Now the woman herself sat to his left, about a quarter of the way down the table. As far away as he could politely put her without having to shout when engaging in conversation.

He'd managed, for her sake, to coax the castle's groan-ing heating system into warming this room, so she'd shed her puffy blue monstrosity of a coat. A blessing and a curse. Because underneath it she wore a dress. Long-sleeved, black, with no embellishments. It should have looked plain and unremarkable, but the simple fabric and cut transfixed him as if the cloth had been woven by magic. The way it wrapped round her slender body... Tied at the waist with a draped skirt swishing at her knees allowing glimpses of the elegant sweep of her calves...

He took a sip of the wine which he'd grabbed from the palace cellar earlier. It hadn't been so long that he'd forgotten how to act around a beautiful woman, but she interested him far too much. It was as if he was a teenage boy again, hoping to catch the alluring swell of a woman's calf, the tempting curve of her breast.

He'd known the moment he'd opened the door to her that she was a distraction, and he'd been right. She may be the answer to one of his country's oldest questions, but Stefano didn't have time to be diverted from his task by errant desire. His siblings were counting on him and he had the terrible sense that time was running out—like watching the last grains of sand trickling through an hourglass.

'This meal's delicious.'

Lucy carefully placed down her fork and looked at him, head cocked a little to the side. Her eyes were wide, golden light gleaming in them from the chandeliers glittering above the table. He should have lit candles. She'd look beautiful in the soft, flickering light, like she had in the glow from the fireplace this afternoon... But this was not that kind of meal, filled with romance and seduction. It was all about fact-finding rather than fanciful thoughts about bathing her in the perfect light.

'You made it yourself?'

'*Sì*. The family chef taught me a few things when I was younger. Said I should learn to feed myself. Also to "impress the ladies". I believe that was his most important consideration for any young man.'

Except Celine had never been enthused by his efforts.

She'd always wanted to dine at the finest restaurants in Lasserno, even when he'd had enough of them and craved a home-cooked meal. Lucy, on the other hand...

He'd spent a tortured half-hour watching her devour the simple pasta dish he'd made. He'd make pasta for the woman every night she was here just to witness her pleasure as she ate it. To watch her tongue dart out almost guiltily, licking some stray sauce from the glorious pout of her lower lip.

'I'm sure you made a huge impression.'

She must have noticed him staring. It seemed to be a strange affliction plaguing him.

She tucked her hair behind her ears, the tips of which were tinted with a faint flush of pink. 'You've impressed me.'

'It was my pleasure.'

Her words shouldn't have moved him, but it was as if an ember had been lit deep inside. A lazy kind of heat slid through him at her enjoyment of the meal he'd made. He couldn't allow it to continue. She was simply another part of the job he must focus upon. Nothing more.

'However, there was no need to dress for dinner.' Her warm winter clothes were much better, with their many layers which hid her from his unruly gaze.

Lucy shrugged, blissfully unaware of his inner struggle. 'I wasn't sure. When you dropped me at my room you did announce, "Dinner is at nine in the dining room. I will escort you there." I've never had dinner in a castle with a count before. It sounded pretty formal.'

She appeared earnest enough. However, the corners of her mouth might have twitched...or perhaps that was his fertile imagination. She seemed to invoke it.

'As you can see...' he held his arms out, motioning to his jeans, his sweater '...no formality here.'

She fixed him with her honeyed gaze and it was as if he were skewered to the spot, like an insect under a pin.

It seemed his words were all the invitation she'd needed, because she was really studying him. Her eyes were on his face, sliding down to his chest, along his arms... Something about the appraisal was as intimate as it was overt. Then she looked away and the release was like a snap, sharp and brutal. He wanted her heated gaze on him again. It seemed as vital as his next breath.

'I'll remember that for next time,' she said. 'If there is a next time. The snow might clear by tomorrow and then Bruno can collect me.'

Not if the weather reports were anything to go by. And even if the snow cleared, she was a woman who might solve the mystery that would pave the way to a kind of forgiveness of his family by his best friend. But most of all he might finally be able to forgive himself. He just needed to remember how to charm. To convince her to stay when it was clear she wished to be anywhere else.

He had been charming once; it was a particular skill required of his job. When the Prince had been required to make harsh decisions, Stefano's role had called upon him to smooth out the sharp edges. Craft messages to soothe and placate.

He needed someone to smooth out his own edges now. All of him felt sharp enough to draw blood. The past few months had been about coercing the reluctant aristocracy into returning gems that weren't theirs. Polite conversation had no place in those efforts. He'd left polite society well behind.

'The weather's set in. But even if it hadn't, you're welcome to stay here rather than in the village.'

She finished another mouthful of pasta. Took a delicate sip of her own wine. Her glass was mostly full whereas his third glass was almost empty.

'That's kind of you, but I've paid for a room in the *pensione*. Plus, it's warmer than here.'

'*Mi dispiace.* I'm afraid my hospitality in that regard is lacking.'

'Well, the room you gave me is lovely. I've never stayed anywhere with frescoes on the ceiling. The frolicking cherubs are sweet.'

'It was a nursery once, and then the nanny's room, which is why it's…sweet. The ceilings of some of the other rooms here serve to remind humanity of all its failings.'

Those were the rooms he now avoided, with their pictures of final judgement and hellscapes. It was as if the building itself judged him, and Stefano didn't need the stones and mortar here reminding him of how far he'd fallen. Anyhow, he didn't want to talk about the castle's many Renaissance wonders—although he could, for hours. He had more pressing things on his agenda.

'What are you hoping to achieve in Varno? Your letter says your grandfather spoke of it and you mentioned your family history?'

He'd found her letter in his desk, bundled unceremoniously with other correspondence he didn't have the stomach for. Most of what was in it she'd already told him—about her grandfather being shot down over Italy and that he'd recently passed away. Meaning she was all he had to solve this old mystery. But they were tantalising hints rather than anything explicit. The letter had been a polite request for a meeting. She'd made the trip sound almost like a kind of pilgrimage.

'You found my letter? At least something's gone right.'

Those words held a worn and tired quality to them. As if a lot had not gone right for her lately. Something niggled at him—a desire to ask why—but he had more important answers to seek, and her problems weren't his to solve.

'I'm sorry for your loss.' Whatever his thoughts on what her grandfather might have done, he had some humanity left. It was the tiniest shred, but for this moment he grasped it. 'You said he passed away recently? He must have been a great age.'

'He was. Ninety-nine. He lived a long and full life, but it's never easy to lose someone you love.'

Lucy toyed with a stray piece of spaghetti on her plate, chasing it around with her fork. He allowed the silence to stretch uncomfortably. He found people often preferred filling it rather than saying nothing.

Lucy gave up her pursuit of the rogue pasta and set her cutlery down. She took a deep breath. Sighed. 'My grandfather used to tell me stories about the great kindness of the people here—especially in the Varno province. I wanted to see for myself. Research my family history a bit. Maybe visit the places he did… see if the people were as kind and generous as he said.'

Desperate and gullible was a better description, for his family at least. With the enemy threatening, they'd hoped a man they'd thought honourable, with allied links to the underground movement, could save the one precious national heirloom they hadn't been able to hide in time. Still, Stefano had never understood why his great-grandfather, Lasserno's Crown Jeweller, had taken the rash action of trusting a random stranger.

'Aren't people in Salzburg friendly?' he asked.

'I made what I thought was a good life there.'

He well understood how what you believed your life to be and what it really was could turn out to be vastly different, though she didn't elaborate. Everything about her seemed distant, cautious… But personal information such as this, whilst intriguing, was not what he sought from her.

'Did your grandfather talk much of the war?'

'No. It damaged him. I think he felt guilt, mainly, for those he'd lost…or couldn't save.'

Nothing about a ring. That would be too easy.

'My great-aunt was only a young woman when she died in the war. My family never spoke of it,' Stefano said.

'Lasserno suffered during its occupation. Sometimes recollections can be too painful.'

'All I know is that my grandfather always remembered the people here. It seemed that he loved the place and had left a little piece of his heart behind from the way he talked about it. In his last weeks he mentioned someone. A woman.'

'Not your grandmother?'

Lucy shook her head. 'Much to my mother's surprise. But in the end his memory was all over the place. He was pretty confused. Anyhow…when he talked about Lasserno he always told me if I loved something, or *someone*, to fight for it. Hold it close because life was short.' She gave a huff of a laugh. Her jaw clenched hard, she stared straight ahead, her eyes distant.

'You don't agree?'

'It sounds romantic, but it only works if a person wants to stay. How do you know if someone loves you as much as you think you love them, or loves you in the same way?'

She turned to him, her eyes tight, as if she was recalling fresh pain. He had nothing for her. Stefano had believed he and Celine would be married by now, yet all she'd wanted was his family name. The title and the position, not the man. More fool him. All she'd proved was that love was for the gullible.

There was no turning back now. His naivety was lost. And he couldn't forget her parting words—was now asking the same question of himself, almost daily. Who was he if he was not working for the Prince? Because that was all he'd been in the end: Alessio's private secretary. Yet he found he wanted to try and give Lucy an answer—one that wasn't steeped in bitterness.

'You can never know. You can only guess or hope.'

She smoothed the fabric of her dress. 'That might be fine for some people, but it leaves the door open to a world of pain. Is that good enough for you?'

Pain was his constant companion now. He didn't want to add more. All he craved was certainty. Not this sensation of life constantly shifting underneath him.

'I'm not much for guessing or hoping.'

She raised her glass in a mocking kind of toast. 'Here's to us.'

With that hard glint in her eye he expected her to down the rest of the glass. Instead, she took a tiny sip. He decided to make up for her reticence. Even though his thoughtless mouthful was a crime committed against the magnificent wine.

'Why are you a cynic, Lucy?' He shouldn't care, but it was a question he genuinely wanted the answer to. What memories made her stare into the distance, with her mouth tight and her eyes strained?

'Life in the orchestra taught me a few lessons about hard work and paying high prices,' she said, torturing the napkin on her lap.

'It must require a great deal of practice.'

'Three to four hours of personal practice a day, leaving aside rehearsals. Or that's how much I liked to do. Some people want or demand more. In the end, I found that… counterproductive.'

'If you need to practice here, you're welcome. We have a music room.'

Lucy's eyes lit up. Such a simple suggestion had made her happy again. Her brightness warmed him. For a moment he never wanted that glow of hers to fade.

'I'd love to see it…even though I'm taking a bit of a break from performing.'

She flexed the slender fingers of her left hand, then pressed her right thumb deep into her palm and rubbed. She bit hard into her lower lip and the troubled look was back again.

'You're free to explore the castle if you wish.'

'Really? Is there anywhere I can't go?'

Strangely, he found he didn't mind where she went. His suggestion appeared to please her. A gentle smile teased her lips and he wanted to keep that look on her face.

'Most of the formal rooms are unused, but you can open any door…look at whatever you want.'

'What if I get lost?'

'You can call me.' He slipped his phone from his pocket. 'What's your number?'

Lucy gave it to him and he sent her a text. Something in her vicinity buzzed with an alert.

'This is exciting. You said you don't allow tourists here?'

'Never. But you've told me you aren't a tourist, so the ghosts of my ancestors shouldn't punish me.' Not for this sin at least. There were many more to haunt him over.

'I'll let you in on a secret,' she said, lowering her voice and leaning forward in her seat. 'I bet I fit the dictionary definition of one.'

He leaned forward too. In these moments the sensation curling inside him was strange and unfamiliar. Like happiness. Around her, he couldn't help himself.

Lucy's eyes widened a fraction. He lowered his voice. 'I won't tell anyone if you don't.'

In response Lucy laughed, and the sound rippled through him with a wave of pleasure so intense he thought he could spend all of his time making her smile.

That was his reminder. As she laughed in her seat, glowing with what appeared to be true joy, he knew he needed to remember the job he must do.

'So, Tourist Lucy, how long do you have in Lasserno?'

He should find out how much time he'd have to try and extract the information he sought—because he needed subtlety. Especially if her family's fortunes had been made on the back of that coronation ring. What would his investigators find? Wealth? A sudden change of circumstance?

But now, as he watched Lucy, it was as if a light's

dimmer switch had been turned down. Everything in her faded. He regretted dimming her glow, because he was sure his words were the cause.

'A few weeks…maybe a month. I have things I need to do in Salzburg. Moving apartments.'

'Your orchestra must be missing you. You have an impressive biography.'

She dug her thumb into the palm of her left hand again, rubbing hard.

'The second violin will slot into my role nicely.' Her voice was sharp and discordant. She grabbed the napkin from her lap, placed it on the table. 'Do you mind? I'm very tired and I think I need to go to sleep.'

Lucy stood, so he stood. How could he tell her he didn't want her to go? Or, even better, tell her that she should invite him to go to bed with her? Keep her warm…

'Please…' Lucy looked at him, her eyes glittering like the chandeliers above them. Were they tears? Before he could say anything, she grabbed her coat. 'I can find my own way to my room. The dinner was beautiful. Thank you again.'

And as she rushed out through the door and left him standing at his seat, it was as if all the lights in the room had finally been snuffed out.

CHAPTER FOUR

LUCY SHOULD BE EXHAUSTED. However, every time she tried to close her eyes her thoughts shifted randomly, like autumn leaves tossed by the wind.

There was no point to them. Ruminating about what had happened couldn't change the reality of her life being a mess. But Stefano…his questions. They'd been the sorts of things any person might ask her in general conversation, but it had become all too much. She'd run before she'd collapsed, weeping into her empty plate.

She rolled over in bed to face the fire, which had died down to cherry embers. The part of the sheet she was not immediately lying on chilled against her body and she shivered. Even with warm socks on her feet, she seemed numb. It was as if she'd be cold for ever.

Although tonight at dinner, the way Stefano had looked at her… His eyes, so dark, had pierced right through her. There'd been a hectic glitter in them when she'd removed her coat and he'd taken in her figure-hugging black dress. The one she'd hastily thrown it into her suitcase when she'd fled her apartment after Viktor's betrayal. *That* look had heated her to her core.

Lucy wasn't sure why she'd put on the dress for dinner tonight. She'd hoped to wear it for their first meeting, had her trip gone to plan. Maybe it's because it was something she'd performed in, and had made her feel competent when nothing about her life over the past months had given her any sense that she knew what she was doing.

Anyhow, what was life if not a performance of some kind? It had seemed for months that she was an actor in her own life, rather than really taking charge. Coming to Lasserno was meant to be her first step in doing that and here she was, trapped in a freezing castle. Shivering, she threw back the cloud-soft down duvet and hopped out of bed, hurrying across the thick carpet to her coat. She shrugged it over her pyjamas, found a pair of fingerless gloves and slid them on before grabbing the duvet, picking up her violin case and huddling in front of the pretty little marble fireplace.

Whilst she was already cracked and broken, her violin wasn't, and she knew the dangers of low humidity and too much cold on the precious old wood. Sitting there, Lucy tried to ignore the pervasive little voice that whispered she was a fraud, even given her position in the orchestra. All those extra hours she'd practised at Viktor's instigation… He'd convinced her he was making her do it out of love, when all it had given her was the beginnings of an over-use injury and a niggling belief that somehow that injury was *her* fault—evidence of an inherent weakness.

What she needed was a cheery big fire…more light to chase away the shadows. Just…*more*. The sitting room had been much warmer, brighter. Maybe she'd find that room, since there was no way she'd ever sleep here—not now. She supposed she could text Stefano to ask for extra blankets, but it was late and she didn't want to wake him…

Her indecision curdled in her stomach, the sensation working its way up, grabbing her round the throat. It was almost like the nerves before a solo performance—but that was a thrilling kind of sensation that overwhelmed most of the fear. There was nothing thrilling about the way she felt now, with this paralysis stealing over her.

'It's not in the stars to hold our destiny, Lucy, but in ourselves.'

That's what her grandfather had always said, as they'd sat together on warm sunny days on the patio of his old home. He'd make a cup of tea and give her biscuits and talk.

She shut her eyes, fought back tears at his loss. He might have been an old man, but he'd been a quiet place of stability compared to the chaos of her father. She knew what he'd been trying to tell her—that she had to make her own way rather than dream about it.

Right now, her destiny involved somewhere warmer for her and her instrument. She stood with her violin case, still clutching the duvet round her, then left her room and padded through the generously carpeted halls filled with gilt-framed artwork and antiques, but happily absent any judgemental family portraits, until she reached a familiar door with an orange glow flickering underneath.

Lucy grabbed the icy handle, opening the door to an empty room. A low lamp still shone, and the fire in the large marble fireplace burned brightly, with a more generous heat than the one in her bedroom. She put down her violin and grabbed some cushions from the couch, dropping them to the floor. Wrapping herself and her violin case in the duvet, she was soon lying down in front of the fire, trying not to think of anything but how warm and comfortable it was on the makeshift bed she'd made.

She watched the flickering flames. And finally her eyelids became heavy and her thoughts drifted…

'What's this? Why are you on the floor?'

Lucy jumped and sat up, the duvet falling from her shoulders. Everything was fuzzy, as if her head had been stuffed with cotton wool. She rubbed her grainy eyes and looked at a clock on the mantelpiece. It was well past midnight.

'I'm trying to sleep.'

Stefano was halfway into the room, holding the neck of a bottle and a short glass, still dressed as he'd been for dinner. He looked effortlessly casual and handsome in a way that almost hurt for a mere mortal like her. His hair, gleaming black and tousled. His jaw grazed by a fashionable stubble.

He glared at the bed she'd made for herself as if she'd committed some personal offence against his furniture. Which she likely had, since she'd disassembled his couch.

'This isn't sleeping. This is nesting like a *topino*. A little mouse.'

'I'm not a mouse.'

Viktor had accused her playing of being timid. It was why she'd practised more…harder. Trying to inject some of the elusive passion he'd claimed was lacking into it. She flexed her fingers, but there was no stiffness or numbness right now. She took it as a small win in months of none.

'I couldn't sleep in the bedroom, so I thought I'd come here.'

Stefano toed the door closed and sank into an armchair. Uncapping the bottle, he poured a generous load of clear fluid into his glass and took a mouthful, rather than a sip. He'd consumed most of the bottle of wine at dinner like that.

She wrapped the duvet tight round her shoulders. 'What are you doing up so late?'

'Working.' He took another hefty swig from his glass and stared into the fire.

'Sounds like you need another job. What's so important that you have to work after midnight?'

'A special project.'

His eyes glittered like obsidian in the golden light of the room, boring into her. She shifted under the intense appraisal. Everything about him seemed to still, like a predator watching its prey.

'I'm trying to find some of the country's lost treasures.'

She swallowed past the sick knot in her throat and placed a hand on the violin case under the blankets, drawing it closer towards her. She could mention the Stradivarius now—it was almost the perfect opening. Except she didn't know the man, or how he'd react...

'What kind of treasures?' Lucy held her breath, waiting for his answer.

His hand gripped the arm of the chair, his fingers denting the fabric. 'Some gems from the royal collection.'

Her shoulders dropped. Jewels—not a lost Stradivarius. 'I'd have thought you'd go to the police about that.'

He dragged his hand over his face and she realised that once she got past how supernaturally handsome he was, Stefano also looked tired. Underneath his eyes his skin had a slightly greyish quality, in contrast to the healthy bronze elsewhere.

'Some responsibilities are mine alone,' he said.

Those words sounded as if they carried the expectations of a nation. He gazed into some unseen distance, as though imagining a future that might be there.

'How's your search been going?'

His focus returned to her and she didn't like it. It was a strange kind of appraisal, as though he was cataloguing her worth. She was well aware of how she must look, her hair likely a bird's nest, wearing her coat and her pyjamas. A mess—kind of like her unravelling life.

'I'm hoping for an unexpected improvement,' he said.

There was something about him that seemed so bleak as he downed the remaining drink in his glass. He uncapped the bottle, poured another shot, seemingly intent on drowning unspoken sorrows. Her heartbeat bounded, sickening and thready in the ominous silence that descended between them.

She wrapped her arms round her knees. 'What are you drinking?'

'Bruno's version of grappa.' He held up the glass of clear, gleaming liquid. 'Do you want some?'

'Is it strong?'

He snorted, his expression brooding and dark. 'It can help a person forget all manner of sins.'

'What sins do you have to forget?'

The corner of his mouth kicked up in the barest of smiles, but there was nothing happy about the way he looked in this moment. 'Too many to count,' he said, taking another hefty sip.

Her stomach turned over in uncomfortable knots, the way it always had when her mum was away, performing, and she had to stay alone with her father. He'd used to like a drink with dinner. Then it had turned into drinks after dinner, then with lunch, and then in the mornings before breakfast…

'Could you…not?' Her voice came out in a whisper, as those memories crept back through the cracks in her consciousness. Memories of staying in her bedroom whilst her dad ranted about needing to 'babysit'. As if he wasn't her father, who should be happy to look after his only child.

'Not what?'

'Drink so much.'

'I have no problem here.' He looked at the glass cradled almost negligently in his long and perfect fingers, then back at her, raising his eyebrow. 'Are you judging me, Lucy? Because if you are, I suggest that you…how do you say it? Take a number.'

There was something simmering underneath here, like magma boiling in the rocks below. You might not be able to see it, but it roiled away nonetheless, waiting to burst through a fissure when you least expected.

'I'm a woman alone in your house and you look like you want to get very drunk.'

She chewed on her bottom lip, almost wishing she'd

said nothing. But surely he could see why the situation might worry her? Of course, he'd probably never been worried by anything in his life...

He hesitated, then put the glass down on a side table and cocked his head, his eyes narrowing. 'You've had experience of this.'

She shrugged.

'Who had the problem? Did they ever hurt you?'

Stefano's voice was low and cool. It might have been soothing in a way, but it carried a steel edge that suggested he wanted to take on the role of avenging angel on her behalf. His cold certainty melted away her apprehension, replacing it with something softer, warmer. These conflicting feelings made no sense. Still, nothing much in her life did right now.

'My father liked to drink. He never touched me, but...'

All those times he'd blamed someone else for his failures. Business ventures going wrong. Bets lost. As a child, she hadn't understood it. As an adult, she'd come to learn that her father had trouble taking any responsibility for his actions or his life. He expected everything to be handed to him. Even her violin.

'Your mother never really gave it to you. She only pretended it was yours to hide it from me. I won't let her get away with it...'

The implication was clear. His alcoholism. His anger. It wasn't his fault. It was her mother's. Hers.

'Words and actions can hurt more than fists,' Stefano said, in a way that sounded far too knowing.

She wondered what could possibly have hurt *him*. He had everything. A title, power, a castle... There was a veneer of perfection about him that seemed hard to crack, although she'd glimpsed a few things. The apparent tiredness. Those moments when his gaze became unfocussed and distant.

'My father's a complicated man. He's an only child

and was doted on by his parents. They gave him every-thing—he just couldn't seem to hang on to it. He likes drowning his sins too.'

Stefano pushed the bottle away from him with two long, elegant fingers. The look on his face was earnest and sure. 'Whilst you're in my home, this won't happen again.'

Something inside her let go, relaxed the tiniest of fractions, and the exhaustion that had threatened all day began to wash over her again.

'You're safe here, Lucy. You have nothing to fear from me.'

After months of not knowing who or what to believe, for a few moments of relief she allowed herself to accept Stefano's words to be true.

Stefano was certain that if he looked in a mirror he wouldn't like his reflection much right now. He'd made Lucy worried, perhaps afraid. Her eyes had been wide, her body tense. What sort of person *did* that? No one good, he was sure.

Having this woman think less of him didn't sit well. Huddled in front of the fire, beautiful and unkempt in the warm light of the room, she looked as if she needed a protector. Once, he'd have been that person. Caring, taking care. Now, he shouldn't be entrusted with anything precious because he'd destroy it. Still, he loathed it that Lucy might believe she needed protection from him.

'You can't sleep here on the floor.'

She curled her arms round herself, fingers gripping the edges of the duvet. 'It's okay. Really.' She grappled with something beside her—something angular.

Stefano frowned. 'What do you have under there with you?'

She shrugged. 'My violin.'

'Your *what*?'

Of all the answers, that was not one he'd expected her to give.

'I'm not the first violinist who's slept with one and I won't be the last.

'Why?'

'It's a three-hundred-year-old instrument, and if it gets too cold and dry the wood might crack.'

It dawned on him now why she was here, in this room with the large fireplace. He felt the sickening sensation of one more layer of guilt joining the rest.

'You're cold. I'm freezing you. Lucy, you should have called me. I'd have found you more blankets.'

'I thought you'd be asleep. Anyhow, I don't think more blankets will work. It's the bedroom. The fireplace is tiny and the fire went out. Don't worry about me—here's comfortable.'

He was the devil who'd done this to her, and he'd make it right. 'Take my room. It has a larger fireplace.'

'I—I couldn't. Where will you go?'

He looked at the long couch where he'd spent many nights sleeping. In his bedroom suite, where every Count of Varno had slept, he was suffocated by the weight of his history. How he'd destroyed it all. That was why he'd taken to this room, with a blanket, a fire and a bottle of alcohol to drown out the self-recrimination.

'I rarely sleep more than a few hours at a time. Please let me show you, then you can decide.'

He stood as Lucy clambered up from the floor in her coat. Then he noticed her feet. 'Are they…socks with unicorn cats?'

Her cheeks flushed a soft pink. She blew out a huff of breath. 'You're really not seeing me at my finest. I'd planned an official visit, where I looked more…competent than this. I promise I know how to be an adult when I try.'

'My sister's studying teaching. I'm sure she has a pair

of socks with cats on them. Not unicorn cats... She would be envious.'

'Don't forget, these are *rainbow* unicorn cats. It's all about the rainbows. My gloves match, too.'

She held out one hand and wiggled her fingers.

'It is a fashion statement I'll never forget. Perhaps I'll try to find some for my sister, as a gift.'

She smiled, and it hit him in the solar plexus like a punch. All the breath left him. That smile brimmed with an innocent-looking joy, no artifice. It lit up the room, taking a grey world and turning it multi-coloured and gleaming, like the rainbows adorning her hands and feet.

'You're a good brother. I can give you the website. I promise she'll love you for it.'

He stilled. If only Lucy knew, she wouldn't be saying these things. His actions had successfully torpedoed his siblings' future. He must never forget this was the woman who might have information that could recover everything for him. That wouldn't happen if she didn't trust him and wasn't prepared to talk—which meant he had to find the shred of humanity he'd buried deep inside.

He was sure she knew something. He'd seen the tightening around her eyes when he'd said he was searching for the nation's lost treasures at dinner. She hid things—he just wasn't sure what.

'Let me take your violin.'

She hesitated before relinquishing it.

As he took the handle of the case their fingers brushed and it was as if time slowed, the stroke of skin over skin seeming to take minutes rather than the briefest of seconds. Lucy made a sound, an exhalation. The shimmering heat of that touch flowed through him. His heart pumped hard and fast. She looked up at him, eyes wide, as if she'd seen him for the first time. Her lips parted.

They stood close, a world of clothes between them, and yet it was as if he was completely exposed. A small sprinkle of freckles dotted her nose, and Stefano wanted to take his time, count each one. He wondered if there were more on areas exposed to the sunlight when the weather was warm, on her shoulders, her chest…

He stopped, shook himself from the fantasy. 'Follow me.' He cleared his throat, his voice rough and raw. 'We need to get you warm.'

That devil's voice in his head began hinting at the many enjoyable ways he could keep this beautiful woman warm and occupied for days. Ways which would allow him to forget the weight of obligation, his failures.

But he didn't deserve that kind of relief. Not the pleasure, not the softness. If she knew anything at all about him she wouldn't be looking at him now with a kind of naked wonder written all over her face.

He began to walk and she followed, still wrapped in the down duvet which trailed behind her like an oversized cape. She appeared regal, almost as if she owned the space, making him feel like an impostor.

'This place is amazing,' she said. 'More like a museum than a family home.'

In many ways she was right, but still, this place *had* been a home to him as much as a showcase. He'd tried to make it so for his brother and sister, when his parents had left them here to pursue their own ambitions, and before those ambitions had become his too, since he really had nothing else.

'The benefits of a five-hundred-year-old family history,' he said.

'I can't imagine the…the responsibility of all that behind you. What that would be like to have always sitting on your shoulders. Or are you so used to it that it doesn't matter?'

It was all he knew. The responsibility simply *existed*. There were expectations he'd accepted because there was no option or choice. It hadn't bothered him in the beginning—especially when the power of that obligation to something larger than himself had become like a drug. When he'd realised as he'd left his childhood and moved through his teens that sitting in the top echelons of his country's society was a good place to be.

That sickened him now, because in his arrogance he hadn't realised the privilege of his position and how easy it was to fall from the lofty pedestal his family had built for themselves.

'I simply…am.'

What more could he say? He was the Count of Varno. The Shield of the Crown. A role he'd never made the most of. He'd worn it like a cloak rather than wielded its power for anything worthwhile. Now the opportunity to do so was lost to him. The sting of self-recrimination was a constant reminder of how he'd failed. He didn't know how to be anything or anyone else.

'Do you ever wish the expectations had never existed? That you weren't who you were born to be?'

They'd reached the door of his room—a blessed relief, because she asked questions it was hard for him to answer, referred to things he couldn't think about lest he dwelled too hard on what he'd thrown away. But to the last question there was only one response he could give.

'Who am I if I'm not working for the Prince?'

Lucy's heart thumped an unsteady tempo, like some kind of wicked drumbeat. He was only being kind, putting her in his room where he hoped it would be warmer than in the chill that had settled over this whole place. More than the troublesome heating, it was an oppression, hanging like a grey pall over the castle. She couldn't shake the conviction that it was coming from the man who had now stopped walking in front of her in long, easy strides. There was a sense of brooding about him…something unfulfilled. She couldn't put her finger on it.

They'd reached a grand door—or at least grander than the other magnificent doors here—with an impressive coat of arms carved into the wood. Stefano stood next to her, a respectful distance away, holding her violin case. It made her prickly, nervous that his hands were on it when the only person who ever touched it now was her. Still, since he might be the true owner of the instrument, she thought she'd try it out for size. It didn't fit.

'You have a unicorn on your door,' she said. It was a fierce-looking unicorn, almost terrifying as it reared against a shield of some sort.

'It's a unicorn rampant.'

'Well, it does look a bit wild, with those eyes and its tongue.'

She turned to look at him and the corner of his mouth hitched. Her breath caught in anticipation, but she still couldn't call the move a smile.

'It's a heraldic term,' he said. 'Since the unicorn's rearing up. But you mustn't forget the dragon.'

How could she miss it? Rearing up as well, looking no less fierce than the unicorn.

'The dragon *rampant*, you mean? Not exactly a restful entrance to your bedroom. I suppose they have some suitably impressive meaning?'

He shrugged. 'Lasserno's herald could tell you more, but a unicorn represents courage, strength and virtue. The dragon is a defender…valiant.'

'A valiant defender with courage, strength and virtue? That's a lot to live up to.'

Stefano stared at his family crest, again appearing as though he was looking through it into a memory. Given the grim line of his mouth and the clench of his jaw, it wasn't a happy one.

'So I'm perpetually reminded,' he said.

This whole place appeared to haunt him. She felt an ache start inside, a sensation of empathy, because at least she'd been able to flee her apartment and her life for a while. Where was his escape, if not here?

'As impressive as it is, your family crest is sadly absent of rainbow unicorn cats.' She wiggled her sock-covered toes and looked up at him. That garnered another of his almost-smiles, and a snort which didn't sound at all dignified or aristocratic.

'After centuries of living with these honourable creatures I can see my family coat of arms is lacking. What do the unicorn cats represent?'

'Hmmm… Happiness, I guess? Which I suppose isn't very impressive.'

'It's an important quality, since so many fail to find it.' His head dropped, and his shoulders slumped in the smallest of ways which told a larger story. 'And I'm certain *you* would be much happier in a warm room and asleep after your long and arduous day.'

Stefano opened his bedroom door, flicked on a light and strode inside. She followed. Whilst what she'd seen of the rest of the castle had been designed to impress, this room was something else. Wine-red carpet as thick and soft as unmown grass. A massive marble fireplace, unlike the tiny elegant one in her room. A lounge suite in front of the fireplace that looked as if you'd sink into it and never want to leave. Walls lined in a deep, rich burgundy silk.

It was bold…sumptuous. Yet as impressive as the whole space appeared, it was nothing compared to the centrepiece of the room. A four-poster bed that didn't look as if it had been built for any mere mortal, with its gleaming polished wood and a rich embroidered canopy in jewel tones completed the opulence of the room.

Stefano placed her violin case gently down in a corner, then moved to the fireplace, working on the fire. All the while she stood silent, just inside the doorway. The breath was tight in her chest. She couldn't sleep here. It was as if by being in this room she'd become immersed in him. It was far too close, too intimate. Like she would sink into him, be pulled under and drown.

'Come in and close the door,' he said, drawing her out of her heated imaginings.

Except watching him poking about in the fire, coaxing it to catch and burn with his sleeves pushed up, looking all manly and competent, just dragged her further into a kind of spell.

He stood and glared at the flames as if daring them to go out, his hands on his narrow hips, the whole move accentuating his broad shoulders backlit by the fire in the hearth. It was a masculine silhouette, but she didn't know why the picture it painted caused all of her to flood with a roaring heat. Really, she didn't need a fire in the room to keep her warm. All she needed was Stefano to stand around and...*brood*.

After a few moments, seemingly satisfied that the fire wasn't about to disobey him, he turned back to her, still stuck in the doorway. Frozen. He frowned. 'If you come inside and shut the door it'll keep the heat in.'

He'd obviously misunderstood her reticence. She probably looked like the frightened little mouse he'd accused her of being, and she refused to be that. Lucy stepped inside and shut the door behind her—then almost backed up against it. Because now he *stared*, as if she was some kind of fool. His intense black gaze was fixed on her. It should have been cold, that fathomless colour, but it reminded her of febrile summer nights in the subtropics back home.

She needed to say something which made sense. 'I *can't* sleep here in your room.'

The words spilled out in a voice that was a little too soft and a lot too breathy and left her exposed—as if she'd stripped off her clothes and was dancing about the room shamelessly naked. And that thought led inevitably to thoughts of him naked too...except he wouldn't be shameless. He would be glorious. Perfect, if the shape of him hinted at under his clothes was anything to go by. Or perhaps not hinted at but shouted out—loudly. With a megaphone.

Her cheeks burned. She wanted to clap her hands to them, to hide what was no doubt a flaming blush, but that would draw even more attention to them.

'If you're concerned about my welfare, I can put your mind at ease,' he said. 'I'll sleep in the room you vacated.'

'It's very flouncy and pink.'

Which was not really what she wanted to blurt out either, but there it was. Even worse, at her words the corner of his mouth twitched, as if he was trying everything he could to hold in his amusement. She almost stopped breathing. Because if this man really smiled, her heart might stutter to a halt and she'd fall dead on the floor.

'I can assure you my masculinity can handle a few flounces.'

Lucy didn't want to talk about Stefano's masculinity. Not here. Not now. Not ever. Especially not whilst he stood in this room, presenting the absolute picture of it.

'Would you like me to put your violin in front of the fire to keep it warm?'

'No, it can't take direct heat,' she said. 'Too cold and it'll crack. Too hot and dry and a similar thing will happen.'

'Temperamental, isn't it?'

'Any instrument can be if not handled correctly.'

'And do you?' He raised an eyebrow. 'Handle it correctly?'

Everything stilled at his question. Something about this moment felt pregnant and full of possibility. An idea of him and tangled limbs and the heat of two bodies exploded in her head and wouldn't leave. She glanced over at the imposing bed, and he did too. Was he thinking what she was thinking? She swallowed, her mouth dry. And even though she wore a coat, and was wrapped in a duvet, she felt completely exposed.

'I'll leave you now,' he said as he walked towards her.

She should have stepped sideways, to move out of the way of the door, but she was paralysed. Stefano stopped next to her, looming large. Hyper-real…more than a mere mortal. And this close she caught a hint of his scent. Fresh and clear, like a bright, brittle winter day in the mountains, with an intoxicating undertone of spice.

She needed to get out of the way. Instead, she took the silk-covered duvet from around her shoulders and thrust it at him. 'You'll need this. It's from the bed.'

'Grazie.' He took it. In the low light of the room his dark eyes glittered as if they were filled with stars from the night sky. Then he motioned to the lock on the door and she stood to the side, looking where he indicated.

'This is the only key, if you feel the need. As I said before: you're safe here, Lucy.'

Stefano opened the door and left without looking back. Closing the door behind him, she twisted the key in the lock, which tumbled with a satisfying click.

In this moment she wasn't concerned at all about her safety. Because she'd locked the door not to keep him out. It was to keep her in.

CHAPTER FIVE

STEFANO SCANNED THE investigator's report, which contained nothing of great interest. Some of it confirmed what Lucy had already told him. That her father came from a wealthy family and had a string of failed businesses and debt behind him. Her mother was a well-respected violinist from a renowned ensemble. The obituary of her grandfather said that he was a reputed war hero with medals to prove it. No riches…nothing to hint at having profited from the sale of Lasserno's coronation ring.

Reading those words on the screen left him feeling somehow soiled and…*less*. Considering what he'd done, it was surprising he had any further to fall, but this intrusion into Lucy's life had made him do just that, and he couldn't understand why it mattered.

Still, she'd come to Lasserno and his castle for a reason. The sweet words in her letter about retracing her grandfather's steps and seeing the country made sense on the surface, but there was something deeper. A pain she hid, behind cute unicorn cat socks and glowing smiles. She might present as sunshine and rainbows, but she was more than that, he was sure.

She was off exploring the castle this afternoon—or that was what she'd texted him. After a morning when the heavenly strains of her violin had faded in and out through the castle halls. She'd played something soulful.

Each perfect note sweeping over him, soothing the constant churn in his gut, the clench of his teeth, replacing it with something else. Something softer. A sense of peace.

In a way, he wished her music would never stop. But it would. The snow would melt and Lucy would leave. He didn't know why that thought ached like a mortal wound.

He shut down the document. Tried to ignore the internet alerts about the royal family. He'd once read them each day, but he didn't need to any more. Still, curiosity pricked at him, to see if the narrative had changed in the way he'd sought to achieve.

The last time he'd checked it had seemed that Alessio was releasing carefully controlled titbits to the press with the zeal of a convert. Joyous pictures of the Prince and his pregnant Princess graced the social pages in a carefully controlled way and the country loved them. Bad news had turned good. The Crown was now glorified, rather than scorned, as it had been when Alessio had first taken the throne, because of his father's antics. Suspicion of the new Prince had turned to accolades.

The twin burns of anger and regret curled tight in Stefano's gut. Those pointless thoughts invaded again. He'd been correct, no doubt. But he should never have ended up here in self-imposed exile. Alessio should have allowed his people to know the good man their Prince truly was. It was all Stefano had been trying to achieve. Except he should have fought for it rather than using subterfuge.

But there was no turning back now—only moving forward.

Stefano rubbed his hand over his face, exhaustion weighing on him like a lead blanket. He'd never required much sleep, but in recent months insomnia had been a regular and unwelcome visitor. He downed the bracing espresso he'd made earlier and settled back to search for more missing gemstones. He had a promising lead on a near flawless emerald which he would not let slip through his fingers.

As Stefano opened another email his phone rang. He checked the number. Lucy.

'*Pronto.*'

'Hi. It's…um…me.'

She still sounded uncertain when she spoke to him, which he found troubling. He wanted—*needed* her to be comfortable around him. For some strange reason it seemed imperative.

'Hello, me. How may I assist?'

She laughed, a musical tinkle of sound that caused warmth to kindle in his chest.

'I've tried following your directions to the music room, but I'm lost. I need some help.'

Her request for assistance touched him in a way he found hard to explain. He glanced at the open email again. Another contact, another phone call to make during which the person on the other end of the line would lie, whine, and then beg to be allowed to keep what wasn't theirs.

'Stefano?'

He shook himself out of his inertia. The call could wait. Helping Lucy would be a welcome break, since he'd been sitting behind this desk for hours.

'I'll find you and take you there. Can you tell me what you're near?'

'Well… I opened a door and it seems to be a room full of boars' heads. Tusks and all.'

'Ah. I won't be long.'

He shut down his computer and jogged to where she described. She stood outside the door of one of the many unused rooms here.

Today she cursed him by wearing active wear for her exploration of the castle: form-fitting leggings that peeked out from underneath her coat and clung to her body, shaping her firm thighs and the swell of her calves. Heaven save him, he couldn't take his eyes from her, and the way he looked at her body was not polite.

She gave him a tentative smile as he approached and he focussed on her soft rose lips, gleaming with a slick of gloss. It wasn't much better.

'There was no need to run. I'm fine so long as I don't open that door again.'

'I should have warned you. My father had a penchant for hunting boar. His trophies aren't to my taste, but I didn't want the boars to have perished in vain, so they now have a room to themselves.'

'You've made them their own shrine. That's kind of sweet, but also kind of creepy.'

'It is my life's aim to do "sweet and creepy" well.'

She threw back her head and laughed.

It was as if sunshine had broken out in the gloomy hall, bright and beautiful.

'Well, you're better at that than in your directions. Where is this mythical music room?'

'Follow me. You aren't far from it.'

He walked ahead and she blew out her breath in a huff, disturbing fine wisps of hair and sending them drifting over her face as she followed.

'You should have given me instructions like, *Turn right at the boars' heads, then proceed straight past the hall of disapproving ancestors and go left at the room of lethal weapons—*'

'You found the armoury as well? You *have* had an adventure today.'

'I suppose I have—though it *was* rather unnerving. What have you been doing?'

Stefano's shoulders dropped, the mere thought of the tasks ahead causing another wave of exhaustion to flood over him. 'More work.'

'I admire your commitment to your job. Do you actually have a life?'

The hot bite of something like anger burned in his gut. He'd had a life once. And status. He'd had everything. But those words came back to haunt him.

'You're nothing, Stefano, if you're not working for the Prince...'

'I had a fiancée. I had more. My work was one of service, but His Highness was my best friend.'

'Was...?'

His pace faltered, and Lucy frowned before he picked up his even stride. She was sharp, this one. Not missing anything. He couldn't admit his disgrace. What sort of a man would it make him? She'd never trust him then— not enough to divulge the secrets her family might have held when he asked her. But for some inexplicable reason he didn't want these blissful moments to end, ruined as they would be by resurrecting events in history neither of them had had any part in.

'Is.'

'Will your fiancée be coming to the castle? I don't want my being here to make things difficult.'

Celine had been reluctant to set foot in the mountains at any time. No matter that the castle was considered a national treasure, she would always say when invited here, *'I am not a goat.'*

Stefano looked over at Lucy, who was worrying her bottom lip with her teeth.

'I'm single now. Our reputations are safe.'

Lucy's expression changed, and her face became painted over with the veneer of sympathy. He'd seen that look on the face of his siblings when he'd told them about the end of his engagement. He hated it. Actions had consequences. He was living his as they spoke. He deserved no misdirected pity.

'I'm sorry,' she said. 'I know what it's like when you have an expectation of how life's going to go, and then it all just…stops.' Her eyes glittered in the low afternoon light, her voice soft and cracked with emotion.

'There's a story there,' he said.

She waved her hand, as if dismissing an irritant. 'It's a miserable one which nobody wants to hear—particularly since you sound like you have one of your own.'

'What if I do?' Strangely, he wanted to know what had chased away her smiles and laughter and replaced them with sadness.

'Let's just say I had a relationship that ended too,' Lucy murmured. Then she stopped, peered into an open doorway. 'Is this it?'

Stefano hadn't noticed where they were. He'd been too absorbed by her. 'Yes. Welcome to Castello Varno's music room.'

She walked inside as if she owned the place, and he supposed that a room like this *was* her domain. He was a mere interloper, even though it was his castle.

Lucy stood in the centre of the space and turned slowly in a circle on the parquetry floor. 'Amazing. I bet the acoustics are glorious.'

'When I was a child, my parents would have recitals here.' The room had regularly been full of people, not a silent space. Now it was an abandoned relic of a distant past.

She walked towards a piano and trailed her fingertips across the dust cover. A shiver of pleasure tripped over his skin at the thought of those gentle fingers on his flesh. Of allowing them to take a winding journey over his body. He took a step back from her. Lucy Jamieson was a risk to self-preservation and common sense.

'I'm assuming it's a concert grand?'

Stefano nodded.

'Did you ever play?' she asked.

'Not officially. My sister was taught piano, and she loathed it. For a while I took over her lessons.'

They'd been moments of true pleasure—something

he'd done for himself, not about what he could give to the Arcuri royal family or his country. He'd relished those secret lessons until his teacher had reported his achievements, in a moment of pride and misplaced honesty.

'My parents stopped them. Time spent on music was considered a waste. They wanted me to only concentrate on things of use in my ultimate role.'

He couldn't prevent a sense of bitterness creeping in. It wasn't as if his marks in other subjects had diminished. His mother and father would never have known had his music teacher remained silent as he'd implored. But to them, anything that was not pertinent to his role as the future Count was unnecessary. They'd ignored the fact it was something he loved. To them, it hadn't mattered. He'd come to realise that in the end all he'd been to them was a cog in their dynasty's wheel. Not a boy who wanted one small thing to claim as his own.

A frown creased Lucy's brow. 'What did you think of that?'

'I was never going to be a musician of your skill.'

'You could take it up again.'

He shrugged. 'That chance passed me by. I had no time. I concentrated on what I needed to assist the Prince in the best way I could. History, politics, marketing, communication…'

'No wonder you're so busy. You must have a heck of a job description. What does the private secretary of a prince actually do?'

Of course he wasn't Alessio's private secretary any more, but she didn't need to know that—not right now. Let her believe that he remained in his role a little longer. It did give him a certain gravitas which 'disgraced count' lacked. How could Lucy ever trust him if he disclosed how untrustworthy he'd become?

'Anything His Highness asks of me, so long as it's legal.'

'If he asked you to…to marry the daughter of a bitter enemy to bring peace between nations?'

'Lasserno has no bitter enemies, but if he asked…' Stefano nodded. 'In centuries past, members of my family have been married off to serve the principality's interests. It made Lasserno powerful and made my family increasingly wealthy and well connected. No one complained.'

Lucy's eyes narrowed, her mouth tightening to a thin and stark line. 'That's…that's *appalling*. It doesn't sound like a best friend and employer relationship but more of a…a hostage situation.'

She seemed to grow taller, as if filled with incandescent outrage on his behalf. He'd never had anyone to support him like this. He'd always supported others. His siblings… Alessio in his role as Shield of the Crown. The burden had become a heavy one. Yet a sensation wound through him that seemed all too soft for his life right now. Almost like relief that there was someone who might think of *him*. Put him first for once.

He shut it down. Whilst he wanted to thank her for her spirited defence, those kinds of feelings led him nowhere.

'My mother and father were the product of such an arranged marriage and it was successful.' At least if politicking and building on the family's name, fortune and brand were any measure. As parents… Well, that was another matter. 'What about yours?'

She wrapped her arms round her waist, turned and looked out through the bank of windows to the cold and grey view beyond. 'Desperately in love once, apparently. Now getting bitterly divorced.'

'So love is no guarantee?'

She gave a small and savage laugh which opened the door to more questions if he cared to ask them. 'Oh, trust me, I'd *never* say it was.'

He could press…ask her about the cynicism that seemed to surround her again. Once, he would have. But now the only questions he should be asking were about her family. Her grandfather.

But he didn't have it in him to do so in this moment. Not when she seemed so lost.

Later.

He had time.

'Don't worry, Lucy. Alessio married for love. And I'm sure he'd allow the same for me, if I believed in it any more.'

'So what you're telling me is that all this is okay and you've never wanted to do anything else?'

He'd never thought of it—not even as a boy. From his first memory, his course had been set. His friendships managed. Everything that he'd done had led him to being the man he was today. Yet somehow he'd still failed.

Lucy made him question the role he'd been born into. But if he began to ask those questions they might never stop…might lead to conclusions that his life and most enduring friendship had been a lie. A hostage situation. And if that were the case, and he was now free, what was he doing tracking missing gemstones?

He had no answers to that question, which sat like an uncomfortable weight in his gut. 'I'm the Count of Varno,' he said. 'Shield of the Crown. This is my life, which I must return to.'

'Then I won't take up any more of your time,' she said, her voice barely above a whisper.

He didn't like the suspicion that Lucy believed she was being dismissed. He wanted her smiles, her laughter. Not these brittle and hard edges that seemed to have invaded their conversation.

'Tomorrow, if you like, I can take you on a proper tour.'

'That would be lovely.'

In the meantime he'd board up his weak points and slip himself back into the Count of Varno's costume. 'For now, do you think you can find your way back to familiar areas of the castle?'

'Don't worry about me. I think I know where I'm going. I'll be fine.'

Lucy turned and looked at him, her golden eyes intense and assessing. And as he left the room, to return to the work pressing down upon him, he couldn't shake the uncomfortable feeling that whilst Lucy was fine, she believed he wasn't.

CHAPTER SIX

LUCY WOKE BEFORE the alarm she'd set on her phone, snuggled deep in a warm bed, her face buried in a pillow. In a haze of early wakefulness she yawned, took a deep breath. There was the scent of sunshine. Crisp, clean sheets. And a hint of something else. An intoxicating spice, rich and deep, that teased, tempted…hit her blood and wound through her on its own seductive journey.

Stefano.

There was a reason it had been a bad idea to sleep here. His name whispered in the recesses of her consciousness. Late last night she'd imagined him lying in this bed, thought how her body touched where his had been, and now it was all she could think about. Except those thoughts had to remain just that—thoughts.

Lucy rolled over, trying to ignore the ache deep inside, the desire for things she couldn't have. Instead she stared at the canopy above her, richly embroidered with an image of the night sky. Constellations in yellows and golds. It reminded her of the few times her grandfather had taken her camping, when they'd looked up into the dark, clear night, and all they'd seen was stars. She missed those stars. The night skies in the larger cities in Europe were filled with too much light pollution to see anything very much.

When was the last time she'd simply looked up, enjoyed something so simple?

Her alarm sounded and she switched it off, checking a message from Stefano. It said he'd provided breakfast and left it outside her door and he'd meet her in the sitting room in around an hour.

She left the warmth of the bed and opened the door to the sweet scent of hot chocolate. On the floor sat a tray with a simple breakfast: some bread, butter, jam. More cheeses and meats.

Something about Stefano's thoughtfulness warmed her. It was considerate and unexpected. She needed to talk to him about the violin, but couldn't seem to find her voice. Because after spending so much time caring for herself, she was enjoying the attention more than was good for her. Plus, she still didn't really know him, and with the thick layer of snow outside she wouldn't be able to escape here any time soon if he didn't react well...

They were thoughts for another time. Today would be fun, she hoped.

Lucy ate and dressed, then made her way to Stefano, excited about his offer to show her around the castle. Her efforts the days before had kept her busy enough, but it had been like walking around a museum without any guide or information. She wanted context, and Stefano's thoughts on growing up somewhere like this, with all that history around him.

Before she rounded the corner Lucy heard him. His voice was raised. Emotive. Speaking in Italian. She slowed her steps. Stood back a little, behind some furniture.

He came into view, pacing back and forth, raking his hand through his dark hair. His jaw was covered in stubble, as if he hadn't shaved this morning.

She didn't need to understand the words to grasp his fury. His body was wound tight, the hand clutching his phone white-knuckled, and the other hand gesticulating and slashing through the air.

Her heart bounded. That sickening twist of nerves was back in her belly. She remembered conversations like this between her parents, when her mother had been on tour, before she'd stopped touring to care for Lucy, because it had become clear her dad had no interest. Her father would rage in the late hours, when he'd thought Lucy was asleep, but she'd heard it all. Seen it, too, on the rare times she'd peeked out from her darkened room and watched her father, instead of hiding under the covers. He'd paced like this, spewing words designed to hurt a woman who was too far away to be able to do anything about it.

And just like when she was that little girl she froze, wishing she could hide, not needing to be reminded of the ugliness of her childhood. At least back then she'd been able to pretend to be asleep through the worst of it.

She really didn't have to look around the castle today with Stefano. Not when he was like this. He hadn't seen her. She could slip around the corner and leave. But as she moved he looked up, his jaw clenched, that gaze of his cold and hard.

'Back into your bed, Lucy, for Chrissakes!'

The breath left her, her heart pounding a sickening rhythm at the memory of her dad bearing down on her. Booze on his breath and hatred on his face. How could he have loved her when he'd appeared to loathe her mother so much?

She held up her hands. 'I'm sorry I'm interrupting.'

Recognition spread over Stefano's face. His eyes widened a fraction. Slashes of colour stained his cheeks. He murmured something into the phone and disconnected.

'Lucy.'

Her name was said with no trace of anger. Instead Stefano's voice ground out rough and almost pained.

'You're obviously busy,' she said. 'It's fine. We can look around the castle another day.'

She was used to changing plans. Her parents hadn't had much time for her. Her mother had often been practising or away performing once Lucy had become a little older. Her father always immersed in some hopeless scheme. Her music had been a blessing, occupying her on many lonely days when she'd suspected her parents were too wrapped up in their own misery to think about her.

'No. I have time for you, and I promised. What would you like to see first?'

His words went some way to obliterating her apprehension over the anger she'd witnessed. Her father had never been able to switch off the emotion so quickly. He was an expert at holding grudges.

'It's your home. Surprise me.'

Stefano motioned with his arm. 'Come this way.'

They began walking in silence. Lucy would have been happy with that had it been a comfortable and companionable one. This wasn't.

She nodded to the phone, still gripped tight in his hand. 'Hard day at the office?'

Stefano looked at the mobile as if he'd just remembered he was holding it, frowned, and slid it into the pocket of his trousers. 'Sometimes people need…encouragement to do the right thing.'

They entered a long corridor. The temperature dropped here, and she assumed it was due to the bank of windows running along the right-hand side, giving an uninterrupted view of the bright snowbound landscape. It reminded her once again that whilst Stefano was treating her like an honoured guest right now, she was trapped here.

'It sounded more like evisceration than encouragement. I thought your family were supposed to be Shields of the Crown, not swords.'

'Sometimes a sword is all anyone understands. Most

of my life has been spent being diplomatic. This is a new development.'

'Do you enjoy it? Being an aggressor rather than a protector?'

He looked down at her, his eyes dark and serious. 'I do what's needed.'

They stopped outside a room and, like Stefano's, she saw this door was heavily carved with a coat of arms, although different from the one on his bedroom.

'This crest isn't yours?'

'No,' he said. 'It's the royal family's.'

'It hasn't got a unicorn rampant either. I call it inferior.'

The corner of his mouth twitched. 'I invite you to tell His Highness. I suspect he'll disagree.'

Before she left the castle she'd get him to smile. But when she did, it would have to be immediately before she walked out through the door, because she was sure his smile would have the capacity to devastate her.

'Why do they get a coat of arms here?'

'This suite's reserved exclusively for Lasserno's royal family.'

'Lucky them. Does the Moretti family get a suite in the palace in return?'

Stefano shrugged. 'I don't stay in the palace. I have a home in the capital.'

That wasn't what she'd asked, but she let it slide. He opened the door and flicked on the lights as they went inside.

'Wow.'

Glittering chandeliers hung from a ceiling which seemed to writhe with frescoes. A heavenly sky…angels blowing trumpets. Thankfully no more gruesome scenes like those she'd come across in other areas of the castle. She didn't need any more reminding of her own mortality. In this room, everywhere she looked something gleamed with the rich burnish of gold.

'Indeed. It's the grandest room in the castle.'

It was all a bit...*much*. 'Do you actually like it?'

Stefano stood in the centre of the room, looking up. 'It's of its time. The whole castle is—though this was a more recent renovation, from the eighteenth century. I find it somewhat extravagant.'

'I was raised in a house in the suburbs.' She tried to stifle a giggle, unsuccessfully. This was so far from where she'd come from. 'You live in a *castle*, Stefano. I think you've cornered the market on extravagance.'

He sighed. 'My apologies. This is my life; it's normal to me. But some days I feel more a custodian of history rather than a true resident.'

'I'm not sure I could sleep in here, with all those angels heralding my divine right to rule and my hereditary magnificence.'

'Most royalty enjoy their own magnificence a little too much.'

'What about Lasserno's current Prince?'

Stefano's mouth tightened and a muscle in his jaw ticked. 'He's a good man.'

There was a world of pain in his expression. She knew about wounds that were kept well-hidden, considering she had a few of her own.

'You should explore,' Stefano said. 'Treat the room like you own it.'

Lucy smiled. 'That's a loaded invitation. You never know what I'll get up to.'

He seemed wound so tight and tense, that she wanted to loosen him up a bit. Untie those mental knots that kept him so firmly bound. She walked through to a bathroom, with bright mosaic tiles on the floor, gilt mirrors, a shower which appeared to be a newer addition. But it was the huge bath which would fit four people easily that grabbed her full attention.

She went to it, peered inside. 'It's hand-painted. With fish and mermaids.' She turned to Stefano. 'Your bath isn't.'

'Praise all things holy. I might become self-conscious, being watched by all those judgemental eyes. Especially the mermaids. Their standards appear…high.'

She had to admit they did look rather judgemental.

'I don't think you have anything to be self-conscious about.'

Stefano raised an eyebrow. 'Really?'

There was a silence again, but this silence wasn't uncomfortable. It was full of things left unsaid. He seemed looser, his gaze softer as he looked at the bath, then at her. She could imagine him lying there, his warm brown skin slick in the water. The feel of him…two bodies sliding together limbs entwined…

Lucy's cheeks heated. 'You *know* you don't.'

His dark eyes twinkled. Again, he wasn't smiling as such, but there was no mistaking the fact that he was… amused.

'Please tell me—I'd appreciate your insight.'

She waved her hand up and down, generally indicating his glorious body. 'Tall, dark, handsome count with a castle. Really, Stefano. You're the perfect cliché.'

His mouth curled and broke into a blinding smile, and then he chuckled, the deep, throaty sound rolling right through her in a wave of heat that warmed her way better than any fire. It was sweeter than the hot chocolate he'd made for her. She wanted to kiss that mouth…the crinkles at the corners of his eyes…as the whole of him stopped looking dark and brooding and simply blazed like the sun.

She was weak for him. Stefano made her as gooey inside as the marshmallows she'd fantasised about toasting. She had to get away. Because if she didn't, she might beg him to kiss her.

She scurried from the bathroom and went through another door. Stefano followed. She could tell he was close from the way goosebumps shimmied up and down her spine at his palpable presence. The next room she walked into was the royal bedroom, with a huge bed covered in a rich blue velvet and gold-embossed pillows. Even worse than the bathroom.

'Have you ever been in here and been tempted to break some unwritten rules?'

'Lucy, what are you asking?'

A wry grin played on his lips. It was a good look on him. It seemed impossible that he could become any more handsome till he'd smiled. Then he became devastating.

'I don't know… Did you ever jump on the bed as a child?'

He put his hand to his heart, his expression earnest, but she knew he was playing along. 'I would never have dared. But how would *you* like to feel like royalty?'

'What do you mean?'

Stefano looked at the bed. Looked at her. Cocked his eyebrow. 'I won't tell anyone if you want to try out the bed.'

Lucy grinned. She couldn't help herself. Her heart beat faster with the thrill of it all. 'Okay, but I won't jump on it. I promise. Kind of…'

She toed off her shoes and climbed onto the soft velvet cover. Flopped down on her back and made the shape of a starfish.

'What do you think?' he asked.

'Why don't you try it out for yourself?' She patted the bed beside her.

He started forward, then hesitated.

'You know you want to… *Your Excellency.*'

Stefano kicked off his shoes as well. Lucy straightened herself out and allowed some room for him as he lay down too, in a dignified, manly kind of way. No flopping to be seen.

He let out a long, slow breath. Moved about a bit as if trying out the mattress. 'I like mine better.'

Even though the bed was enormous, lying there with Stefano was still too close. Lucy closed her eyes for a moment, tried to shut him out as they lay in silence, but she still caught a hint of him. A scent like warm spice. That smell had invaded her dreams, as had the man himself. And, whilst she couldn't really remember what had actually happened in them, all she knew was that she'd woken up with the sheets tangled round her legs, the whole bed in disarray, and a delicious warmth sliding through her.

'I think that I prefer your bed too.'

Lucy opened her eyes. Her voice didn't sound like her own. More of a sultry whisper than a statement of fact. Stefano turned his head, his dark eyes blacker than usual, the pupils drowning out the espresso-brown. Her heart thumped. That familiar rush of heat which she'd woken up to was now rushing through her. Enticing. Intoxicating. She knew what it was—desire. And she couldn't, *shouldn't* desire this man. Not when her life was such a mess. Especially not when she was keeping secrets from him.

Then his lips parted, his fingers flexing on the coverlet. The moment swelled with possibility.

'What do you like about my bed, Lucy?'

The smell of you. Imagining you in it naked. With me.

But she couldn't say any of those things.

'The canopy. The constellations. I miss seeing the stars for real. There's too much light in the big cities here.'

A look passed across his face. Stark, blank...almost hopeless. Stefano turned his head to stare up at the ceiling. Then he sat up, ran his hand through his hair. 'The castle's large, and there's much more to show you.'

She regretted the change in mood. That she hadn't taken a leap of faith and told him what she really felt. But she wasn't sure she could trust him. She hardly trusted herself.

'I promise I won't have you breaking any more rules,' she said. 'Even though I think you kind of enjoyed it.'

The corner of his mouth kicked up in another wry kind of grin which made him look younger, almost devilish, and her silly heart tripped over itself.

'It's one more sin to add to a list of many,' he said.

Yet despite that lightness his voice carried a weight heavy enough to break a person. She wanted to reach out, clasp his hand, ask what was wrong, but she wasn't sure he'd accept it or give her an honest answer.

Instead, Lucy slid off the bed. She straightened the crushed covers and dented pillows as he did the same on his side. Their movements struck her as intensely intimate and domestic.

She swallowed, her mouth dry. 'Where to now?'

'Perhaps the portrait gallery, so you can view the members of my noble family?'

She didn't want to see that—all those pictures of his deceased and judgemental relatives. She wanted to know more about *him*, the man, with a ferocity that completely overtook her.

'Do you have a favourite place here? One you love more than anywhere else?'

'*Sí.*'

'Then take me there.'

He needed to get out of here. Escape this room. Lying down next to her had been a mistake. Not because he was concerned that only the bodies of royalty should lie in the hallowed bed they'd lain on together—that was the flimsy lie he'd told himself. It was more.

The naked avalanche of desire that had struck and mown him down, crushing his will. Seeing her lying on that royal bed, with her strawberry blonde hair spilling over the pillows, he hadn't been able to help but think of her in *his* bed. Which had led to inevitable thoughts of being in that bed with her.

It had been all he could do when they'd lain on the pristine covers not to invite her into his arms. Kiss her. Evoke soft moans of pleasure as he made love to her, burying himself in the warmth of Lucy's body and forgetting everything. But forgetting wasn't an option. Not for him. He needed to remember, to dwell on his pain. Because he hadn't served his penance yet and might never do so.

He went to the door of the Royal Suite. She wanted to know his favourite place here? He'd show her. That was safer than this fever which gripped him in its thrall.

They walked together through some of the service corridors, utilitarian spaces of rough-hewn stone and little embellishment.

'I don't know how you find your way around,' said Lucy. 'Do you ever get lost?'

Stefano looked over at her. Her cheeks were red. She seemed a little puffed.

He adjusted his stride and slowed down for her. 'As children we ran wild in this place.'

'A game of hide and seek must have been impossible. You'd never find each other.'

'Mainly we hid from the nanny and our lessons. But I came away with an excellent mental map of the castle.'

'Where were your mum and dad?'

'Politicking. Their favourite pastime. Here we are.'

He grabbed the hem of his sweater and pulled it over his head. Dropped it on a chair outside some double doors. The chill of the air on this side of the castle was an immediate shock after the warmth of his clothing.

'What are you doing?' Lucy asked.

She was staring at him with a mixture of surprise that he should be undressing in the cold, and something else.

With her eyes a little wider, and her mouth in an unspoken *oh*, it looked a lot like…fascination.

He preferred her looking at him like this, with a kind of wonder on her face. Not the way she'd been earlier, when her eyes had been wide with trepidation. Stefano hadn't wanted Lucy to witness his ugliness, what he'd become in his pursuit of redemption. It was important that she think well of him, and he didn't stop to analyse why.

'Trust me when I say you won't need your coat here.'

Lucy narrowed her eyes, but she shrugged her coat off, dropped it on the chair over his sweater. Her long-sleeved knit top hugged her figure, gave him a tantalising glimpse of her slender waist, the perfect swell of her breasts. She was his guest—in his care. He shouldn't be lusting over her. But she was all beauty and sunshine and he craved the light.

She wrapped her arms round her waist. Bounced up and down on her toes. 'Okay, I'm officially freezing.'

'You won't be for long.'

He pushed the double doors open into an entrance hall. A rich, earthy smell permeated the space. The temperature here was warmer, the air more humid.

Lucy relaxed a little, her arms looser by her side as she seemed to unknot. 'Where *are* we?'

Stefano smiled. 'One of the castle's greatest treasures.'

He walked towards some glass doors which were fogged, with rivulets of moisture running down the inside, and opened them. Heat and humidity blasted them like a palpable hit from the expansive tropical conservatory. Full of palms and ferns, it was a wonder of his mountain home. Even though he'd been here numerous times, it never failed to amaze him.

'This is incredible,' Lucy said, her voice full of breathless wonder. 'I can't believe the castle has somewhere like *this*.'

Condensation covered the glass, so it was difficult to

see outside. On the days when you could it was a kind of magic, standing in the tropics whilst the world outside lay gripped in the depths of winter.

'One of my ancestors was a renowned horticulturalist who designed and built a famed Italian-style garden at the palace. But his first love was the tropics. He sought to create the same here. In many ways, this conservatory was considered his folly.'

It's what had prompted his brother to study horticulture. As children they'd spent so much time here, paddling in the tropical pond, hiding in the ferns. On returning from the capital, it had always been the first place in the castle Stefano visited after speaking with the staff. Whenever he walked in here, breathed the warm air, it was as if all the stress he carried was untangled.

Perspiration pricked at the back of Stefano's neck. It wouldn't be long before it was too hot in here for either of them, wearing all their winter clothing.

As if reading his mind, Lucy peeled off her long-sleeved top, leaving herself in a clinging strappy under-shirt, with a shadow of perspiration at her lower back.

Palms fanned out overhead, the whole place lush and fertile. The only sound in the space was the crunch of Lucy's boots on the gravel path and the plink of water dripping into the pond.

'It's almost like the rainforest I went bushwalking in as a child…'

She turned to him and held her arms out wide, looking up at a tree fern like a huge green umbrella above them. A few droplets of condensation from its fronds dripped on her face.

She smiled, wiped them away. 'Who looks after all this?'

'It's my brother's project now. Some gardeners help, but I sent them home with the rest of the staff. Most of the water is controlled by computer, but Gino tells me what else is needed. He asks for photographs of the plants that worry him. Sometimes I'll hand-water, if what's provided by the sprinkler system isn't enough.'

'I can't believe you don't spend all your time here. It's almost like you're punishing yourself, living this ascetic life in a few cold rooms.'

How close she was to the truth. 'I'd hardly call living in a castle "ascetic". You said it was extravagant.'

She narrowed her eyes. 'You're being obtuse and know exactly what I mean.'

What would she think of him if she discovered the full extent of how far he'd fallen? He didn't know why that thought filled him with dread.

Luckily, she didn't question him any further. Instead, Lucy walked towards the pond, trailed her hands through the water which, from experience, he knew would be warm. He was only sorry the water lilies weren't in bloom. Lucy would love the water lilies.

'Why is the temperature in the rest of the castle so cold when in here it's like this?'

'If the temperature falls in this place, it will all die.' After everything else he'd done, he would not lose this too. 'What does it matter if I'm cold? To protect it until Bruno can repair the heating, I'm diverting most of the resources to the conservatory.'

She frowned. 'You're diverting some to me too. I should go and leave you be. Not add to your worries.'

'You're welcome here, Lucy. And I don't want you to leave until I've heard you play.'

She pressed the thumb of her right hand deep into her left palm and rubbed, staring into the distance. He wondered if she even knew she was doing it—the action seemed almost reflexive. She moved further into the space, gently brushing aside some plants hanging across her path.

'This is such a special place...'

'It's where I proposed to my fiancée.'

He didn't know why he'd made that admission. It was one of the reasons he only came here out of necessity lately—although with Lucy's presence the pain of the memory seemed somehow distant. Not so bright and fresh…more like a sun-faded photograph.

'Thank you for bringing me here, then. It must be hard, with those memories. Especially since this is your favourite place in the castle.'

When he'd planned his proposal his intention had been to take Celine to a tropical island, chasing summer. But Alessio's father had abdicated, throwing Lasserno into crisis. Instead he'd brought her here, because the conservatory had always seemed to him like another world.

'She didn't really like it. Said the humidity made her hair kink.'

Lucy stared at him but said nothing, and he appreciated her silence. He noted that in the humidity her hair had developed a distinctive curl to it. She didn't seem to mind—or perhaps she didn't even notice.

Lucy strolled back towards him, a fine sheen of perspiration across her skin, making her gleam. 'I hope you don't mind me asking, but why did your engagement end?'

The real truth he couldn't admit. He wouldn't have Lucy thinking less of him—not when in this moment he felt as if life had some hope again. The sensation would fade soon enough, when reality intruded, but for now he wanted this. To keep it and hold it for himself. Where was the harm?

He shrugged. 'I've taken a…a step back from my role as His Highness's secretary to repair the castle. My fiancée liked my status and links to the Crown more than she liked me.'

Lucy's eyes widened. 'Gosh, I'd marry you for the conservatory alone. Who cares about a prince?'

Laughter burst from her. The joy on her face was infectious. He couldn't help himself. He laughed too. She did that to him—brought back the connection to his humanity when before it was as if he'd forgotten how to have fun. And that feeling—the shining light of happiness and his enjoyment of Lucy's company—flared inside him, strong and bright.

'You're worth more, you know,' she said. 'You're not your work. No one is.'

His role was all he had. All he'd been born to. All he'd aspired to. All he'd ever wanted. He and Alessio against the world, carving their own path. But he wondered now, as he watched Lucy nibbling on her lower lip with an inward-looking expression on her face, whether she'd been speaking to him or herself.

'How would you know?' he asked.

She seemed to shake herself from that introspection and come back to him.

'You're dedicated to what appears to be an unpleasant job right now. You're here in the castle on your own, freezing yourself, making sure that the conservatory your brother loves stays alive. You've taken me in—some muddy stranger on your doorstep. You seem like a good man, and finding a good man is hard.'

'I'm simply a man, Lucy. More flawed than most, I promise you.'

It was a warning to her not to get close. A reminder to himself not to forget who he was and what he had to do here—even if the reasons seemed to be a little fuzzy and out of focus today.

'My mother says that if you break up with someone you should reclaim the places you went together as a couple just for yourself. To own them again. I did that after...'

'After you broke up with your boyfriend?'

She let out a deep and heavy sigh. 'After I found my ex-boyfriend in bed with another member of the orchestra. A pretty young viola player.'

A hot burst of anger roared through him like a flash fire. How could anyone do that to her, especially someone he supposed she'd loved?

'You're a beautiful young violinist, and he was a fool.'

Her lips turned up in a soft smile, but her eyes remained sad. 'Thank you. I'm trying to think that, but it's been hard. At least we weren't engaged. But the point of this isn't to get sympathy for myself. There was a little café in Salzburg we used to go to during rehearsals. It sold the best pastries. Just before I came here, I went there. Ordered a coffee and cake and sat. Enjoyed it on my own. I took the café back. That's what *you* need to do—make new memories for yourself.'

'Perhaps I will.'

She was so bright—like one of the vibrant orchids which bloomed here. A splash of colour in all the green. Any thoughts associated with this place would now seem full of her.

'What would it take for me to capture good memories here, to reclaim this space, Lucy?'

She hesitated. 'I—I don't know. But…something momentous?'

Her face and cheeks flushed the colour of a newly opened rose. She looked like summer, standing there in her strappy top, with the bare skin of her arms exposed and pale. Everything here smelled raw, like life and earth, except for her. Lucy was the delicate hint of flowers. She wasn't merely beautiful, but achingly so. The warm gold of her eyes glowing in the light.

All Stefano could think about now was the pout of her exquisite mouth…how he wanted to run his thumb over her lower lip to see if it was as soft as it appeared. He reached out. Hesitated a moment. She didn't move away. Instead, she leaned into him. He drifted his thumb over that perfect lower lip and it was as silky as he had imagined. Her eyes fluttered closed, her eyelashes fanning over her cheeks.

A kiss would do it—chase away any remaining memories of a day that was supposed to be special and instead had somehow *lacked*. But kissing Lucy would be wrong. It would be madness. And still he stepped towards her, eased his arms around her waist.

Her eyes opened, then widened, and she slid the palms of her hands flat on his chest, splaying her fingers over his muscles. A tremor ran through her. Not cold, but goosebumps, which peppered her skin under his fingers. He dropped his head and she rose to meet him.

The merest brush of their mouths and he was lost. Lucy was black ice. She was danger. Someone who diverted him from what he needed to do, from what was right. And yet he didn't care. Instead, he let go. Allowed himself to slip and to fall.

A flame of desire ignited and took hold.

Lucy made a sound, almost pained, pressed harder into his body as if she couldn't get close enough. So he tightened his arms till there was no space between them. Her lips parted under his as their tongues touched, slipped over one another.

It didn't seem like a first kiss, where two people needed to learn one another. This was more knowing. A passionate give and take. Nothing tentative. A kiss driven only by instinct.

Stefano was hard, aching. Almost desperate. He should stop, but the kiss only deepened. She must know—she'd have to feel his need, pressed together as they were. Still, she didn't pull away, and he hoped she never would. This was desire in its purest form—a welcoming of two bodies together in perfect harmony. They shouldn't, but he wanted to have her here. Except there was nowhere to lie. And this was a woman who deserved a bed with soft covers and crisp sheets. Not ravishment on a garden bench or moist earth.

His mind catalogued the places close by. He could swoop her into his arms, take her back to the Royal Suite and make love to her there…

Then he noticed her slowing, pulling away. He wanted to chase the kiss. Fight for it. But instead he stopped and pulled back too, even though inside he howled like a wild animal. He looked down at her lips, plump and red. Her breath coming in heavy gusts, mirroring his own. He loosened his arms, even though he wanted to tell her she should never leave them.

'I…' It was as if Lucy couldn't get out any words. Her eyes were glazed, her pupils wide. Her dumbfounded look mirrored how he felt.

'If that's not what you wanted, I'm sorr—'

'No. It was perfect…' She raised a trembling hand to her mouth. 'The perfect way for you to take this place back. I'm glad I could…help.'

Lucy stepped away from him.

He knew he should stop her, but she turned and fled. Stefano could do nothing but let her go.

CHAPTER SEVEN

LUCY LOOKED OUT of the window of Stefano's room. The sun was out, the snow no longer falling. She'd had dinner in here last night, after getting a text saying he had to work and would leave a meal in the kitchen for her. She'd welcomed the breakfast tray he'd dropped outside her door this morning, giving her some space. Apart from texts, they hadn't spoken at all.

Did he regret what had happened?

She lifted her fingers to her lips and closed her eyes, revisiting the kiss that had kept her awake half the night. The pleasure of it was still humming through her veins. How she'd never wanted it to stop, but known it *had* to.

She still hadn't told him about the violin, and something about keeping that secret now didn't feel right. When she'd first arrived, she hadn't been sure of him and how he might react to what she had to say. Now she didn't want to ruin this growing understanding between them that was as confusing as it was precious.

Only the pure force of the iron will which helped her practise through boredom and sometimes pain had her running away from Stefano in the conservatory as if their kiss had meant nothing but a mere favour. Who was she kidding? It hadn't done any favours for her. It had rocked her world.

Lucy wasn't sure what it had done for Stefano. She

wasn't completely naïve. He'd been hard. Aroused. But she figured that simply happened when a man got up close and personal with any woman. And maybe when she'd stepped back he might have had a confused look, as if he'd taken a hard knock to the head, but she didn't really know. She hadn't been thinking very clearly herself.

Which was why she was here with her violin, looking to play. It grounded her, losing herself in the music. Reminded her of who she really was. Trying to achieve the perfect pitch and those notes that sang through her and her instrument so she could forget the wallop of passion she hadn't realised could exist between two people.

In her limited experience, with only one boyfriend, it had never occurred to her that there was something in the world better than the feeling she could get from her playing. But Stefano's lips on hers had eclipsed it all, and they'd been fully clothed. She'd never wanted the moment to end.

Lucy tried to ignore the wicked hum inside that tempted her to think of him less…*dressed*. She couldn't. Wouldn't. Some might say that thoughts were free, but that kind of thinking would take her nowhere.

Lucy started with the exercises her physiotherapist had told her to work on, warming up her hands and gently stretching them before picking up her violin, her bow. So familiar they were like old friends, like part of her. She played some simple scales first. Her fingers might be a bit stiff but there was no pain today, so she started a more complicated exercise.

When she'd finished a knock sounded at the door. Soft, not a demand, more a polite request to enter.

Her heart rate jumped from *lento* to *presto*, and it was only luck and good fortune that stopped her bow slipping from her fingers and falling to the floor.

'Come in.' Her voice sounded thready and faint. She swallowed as the door eased open.

Stefano entered the room slowly, as if he wasn't sure what would greet him. She supposed she had fled from him and the conservatory the day before like a vampire trying to escape dawn. It hadn't been a dignified exit.

He stood there in his usual clothing. Jeans, boots, sweater. Effortlessly casual and artfully dishevelled. She, on the other hand, was a mish-mash of figure-hugging active wear and a warm pullover that had seen better days but was soft and warm as a hug.

It didn't seem to matter to Stefano. He looked at her as if she was a steaming cup of coffee after a long, sleepless night. How she wanted him to drink her right down. And all she could think about now was the contrasts of him. Hard body, gentle lips, a kiss that stopped time...

'Please. I heard the music,' he said. 'You don't have to stop for me.'

Lucy tried not to think about how perfect it had been, having his arms wrapped tight around her. 'I was only practising a little.'

'Would you play something?'

'I don't have any accompaniment.'

It was a cop-out. She didn't need a soundtrack. What stopped her was the nerves churning in her belly like that hive of bees again, intent on stinging her. She wanted to know what he thought—whether the kiss had stunned him as much as it had her. It shouldn't matter, but somehow his approval seemed vital. Because something had changed in those moments in the conservatory. Things she couldn't give voice to.

'If you did, what would you play for me?'

Light filtered through the mullioned windows. Outside the landscape lay crisp, cold and perfect. That pristine beauty masked a creeping danger to those who were unwary. And that sense of hidden peril was a lot like the way she'd come to view love—though why *that* word should enter her head now she didn't know.

'Vivaldi. *Four Seasons.* "Winter".'

Stefano pulled his cell phone from his pocket and smiled. 'For a woman who hates winter, you have an affinity for it.'

'I can admit it looks pretty,' she said, as he unlocked his phone and began scrolling through. 'You know my feelings otherwise.'

He raised a dark, perfect eyebrow. 'Are you comfortable here?'

The question was a loaded one, but gently asked. She gave a truthful answer. 'I am, thank you.'

Lucy wasn't apprehensive the way she had been in the beginning. She was more afraid of herself and her feelings, which seemed to want to leak out all over the place—especially all over him.

He nodded, and something about him relaxed. His stance appeared a little looser, as if he'd been worried before and was not so much now.

After a few short minutes Stefano seemed to find what he was looking for and held up his phone with the screen facing her. 'Is this you?'

She walked forward, peered at the screen. It was a video of her charity performance with a string ensemble a few years earlier. She swallowed through the knot in her throat. 'Yes.'

His lips curled into a smile. 'Then we have accompanying music—of sorts. I can cast the sound to the speakers here. I would love to hear you. The snow's stopped falling. If it stays that way, the roads will be clear soon enough.'

Meaning she'd be able to go. Walk away from here and never see him again. She didn't know why that thought hurt. But this was a wish she could grant for the kindness he had shown her. She'd needed a soft landing after all she'd been through, and even though he might not have realised Stefano had given her that.

'Okay. That should work.'

She would be better than the performance on video, so that would compensate for her lack of practice. She could do this. It would be just like playing along, and the background sound would hide any stumbles from the fingers that still didn't work so well.

Stefano walked to an armchair in front of the fire and sat. 'Ready?'

She took a few moments, a deep breath in, a slow exhalation, settling the churn in her belly. Something more than the normal apprehension she might experience before a concert. It was as if this performance was the most important of her life. The need gripped her to be perfect for him, an audience of one.

Lucy positioned her violin, her bow. Nodded. He pressed play and there was a pregnant silence before the staccato sound of strings filled the room. His eyes were on her, intent, as Lucy waited in those thrilling moments full of expectation before she struck the first notes of flawless sound, vibrating through her and her instrument. It settled the cracking nerves, soothed the bumps of fear. And then that sense of release overwhelmed her, and she was nothing but the flow of sound as her fingers worked and she drew her bow across the strings. Immersed in her playing, ceasing to exist bar a pinprick of consciousness where the music became everything.

But all the while she knew.

Something about this was different.

It was more than the joy of the music. She played for *him*—Stefano. All the words left unsaid after their kiss in the conservatory were poured into her playing, and she hoped he heard what she'd been unable to voice, what the music allowed her to feel. Hoped he had the sense that she'd shared part of her soul with him.

Then she closed her eyes, let the memory of their

perfect kiss wash over her, flood her playing, and sank into the music and her message, allowing herself to be carried away.

As patron of Lasserno's orchestra Stefano had seen a great deal of music performed live before, by some of the best musicians on the planet. He was privileged in that regard. But this was something else…having music played for him alone by Lucy.

It was a revelation.

He couldn't take his eyes from her… He felt the intimacy of this moment as he had in those perfect seconds as their lips had touched the day before. When he'd thought there could be nothing much better in the world than the way his need for her had hit his blood like a shot of spirits.

It was like that now, watching her play her violin. Her eyes half closed. Her face serene at times, agonised at others. He became immersed in the music as each note struck him, like an arrow to the chest. The sound embedded inside him, swelling and growing till the passion in her playing filled him.

It could crack you in two this music. How could someone take wood and strings and create a sound like from heaven?

In those moments it filled him to overflowing, as if the emotions in the music would spill out of him too. Lucy's performance—the brilliance of her—had stolen his voice. His breath. It had stolen everything. He was lost in her. The perfect sound reverberated from the walls, flooded through him as if it could cleanse his very soul. He'd experienced many things in life. Beauty, pleasure, joy. But nothing could eclipse these moments now, when she played for him. It was as if every note carried a message, inscribed on his soul in permanent ink. An indelible mark.

Then, in a flurry of brilliance, fingers and bow, the music ended too soon. The crowd on the video applauded and he wished he could provide a true crowd here, to fete the genius he'd witnessed. But there was only him. Unworthy in all ways. He still clapped, though, because what more could he do? She deserved the accolades, the cheers of *Bravo!* that the audience on the video provided for her in a standing ovation.

He stood as well, whilst she clutched her violin with a beatific smile and bowed. Colour sat high on her cheeks. She breathed hard, looking like a woman who had experienced ecstasy.

In a blinding moment he wished he'd been the one to put that look on her face.

'You're magnificent,' he said. His voice didn't sound like his own. It was strangely hollow, almost as if he were speaking outside himself.

'Thank you. I haven't performed for a while. I made some mistakes.'

'I would never have guessed. I don't know how you do it.'

He approached her and she looked up at him, glowing. 'Easy. Fingers. Bow. Practice.'

'Don't undersell yourself. What you do is *not* easy. I wouldn't be able to play a single note.'

'Of course you could. I could show you.'

He looked at the precious instrument which she held so lightly in her brilliant hands. Stefano knew the value of a violin so old—both in monetary terms and to a performer like her. She'd been willing to sleep with it to prevent it getting too cold. To let him touch it…?

'One note?' he said.

She smiled, and the warmth of her happiness filled him with the same joy as if she was still playing her violin for him.

'We'll start with the bow. Thumb here in the space.' She showed him and it looked effortless. A light touch which created magic. 'Middle fingers curled over. Tip of the little finger on the top of the bow.'

Lucy gave the bow to him and Stefano followed her instructions.

She nodded. 'Pretty good. Now, take the violin and hold it firmly round the neck.'

She held it out to him and he grasped the wood, still warm from her hand, as she circled round behind him.

'Don't drop it, but don't throttle it either.'

Her voice was close, and he could still hear the smile in it.

'Stand with your feet shoulder-width apart and relax.'

'I'm holding the three-hundred-year-old instrument of a renowned violinist, Lucy. I'm unable to *relax*.'

That, and he could sense her warmth. The knowledge of her standing close was sending a shiver down his spine.

She snorted. 'Fair point. Now, put the violin on the top of your shoulder, cheek and chin on the rest, try not to tense up…'

He simply listened to her lilting voice, followed what she told him to do.

'I just need to adjust you a bit, okay?' she said.

'Of course.'

Her hands were on him then, and he was captive to her gentle touch, changing his position. Hers to move however she pleased as she murmured words of encouragement. He lost himself in her, forgetting about the valuable instrument he held, focussed entirely on her because nothing else existed. He wondered if anything ever would again after this. It was as if the longer she was here, the more she was changing him.

Lucy stood back a little, inspected him. 'You're perfect.'

He wished he was…but that man didn't exist any more. Still, he would pretend—for her.

She approached again, from the front. 'Now, draw the bow across the strings.'

Stefano did, and the violin gave an unearthly screech. He stopped immediately.

Lucy laughed. 'Everyone does that the first time they play—even me. It's not about failing; it's about not giving up. Here.'

She adjusted the bow's position a fraction, her fingers warm on his skin.

'Try again.'

He did, and the note reverberated through him, a clear, crisp sound. One. Perfect. Note.

'You did it!'

Her smile was like the midday sun hitting snowfall. It blinded him.

'A beautifully played D! I know it's not a piano, but you said you'd always wanted to play an instrument. Maybe you can learn?'

He handed her back the violin, her bow, and she did what she needed to with them before placing them safely back in the case.

'Thank you.'

His voice sounded cracked. He'd enjoyed many advantages of his birth, his position, but of all the things he'd been able to do this moved him more than any other. Her thoughtfulness, everything about her, called to him. All he wanted to do was reach out…touch. Let her brilliance cleanse him of his many sins.

Lucy shifted her violin out of the way and flexed her hand. Pressed her thumb deep into her palm.

'You do that often,' he said.

She shrugged. 'I suffered an injury and I've had to rest it. But since I've been here it hasn't been too bad.'

'And I asked you to play for me. I'm sorry. I didn't know.'

She'd been reluctant to play when he'd asked and perhaps this was the reason why.

'It was good. I've been at a…a crossroads. Playing hasn't been as joyful as it once was. I've been wondering if I should stop—but then who would I be?'

It was a terrifyingly familiar sentiment.

Lucy continued working her thumb into her wrist and then into her forearm. He hoped her playing today hadn't hurt her. If it had, it was just another thing to feel guilty for.

Stefano reached out to her, hesitated. 'May I?'

Lucy held out her hand, palm up. He took it, cradled it in his own. The tips of her fingers were flushed pink. He brushed his own over them, then her palm. She gave a sharp exhalation.

'Do they hurt?' he asked.

'Not for a long time. I have calluses there now.'

Her voice was a whisper as he touched her skin and held the true instrument of her brilliance—not the violin, but her hands. He stroked his finger along her palm, then down each of her fingers. The pupils of her golden eyes flared wide and dark.

'Who would think that flesh and bone could contain such skill?'

'I've worked hard and my body's suffering for it.'

'Is it painful right now?' He pressed his own thumb where he'd seen hers go so often during her short stay here.

She moaned softly. 'You're strong. Better than my physiotherapist.' She looked up at him. 'That feels so good.'

He shouldn't be this close to her. He shouldn't be touching her. Because all he wanted to do was kiss her pain away. Their kiss in the conservatory had been a revelation. Lucy in his arms…confusing everything that he'd thought he wanted or needed. The way they'd fitted together so perfectly had made him question his place, where he should be—because now there was no more important place than here. In the mountains of his ancestral home. Alone with Lucy and her music.

The sound of it had awakened something in him—as though for years he'd been walking through a fog and then she'd entered his life and it had lifted to reveal a brilliant, sunny day he hadn't realised existed. Burned off the mist of despair to give him something dangerous, like hope. Hope that underneath—somewhere buried deep—he was still a good man.

'You are a miracle,' he whispered.

He took her hand and placed it on the flat of his chest, his own hand over hers. The warmth of her palm almost burned through his clothes. She looked up at him, her lips parted, cheeks still flushed a sunset-pink. The pupils of her eyes were wide and dark, almost obliterating the warm honey-brown.

'Not a miracle…just a woman.'

'No, you're more.'

He cupped her jaw with his free hand and lowered his mouth to hers. She met him halfway. Their lips touched and it was if something inside them exploded as they burst into life. She slid her hands up, over his shoulders and into his hair, gripping tight as if never wanting to let him go. He wound his arms around her, pressing her into him. Her body against his was still the perfect fit.

The fire crackled low in the hearth, warming the room, filling it with a dusky glow. There was no one here but her and him…two people shipwrecked together. The world would exist again soon enough, but today he needed to pretend. His whole life had been set out for him, directed as if it were a play and he a mere actor. Lucy wasn't written into any script, but for once he craved to do what he wanted rather than what was required of him.

Lucy was unexpected. A bright, perfect burst of passion in what had otherwise been a passionless life—one of duty and honour but somehow *lacking*. He hadn't seen it before, but he knew it now, with brutal clarity as he held this woman in his arms and simply allowed himself to *want*. Nothing would intrude—not his duty to his siblings, not recovering the Crown Jewels. For now he was simply Stefano Moretti the man. Not His Excellency the Count of Varno, Shield of the Crown.

He slowed the kiss before passion completely overtook him…pulled back. Lucy made a muffled sound of protest.

'I crave you, Lucy. Crave to make love to you and to hell with tomorrow. Tell me you want that too.'

She looked up at him, her lips a deep blush-pink, her golden eyes searching his face. She wasn't pushing him away, but he loosened his arms nonetheless. Stefano recognised the disparity of their positions. He didn't want her to feel beholden to him, for giving her shelter in the castle. He was in the position of power, but he needed her to know she had all the control.

'If you don't want what I do I'll walk away. You've nothing to fear.'

The corners of her perfect mouth tilted as she threaded her hands into his hair once more. His heart thumped hard and fast, beating in his chest like timpani.

'I'm not afraid of you.' Her voice was soft, like the sound of the world in the moments before snow fell. 'Take me to bed, Stefano.'

He groaned and swept her into his arms. Her lips had parted and her eyes were bright with a glorious flame. He walked the short distance to his bed, placed her gently on the covers. She needed care, reverence, this woman who played like an angel and injured herself for her art.

That heady drumbeat in his chest drove him, spurred him onwards. But he was tired of a life that was hard and fast. All he craved was softness.

He kicked off his shoes, lay over her. Lucy's body was supple and pliant under him. She parted her legs and he settled between them, resting in her warmth, aching with desire. He dropped his lips to hers again and she welcomed him. Their tongues touched and he was lost. The scent of her was rich, like raspberries and cream. Like the perfect dessert at the end of a meal. It was a promise of something that might be out of reach for ever, but for today was his to grasp.

He slid a hand under her top, skating over her side, her ribs, and she quivered.

'Cold?' he murmured.

He should get her under the covers, but for the moment he simply wanted to be here…with her. She wrapped her legs around him, pressing herself up into him, and his breath hitched.

'Not around you.'

His hand rose higher, over her bra to the tight knot of her nipple. He circled a finger over it. As his lips plundered hers, Lucy's back arched and she gave a pained moan.

'Like that?' he asked.

'More…'

He smiled as he gazed down at her, Lucy's eyes were glazed and distant as she panted underneath him. 'Greedy.'

But he obliged, happy to feed her desire till she was full with it. His touch was firmer now, like a pinch, and again she arched her body into his palm. He didn't care about himself—not in that moment. All he cared for was Lucy's pleasure, her gasping breaths, the way she quivered under his touch.

He needed to explore all her glorious skin in the warmth of this bed. He moved off her. 'You're wearing too much.'

'So are you.'

Her chest heaved, her gaze glassy and drugged from mere kisses. He couldn't wait to see how she'd look when he'd made love to her for hours.

Stefano wanted to wreck them both.

He hoped the smile he gave her showed his wicked intent. 'I'll come later. For now, this is about *your* pleasure.'

He slid his hands up her body to the top of her leggings, began to drag the fabric down her long legs. She wriggled, trying to help. Made a sound of frustration.

He lifted his hands from her. 'Shh… Be still. Trust me to look after you.'

She stopped moving, lay there quietly with a glorious pout on her lips. 'Hurry.'

He'd prove to her the benefits of going slow.

Little by little the pale expanse of her skin was exposed. He tossed her clothing aside with her socks. Leaned over her with his hands either side of her waist. Dropped his head to touch his lips gently to her belly. Kissed her lower and lower, tracing his tongue over her warm flesh till he reached her underwear.

Then he kissed the heart of her. The scent of her arousal teasing his senses. Driving him on. He hooked his fingers into her panties and tugged them down. Tossed them over his shoulder as his gaze feasted on the curve of her waist, the neat thatch of golden hair between her thighs.

'Open your legs for me.' His voice ground out of him, barely in control.

She did, and he kissed her there. The salt-sweet of her. He closed his eyes and traced his tongue along her overheated flesh. Stroked her inner thighs with his thumbs as she quivered and shook, then speared her hands into his hair and gripped hard. His name on her lips was soft at first, the merest whisper, but it became a chant as he slid a finger into the slick heat of her, then another, and carried her screaming over the precipice.

She lay back, her breaths gulping sobs. The skin under his fingers pebbling with goosebumps. She'd be cold and he was still wearing far too much clothing. He stripped as she watched him, the darkness of her pupils obliterating the gold of her eyes.

'Take off the rest of your clothes.' His voice was all command.

She sat up almost in slow motion, as if moving was too hard, her arms lax and limp. She slipped her top over her head. Unclipped her bra. Her nipples stood tight and high. Stefano's mouth watered. He wanted to give them, and her, the attention they deserved.

Soon.

He thrust his trousers down his legs. Stepped out of them. Kicked them aside, trembling with desire. The need to touch her again drove him on. To make her scream his name once more—louder this time. Because there was no one here who could be witness to the pleasure they shared.

He walked to the side of the bed, drew back the covers. She scrambled under them, her strawberry blonde hair spilling over his pillow as he joined her, gathering her close. She wrapped her arms around him. Traced her roughened fingers over his back, the calluses from years of playing teasing his skin. He thrilled at her touch, at the evidence of her dedication and hard work.

'I need you,' she whispered.

'And you'll have me.'

He rolled over, found protection in his bedside drawer, sheathed himself. Then he rolled back to Lucy and gathered her softly in his arms. There was no sound in the room other than the panting of their breath and the crackle of the fire. They'd make their own music soon.

He moved over her again. Notched himself at the juncture of her thighs. Took a few breaths to steady himself. He wanted this to last for hours, so both of them could forget. Him, the looming disgrace he'd brought on his family. Lucy, her pain. Her injury. The cheating ex who'd never deserved a woman so precious.

They would each immerse themselves in each other for a while and pretend the real world couldn't touch them.

And as he slid inside her he lost himself to the rhythm of their bodies and time ceased to exist.

Lucy's whole life had been all about music. The quest for perfection. Hours when it had felt as if she'd never get anything right. The gruelling travel to another town, another city, when sometimes she hadn't felt settled into any place she could call home.

She'd never thought there was anything else for her and she'd never wanted anything more—till this, and Stefano. His touch was like the music, filling her with the same wondrous heat, like a miracle.

His mouth dropped to hers now, his kisses slick and lush. There was no uncertainty. It was as if they'd been kissing each other for years—as if, for her, there'd been no one before him.

His hands stroked her body with reverence. Setting her on fire. Nothing mattered but the here and now and Stefano deep inside her body. As if he was connected to her soul in the rightness of how they moved together.

She wrapped her legs around his muscular thighs, the movement of him slow, aching, and every part of her shivered with the perfection of it. Of the time taken to pleasure her. Of the slow, inexorable burn in her core, the sweet ache that wound higher and tighter.

They moved together in perfect tune, as if they were made for one another. Tears pricked at her eyes. The sensation overwhelming her, hovering on the fine edge of pleasure and pain, held there for what felt like hours. She didn't want it to stop, even though she knew things like this couldn't last.

It would all fall down, this house of cards they'd built around themselves. But for however long it lasted, she would take it. She didn't care. For all her life she'd been rooted in reality. Now she wanted to lose herself in the fantasy of them together.

The way he'd looked at her with wonder when she played—not with the critical gaze that everyone else employed, but with one of pure pleasure—was the same way he gazed at her body now, as if she was the most beautiful woman he'd ever glimpsed. And yet she couldn't fall over the edge, still chasing it like some competition to finish.

'More…' she whispered against his lips.

'I want you all afternoon. I want you into the night. And I want to make sure the pleasure lasts and lasts for you, *cara*.'

She couldn't remember anyone who'd only thought of her. She had never really thought about herself—always about work, about practice, about what others would think. This…her pleasure being his sole focus…was like a bomb going off inside her. Not a slow burn, but an explosion that stole her breath, brought raging heat burning out from her core.

She wrapped herself around him and let it take her, until he joined her in a rush of ecstasy…

CHAPTER EIGHT

LUCY DRIFTED INTO wakefulness surrounded by delicious warmth. There was a comforting weight over her waist. A hard body spooning her back.

She opened her eyes. The weather outside was gloomy again. But everything inside this room seemed to be bursting with sunshine.

The night before had been...astonishing. She'd only ever had one boyfriend. Her work and her practice had meant that there was little time, and with Viktor their passion had been in the music. It had hardly mattered that the physical side of things hadn't set her on fire.

What a fool she'd been. Stefano was like nothing she could ever have dreamed. The way he'd cared for her, her pleasure, above everything...

That wicked slide of heat began its relentless journey through her again. The need inside urging her to turn in his arms, to kiss him and spend the day in bed, revisiting what they'd shared during the night.

Except she still hadn't said anything about her violin. About the copies of the diary entries she carried. Before, she had been unsure of him. She had no excuses now...

The arm round her waist tightened, and with the merest brush of lips against her neck she forgot all else. She wriggled into Stefano, slick and aching. Felt the press of hardness in her back.

He chuckled. 'I see your passion is not only in your playing.'

'That's not what other people have said.'

Stefano sat up and she turned. The covers had fallen from his body. She relished the hard etched muscles, the strong arms, the hair on his chest arrowing down to the juncture of his thighs. This was a man in his absolute prime and she craved every part of him.

'What fools have said those things about you?'

Viktor. He'd made her practise and practise. He'd always said there was something 'lacking' in her music. Something she needed to find because if she did she might be extraordinary. She'd listened because, whilst he wasn't first violin, he was a brilliant and renowned musician in his own right and she'd thought he had her best interests in mind.

All it had done was make her question her playing. But it felt wrong to mention him now, in this bed, after Stefano had made love to her all night. Had made her forget all her problems and replaced them with only the midnight certainty that she was beautiful and cherished.

Stefano's eyes narrowed. 'It was that ex-boyfriend, wasn't it?'

'He said my playing…"lacked".'

Stefano spat out a string of words which she was sure were profanities from the way he said them, as if they were poison in his mouth.

'Nobody who listens to you could fail to hear the passion in your music. *This* is where I feel it. Right here.'

He took her hand and placed it on his chest, over his heart, which thumped a steady, comforting rhythm under her palm.

'I do think I became lost in my playing…'

'You play like an angel whose heart has been broken and is about to fall. I don't cry, but I wanted to weep at the sound of your music.'

She'd had confidence once, but had begun to feel it was misplaced—slowly chipped away because of her desire to be better, to be perfect, till she'd stopped thinking she could play at all. Once, she'd thought she could achieve anything. When had she begun to believe she was a fraud?

'He was your partner. He should have loved you rather than tried to diminish you. People can be envious of success. He wanted to take yours as his own.'

She looked up at Stefano, so adamant for her when he barely knew her. 'He's acting first violin now in my place.'

'Because of your injury?'

She nodded, the burn of tears stinging her eyes. She wiped them away. Stefano took her hand, began massaging deep into her palm, working his way up her arm. The pleasure of that touch, his care, rippled through her.

'That, and because there were rumours that I'd been saying things about other members of the orchestra... about the conductor. I denied it, but I'm the newest member. The youngest. I didn't tell anyone I was hurting because it almost felt...shameful, how my body had let me down. I hid it from them, thinking I could sort it out myself. It made everyone suspicious about what else I might have hidden. I'm the link between the orchestra and the conductor. I can't do that job if people don't trust me.'

'People are jealous of your talents. That's all.'

'I was told to take some time to think about my future. To try and fix myself. And I don't think they meant physically.'

'There is nothing to fix, *cara*. You're perfect as you are.'

Stefano's touch gentled, became more a stroking, and she moaned. His eyes darkened and the intensity of that gaze was too much. It was as if he saw her in ways that no one else did.

'You are a beautiful, passionate woman and you should

not allow *anyone* to try and convince you of otherwise. Your orchestra…? They don't deserve your brilliance.'

The words caught in her chest like a hand grabbing at her heart and twisting. She'd spent her life in a world of competition. A world of music and beauty, sure, but you had to be strong. You didn't always get praise. Most of the time you received criticism. Some of it constructive, a lot of it quite cruel.

Stefano's accolades meant more that he could ever know, and yet she was repaying him by not being honest. The sting of bile rose in her throat. What would he think of her if she were?

'Thank you. But—'

'Accept the praise. You shouldn't qualify it. Don't pay attention to people who try to reduce you to their own mediocrity.'

He picked up her hand and brought her fingertips to his mouth. Kissed them. The heat of his breath, warm against her flesh. She didn't say anything, just lay there, relishing the attention like a cat being stroked. Her eyes drifted shut as she absorbed the pleasure of it all.

'Okay…'

It was all she could say. His gentle ministrations, his defence of her, had stolen her words and left her only with complicated feelings swirling inside. Soft, warm feelings that she craved to give in to but wouldn't voice.

'I cannot believe that after last night in my bed we're even speaking of another man.' His voice had taken on a deeper tone. Rougher.

She opened her eyes then and he was staring at her, focussed and intent. 'You think you're that good?' she teased.

Stefano raised an eyebrow. The corners of his lips twitched in a smile that wouldn't break free. Yes, he *was* that good—and he knew it. Her body had given her away. Last night had been a revelation of pleasure.

But she didn't want to stroke his ego too much, since he was sitting there looking so assured of his own abilities. Another tease slipped out. 'Or are you jealous?'

'I'm protective of what's mine.'

The force of those words tore through her. *Mine.* She should be outraged that he was so…possessive.

'Oh, I'm yours, am I?'

She'd never truly felt like anyone's before. This sensation—it was fresh. Sharp and bright like the cold fall of snow. And she loved it. A lot too much.

Stefano truly smiled then, and in his smile was something sultry and wicked that told her she would pay, and that he'd enjoy meting out the erotic punishment.

'Should I remind you whose name you called out all night? I owned your pleasure in the early hours. I'll own it again.'

A shiver of desire ran over her, goosebumps peppering her skin. She raised an eyebrow of her own. 'Will you, now?'

'I want you,' he growled, 'and I don't want to be gentle.'

Her breathing came sharp and fast in anticipation of what he might do. 'Then don't be.'

He pounced in a flash. Her hands were pinned lightly above her head under one of his own and his strong, muscular body was covering hers. Lucy's heart beat a wild and uncontrolled rhythm—not out of fear, but with the thrill of being mastered by this man. She opened her legs, his hardness between her thighs. She wanted him inside her so she could forget everything but the pleasure he could bring her.

'Let me see… Where do I start, hmmm…?'

The way the corner of his mouth tipped up in a wicked smirk told her he *knew* what he did to her. The lazy heat running through her veins exploded into something hotter, more potent. She didn't care. She arched her back, trying to get him in the right position, to ease the ache inside that built and built. But the weight of his hips on hers held her down. He could ease up if he wanted to. He was doing it to torment her, make her beg, and she didn't care.

He let go of her hands. 'Don't move them,' he growled.

She froze as he dropped his head, his teeth scraping her nipple. The pleasure of it sizzled through her, arrowing straight between her thighs. She squirmed underneath him. He moved his hips then, sliding over her. She was slick. Wet already. With one change of angle he could be inside her, but he didn't give her enough room.

'Stefano…'

Her voice was a whisper, like a breath of air, and she wondered if he'd heard her. She didn't want to seem as if she was breaking yet. She was trying to extend the pleasure, stretch it out till it snapped with force.

His deep, resonant chuckle was pure wickedness reverberating right through her. And, as much as she needed him, a small, rebellious part of her didn't want to give him the satisfaction of knowing what he did to her. It was a game being played to see who'd succumb first. Except she knew it would be her. Every part of her body strained for him, the pleasure from his touch making her tremble.

'What did you say, *cara*?' He hadn't moved his head far from her left nipple and his breath was warm against her.

'Nothing at all,' she panted.

He took her pebbled nipple into his mouth again. Sucked. Another arrow of pleasure speared between her thighs where he rocked against her. He pulled back again and blew on her, the chill of that stream of air over her damp skin causing her nipple to tighten further. It was hard. Over-sensitive. Too much and not enough all at the same time.

'If you can speak a sentence, I'm not doing a good job.'

If he did any better, she'd die. Right here on the bed. And her reasons for wanting to win this little game became hazy as her body began succumbing to his onslaught. To the slide of him as he flexed his hips against the folds of her, to his attention at her nipple. She held her hands above her head because it was what he'd demanded of her and she hadn't thought to question him. Her body was completely at the mercy of his.

Another rough scrape of his teeth against her over-sensitive nipple almost undid her. 'Stefano!'

'Ah, *cara*, are you feeling neglected?'

'*Please*. I—'

'Shh… I'll look after you now.'

He rolled from her and found protection. Then he was back. Wrapping her in his arms. His kiss was hot, hard.

'Are you ready for me?'

His voice was pure gravel and it scraped over her in a shiver of pleasure. He was as affected as her by this thing between them.

'Yes.'

'Then hold on to me.'

She wrapped her arms around his back as he rose over her, settled between her thighs and thrust into her. She almost broke then, at the pleasure and the pain of him deep inside her as he moved. Hard, just as he'd warned. Desperate, just as she felt. She clung to him. Moved with him. Chased her pleasure as he drove into her. The burn inside her building and building till it overwhelmed her. Exquisite, electric…

'Say my name.'

His breath was warm against her throat. His voice all command and she didn't care. She wanted it. Craved his assertion. He scraped his teeth against the side of her neck and the pleasure rippled through her.

'*Stefano…*'

He groaned. Changed his angle to thrust even deeper. And that was all it took. She was flung over the precipice, soaring into the void with his name once again screaming from her lips.

CHAPTER NINE

STEFANO STRODE THROUGH the castle halls to his room. He'd texted Lucy to meet him there, with instructions to dress for the cold. The weather had cleared, so he'd spent a good part of the afternoon preparing his surprise for her in another of the places here where he'd spent time as a boy.

He didn't know why it was important to show her but, like the conservatory, he thought she would love this too, and her pleasure had become important to him. Vital, like breathing.

When he arrived at his room she was standing outside dressed in her coat and jeans. There was a black and white knitted cap on her head. Fingerless gloves on her hands.

'Cows?' he said, and smiled. 'Do your socks match?'

'Of course.' She held out her hands, showing him that her gloves matched too. 'It wouldn't be me if they didn't.'

'I hope to see them later.'

She raised an eyebrow. 'Only if you're very good.'

Stefano moved close, backed her up against the door. He leaned down and murmured into her ear. 'I was hoping you'd want me to be very…bad.'

He relished the scent of her like a delectable dessert. Lucy gave a pained exhalation. Her hands on his chest, sliding over his shoulders and drawing him close. 'Stefano…'

All he wanted to do was open the door and tumble her

into his bed, stay there with her for hours. His willpower was a threadbare thing, but he mustered it nonetheless and stepped away.

He chuckled at her disappointed pout. 'You have the capacity to make me forget everything I'm meant to be doing. But I have something to show you and I won't be swayed.'

'You're being enigmatic.'

He'd wanted her trust, and yet he knew that after what she had been through with the betrayal by her ex it would have to be earned.

'You asked about my favourite places here. I've another to show you—somewhere I particularly enjoyed in my early teens. It's a surprise.'

He began to walk and she followed. Her smile was bright and happy. The look on her face could chase away all the cold in this place.

'Did you spend much time in the castle when you were younger?' she asked.

'Until I was in the equivalent of your high school, yes. We lived here with whichever nanny and specialist tutors my parents had employed, whilst they were in the city during the social season and for work.'

Her eyebrows raised. 'So you were left alone?'

'My parents subcontracted their responsibilities. Their main aim was to ensure we didn't disgrace ourselves, but once the future of the Moretti name was assured by my birth, and then that of my brother, they felt they'd done their duty. Their role was to maintain their status as one of Lasserno's premier families, which had always been their main interest.'

'What about you?'

Stefano shrugged. 'There are many things children can do when the eyes on them aren't as watchful as they should be. It wasn't all bad. Given that my role as the future Count of Varno was assured, I had no real concerns.

I watched out for my siblings. I was in charge of them in many ways.'

'That sounds…lonely.' Lucy frowned. 'What about friends?'

He shrugged. Sometimes he'd missed the company of children his own age, but occasionally the staff here would bring their children to the castle, for him and his siblings to play with. His parents would have been horrified, so no one had ever told them.

'Alessio's was the only friendship that was really encouraged.'

Lucy placed her hand on his arm as they walked. 'That's sad. You realise, don't you?'

Her sympathy, her support, almost stopped him. She could never understand how much it meant against the pain from that time, of almost losing his sister and being forced to accept responsibility too young. Not being encouraged to mix with others like a normal boy. He hadn't recognised back then how it had shaped his life.

'Perhaps—if we hadn't liked each other. Luckily, we did. He became like another brother to me.'

It was as if a hand had plunged into his chest, tearing out his heart at that acknowledgement. The loss of Alessio's friendship was a wound that would likely never heal. But there was so little he could tell her. He didn't want this moment ruined by the admission of his failings, but there was so much he wanted to say.

'Since I've been back taking care of the castle's repairs it's the first time in years we haven't worked together in some way. That's been…challenging. It has always been my role to assist him in whichever way was best.'

It wasn't exactly the truth, but it gave voice to a small part of his reality.

Lucy frowned. 'I can't imagine that kind of expectation.'

'What about you?' he asked. 'Did you always know

you wanted to play the violin, or was it something imposed upon you by your parents because of your mother's talent?'

'How did you—?'

'Internet.'

He smiled, trying to recover from the error of that admission. He knew far more about Lucy than she'd disclosed to him. He should probe her about the coronation ring now. In his not doing so there was a lack of truth between them which needled his conscience. But now was not the moment. He intended to put another of those blazing smiles on her face. And whilst they were snowed in, there was still time...

'You have a history. Some might say you're living up to it.'

'My mother encouraged me, and from the moment I saw her playing it was what I wanted to do. I never questioned it until recently, but now I'm wondering who I am if I can't play.'

It seemed they were both questioning their place in the world.

Celine's words inched into his consciousness again. *'Who are you...?'* He shut them down.

They'd moved into some of the lesser-used service corridors. Places he'd played in as a child, creating fantasies of knights and of dragons he and his siblings were required to slay. As children, they'd always been victorious. It was only as an adult that he'd come to realise that life didn't always work out the way you thought it would.

He glanced over at Lucy again. He'd like to slay *her* dragons. She didn't deserve the treatment that had been meted out to her, causing her to question her playing, her talents.

'Where on earth are you taking me?' she asked.

'You'll have to wait and see. Ah, here we are.'

They'd arrived at a wooden door made of rough-hewn

slabs of wood and hand-forged cast iron hinges. He'd unlocked it earlier, when he'd come to make the space ready for her.

Stefano tugged at the handle and the door creaked open to reveal a dimly lit stone staircase.

'How many steps are there?' she asked.

'I've never counted them—but, trust me, the effort is worth it.'

He'd set up his own space here as a teenager, for those times when his siblings had become too much and he'd wanted a place to be alone. It had given him perspective. A reminder that there were things bigger than himself, and that his problems were small compared to the vastness of the universe before him. He'd studied here, dreamed here of a life and a future that he'd thought would be grand and important. Of how he might be better than all the Counts before him, stamping his indelible mark on the role.

How naïve he'd been. Those dreams all seemed so futile now. He'd marked the role with a blot of ink so black and dark it might never wash clean.

They'd reached the top of the stairs and Lucy waited whilst he opened another ancient door into the room he'd readied for her. He'd never brought anyone here before. It was the one place in the castle he'd kept all to himself. Not even Celine had seen this place…his teenage sanctuary. She wouldn't have been impressed, given it lacked the grandeur of the rest of the castle.

What would Lucy think of it?

He wasn't sure why the answer to that question was so important.

He turned on the torch, then took Lucy's hand and led her through, closing the door on the dimly lit stairwell behind them. At least the room was a bit warmer than freezing, with the space heater he'd placed in the corner working hard to heat the area. It was a difficult task since there was so much glass around them.

He moved to the edge of the room, out of the way of the furniture, and turned off the torch again.

Lucy's fingers squeezed his. 'Where are we and why are the lights out?' she whispered.

'We're in the eastern turret. Let your eyes adjust.'

In days long past the room had been encased by windows, rather than leaving it open, and it was the perfect place to view the province his family had supported over centuries. Tonight there was little light outside, the moon a bare sliver, which was perfect for what he had in mind. The only sounds were their breathing and the gentle brush of a cold breeze.

He tugged on her hand. 'This leads to the ramparts. I hope you're not afraid of heights.'

There was no risk of falling, the walls were higher than his own waist, but they were a long way above ground. Still, it wasn't looking down that he was interested in.

'I'm not afraid if I'm with you.'

Lucy's words struck at the very heart of him. In those moments he believed that he was once again a man of honour, of worth. She followed him with no hesitation.

He stepped out first to test the temperature, and the frigid air hit him like a slap. Lucy wouldn't like it, but he hoped what he had to show her would compensate for the cold weather she loathed.

'It's freezing,' she said, her breath like puffs of smoke in the night air.

'I know, but we won't be here for long and I'll keep you warm.' He stood behind her and wrapped his arms round her body, barely able to feel her under the downy coat she wore. 'Look up.'

Her head moved back against his chest. 'Oh. *Wow.*'

He looked up himself, and saw the clear black night sky was peppered with thousands of stars. The wonder of it caught him the same way it had when he'd first seen this as a boy, climbing into the forbidden tower and realising that the world was a far bigger place than just him and his family. The perspective had been a humbling one.

'You wanted to see stars.' He tightened his arms round her and rested his chin on the top of her head. 'Whilst these aren't the stars you see from your home, I hope they're enough.'

'This is so special. What an amazing place...' She turned in his arms. The slender moon's glow washed over her face, pale and ghost-like in the silvery light. 'Thank you.'

'It's my pleasure to share this with you.' It meant everything to hear the wonder in her voice. To see how she appreciated his retreat, its beauty. 'I've never brought anyone here before.'

She had given him her music, and he had nothing to give in return other than what he could show her. The conservatory...this secret place. The areas of his home most special to him...

He'd given her a key to parts of his life few had been allowed to glimpse. And in doing so, it was terrifying for him to feel how *right* this moment seemed, when everything else in his life was wrong. She'd given him that without realising, and he didn't know how to thank her without divulging all his sins. He didn't want her thinking less of him. Better for tonight to live in the delusion that things between them could stay just as they were.

Silhouetted against the glimmering lights of the city in the distance, Lucy tilted her head back again. There was the merest of sparkle in her eyes as whatever light was available caught there and glittered.

'I've missed seeing the stars.'

He cupped her face in his hands, his thumbs sliding over the soft skin, slick in areas with what felt suspiciously like tears.

'It's so beautiful...'

There was a sound to her voice, a crack in it. As if it

was broken with emotion. It cracked something inside him, too. Stefano was almost certain her tears were happy ones, but he didn't want her to cry. He wanted to bring her joy. The need for that overwhelmed him—the need to comfort, protect. To make her...*happy*.

'Lucy...'

He dropped his mouth to hers, found her lips warm and soft under his own. Parting, letting him in. And once again he was lost.

Lucy tightened her arms round Stefano's waist. Her bulky jacket, her gloves, were an interruption to the feel of his body against hers. Still, the heat of him rushed through her like a burst of hot water. She couldn't get enough of him. He seemed like such a hard, uncompromising man, but his kisses...they were all gentleness.

This was beyond what she'd already experienced, the passion. There was something more. He'd trusted her with this special place, which he'd never shown another. It all overwhelmed her, like her music, and she was lost in him, trembling in his arms again.

His kiss slowed, stopped. His heavy, warm breaths gusted for a moment against her cheeks. He pulled away and she wanted to shout *No!* To drag him back to a place where they could both get lost in each other. Forget everything but the magic they made together.

'Come inside. You should get warm. With all the windows, you can still see the stars. It's freezing out here.'

He took her hand, laced his fingers through her own and walked her inside. The room seemed quite cosy, considering they were in a turret, and it was frigid outside, but she couldn't get a good view of the space in the darkness. She'd only caught glimpses of it in the torchlight.

Stefano unthreaded his fingers from hers, left her standing in the centre of the room. Even through her soles of her boots the floor seemed softer here. A rug, per-

haps? There was a striking sound, a hiss, and the glimmer of light from a match as he lit something. A candle.
Then another. And another. Stefano went through three
matches before a golden light glowed in the room. Then he
walked towards her, guided her to a plump couch where
she sat down.

She could see it now, the small square space. A single
bed, a desk… The bulk of the floor was covered in a plush
rug, as she'd guessed, and the rest was polished stone.

'Here's a blanket.'

He handed her the heavy, silky-soft fabric and she
wrapped it around her knees. Then he reached for a vac-
uum flask and unscrewed the lid. He poured out a cup
of something and the scent of chocolate teased her nose.

He handed it to her. 'This will help.'

'Thank you.' She took a long sip of sweet, perfect hot
chocolate. 'It's not as cold in here as outside.'

'I turned on a heater, but it's not the most efficient way
of warming the space. This place was meant for protecting
the castle. I'm sure my ancestors didn't want the people
guarding it to get too comfortable.'

'It looks like it's been made comfortable.'

This would have taken time and effort. The candles,
the heater, the drink… Walking up and down that flight
of stairs multiple times, because it likely would have taken
more than one trip. He'd thought about this. He'd done
it for her.

The burn of tears teased at her eyes again. This man—
he was all risk. And she was deceiving him by not telling
him about the violin, by allowing herself to be lost in this
world that they inhabited together rather than ruining precious moments like this, in a fantasy place where everything going on outside the castle didn't matter.

But for now she'd relish the time with him. This big,
beautiful grand gesture from a man who would likely not
admit to any softness.

She blinked the errant tears away. Settled back into the cushions as he sat beside her. 'What is this place used for now?'

He looked around the room and an expression crossed his face. Something almost wistful. 'Not for anything. I keep it furnished for sentimental reasons. It was my escape when I was younger. Being in charge of the castle and my siblings when I was only a teenager was difficult at times. At my request, the staff took some furniture from the lesser-used rooms and made this place for me.'

'It must have been hard, being so responsible.'

He sat staring at the candles on a small table, his eyes unfocussed. 'It wasn't all responsibility. We ran wild much of the time. I was their leader. For the most part we had fun.'

'For the most part?'

'Children aren't easy to look after, and my younger siblings felt neglected by me at times, I'm sure. They certainly felt neglected by my parents. One evening my younger sister decided she wanted to see my mother, who'd worn a grand ball gown to go to the capital. Emilia packed a bag and left the castle. It was winter. We were lucky that dinner was early that night or we'd never have noticed her missing. Even luckier that fresh snow had fallen and we could follow her footprints, or we would have lost her. From that day on, I never forgot my responsibility to my siblings. To keep them safe. To protect them.'

Lucy reached out and laid her hand over Stefano's for comfort. His skin was warm under her fingers. 'At least they're adults now.'

'I'll always be responsible for them. Lasserno can be unforgiving—especially for my siblings. Social climbing is an aristocratic sport here, and my brother and sister aren't interested in playing that competitive game. I had the protection of the Crown, but they wanted something different from life… What I do has an impact on them and always will.'

Stefano was so responsible. He was looking after *her*. She wished she could look after him for a change. He desperately needed someone to give him a little softness in his life.

'Thank you for showing me this place. Your home is beautiful. You must miss it when you're not here.'

'I've been neglecting it. Celine didn't like the castle, or the mountains. The things she used to say about them…' He laughed, but it was a bitter sound with no pleasure in it. 'So I stayed away when I should have been here. My brother cares for the conservatory but that's all he's really interested in. My sister is busy studying. The responsibility for this place is mine and I've failed it. You're suffering the consequences.'

'I'm getting used to the temperature.'

'You shouldn't have to.' He took her hands between his and the heat of them slid through her fingers. 'Are you cold now?'

'Never around you.' It was as simple and as complicated as that. He might be dark and brooding, and there was something around him that wasn't entirely happy, but Stefano carried the heat of sunlight. It was a truth she could admit when other things between them were a lie.

She wished she could talk to him, tell him what she needed to before her secrets eroded everything beautiful between them, but she couldn't find the right words. Not here in this space together, cocooned against the world, where she could kid herself with the fantasy that reality couldn't touch them. She'd allowed a sense of inevitability to overtake her. As if there was nowhere else they should be.

She didn't know who moved first—her or him—but somehow they were closer and their lips touched again. She opened underneath him. His mouth was a gentle tease against her own and all she craved was more, *deeper*. She could forget when his lips were on hers, when his arms were banding her body, when he was inside her. Her worries dissolved and her pain disappeared with the pure and perfect need. Nothing mattered. Not the orchestra. Not her violin. There was her, and him, and it was enough.

Her hands skated around the waist of his hard body, tugged at the warmth of his sweater. She slipped them under his shirt to stroke his hot skin and he flinched away, a smile on his lips.

'You say you're not cold, but your fingers are.'

'Then keep me warm.'

Stefano moaned and took her in his arms. His lips crashed onto hers in a move that took rather than gave. She didn't care. She wanted to forget again, and she would give everything in this moment for their bodies to be skin to skin, with his hard, muscular frame covering hers.

His sure hands unzipped her coat, pushed it from her shoulders. The cool air of the room held a sting, but it was nothing when compared to the passion and heat that they generated together. He broke from the kiss and stood, holding out his hands to her. She placed her chilled ones into his and he helped her stand. He walked them to the narrow bed and drew back the covers, then hesitated.

'I'm sorry…perhaps we should go somewhere else.'

Lucy looked up into his black eyes, gleaming in the candlelight. She cupped his cheek and the stubble teased her palm. 'No, here's perfect.'

'Good. I'm not sure that I can wait.'

He undid the button of her jeans, slid down the zip and eased them from her hips, down her thighs, as his hands skimmed her legs. He crouched on his knees before her and pressed his hot lips to her belly, then lower, his warm breaths gusting over her skin.

'You are so beautiful…' he murmured against her flesh as he kissed her at the juncture of his thighs. Moving her underwear aside, he let his tongue explore, gently toying with her, and she was frozen in pleasure till he stopped. The only sound in the room was her panting breaths.

He helped her out of her boots, her jeans. 'On the bed,' he said, his voice dark and rough.

She trembled at the need his words exposed, at the fact that she'd done this—moved such an implacable man. She lay down, the sheets cold and crisp underneath her.

Stefano shucked his own trousers, the rest of his clothes, till he stood perfect, naked and erect, in the soft glow of candlelight. The illumination etched the shadows of his muscles deeper, made them magnificently defined. She lay back, glorying in the masculine perfection of his hard, male body, admiring the work and dedication he must put into it. Into everything.

His dedication and attention now being directed towards her.

He joined her on the bed and pulled the sheets and thick down cover over them both. His hands skated under her top to stroke her skin and she shivered at the pleasure of his touch. A sweet ache built deep inside her.

Stefano unclipped her bra and his hand reached for her breast, stroking her nipple till it beaded. The sensation stung like an electric shock through her, between her legs. His muscular body was against hers, the crisp hair on his legs teasing her skin. His head dropped to her nipple, his tongue smooth and insistent as her flesh responded to his ministrations, her hands clawing into his back.

Stefano chuckled, then the sound was cut off as he wrapped his lips round her nipple and sucked, slipping a hand between her thighs. She was close. This man set her aflame. She might have once thought music was her only passion, that playing the violin was everything to her, but Stefano Moretti was fast turning into a dangerous obsession.

She shook under his ministrations, not wanting to tip over the glorious edge without him. 'I need you...'

'You have me,' he murmured against her skin, and a rush of heat coursed inside her at the desire that once again roughened his voice. But he didn't stop his insistent stroking of her overheated flesh.

'Inside me.'

All of him stilled. 'Whatever you want that is in my power to give you, Lucy, I will.'

His touch and his body might inflame her, but those words... They spoke of more than sex or infatuation. More than passion. They speared right to the heart of her, and she couldn't think or even dream of what they might mean.

She held a secret, and now it almost felt like a betrayal not to tell him. Some might say it didn't matter—that the violin had been in her family for over seventy-five years and why should she care where it had come from after all that time?

But to her honesty was everything. She'd seen how her father's lack of it had eaten away and destroyed things. How Viktor's cowardice had meant his having an affair rather than confronting the failure of their relationship. She always wanted the truth, even if it was brutal and hurt her, left her bleeding. Better that than living in blissful ignorance only to have life as you knew it pulled away from you at the last minute.

'Where did you go?'

Stefano's words dragged her out of those dark thoughts. She should say something, but his hands were stroking her again, drifting over her skin, and all she craved was to shut her eyes and give in to the sensation.

She reached up to his face and drew her thumb across his lips, gazed into his meltingly dark eyes that gleamed with flickers of gold in the light. 'I'm right here.'

'If you're still coherent, I'm not doing my job.' He

grasped her top and bra and took them off in one go, tossing them on the floor. 'That's better. Now there's nothing between us.'

But there was. He deserved more than this. But she didn't know what to say when all she wanted was to lose herself in him again. 'Please, Stefano.'

He reached down to his trousers on the floor. Grabbed protection. Sheathed himself, then settled over her.

'You came prepared.' She parted her legs, gloried in the feel of him notched between her thighs. Awaiting the pleasure that was so close, everything to come.

'I always want you. It's like an obsession.'

In that way their feelings were terrifyingly mutual, but there was something else which screamed of a desire for much more. Permanence.

Stefano dropped his mouth to hers, his kiss slick, hard and intent. As their tongues touched and she wrapped her arms tight around his body once more he slid into her. Her back arched at the pleasure of him deep inside her body. She was so close, even now. This man inflamed her, set her alight.

He moved and their bodies melded, the beautiful song of their lovemaking echoing round them in the small, intimate space. Lucy tightened her arms around his torso. Wrapped her legs round him. Glorying in the feel of his hard body against hers.

The way they moved together was pure instinct and an innate knowledge of each other's desires. She didn't want this night to end. That need chanted in her head as her body tightened, climbing higher and higher. The burn building inside her. Waiting for the brilliant snap of pleasure that he held just out of reach.

He murmured words—some in English, some in Italian. Gentle things about her beauty, words of encouragement, telling her how much pleasure she gave him. None of them pushed her off the delicious edge she walked, held in an endless fog of pleasure. Then there were more whispered words, ones she wasn't sure he'd want her to hear, lost as they both were in the moment together.

'How will I get enough of you?'

They were like a match to kindling. She burned with the ferocity of petrol flung at a fire. An explosion of pleasure she wasn't sure she'd survive as the sensation burst inside her, rending her in two, and she sobbed his name to the stars.

CHAPTER TEN

LUCY LOOKED OUT of the window of the music room, where she'd decided to play—perhaps one of her last chances to do so. The snow had stopped. There was little question that the roads were passable and there was now no excuse for her to stay. Except she didn't want to go.

She'd moved from thinking she could never allow herself to be vulnerable with a man again to sharing some of her deepest fears and dreams with Stefano. The thought of leaving him stung like an open wound in the sea. So she took the pain and did what she had always done with it.

She played.

The piece was a simple one, but something she loved. The perfect acoustics of the room amplified the tune. Sweet and gentle. Almost hopeful. It was how she felt—about her playing, at least.

Without the pressure of performance there wasn't any stiffness or pain in her hands. Her fears over her injury had lessened, and she'd begun to love the music again. It was what she'd missed. Not learning something complicated to thrill a crowd, or a piece she didn't enjoy because that was what her performance schedule required. There was no need to strive, because she was enough. Lucy knew now that she wasn't a fraud. You didn't get to the position of first violin by fooling anyone. You either had the ability or you didn't.

Stefano had given that back to her. Restored the confidence that had been slowly yet relentlessly eroded till she'd questioned everything. She allowed herself to see her musicianship through his eyes. Remembered the wonder on his face as he'd watched her play. It was a feeling she allowed to be mirrored inside herself, because he believed in her abilities. Believed in *her*.

And she'd begun believing in herself again too. Cocooned here in this place, it was as if her creative well had been refilled, with passion blossoming. Somewhere along the way something had happened to her with this brooding, complicated man. A man she didn't want to leave.

She still hadn't been honest with him about her violin. In the beginning she'd been scared to say anything till she had the measure of him. Now…? Now she had no excuse other than the realisation that telling him would change everything. The guilt of keeping her secret after the care he'd shown, after they'd made love, was a brutal voice that whispered in her ear about how she'd failed him.

She was sure he'd think that too, the moment she said something. There was no excuse for leaving it so long other than her selfish desire not to change this fragile, beautiful thing between them. To pretend that the outside world didn't exist, protected as they were by the winter around them. But reality always intruded.

She finished her piece, loosened the strings of her bow, and packed her beloved violin back into its case. Her parents' lawyers were still arguing over whether it formed part of the marital property pool, but it didn't matter. She'd come to realise that even in wartime you didn't hand such a valuable possession to a stranger without it involving some obligation.

Her grandfather had carried that obligation and his sense of guilt till he died. His carefully written diaries hinted at the weight of it—how it had almost crushed him some days. His final words in those last weeks, whilst confused, had spoken of a loss and guilt that plagued him. Of taking something that wasn't his, to save himself when everything else around him was lost.

It was time for her to complete the mission he'd started over seventy-five years ago. Time to set his memory free.

The door cracked open and her heart began to thump in an excited kind of rhythm. It was like the anticipation of waiting in the wings backstage, just before walking on to perform.

Stefano came into the room and shut the door behind him. She wasn't sure she would ever get enough of this man. In her quieter moments Lucy realised that she wanted to make her reality here, if only she could ignore her fears of bursting the shimmering bubble of possibility that surrounded them.

She smiled, but that smile rapidly faded. An energy she couldn't place crackled round him like static. His eyes were dark and glittering as he stared at her with an intensity that caused a shiver to race over her spine. Something was wrong. She knew it. Could feel it intuitively. It was like the sound of a violin when its strings were overtight. Everything about him was discordant. Too sharp.

'You seem…tense. Everything okay?'

Stefano's hands clenched, released. He flexed his fingers. 'I took a phone call assuming it was you, so I didn't check the number before answering.'

His voice cut her, sharp and cold, like the whistle of the wind in the ramparts of this place.

'Instead, I was forced into conversation with His Highness's private secretary.'

'I thought *you* were His Highness's private secretary and you were just here repairing the castle?'

Pain was etched on every part of him—in the tense set of his shoulders, the tightness around his eyes, the brutal slash of his mouth.

'Don't believe everything you read or hear.'

Lucy walked up to him, reached out and placed her hand on his chest. The heat of him reassured her, when he otherwise appeared wrapped in cold and darkness. The moment seemed fragile and hesitant, and then Stefano dropped his head, took a step back and away from her. It might have been only centimetres, but it felt like an uncrossable chasm.

'Stefano, who hurt you?'

If she hadn't been staring at his face, searching for the answer, she might have missed it. But there was a flinch, as if he'd been waiting for a strike.

'Some of the deepest wounds are self-inflicted.'

Each word sounded as if it had been ground through glass, shredding him as it was spoken.

'Recently I've come to think most things can be fixed,' she said. He'd allowed her to believe that—one of the many gifts he'd given her in her brief time here.

Stefano gave a short, sharp laugh, more mocking than amused. 'I wish I had your naïvety. Some mistakes can't be repaired.'

Time for her to discuss her own error—not talking to him earlier about the violin and what she knew. She needed to leap into the void and trust that it would work out, because somewhere in her time here she'd begun trusting him. First with her safety, with her body, and then with her heart. It terrified her, because there was only guessing and hope. But she realised now what she'd tried to ignore: this endless warmth suffusing her, the catch and thrum of her heart every time he came near, the emotions she'd refused to give voice to, could only mean one thing.

She loved him.

And she wanted him to love her back.

Maybe she was naïve, as he'd accused her of being, but the future she hoped for could only happen if there was truth between them. She couldn't go back to the beginning, so they'd have to start again today. She'd found the courage to do so now she believed in herself, and more importantly in him. Because she'd come to understand one thing in the time she'd been here. In a world of men who'd let her down—her father, her ex-boyfriend, and in a way her grandfather, with all his human failings—there was still a man who'd proved he could be honourable.

This man who'd shown her the stars.

'You're a good person, Stefano.'

His eyes narrowed. His look was piercing and hard, as if he was assessing her worth and somehow finding her lacking. 'Would you forgive a man who betrayed you?'

Betrayal she knew all about.

She wrapped her arms around her waist. He could be talking about Viktor, but she was sure there was more than one meaning in everything Stefano was saying right now. A riddle she was being forced to solve.

What else could he mean? He'd said he no longer had a fiancée—maybe he'd lied about that? Nausea churned in her stomach, as if she'd taken a hefty swallow of sour milk. What did she really know of him, anyhow? She'd only been here a week, and he'd promised her nothing.

No. He'd promised her she was welcome. He promised she'd be safe. He'd given her both of those things. Whilst she hadn't much trusted her instincts over the past months, she didn't believe his sincerity had been faked.

'I *know* you. You're not like Viktor.'

'Not in deed, but in every other way I'm the same. You say you know me...' He stabbed his fingers at the middle of his chest, as if punctuating every word on his flesh. 'Maybe I should tell you who I really am in the spirit of honesty. Honesty between people is important, isn't it?'

He turned his back on her and stalked to the window, and as he did so she caught a glimpse of his expression. Lip curled in a sneer, dark and ugly. But she didn't think it was directed at her, given he was now staring into the melting landscape outside, towards the capital. It was as if he *loathed* himself.

She shook her head. 'You're the man who took me in. Gave me his bed. Showed me his home. You're someone who's kind, considerate—'

He whipped round. Took a few steps towards her. Stopped. 'I resigned my position as the Prince's private secretary after betraying him. My best friend. Reporting his private movements to the press. I brought dishonour and disrepute to my family.'

She didn't know what to say. Her voice had been stolen by his revelation. He'd been pretending he still had the role all the time she'd been here. How could he have done something like that? They'd talked of it—the responsibility, the obligation—and it wasn't a job he held at all. What had he been doing when he'd claimed to be working, locked in his office during the day, and on some evenings well into the night?

Lucy swallowed down the knot in her throat. Tried to dig up the trust in Stefano she'd found over the time she'd been here rather than turning away and leaving. And whilst the voice of warning in her head whispered that he was a liar and didn't care about her, she saw that Stefano wasn't standing before her uncaring. He'd dropped his head. His shoulders rose and fell as if the weight he carried would soon crush him. It was as though he'd taken a fatal wound and was about to bleed out on the floor.

Lucy knew that nothing would help this type of injury, because it looked as if it had damaged Stefano's soul. Bad people didn't give a damn about that kind of wound. Guilt was only suffered by those who had a conscience, who knew right from wrong and regretted their actions and the hurt they'd caused to others. That knowledge was all she needed to keep her in the room.

'Why did you do it?' she asked. 'Because intention is everything.'

'My reasons may have been sound, but the "why" is irrelevant. I have a meeting at the palace in one week. It's not enough time for me to finish the work I've started. You have kept me from it. Distracted me in *every* way. And now my time's run out.'

He looked at her then, and his eyes were narrowed. Cold, like black ice chips.

'You have something I want.'

Dread flowed over her like a shower of iced water. He'd told her nothing whilst she was here other than he'd been looking for jewels. Stefano couldn't know about the violin, could he?

Lucy took some long, slow breaths, as if preparing herself for a performance, and in many ways she was. The performance of her life. The future rested on what she was about to say.

'I think you're right. That's what I need to talk to you about. The real reason I'm here.'

For a few precious moments Stefano had hoped that Lucy would have no idea what he was talking about, no knowledge of the past that had entwined their families and cursed him. Her words ended that lingering fantasy.

She'd stayed here with the knowledge all along. Eating his food, sleeping in his bed, sleeping with *him*—and for what? She was just another woman using him for her own agenda, like Celine. But what did it matter when his life was now on a collision course with Alessio?

The message had been polite, yet firm and clear. The meeting was non-negotiable. Letters could be ignored, as he'd successfully done over the past few months. A personal demand could not.

The words of Alessio's new private secretary still buzzed in his ears like violent white noise. There had been mention of Stefano's role as patron of the orchestra, and an important but undisclosed personal request.

Now he could barely contain the heat inside him, which reached volcanic levels as he battled the tide that threatened to burst free. The anger at himself for his failure, for allowing Lucy to distract him.

This was his last moment to make things right for his siblings. Whatever the cost, he would not fail them again.

He walked towards Lucy. She looked up at him, her golden eyes wide, her teeth worrying her bottom lip.

'In the dying days of the Second World War, as the enemy approached to occupy this castle, my family gave Lasserno's coronation ring to an Australian soldier with links to the underground movement, to take to safety.'

'Wait...what?'

A frown creased her brow. She appeared confused. But there was no confusing what he'd said. The facts were incontrovertible.

'I don't know anything about a ring. I only know about my violin.'

It was a delightful and compelling act—but then Celine had fooled him for five years, professing love and adoration when it had all been lies. It simply proved how easily he fell for a beautiful face. A willing body.

'I am not interested in some fiddle.'

'It's no *fiddle*—and there's no ring...only the violin and what my grandfather's diaries say. Something about it being Lasserno's heart.'

Stefano's own heart stuttered, missed a beat. Those words alone were enough to confirm what he knew. But to have *diaries* as evidence?

'Another name for the coronation ring was the Heart of Lasserno, after its flawless central ruby. How could your grandfather talk about Lasserno's heart if he didn't have the ring? It's no coincidence.'

His words were hissed through clenched teeth as he began to pace, trying to hold back his frustration at her equivocation when *everything* rode on this.

'And yet my investigations show that your family has no great riches. It's unremarkable except for your father's parlous financial history.'

Lucy rocked back, a hand to her chest. 'You had me investigated?'

In a moment of weakness Stefano hesitated, almost reached out to steady her, to take her in his arms and whisper that everything would be okay. But *nothing* here was okay.

'Exactly how long have you suspected that my family had something valuable of yours?' she asked.

'When you mentioned your grandfather's name. Arthur Hunter. "Art", you called him. My family archives talk of a man—Art Cacciatore. Despite extensive searches I could never find him, but *cacciatore* means "hunter" in Italian. Something else that's no coincidence.'

The colour ran high on her cheeks. Two ruddy red strips on her otherwise pale skin.

'You knew from the beginning. All this time.'

She shook her head, almost as if disappointed. As if he was yet another person to add to a growing list. But she was no innocent in this twisted tale. Her feelings didn't matter here—only his brother and sister did.

'Where is the ring, Lucy?'

She threw up her hands. 'I keep trying to tell you. There's only the violin. My grandfather's diary mentions someone telling him to save himself, and he says that Lasserno's heart saved him. You say it's a ring, but the violin saved him. I've told you this story. In his last days he seemed crippled by guilt over it all.'

What did he care for the violin? He'd not completed the task he'd set out to achieve. There would be no glorious homecoming for his nation's treasure. His quest for redemption had come to an ignominious end.

Stefano shoulders slumped, and exhaustion threatened

to cut him down at the knees. How would he free his brother and sister now?

'That coronation ring was priceless…'

Lucy took a step forward, looked into his face, faltered. She stepped back. 'So is the violin. I was told my whole life that it was one of many valuable reproductions, but when my grandfather died and we found his diaries we discovered that it was real. A Stradivarius.' She pointed, jabbing her finger at the case where it now sat, on top of the grand piano. 'Up until now it's been thought that all the existing Strads are known. A new one will create history—a storm in the music world. My grandfather talked of the violin being Lasserno's heart and Lasserno's heart saving him. What if…? I don't know…'

Lucy began to pace, clenching and unclenching her hands. 'What if they're one and the same? Maybe he swapped the ring for the violin whilst on the run? To keep himself alive? A jewel couldn't help him, but a violin could. Maybe he saw the Stradivarius as fair trade, because he knew the value of what he was being given? Swapping one priceless object for another. It's all a guess, but I can't be sorry about it. Because without the violin I might not be here.'

Sorry… It was a mere word. It wasn't enough. She'd travelled to Lasserno for this reason and stayed silent.

'You came to my home with that knowledge and you did not say *anything* to me.'

Lucy reached out her hands, as if imploring him to engage his softer feelings. Her entreaty was wasted. Any remaining softness inside him had suffered its final death throes.

'You knew as well—maybe not about the violin, but about my grandfather. We've both been hiding from this, Stefano. But I was always going to say something. My grandfather *loved* Lasserno. He talked endlessly about it. I said to you before that I believe he left a part of himself here. I genuinely came here to…to learn about you and your family.'

Her words were pretty, but they didn't change the truth. 'One thing is clear. You didn't find me worthy enough to tell the story.'

'That's not what I said. And if you believed my family had the coronation ring why didn't you say anything to me?'

He gritted his teeth, fighting the bile that rose in his throat. 'There's an Italian saying: *To trust is good; not to trust is better*. It's now my motto to live by. I would *never* trust the words of someone like you, whose relative stole from my family. My country. Who didn't say anything until she was caught out.'

All this time Lucy had looked as if she was ready for a fight. She had been standing tall and proud, almost regal in her demeanour—and he knew royalty. But after those words it was as if she was a tree, felled by the fatal blow of an axe. There was a desperate final teeter and then she seemed to topple.

'And I thought I'd fallen…' Her voice hitched. Her mouth was downcast, her gaze hollow and blank, her eyes glistening. 'We…we made love and you didn't trust me at all.'

'What we did had *nothing* to do with love.'

The lesson was a painful one, but it was one she should learn. All her talk of him being a good man… She couldn't have meant any of it. Because if she'd truly believed he was good she would have said something to him before he'd confronted her. Well, he'd show Lucy now. Her faith in him was utterly misguided. There was no good left in him.

'And now you learn the man I truly am, *cara*. You know it all.'

'You're right. Trusting someone's good intentions hurts too much. Not trusting is *much* better.' She dropped her head. Scuffed at the floor with her booted foot. All the brightness in her had died, like a candle snuffed out. 'Now the snow's gone I assume Bruno can reach the castle? I'll call him and leave.'

She turned. Began walking to the door. Stopped. Her shoulders rose and fell but she still faced away from him, as if she couldn't bear to look at him ever again.

'My grandfather always said the violin saved his life. Recently, to me, it's felt like an impossible burden. For you, Stefano... I hope it sets you free.'

Stefano sat outside Alessio's office in the palace visitors' area. He'd never thought he'd be waiting like a stranger when this place had once been so familiar to him it had been a second home. He hadn't wanted to walk through these doors again until his self-appointed work was complete. The call had come too early. He only hoped he'd done enough, since he hadn't retrieved all the Crown Jewels yet. And as for the coronation ring...

Distraction had come into his life, taken him away from what he had to do. An arrow of pain shot through him. He wouldn't think of that distraction now. He wouldn't think of *her*. He tried to shut down the visions tripping through his mind of sunshine, of strawberry blonde hair. Of freedom and allowing himself to dream rather than settling himself into cold reality.

The cold was where he belonged.

In his hands he held what he hoped would be his family's redemption. That was all that mattered. His brother and sister would be free. They would leave Lasserno, and be able to escape any misplaced censure for his personal failings. It was what he wanted for them. His own future was meaningless now. He'd held a glimmering possibility in his hands for the briefest of moments, shining brighter than the gemstones he'd recovered, till he'd rejected it all.

He would never forget the lines of hurt etched on her beautiful face as he'd said what he had.

Lucy.

He gasped against the pain, like a soul torn in two. It was nothing. *She* was nothing. She couldn't be. Who would want someone like him? He simply wouldn't think about her.

Yet as Stefano placed the precious violin case on the ground, he almost doubled over with the agony of it all.

The ornate door in front of him cracked open. It was time, but his ruined heart barely changed its rhythm. He wasn't sure it knew how to beat. It was as cold and dead as it had been when Lucy had first walked into his home.

'Your Excellency…' Alessio's private secretary hesitated for a moment. 'Are you all right?'

'Of course.' The lie slipped easily from his lips, when in truth he didn't know what 'all right' felt like. Not now. Not since he'd ejected the only person who had made him feel human again from his home.

Not ejected. She'd left. Without turning back. Without a fight. Just as she should have. He'd as good as forced her. Because he really wasn't worth fighting for.

'If you'd like a moment—?'

'No.'

Stefano grabbed the case from the floor and stood. He might be broken but he wouldn't be cowed. Some pride remained. It was hanging by the thinnest of gossamer threads, but it was there, and he clung to it because it was all he had left.

He walked into the room and Alessio's secretary slid out behind him. Shut the door with a solid click.

Alessio sat behind his desk, looking as regal as his title dictated. He'd always worn the weight of his role with distinction, born to it and accepting of it. His only flight of fancy had been his wife, Hannah. A saving grace, it seemed, because Alessio looked well.

Stefano supposed love did that to you. He wouldn't know. For him, love was simply another arrow of pain to shoot into his heart. It was as if the universe enjoyed using him for target practice.

He bowed, short and sharp. 'Your Highness.'

The words were hard to say when they had to be meant formally, rather than as a mere greeting between friends. He clenched his jaw almost hard enough to crack teeth. It all angered him. The familiar surroundings where he was now a stranger. The situation he'd created when he should have fought Alessio for what he believed was right, rather than taking matters into his own hands. Alessio too, for his silence.

There was no sign of emotion on his impassive face. He'd always been a master of control. Yet Stefano wanted him to shout and rage, as if this meant something. He wanted Alessio to care as much as he did about what had been lost.

'Your Excellency. Thank you for *finally* responding to my requests.'

Alessio didn't invite him to sit, so Stefano remained standing. Once he would have sat regardless. 'As I told your private secretary, I've recently been snowed in.'

A flicker of something passed across Alessio's face, so fleeting Stefano couldn't be sure what he'd seen.

'I hope you found a way to stay warm.'

Stefano's thoughts ran out of control with the memory of Lucy. How they'd fitted together in a way that had felt like for ever.

His breath hitched. He couldn't think of her. *Wouldn't.* Yet again she was distracting him from what he had to do.

He took a deep breath, and returned to the task he'd set himself in the months since he'd walked away from the palace. 'I assume you didn't summon me to discuss the weather?'

'It seemed the polite way to begin, since you didn't respond to any of my earlier attempts.'

Alessio's gaze slid over the violin case Stefano held in his hands. His palm was itching to release it.

'Please take a seat.'

'I'd rather stand.' Stefano placed the violin case in the middle of Alessio's desk to rid himself of the instrument, which had taken on the feeling of a time bomb on its final countdown.

'What's this?' asked Alessio.

'This is what's become of the Heart of Lasserno. A violin. A Stradivarius. Swapped for the ring in the war.'

He'd thought saying the words would change everything, but there was no lightning bolt of forgiveness from the heavens. All Stefano wanted to do was to snatch the violin and take it away from here, return it to the woman who made it sing.

Instead, he clasped his hands tight behind his back.

Alessio's eyes flared wide, then his face settled into its cool, regal demeanour once more. 'Where did you get it?'

'From a violinist. Signorina Lucy Jamieson. Her grandfather brought it home after the war. It's been with her family—'

Alessio's eyebrows rose so high they almost disappeared into his hairline. 'You *took* her violin?'

Wait... What? Alessio knew of Lucy's presence in his castle?

The surprise of that almost took his legs from underneath him. Stefano sank into the chair he'd earlier refused. 'How did you—?'

'I need to know everything that's happening in this country, so I'll never be surprised again.' The corner of Alessio's mouth curved in the merest of movements, but for him it was the equivalent of a sly smile. 'Bruno proved very informative about "the angel in the castle who is too beautiful for a devil like Moretti." They were his exact words, only partially said in jest.'

Lucy *had* been an angel. One of redemption. In the dark and lonely nights since her departure he'd had long hours to think about her time in the castle. She'd been a woman alone, trapped with a stranger. He remembered her apprehension when she'd first arrived. Of *course* she wouldn't have told him about the violin immediately. She couldn't have known how he'd react in those early days, and his terrible behaviour in the end proved any lingering fears were well justified. It had been unfair to blame her when he hadn't pursued the issue either.

In that way he wasn't a devil, as Bruno had accused. He was a vampire who'd slowly tried to suck the life and the joy from her to make himself feel better. So he could forget about his own failings and relish her attention. Which was why he'd said nothing about the coronation ring.

Still, something didn't make sense here. It was as though he'd entered a room halfway through a conversation and had to catch up on its meaning.

'You've been…keeping an eye on me?'

'Someone had to. You weren't responding to my correspondence, and you looked like hell. Although at the time of Bruno's report I did wonder whether you were auditioning a violinist for Lasserno's orchestra in your role as patron. She would be a coup.'

His heart rate spiked at the mention of his patronage. With it, he would be able to ensure the violin's protection. Allocate funds specifically, so it remained treasured for another three hundred years.

'I'm not giving up that role too,' he said.

If he had to, his punishment would be complete.

'I'd never ask you to.' Alessio frowned, waved his hand as if in dismissal. 'But that's not important. Where is the evidence that this violin is what's become of the coronation ring?'

Alessio steepled his fingers and pinned Stefano with his steady, impassive gaze. Stefano had witnessed people wither under that assessment, which Alessio could hold unchanged until the other person cracked and divulged all their sins.

Stefano tugged at his tie…straightened it. He wasn't like those people because Alessio knew his sins. Most of them, anyhow.

'There's a story. Some diary entries.'

Lucy had left them behind on his bed when she'd gone. Stefano had yet to get to the bottom of what they meant. He still had more documents to search through from his own family's archive, although he had enough proof regarding the violin for today's meeting.

'Is there any provenance? Or only family stories about Signorina Jamieson's violin.'

'It's Lasserno's violin, not hers.' Except the words didn't ring true. They sounded hollow and false in his mouth. 'I've asked an expert to appraise it, and he believes it's a Stradivarius. Dendrochronological dating will confirm it.'

Alessio stood and moved out from behind his desk. He leaned against the front of it, his hands gripping the antique wood. The move forced Stefano to look up at him, when before they'd always treated each other as equals. In the strangest of ways, it was only now that he felt judged and found lacking. Even when he'd resigned from his position Alessio hadn't looked down on him like this.

'I knew you were strategic. Ruthless, too, if the stream of anonymous packages full of gemstones coming across my desk is anything to judge by—for which I will endlessly thank you. But I didn't realise you could be cruel.'

'She gave it to me.'

He knew he sounded like one of those whiny aristocrats who'd taken the gemstones Alessio's father had given them. They'd had no right to them, but this was different. He was doing his duty by his country, as anyone else would.

Wasn't he?

Nothing seemed certain any more. It was as if everything he'd thought he knew had shifted underneath him.

'She *gave* you a multi-million-dollar instrument that has been in her family since the war? The tool of her trade? Ask yourself why she did that, Stefano, when she could have said nothing.'

'I thought I'd fallen...'

No. It had been the right thing to do. Lucy had known in the end that the violin wasn't hers to keep and she'd left it behind. Even though he would never have stopped her if she'd picked up the case and walked away.

'I hope it sets you free...'

The pain of her last words scoured like acid through his veins. He couldn't respond to Alessio. He was struck mute by the realisation trying to break through, tapping at the inside of his consciousness like a rock hammer. He ignored it.

'I see you refuse to answer that question. So how about this one?' Alessio crossed his arms. 'What am I to do with it?'

'You said that if I found the coronation ring I could have anything I wanted.'

That was what he'd come here for. His brother and sister. He'd forgotten them somewhere in the conversation, since it wasn't going the way he'd expected.

'That was youthful rambling, when we were both insecure about our place in the world we'd been thrown into too early and underprepared. I never required *this*.' He motioned to the violin case on the desk. 'All you've ever needed to do is ask me for what you want. So what is it?'

Stefano wanted so many things. He wanted his brother and sister to be free of the weight of his family's obligation to the Crown. He wanted his friendship with Alessio to be repaired. He wanted…what he couldn't have. What he'd pushed away.

Better to ask for something which could be granted than wish for something that couldn't. 'I want you to free Gino and Emilia.'

Alessio's eyes widened. 'Your brother and sister aren't my prisoners.'

'Both want to travel overseas for work. That means leaving their roles here.'

'They go with my blessing.' Alessio rolled his eyes in a way that was entirely uncharacteristic and no part of his normally regal demeanour. 'Is this really how bad things have become between us? I thought I'd created a modern principality, whereas your family believes we're trapped in some medieval realm. It seems I'm failing as a benevolent monarch—but at least I have a priceless violin. Thank you for small blessings.'

Stefano's anger spiked then, mingled with the pain of the things he'd thrown away. A picture of his last moments with Lucy was filling his head. Her face… How wounded she'd been…

He launched himself from his seat, unable to sit still, to sit being…*judged*. Alessio leaned back a little to let him pass, as if Stefano might lash out. It made him wonder how he looked, because in this moment he felt feral. He began to pace, to burn off the excess energy that welled inside, clawing at him, wanting to tear free.

'Doesn't *any* of this matter to you?'

'Many things matter. Love, friendship. The rest is ephemeral. Right now, you're trying to buy redemption. Trust me—redemption won't come until you've forgiven yourself.'

Stefano stared at the man who had once been his closest friend. Everything ached, as if nothing would sit right with him ever again.

Alessio sighed. 'Hannah warned me about writing missives, but I didn't know how else to reach you when you wouldn't take my calls. I've failed as a monarch and now as a friend. I should have listened to your counsel. You were right about the press. So what do you need to end this distance between us? Because I miss you. Hannah misses you.'

Stefano stopped dead, not sure of what he was hearing. 'It can't be this easy.'

'None of it has been. I've been enraged, hurt—and confused by what you did. You blindsided me. But in the end I've learned a great deal about love, generosity and forgiveness from my wife. Though I *would* appreciate another grovelling apology.' Alessio smirked. 'It only seems right.'

Of all the things to be asked of him, an apology was the easiest to give. Stefano walked over to Alessio and stood in front of him, head bowed, paying due respect to his monarch and to the friend he'd wronged. 'I'm sorry. I've regretted my actions every day since I walked from this room.'

'I guessed. Locking yourself in your castle and taking to Lasserno's aristocracy like an avenging angel suggested a great deal of contrition. But that's in the past. It's time to turn to the present and the future. Now you've told me what your siblings want, what do *you* want? Your old job?'

Stefano rocked back on his heels. Months ago this would have been like an answer to his every prayer. Now...? Now nothing seemed right without Lucy in his life.

'No.'

Alessio flinched, pain etched over his face. Stefano didn't wish to hurt his friend again, but he needed to find his future rather than step back into the past, which was what Alessio offered.

'The things I want aren't in your power to grant, because they involve someone else.'

Lucy. She was all he desired. Since she'd left the castle he'd been plunged into a silence so stark that in the absence of her music it was as if he was the only living being left on earth.

'Ah… I think I know where you are and I sympathise,' Alessio said. 'Though I do have a request. Hannah's due to give birth any day, and we want you as the godfather of our child. I have a suspicion she's holding on until you say yes…until I make this right.'

The roiling emotions inside Stefano stilled. He was having trouble making sense of the question—such a privilege being asked of him after all that had passed between them.

Then those words of Celine's crept back, whispering in his ear… 'What if I'm not worthy of the role?'

'Listen to what I'm saying.' Alessio laid his hand on Stefano's shoulder, the comfort of one friend to another. 'You're worth more than you ever knew. I'm sorry that you ever felt less, but you are and will remain my closest friend. I don't care about your role as Shield of the Crown, or your title. It was your friendship that I needed, and you gave me that unfailingly. What you did—misplaced as it was—freed me to follow my heart with Hannah. Although the execution was poor, your intentions were good, and in the end that's all that matters.'

'Intention is everything.'

They were Lucy's words. She'd been right. He should have listened to her. Instead he'd cast her aside, because he hadn't been able to trust or forgive himself. He'd been inexcusably cruel when she'd handed him his means of salvation. She'd handed *everything* to him, without asking for anything in return, and he'd thrown it back in her face.

Stefano couldn't ignore the truth. He loved her. He didn't deserve her.

And yet if Alessio could forgive him, then perhaps Lucy could too.

CHAPTER ELEVEN

BRIGHT LIGHTS BORE down on her as Lucy stood on the stage. The applause from the Parisian crowd was thunderous as she took a deep bow. She'd been asked to perform a single concert on a Stradivarius that was being sold by a consortium, to showcase the instrument for potential purchasers. By the measure of the applause she'd done the violin justice.

It had been an extraordinary instrument to play—a thrill all its own—but it hadn't been *hers*. The tone was still magical, but subtly different, without the same sense of wonder and joy attached to every note.

It had been easy enough, though, to pour the emotions of grief and loss into the mournful music she'd played. Once, she'd thought she understood those feelings. Yet until she'd walked away from Stefano she'd had *no* real idea of pain's true depths. They'd had so little time together, and still his impact was like being hit by a meteor.

World-ending.

She was left with a deep and unrelenting ache. Missing him. Missing her violin.

She had many regrets, but in the end leaving the violin she'd played for years was not one of them. Her father was furious, but he and his solicitors couldn't argue against the evidence. The violin was Lasserno's heart, and she'd given it back. It was now safe from a fate similar to that of the violin she'd just performed with: being seen as an investment rather than the treasure it was.

She wondered if another violinist played it now, in Lasserno's orchestra, or whether it was locked in a glass case somewhere, on display for all the world to see, with the story of the coronation ring and her grandfather.

The loss of Stefano and the violin was woven into the fabric of her recent past. She didn't understand how she could unravel it, so all she did was stand there, basking in the acclamation of the crowd, until the applause died away.

Her time was done. She took her final bow and went backstage, handing the Stradivarius to a team of security guards, who locked it back in its case and whisked it away. She accepted congratulations, said goodbye to those in the ensemble who'd played with her, and then exited through the stage door.

A small crowd stood there waiting for her. She smiled. Signed autographs on programmes until the well-wishers thinned. If she'd been carrying her own violin she would have found some transport to take her back to her accommodation. But tonight she would walk.

It was a cool evening, with a chill reminiscent of the mountain castle which had changed her for ever. She wanted that chill to seep into her bones. A reminder of what she'd lost in those beautiful, frozen days in Lasserno.

As she stepped away from the stage door, ready to walk to the boutique hotel the organisers had arranged for her, she glimpsed a final person standing in the shadows, waiting. She readied herself with one more smile for one more autograph. Then the person stepped out of the darkness into the light.

Stefano.

He stood immaculate in a dinner suit, white shirt and black bow tie. The cloth lovingly clasped every inch of his impressive frame. The perfection of his suit was in vivid contrast to the rest of him. His hair was more unruly than she'd seen it before, teasing the neck of his collar. And the ever-present shadow of stubble on his face was now more of a beard. The temptation to reach out, to touch and see if it still prickled under her fingers, almost overwhelmed her. Instead, she clenched her fists tight.

'Your performance was magnificent,' he said in a voice that was rough, as if he'd almost forgotten how to speak—just like that first day she'd met him in the doorway of his castle, looking like some gothic hero.

But he wasn't any kind of hero. He was just a man. And she knew that her performance, the emotion and the ache of it, had all been down to losing him.

'Thank you.'

She wondered if he'd heard it in her music. What he'd thought if he had.

A sharp breeze gusted down the narrow street past the stage door. She trembled, but not from the cold. Stefano blazed in front of her. He'd always been heat enough to keep her warm. She dug her fingers reflexively into the palm of her hand.

A deep frown interrupted his brow as Stefano took a step forward. 'Are you hurting?'

Hurting? The ache was relentless—almost like a living thing, gnawing at her insides, day after day. If not for her music it would have broken her irretrievably. And, yes, she still felt as if parts of her were missing.

Lucy took half a step back. Better that than running into his strong arms and hoping he'd catch her when she fell against him.

'I'm doing fine.'

That was the partial truth. She wasn't hurting herself in a quest for perfection, or at the demand of another, because she realised now that she was *enough*. She always had been. And she deserved someone who could love her with an open heart. No artifice. No agenda.

She was someone with a warm heart herself, brimming

to give away some of the love it held. This man in front of her didn't believe that he could give her that…that he was deserving of what she offered. And she wanted the love, the adoration… Everything she believed she'd experienced in a week trapped in a castle with him.

'What are you doing here, Stefano?'

'I came here for your performance. I came here to see you.'

Her heart jumped as if it had been shocked. Behind her, light spilled onto the road as the stage door opened. A few of her fellow musicians came out, stopped.

'You okay, Lucy? Sure you won't come for a drink?'

This was her perfect escape. She could leave with these people whose company she'd come to enjoy and escape Stefano for ever.

But she needed closure. She hadn't had it when she'd fled Castello Varno in those icy mountains. When a sympathetic Bruno had heeded her call, picking her up and driving her to the *pensione*. Maybe seeing Stefano would help plaster over her damaged heart—because whilst she hadn't been broken, she'd been left emotionally bruised and bloody.

'No, thanks. I'm fine,' she replied. 'I've got things to do.'

They nodded. Said their final goodbyes. Stared at Stefano.

He didn't acknowledge them at all. His gaze didn't leave her. It was intense, almost…*hungry*. Scanning over her as if he was looking for missing pieces. He shouldn't look for them here. She'd left them behind in his castle, when she'd walked out through the great wooden doors trying not to look back to see if Stefano was watching her.

'Allow me to give you a lift to your hotel.'

He motioned to a black limousine, which sat cloaked in darkness. She shook her head. Standing metres away from him was bad enough. She'd never cope being cooped up in the cabin of a car with him.

'It's a nice night and it's not far.'

Lucy looked up at the sky. The lights of the city obliterated most of the stars. Unlike in Varno, at Stefano's castle, where on that clear night on the ramparts she'd felt as if she could reach out and touch heaven. And then afterwards, in the turret with him, she had.

'I'll walk.'

She needed to work off the performance. The adrenaline of the concert still coursed through her blood, leaving her light-headed. Reckless. That wasn't a safe way to be around Stefano.

'Would you allow me to walk with you?'

Whilst she always felt safe in Paris, it still seemed like the sensible thing to do, and she needed to find out why he was here. Curiosity won. She hoped it didn't kill this cat…

'Sure. Why not?' Lucy let out a slow breath and wrapped her arms around her waist.

Stefano stepped forward. Stopped. 'Are you cold? Would you like my jacket?'

'I'm…'

He reached for his button, undid it. Shrugged out of the fine black wool with its satin lapels. He approached her with some hesitation. She didn't object. Partly because she was cold and had forgotten a wrap. But partly simply wanting him to be close, if only for a few moments.

He draped his jacket gently round her shoulders and the warmth of the fabric from the heat of his own body engulfed her. The scent of him was crisp as winter, dark as spice.

When he stepped away, his eyes glittered like black diamonds in the streetlights. 'I know you don't like to be cold.'

'Thank you.' The sting behind her eyelids hinted at

threatening tears, but crying would get her nothing other than puffy eyes and a red nose. 'Let's go.'

She began to walk, thankful for the ballet flats she wore. He turned and caught up with her in a few easy strides.

'You're looking…well,' he said.

A tiny spark of pleasure lit inside her, but she knew he was only being kind. She looked haggard. The dark rings under her eyes from sleepless nights were not so well hidden by make-up. In the nights since leaving Lasserno she'd done a great deal of thinking—about him, her life, her career… None of it had been easy.

'As are you.'

There was more truth in her comment than in his, even though something about him appeared wild. His frame was leaner than it had been all those weeks before.

He made a noise like a snort. A scornful sound, as if he hated this stilted formality between them as much as she did.

The people of Paris bustled about them. The city of love was still alive at this time of night. It left a bitter tang in her mouth, a clench of pain deep inside her, that here she was with the man she'd fallen in love with and there was nothing here for her.

But it wasn't all wasted.

She'd recognised a thing or two after she'd left the violin with Stefano. When she'd played in her orchestra on her return…played here tonight. It wasn't the instrument that defined her. She was good at what she did on her own, no matter how much she missed playing the violin that had become like a part of her.

'You're back with your orchestra.'

Stefano didn't ask it as a question, and a tiny thrill ran through her at his knowledge of what she'd been doing before she shut it down. Her return had been on the orchestra's web page for anyone to see. Still, he'd checked…

'I am.'

'Did you have any trouble?'

'I took back what was rightfully mine.'

She'd refused to accept the way she'd been treated. Made it clear the injury was no fault of her own and any rumours were just that. Without proof. She liked to think that in the end everyone had seen through the lies. What she hadn't expected was the support from some of the other members of the orchestra who valued her leadership. Then there had been the letters from fans, wishing her well in her recovery, waiting impatiently for her return.

'And how is it?' he asked.

They'd almost reached her hotel. She would say goodnight to him and then they'd part. He was on his own journey, she was on hers, and they didn't converge. All she had left was the empty space in her heart where he had been, which tonight she'd filled with music. She'd return to Salzburg and they'd both move on.

She didn't know why that thought felt like a death.

'I'm thinking of resigning my position,' she said.

'No! Lucy, you can't. Has that *bastardo* Viktor—?'

'It has nothing to do with him.'

Stefano's vehement defence sent another shiver of awareness through her, but she couldn't allow it to mean anything. He'd made himself clear the day she'd walked out of his life and back to her own.

'I wouldn't resign for that man—not after I've fought to keep my position. The fact I'm back at the orchestra shows his undermining of me didn't work. In the end I won. He lost.'

She realised the truth of that now. But, more importantly, she knew she needed to work with people who wanted to create something beautiful rather than people who'd stab each other in the back trying to improve their position. In that way, deciding on her future was becoming easier.

'Of course he did. I've looked at some of his playing. He can't match you—in *any* way.'

The passion contained in those words slid through her veins, sparking flares of heat deep inside. But there was nothing for it. They'd arrived at her hotel. Now she and Stefano would part, and that would be the end of them. She would be gracious, even though her insides felt as if they were being shredded by razor blades.

'That's kind, but we're at my hotel.' She looked at the doorman and smiled at him as he held the door open for her.

'Mademoiselle Jamieson. Your Excellency.'

She turned to Stefano. 'How does he know you?'

Stefano slipped his hands into the pockets of his trousers, shrugged. 'I'm staying here as well.'

Lucy hesitated. The tumble of emotions inside her was strange and confusing. 'That's kind of creepy, Stefano.'

'You've made that accusation before. It appears I do "creepy" quite well—even though it wasn't my intention, and there are good reasons for my being here.'

'Staying at the same hotel as me should have been where you started our conversation. Could you not have said something earlier, like back at the concert hall?'

'You would have found out soon enough. And I was enjoying the walk with you.'

She strode through the foyer and to the lift. Slipped off his jacket and handed it to him. He looked at it for a moment and frowned, as if the thought of her returning it almost hurt. Still, after some hesitation he took it, and folded it over his arm.

'It's been nice seeing you, Stefano, but I've had a long day. I wish you all the best for your future. Goodnight.'

He flinched, and she didn't care. She couldn't allow herself any kind of softer feeling, like sympathy, since he had none for her.

'I… I want to keep talking. Could we take this to my room?'

Her heart did a silly backflip, but she ignored it. Frowned. 'What for?'

How could she go to his room when all she wanted to do was fall into his arms and be held?

'Because there's a lot that I have to say, and it's clear my attempts so far have been poor.'

'I don't owe you any more of my time.'

Seeing him again had brought all that pain she'd tried locking down into sharp relief. She'd set a clock on her grief over Stefano. Six months. Six months in which she'd immersed herself in it and hoped not to drown. Now she'd seen him again that clock had restarted, and the day she'd walked out through the door of his castle came back with the fresh, bright sting of a papercut.

She stabbed at the button for the lift, needing to get away.

'No, you don't owe me anything,' Stefano said, keeping his voice low as a few people in the foyer were watching them both. 'However, I owe you a *great* deal. Please, Lucy.'

At a distance in the concert hall, she'd looked luminous. Playing the instrument like an angel. Stefano had almost wanted to purchase the violin, to capture its heavenly beauty, but it was only wood and strings. The real genius was Lucy.

He wished he could trap it, bottle it.

Keep it to himself.

Never let it go.

But there was a saying about loving someone and setting them free. In that her grandfather had been wrong.

Stefano knew he hadn't been able to hold her and keep her before because he'd been in no fit state to offer her anything. He only hoped he was better now, because her absence in his life had left a hole so great nothing could fill it. He'd thought the chasm between himself and Alessio bad enough. It was a mere crack in the pavement compared to this. Without Lucy, his life seemed wholly lacking, and he had no idea if he could fix what he'd deliberately, callously broken.

'We don't owe each other anything, Stefano. If you feel an obligation to me in any way, I'm releasing you from it.'

'I only want to talk.'

And he hoped that words would be enough. Though he'd already hurt her terribly with his words. Words not meant. Words spat out in fear because of self-loathing. He knew his actions would need to match the true meaning of what he said tonight *exactly*, or he would lose her for ever.

If he hadn't lost her already.

'If I come up to your room and listen to what you have to say, will you then leave me alone?'

'Of course.'

Every part of him objected to his promise, but if all he could ever have of her was her music, then that would be enough. It had to be. He'd become her most ardent yet silent supporter.

'There are conditions.'

She stood there so fierce, dressed all in black—presumably so nothing would detract from the music she played—but all he could see was *her*. She filled the foyer of the hotel, luminous with her strawberry blonde hair in a flawless chignon, her honey eyes glowing with a furious fire. How everyone in this space was not as transfixed as he was, he could not explain.

'Whatever you want, Lucy.'

She looked stricken. 'You stay on your side of the room. I stay on mine.'

For a moment, hope flared. If she didn't want to be close to him then maybe she felt it too—the indefinable, shimmering desire between them. And, whilst she looked magnificent, no amount of make-up could hide the bruised shadows under her eyes, which Stefano was sure *he'd* caused.

He craved to touch her, comfort her, soothe away her pain. But he'd hold those demands of hers sacrosanct. It was a small price to pay if it allowed him to say what he needed to. And when he had, he'd open his arms and hope she'd walk into them.

Not sure of his voice in this moment, he nodded.

'I need the words, Stefano.'

'I accept your conditions.'

The antique lift door rattled open. Her eyes widened, almost as if in fear, and then she went ahead of him. He keyed in the number for his floor as she took one corner, fixing her gaze resolutely on the moving numbers as the door clanked shut before them. He stood in the other corner, closing his eyes so he didn't have to watch those same numbers pass him by like a terrible countdown.

Probably to the end…hopefully to the beginning.

The lift eased to a stop and he followed Lucy out to the only door—that of the Presidential Suite. He opened it and motioned for her to go inside. She entered, then stopped. A mountain of a man rose from a chair. He'd forgotten about the security guard following him, and saw Lucy stare at him with concern.

'You may go now,' Stefano said. 'I'll call with further instructions if required.'

The man nodded. 'Of course, Your Excellency.'

'Please excuse the necessary security,' Stefano said, as Lucy watched the man leave. He took himself to the furthest corner of the room, since that was what she wanted, and draped his jacket over the couch. 'Would you like something to drink? I can call for tea, coffee…hot chocolate?'

'This isn't a social visit. You said you had things to say.'

She crossed her arms, standing straight and tall just

inside the closed door of the room, but her voice… He could hear the desperation of it. Then her watchful gaze looked him up and down. Did she want him still? It was time he played the cards he'd been dealt. He hoped it was a good enough hand.

'I have a message from His Royal Highness.'

'Are you speaking again?'

'Yes.'

If there had been one moment of relief in the disaster of these past months, it was that. His friendship with Alessio had been healed over a long night of dinner and of talking in a way they hadn't for years. If it was possible, their friendship had deepened. He was even going to be godfather to the beautiful little princess born two days after he'd accepted the honour.

Once he would have thought his life was perfect, but now he knew it wasn't. Not yet.

'Has he given you your job back?' she asked.

'His Highness has a perfectly good private secretary. It's not a role I want. Not any more.'

Right now, he couldn't think of any future without Lucy in it. He'd told Alessio as much, and his friend had understood. Stefano couldn't contemplate a life without her. They'd only been together for the briefest of times, and yet already it seemed that they were inevitable. His whole future lay in her brilliant hands.

He had done so much to hurt her, and if he could revisit those last days, he would change everything. He saw now that they'd both been afraid because they'd found something precious and yet both of them had held knowledge that could tear them apart. By taking the Stradivarius he'd thought he'd found the means to his salvation. Whereas if he'd really understood the truth he would have seen that salvation only came from within himself.

'What *do* you want, Stefano?'

Her.

Always. Only. Ever.

'His Highness asked me the same question...' All he could offer Lucy was a polite smile. Telling the truth now might have her running away from him. 'But I have an offer from him for you. Please wait here.'

He walked into his bedroom, grabbed the case that had been sitting carefully on his bed. Hoped that this would at least put the spark back in her eyes—the one he'd seen that first moment when he'd opened the door to his castle and found her on the doorstep. The bright gleam he'd witnessed when he'd moved inside her as they'd made love... when he'd shown her the stars.

On his return to the sitting room, Lucy stood looking out of the windows, staring over the city of love. The place where he hoped he could show her what she meant to him.

She turned, and her eyes widened when she saw what he held. Her fingers flexed.

'I've been asked by His Royal Highness Prince Alessio of Lasserno to bring this to you. On permanent loan from our country.'

He placed the case on a coffee table, opened it with the reverence such a precious instrument deserved. The Stradivarius lay in all its burnished glory inside. In the end a committee of experts had examined it with excitement and confirmed what they had all known. They had assured everyone that it was still perfect, before returning it to its rightful owner.

Because he'd come to an understanding, after reading her grandfather's diary entries and researching more of his family's papers—out of love, not anger or desperation—that this violin was as much a part of a love story as an object of salvation from the war. A decent man would have let her keep it when she'd offered it to him, but somewhere in those bleak months he'd lost his humanity...lost himself.

It had taken Lucy to help him find himself again.

'Is this…?'

Her voice was breathless, choked. Tears sparkled in her eyes. It took all his willpower not to go to her, but he'd made a promise and he wouldn't break it. He'd broken too much already.

'Your violin.'

'It's not mine.'

'It is if you want it. My country will provide permanent security, so it never feels like a burden. It will always be safe and so will you.'

Her eyes were wide, staring at the open case. A tear dripped onto her cheek and she scrubbed it away. 'Why?'

He stood firm in his place even as her tears continued to fall unchecked. Not until she asked would he approach her, and if she never did then here was where he'd stay till she walked out through the door.

'You solved a mystery. You brought a part of my country's history back to us—even if it wasn't the coronation ring I'd been searching for. You brought a story of my family and yours. A story of love and wartime. The diary extracts you left for me tell part of the tale, but there's more.'

He hoped it would give her an explanation, and put her grandfather's memory to rest with some peace.

'Your grandfather's diary said, *"The violin is Lasserno's heart, not mine. Mine belongs to another."* I believe the precious object being taken to safety by your grandfather as the enemy marched towards the castle was not a ring. It was a person. My great-aunt.'

Lucy gripped the back of an elegant brocade armchair in one hand, wiping away tears with the other. The shock and the pain of seeing Stefano again and now this? She didn't know what to do. She wanted to walk to her violin, take it and run. But she also wanted to run to Stefano and fling herself into his arms.

All those conflicting emotions had her frozen, hanging onto the chair, because she wasn't sure that her legs would carry her if she tried to move.

'How did you work that out?'

'You told me your grandfather had talked of another woman. One of his diary entries said, *"We used Lasserno's heart to save ourselves, yet I couldn't save Betty."* That was a clue. With the Australians' love of shortening names I wondered if Betty might be a reference to my great-aunt Elisabetta. In my search for answers about the ring I'd scoured my great-grandfather's papers. It wasn't until I saw your grandfather's diary entries that I thought of looking for any of hers.'

'What did you find?'

'Not as much as I'd hoped. A few notes on scraps of paper, tucked into the cover of a book recording the birthdays of my family members over the generations. Some words of love and admiration in handwriting that looked like your grandfather's. Was Arthur's birthday the sixteenth of March?'

Tears filled her eyes again, spilled onto her cheeks. She wiped them away, nodding, unable to speak.

'His name is in that book. I'm sure she never meant to forget him.'

'You said she died in the war?' Her voice trembled and broke.

Stefano nodded. 'I told you she wasn't spoken of much. Grief gives some people the need to recollect, and others the wish to forget. My family were in the latter category. From what I could piece together, it seems Elisabetta was a bright, bold young woman, who did not like Lasserno's neutrality in the war when she'd witnessed so much suffering elsewhere. But even more information came from your grandfather. Having his true name meant my investigations could determine his service number, and with that I was able to search your country's archives. Your grandfather wrote a report to his superiors, explaining his time on the run.'

Lucy's breath hitched. She and her mother had never thought to look into her grandfather's war records. The shock of the diaries had been enough. Nothing else had entered their minds.

'What did it say?'

'His report told the story of his time in Lasserno, being sheltered by my family. He fled with my great-aunt, who'd helped people via the underground movement before, making her a target. They were caught in a firefight and Elisabetta was injured by shrapnel. He tried to save her, but she was mortally wounded. Arthur had to keep running so he wouldn't be captured. He reported that Elisabetta's remains were taken by members of the underground movement who said they would inform my great-grandfather.'

'Anything about the coronation ring?'

'Not as such.'

'I'm sorry.'

Stefano shrugged. 'It's more than I've ever had before. More than I could have imagined. You gave that to me. To my country. Arthur mentions the violin and his playing, which allowed him and Elisabetta to hide their identities. He doesn't say how he acquired it—however, your guess that he swapped one precious object for another fits. How else would he have obtained a Stradivarius? It's what I would have done to save the one I loved.'

His gaze was fixed on her with an intensity which made Lucy light-headed.

'In my family's documents I also found this.' Stefano reached into his pocket and pulled out a yellowed piece of paper. He handed it to her. 'A letter.'

She took the thin, worn document and opened it to read the neat black script that looked a lot like the writing in her grandfather's diaries. It was dated after the war ended, and addressed to the then Count of Varno.

I am sorry for everything precious of yours that I could not save. Forgive me. For I will never forgive myself.

There was no signature, just the initial 'A', but it was enough. She looked at Stefano, who had a soft and tender smile on his face.

'My grandfather carried guilt over this his whole life, and never more than in his final days,' she said. 'It was awful. He kept saying, "I'm sorry." We didn't know what for.'

'I never understood why your grandfather, a stranger, would have been entrusted with something so precious as the country's coronation ring. But the story comes together if Elisabetta died trying to get the ring to safety, whilst your grandfather was trying to protect them both. I'm sure he loved her, and she loved him.'

'All those times he talked to me of holding on to love and never letting it go... I wonder if he couldn't face your family because of the shame of losing your great-aunt. That's what he was asking forgiveness for—especially if they were in love.'

In a terrible, heart-breaking way it all made sense.

'It wouldn't surprise me,' Stefano said. 'Even if it wasn't your fault, losing someone you loved and were meant to protect would plague you with guilt for eternity.'

In the soft light of the room Stefano's dark eyes glowed with a banked heat which lit inside her too. No matter how cold it was, he'd always kept her warm. Then he held out his arms, almost like an offering for her to come to him.

'So here we are. Two people brought together by this story.'

As much as his open arms were a temptation, Lucy

held her ground. The reason he'd come to Paris was to deliver the violin. Without it she would never have seen him again, she was sure. He didn't really want her. He certainly hadn't trusted her. She wondered if he would trust anyone. Something about that crushed her heart like the wings of a doomed butterfly.

'The story you've given me is a beautiful one. Thank you. And now your job's done you can go back to Lasserno.'

She wouldn't subject herself to more pain, to more hope for the heart of a man who probably still hadn't found his own. Who didn't know what he wanted out of life. Because she'd asked and he'd had no answer. He certainly didn't want *her*.

'My job here has only just started, *tesoro*.'

Her eyes widened at the endearment which had slipped out unchecked, and his gentle words slid under her ribs like a knife, stabbing at her with a hope she shouldn't have.

'Don't think too hard, Stefano. Let's just agree that I was rebound girl, and you were rebound guy. A palate cleanser—even though I did get left with a nasty taste in my mouth at the end.'

He shook his head. 'If you're deliberately trying to hurt me, you're succeeding. But take comfort that nothing you say can hurt me more than I have hurt myself. I was a fool to realise too late that you'd stolen a piece of my heart. And now I'm offering all of it. Because whilst I don't deserve you, I cannot help having fallen in love with you.'

Her breath caught. There might not be enough oxygen in the room to fill her lungs after such a declaration.

'But wasn't what happened between us all a lie?'

She'd tried not to believe his cruel words *'What we did had nothing to do with love.'* On those dark nights alone she'd thought of their time together. The things he'd done for her. His kindness. She desperately wanted to believe that it had come from somewhere deeper, a true caring, but it hurt too much to allow that fantasy in the unforgiving light of day.

'I told myself lies about many things. About how without my role as Alessio's private secretary I was nothing. How I could never be forgiven for what I'd done. How there was no one I could trust. But the worst lies I told myself were about us. I ignored that what I felt for you was the one truth—the one thing I should have trusted. Instead, fear won. My decisions had been so poor. Talking to the press about Alessio... Even my engagement... Because it's clear Celine never genuinely loved me. How could I trust my feelings for you when I couldn't trust myself?'

She wrapped her arms around her waist. A trembling had started through her body and it wouldn't stop. Not cold. Not fear. Just a well of emotion she didn't know what to do with. So she tried to hold it in. If she let it out—if she *hoped*—she didn't know how to survive rejection again.

'But how can *I* trust what you're saying is true?'

'There is one reason I haven't accepted any role from Alessio. I can't contemplate a life without you in it. I don't know what shape it can take. This is not meant as pressure, but to explain. You're not responsible for me, Lucy. You're not responsible for my happiness. But I can only decide what I'm going to do when I know what you want too—because I love you with all that I have.'

This was everything she'd craved, and yet she was terrified to reach out and take what she thought he might be offering. 'I don't know if I trust *myself*. My choices haven't been great either.'

'You were betrayed. It leaves scars. But a wise friend said to me, *"Many things matter. Love, friendship. The rest is ephemeral."* Trust in the way I feel for you. Trust in my love for you. That's what I know. That's what I'm sure of. But I'll wait until you feel those things yourself. I'll follow wherever you wish to lead me to make that happen. I want you to be my future…if that's what you want too.'

He stood under the lights as if spot-lit on a stage. Delivering a soliloquy that spoke to her alone, filling her with light and warmth and something that felt a lot like the hope she'd thought she might never find again.

'What are you asking?'

'I'm asking you to be with me.'

He dropped to his knees as if in slow motion. This magnificent, proud man was on the floor over at the other side of the room. His focus only on her.

'To marry me, if you'll have me. To be the Countess of my heart and my home. All I have to give you is the man. I hope he can be enough. Because I am only half a man without you, Lucy. You are my missing pieces.'

She couldn't stand still. She rounded the armchair, walked towards Stefano, trying not to run. When she reached him he looked up at her, and she saw the love she felt for him mirrored in the dark heat of his gaze. She cupped his cheeks in her hands. The weeks-long stubble there teased her fingertips.

'You were enough before, and you're even more so now with that declaration.'

He shut his eyes for a moment, then opened them again. They glinted in the lights of the room, brimming and full. One overflowed, a tear tracking from its corner.

She wiped it away with her thumb. 'You said you don't cry.'

'Only for you. You break me, Lucy. The day you left, the music in my heart died.'

He could break her too. Her own vision began to blur, but these weren't tears of sadness. 'Oh, Stefano.'

'May I touch you now?'

His voice was raw with emotion, quiet and cracked. As cracked as she felt. But she hoped that in each other's arms they could put themselves back together again.

'Please.'

He stood, wrapped her tight as she nestled against his hot, hard chest. It was as if everything was right once more. Whole and perfect. She breathed in the scent of him, cool and crisp with a hint of spice. He would remind her of winter for ever. It might become her favourite season…

'I have something for you.' He murmured the words into her hair. 'It's in my jacket, but I need to let you go to reach it.'

She looked up at him. Traced her fingers against his beautiful mouth. His lips parted. 'I've only just got back into your arms.'

Stefano kissed her fingertips, then loosened his embrace. 'It'll be for a moment. Then I'll be back and never let you go again.'

He went to the jacket draped over the arm of the couch and reached inside, came back to her holding an antique leather ring box. He opened it. Inside lay an extravagant ring. A large oval diamond surrounded by a halo of smaller round diamonds. It sparkled under the lights of the room, pristine and white, like fresh-fallen snow in the sunshine.

'I wanted something that shone as brightly as you. To show you how much you've brought to my life. You've brought music, you've brought happiness, but most importantly you've brought love. *Ti amo*, Lucy. Be mine.'

She smiled, her heart so full of love for this man that she wasn't sure there was room left for anything else. 'I already am. I've never stopped.'

Stefano moved back, giving himself a little space, and gently slipped the ring onto her finger. The perfect fit celebrated the bright new bond between them.

Then Lucy placed her hand over his heart, which beat strong and sure under her palm, marking out the tempo of their love. 'How could I not marry the man who showed me the stars again?'

EPILOGUE

LUCY WALKED TOWARDS the giant Christmas tree that stood in the corner of Castello Varno's sitting room. As the new Contessa, she'd spent a month decorating for the season. All Stefano's staff had joined her with enthusiasm, saying it had been too long since the castle had seen a proper Christmas.

She adjusted a few glittering silver stars, a strand of tinsel, as the gentle chords from a distant piano drifted into the room. Stefano had begun taking lessons soon after their engagement had been announced.

Her heart swelled with pride as she heard the song he was learning in order to accompany her at Lasserno's New Year's Eve Royal Gala Ball. Whilst she was guest violinist for a few pieces with the orchestra that night, their personal surprise was to be their playing of the first movement of Monti's "Czardas" together, for the crowd.

Almost nothing had been so special as those moments practising together, when she and Stefano had been able to share their love of music. The only thing eclipsing it had been their wedding, a little over twelve months earlier, in Lasserno's Cathedral.

It had been a celebration befitting the Count of Varno, Shield of the Crown. But to her it had seemed surprisingly intimate, even if they had married in front of hundreds of people. Alessio had walked her down the long aisle that day. She'd never forget the words he'd murmured to her before moving to Stefano's side as his best man, in that moment showing his enduring support for her beloved husband.

'I am so glad you found him...for us all.'

She was glad she'd found him too—in more ways than she could ever express. Stefano's presence in her life had restored her trust. With him, it never wavered. The promises he made were always kept.

He'd followed her to Salzburg, wanting her to be sure that the decision to leave her role as first violin was one she was happy with, and in no way influenced by him. In the six months they had been there he'd helped her take back the whole city for herself.

His siblings had happily put their own desires on hold to care for the castle whilst allowing him time to be himself. Not the Count of Varno. Not the Shield of the Crown and Alessio's confidant. Simply Stefano Moretti, the man she loved.

She hadn't noticed that silence had fallen, lost in her own thoughts. The door to the sitting room opened and Stefano walked inside. Goosebumps skittered over her. Each time she saw him she had the same thrill as the first, when he'd opened the castle door to her and in many ways opened the door to the rest of her life.

'I thought you'd be toasting marshmallows,' he said.

She placed her hand on her stomach and laughed. 'I think I've been eating too many.'

His eyes flared with banked heat. 'You've certainly been taking to winter activities with great enthusiasm.'

'I've realised it's a wonderful season if you spend it with the right person.'

A sultry heat of her own flushed her cheeks. She'd come to learn that there were many ways to spend a cold, snowy day. Stefano seemed determined never to let her be cold again.

The corners of his mouth rose into a wicked smile which curled her toes. 'Nice to know you believe you made the right choice.'

'You're learning a complicated piece for the piano to join me in playing before your country. Who else would do that for me?'

He chuckled, and the sound rippled right through her in glorious waves of pleasure. 'I hope I do you justice.'

His piano teacher said Stefano had real talent. But whilst *she* knew he had nothing to worry about, Lucy understood his fears, because the first time she'd performed in front of a crowd she'd been terrified.

She went to him, stood on her toes, and gently kissed his lips in encouragement. 'You're wonderful and your playing is wonderful.'

He slid his arms around her waist and deepened the kiss, holding her tight. All of the man was hard, but now he was a little bit compromising—at least where she was concerned.

Lucy fell into the kiss, into him, and relished those precious moments before pulling back.

Stefano's breathing was heavy, his breath gusting against her cheek. 'Why stop?'

She laughed. 'Later. I want to give you your Christmas present.'

'Now?'

Her heart thumped a little harder as she went to the tree and grabbed a small rectangular box from underneath, which she'd only wrapped and placed there that morning.

'Before everyone arrives.'

Stefano's family was joining them for Christmas Eve the following day, and staying until it was time to leave for the capital and the ball. She loved his brother and sister, but she wanted these next precious moments to be shared with her husband alone.

She handed him the gift and he took it from her.

Shook it. The box rattled. He raised an eyebrow. 'Do I get a hint?'

She took his hand. 'No. Come and open it.'

He twined his fingers with hers in a gentle squeeze as she led him to the couch. They sat in front of the fire and Stefano turned his attention to the wrapping.

Lucy swallowed, her mouth dry. It was silly to be nervous, but every day she tried to make Stefano happy, to remind him that he was a good man. That he was loved.

He tugged at the silver bow, picked at the tape, and carefully peeled open the green paper, leaving him with a plain white box. Lifting the lid, he stared inside. His eyes widened, and then the plastic stick it contained, with its two prominent blue lines, tumbled to the floor.

'Tesoro...' Stefano jumped from the chair and gathered her into his arms once more. 'La mia stella.'

My star.

She'd begun to have suspicions a few weeks earlier that her expanding cleavage, which Stefano loved so much, had less to do with the toasted marshmallows and hot chocolate she'd been consuming and more to do with the fact that on some days they'd been casual with contraception.

Stefano cupped her face in his hands. 'You have been looking more beautiful than ever. I thought it was happiness...' His voice was filled with wonder, a reverent whisper. 'But this is more than I could have dreamed. How far along are you?'

Tears pricked at her eyes. This was more than she could have dreamed too—the joy that filled her in this moment. 'Still early...maybe five or six weeks. A scan will tell us.'

His eyes widened. 'The ball...the performance. We should cancel. You need to rest.'

She pulled back laughing. 'I'm pregnant. Not an invalid. We're playing together, and you're being formally announced as Special Advisor of State to His Highness. There is *no way* we're missing the ball.'

When she and Stefano had returned to Lasserno permanently, Alessio had reached out to suggest the role and Stefano had accepted. Not because of the weight of family history or any sense of obligation. Because it had been a deeply heartfelt offer from one friend to another.

Anyhow, Stefano was already a true Shield to the Crown. A protector at heart. He'd nurtured and protected her.

'So long as you're sure.'

He placed his warm hand on her stomach, looked deep into her eyes, and the emotion she witnessed there would have cut her off at the knees if she hadn't known he would always hold her up.

'I've never been surer of anything. I'm so proud of you, Stefano, and I want everyone to see how much.'

'You are the song in my life. The music in my heart. My love for you makes me better at everything I do. Yours are the only accolades I'll ever need.'

He bent, swung her high into his arms, and Lucy threw her head back, laughing at the happiness of yet another perfect moment.

'And now, *tesoro*, it's time for me to show you the stars again.'

* * * * *

DESERT PRINCE'S
DEFIANT BRIDE

JULIEANNE HOWELLS

MILLS & BOON

For Paul.

Thank you for the endless encouragement and unfailing belief, for valiantly trying not to glaze over when asked for the hundredth time to reread a scene, and most importantly for all the years of love and laughter.

What more could a girl need in her hero?

CHAPTER ONE

THE RECEPTION ROOMS of the Surrey mansion were thronged with the great and the good. Not a soul amongst them would have declined the invitation to this charity event. It was worth the cost of the hefty donation alone just to be in the same room as its host: the achingly glamorous Sad Prince.

Officially he was His Royal Highness, Crown Prince Khaled bin Bassam al Azir, but unless addressing him directly, who used his official title? Certainly never the press. They preferred the poignant epithet; it suited him too well.

'Of course it does,' said one of their number, a society columnist holding court amidst a gaggle of guests. 'Can you recall a single image where the Prince is smiling?'

Beside her, the woman's husband shook his head. 'Not a one. Always looks so melancholy, poor devil.'

'Poor? Nabhan may be a desert kingdom, but first there was the oil, and now it's a financial hub. The man's as rich as Croesus. And he's what? Thirty-two? In his prime, with the world at his feet. What's poor about that?'

'I suppose,' her husband said, snagging a glass of champagne from a passing waiter. 'But when does he take time off to enjoy it?'

It was seven years since the King's ill health had forced his retirement from public life. His only son had assumed the workload of prince and monarch, and by all accounts, not stopped working since.

'Things might have been different had the older brother

survived that accident, of course,' the husband said mournfully into his glass. 'But who was surprised when it ended badly for him? Always too reckless, that one.'

There were murmurs of agreement from the little group. *'A horrible business, losing your sibling like that.'*

'No wonder the Prince looks so tortured.'

Sensing an unwelcome shift in their attention, the columnist said loudly, 'But have you heard the rumours? Apparently he's about to choose himself a wife.'

There was a collective 'ooh...' and all eyes turned back to her.

'The Palace has denied it, of course, but who believes that? Not when he's been conspicuously single for six months.' She cast a meaningful look around her audience. 'Now there's a man preparing the way for his bride...' Seeing the meat and bones of tomorrow's piece, far more juicy than this dull old charity event, the columnist added, 'And did you notice how he disappeared promptly at eleven? Maybe the girl's actually tucked away here.'

She placed a hand to her bosom and gazed feelingly into the distance.

'We could say we were there the night the Sad Prince proposed to his future princess. Oh, the romance of it.'

'Romance?' her husband scoffed, quite ruining the moment and earning a filthy look from his wife. 'She can forget all that. With that one she'll be lucky to get so much as a smile.'

For the young woman who was indeed hidden away in a private part of the house, the Prince's smile, or lack thereof, was not her most pressing concern. Neither was there any romance in the air.

At that moment, though, the Sad Prince was in his suite and removing his clothes. Far from entertaining some fortunate female he was, in fact, alone.

Lily Marchant knew this for a certainty.

She knew this despite being neither his prospective bride

nor his new girlfriend, nor yet being on the guest list for the event still in full swing downstairs. Nor, before this evening, having even set eyes on the man in over a decade.

She knew this because she had a ringside view from her hiding place behind the louvred doors of his dressing room—the only place to suggest itself for concealment at extremely short notice.

The Prince had already slipped off his impeccable dinner jacket. The obligatory bow tie hung loose at the collar of his crisp white shirt. Even now his fingers were going to the buttons, revealing a tantalising glimpse of toned chest.

Lily knew the decent thing would be to look away—the man had no idea he was being observed after all. But this was Prince Khaled al Azir. He of the film-star looks, the heart-stopping sex appeal. And once, before she'd grown up and understood how nonsensical it was, the very epicentre of all her romantic hopes and dreams.

His olive-toned skin and raven-dark hair he'd inherited from his Nabhani-born father. From his English mother came impossibly high cheekbones and deep-set pale grey eyes. The sensuous mouth and the look of cool hauteur were all his own, and he was, quite simply, stunning.

Even with his clothes on.

Lily sneaked closer to the gaps in the doors.

A gold watch fell with a clatter to the bedside table, followed by a pair of cufflinks, their diamond studs glittering in the soft lamplight. Both so casually discarded and probably worth a king's ransom. Certainly more than she or her stepbrother could ever hope to afford.

Lily's mouth tightened as she was reminded of why she was there.

Because of the kind of man the Prince had become.

Ruthless and heartless.

At least enough to abandon his closest friend precisely when he needed his support the most. Meaning Nate had had to turn to her for help.

Lily was still reeling from that morning's phone call.

'Baby Sis, I'm in trouble and you're the only one I can trust.'

Baby Stepsis, she could have corrected, though it hardly mattered. Nate was all the family she had, or the only one who would acknowledge her, at least.

Her big, handsome stepbrother, whom her friends swooned over. But to her was just Nate, her lifeline, the only person who'd ever tried to put her first.

Whether that had been ditching his own plans to take her shopping for her first grown-up party dress and then being there to collect her after the dance, or rearranging his diary to attend school sports days or prize-givings. The only adult in her life who ever had.

Nate was her hero. She'd help him come what may.

'Funds have disappeared from the charity account and Khaled thinks I'm responsible,' he'd told her.

The men had been friends since school. Nate even worked for him now, as director of the charity benefitting from to-night's event. How could Khaled believe such a thing?

Through the slits in the doors Lily glared at the real villain here. But then off went that snowy white shirt, sliding from a perfectly sculpted back.

The dressing room became rather airless.

She'd seen photographs. Who hadn't? He was one of the most photographed and photogenic men on the planet. She'd even seen him close up before. Twice.

None of that quite prepared a girl for the effect of seeing the man he was now. Though there were traces of the teenage boy she'd once known, this bare-chested Adonis was all power and physical confidence.

As he crossed the room Lily gazed after him—and almost toppled into a row of neatly hung suits. A hanger creaked as it swung on the clothes rail.

The Prince stopped.

Right next to the small table set in the window recess.

Where her stepbrother's laptop now lay.

Where there had been only an *empty* tabletop when she'd entered the suite.

She gnawed on a finger. Why hadn't she brought the wretched thing in here with her?

Frantically she tried to remember Nate's advice should the worst happen.

'Improvise.'

'Improvise how, exactly?' she'd asked.

'I don't know... Cry, throw yourself on his mercy, or...'

She'd waited for something useful.

'Don't get caught.'

Don't get caught? When Khaled stood right next to evidence that he had an intruder.

But after trailing a long finger across the computer lid, he turned, disappearing into the bathroom opposite her hideout.

Lily deflated on a long sigh. There was still a chance to get out of this. The Prince was otherwise occupied. From the bathroom came the sound of a shower running.

Nate needed her to get his laptop. He wanted to check for evidence of how the money had been taken. He had his suspicions, he'd said, but he couldn't tell her. Not yet. He didn't think it was safe. Khaled had it with him, and the best chance to retrieve it would be for her to attend the charity event he was hosting.

Penny, Nate's secretary, was on the guest list but had fallen ill. *'You can pretend to be her. If we're lucky no one will check.'*

So Lily had dug out her one good dress, taken the hour-long train journey from London, followed by twenty minutes in a taxi, all the while nervously practising a plausible speech which in the end hadn't even been needed. With the barest of checks, she'd been allowed in.

Accessing the private part of the house had, however, proved to be altogether more difficult.

After mingling on the ground floor she'd sidled towards the main staircase. Only to be halted by a besuited, polite, but totally intimidating guard.

She'd needed a plan B.

A line of French windows had been thrown wide, allowing cooler air to flow in and overheated partygoers to stroll out. Lily had joined them on the terrace where, by luck, she'd found an alternative route to the first floor.

It had been tricky, but she'd actually made it into the Prince's private quarters, and there had sat Nate's laptop, in broad view on the desk.

She'd moved it to the table by the window and, because she'd lost the folding tote she'd brought for the job, had been searching for something to carry it in when she'd heard voices along the corridor.

There'd barely been time to race to the dressing room and close the door behind her before the Prince had walked into his suite.

Now here she was, surrounded by rows of expensive tailoring that had a delicious scent of citrus and spice, wondering how to get out unnoticed.

She almost leapt from her skin at the trilling of the bedside phone.

Khaled reappeared, a towel slung low around his hips. He took the call, looking directly at her hideaway as he spoke. Lily lurched back. Her elbow collided with a row of shoes, catapulting two into the air. She caught them just before they slammed into the door and puffed out her cheeks in silent relief.

Khaled replaced the receiver.

'It appears we've reached an impasse.'

His voice was a low, rich rumble. She remembered that sound: its timbre, its pitch, the perfect English with its precise, upper-class diction. What she didn't remember was the curious tingling it sent along her spine.

And just who was he talking to?

She squinted through the gaps in the doors. Was someone in the lounge beyond the bedroom?

'My car is ready and I need to dress. So either I pretend I

don't know you're in there, and risk a scene when the door is opened, or you come out now and spare us both the drama.'

Lily went hot and cold all at the same time.

He knew she was there.

The Prince stared at the dressing room, then with an exasperated sigh strode towards it. The door was flung wide and there he was, staring right at her: taller, broader, and so much more *naked* than he'd appeared from behind the safety of the slats.

'Miss Marchant, what a pleasant surprise.' His icy tone suggested he felt the exact opposite. 'Please, do join me.'

He made no attempt to move aside, so her nose almost brushed his bare chest as she slid from the shadows and into his bedroom.

Blinking in the brighter light, she raised her eyes to the Sad Prince—to six foot three of powerfully built, barely dressed, angry adult male looming over her. He wasn't looking particularly sad right now.

If ever improvisation skills were needed…

'Hello, Khaled,' she said jauntily. 'We must stop meeting like this.'

His brow knotted. 'I don't see any similarity. As I recall, last time it was your cloakroom you were hiding in, and I definitely had not broken into your rooms.'

He reached for the shoes she still clutched.

'I also didn't steal anything from you. What are these for?' He held them aloft before tossing them onto the bed. 'A souvenir of your visit?'

'I'm really sorry, I know I shouldn't be in here, but I got lost trying to find the…the ladies' room.'

One ebony brow lifted, but that beautiful face didn't soften for a moment.

'I genuinely came in here by mistake, and then when I heard you outside I'm afraid I panicked and hid.'

'Indeed?' His fierce gaze didn't waver. 'You were lost and yet you didn't think to ask any of the guards stationed along the corridor for directions?'

'Guards?' Lily swallowed, and shot a glance to the suite doors, imagining the fearsome figure from earlier waiting beyond them.

'Yes, several. Stationed between here and the reception rooms.'

He was still disconcertingly close. Lily watched, fascinated, as a droplet of moisture dripped from his hair to trail in a sinuous pattern down that muscled torso.

She dragged her gaze away. 'If I'd seen them I would certainly have known not to come in here.'

'And had they seen you they would have prevented you from doing so, I assure you.'

'But I saw no one. Perhaps they had slipped away to… to powder their noses, or something?'

The look he bestowed on her was one of pure disdain. 'They're all ex-special forces. I doubt they've powdered a damn thing in their lives.'

Lily could believe it, but thought it wise not to comment.

Arctic grey eyes bored into her. 'So you entered these rooms in error. But please, enlighten me, why were you in my house in the first place?'

He was looming again; her five-four frame was no match for his soaring height.

'For the charity event, of course.' She injected a little disdain of her own into her voice. 'Why else would I be here?'

He folded his arms across that broad chest. He must work out a lot. Muscles like that were no simple gift of nature.

'You weren't on the guest list and it was invitation-only,' he said.

Ah, this she was prepared for. 'A friend was due to attend, but she's ill. She gave me her ticket. She knew I'd want to come.'

'I see. You have an interest in the cause?'

'Of course,' she lied. Well, she might have if she'd bothered to find out what it was. 'It's such a worthy cause and it's long been close to my heart.'

'The endangered flora and fauna of the Nabhani marshlands?' He looked disbelieving. 'And how long have you supported the charity?'

'Oh, you know,' she said, waving a hand through the air, 'absolutely ages.'

'Miss Marchant, the charity was officially launched this evening.'

She opened her mouth to answer, but nothing sensible came to mind. Except to curse, despite their perilous state, all the beasts and flowers of the marshes of Nabhan. Wasn't it a desert country? How could it have marshland?

'I must have confused it with another charity.'

'Evidently.'

Her weak smile garnered no response. Evidently it was time she got out of there.

'Well, it's been lovely catching up, but I really ought to be going.'

Strong fingers closed about her bare arm. 'I think not.'

The impact of that skin-on-skin contact arrived at her legs just as she required them to move. She was being marched to the lounge area of the suite.

On another occasion she might have admired the tasteful decor, the watered silk wall coverings, the richly hued rugs underfoot, but right now all she could digest was the shocking heat of that touch and the debilitating effect it was having on her ability to walk.

'Sit,' he said, pushing her onto a sofa.

Hardly necessary. Her knees buckled of their own accord.

Khaled snatched up the remote control for a TV standing in the corner of the room. He scrolled through channels until images from a security camera appeared on the screen. The footage showed the exterior of the house, the balcony outside this bedroom, the ivy-clad wall below.

He perched on the desk. Lily tried not to stare at the extra inches of muscular thigh revealed as the towel rode higher.

'So, let's clarify. You claim you are here as a long-time supporter of a charity which was only launched this evening. I find you lurking in my private rooms—which, you maintain, you entered by accident.'

Above the fireplace hung an eighteenth-century hunting canvas. Riders, horses, and a pack of baying hounds streamed across the foreground, whilst in the distance a fox ran for its life.

Empathising with that harried speck of orange, Lily said, 'Yes, of course. I've already explained. I was lost.'

His mouth tightened at her response.

'Then kindly explain this.' He punched a button on the remote.

On screen, the figure of a woman appeared, creeping along the base of the wall. She peered up at the balcony whilst she slipped off her sandals and snagged their straps between her teeth. A clutch bag was tucked down the front of her dress and then—Lily squirmed at this—she hitched up her hem and tucked it up into the legs of her knickers. The woman grasped the ivy and began to climb.

Khaled snorted in disapproval and Lily looked away. She knew what came next.

Halfway up, the climber lost her footing, and as she swung about, fighting to regain her grip, the shoes slipped from her teeth to fall into the rose bed below.

Lily curled her bare toes out of view.

Eventually the woman reached the balcony, heaving herself over, only to scrabble for the bag as it tumbled from her cleavage, joining the missing shoes. Worst of all, the hem of the dress had worked loose, got caught on the railing and hitched higher, revealing, in mortifying detail, an expanse of lace-clad bottom.

Lily slid her fingers across the tell-tale tear in the hem of her dress. She could do nothing about the burning heat of her face.

'She's very enterprising,' she said. 'Is she a groupie or something?'

Khaled stared at her. 'You're actually going to pretend that isn't you?'

She doubted crying or throwing herself on this man's mercy would help. All she had left was bluff.

'You think I could make a climb like—?'

'Enough!'

She jumped as the remote clattered onto the desk. 'I've given you the chance to be honest with me, but it seems you're determined to continue with this nonsense. I don't have time for it. So here are your options. One, we call the police and allow them to get the bottom of this.'

Lily swallowed. 'And option two?'

'We take the more civilised route. I have business in the capital. You agree to come with me. Take some time to consider your position. Then, if you're wise, you'll answer my questions about your stepbrother.'

Right now, anything was better than being arrested.

'I've missed the last train back, so a lift home would be good,' she said. 'I'll go for the second option—though what more we have to discuss I can't imagine.'

An odd, almost triumphant expression crossed his face. 'Finally you show some sense.'

He called out to whoever was waiting on the landing beyond his suite.

A man entered. His black suit was finely tailored, but his solid frame and watchful eyes belonged to a much tougher existence. He was reassuring, or formidable, depending on how you looked at it—and a familiar face Lily realised.

'Hello, Rais,' she said to Khaled's personal bodyguard. The same man who had protected the teenage Prince all those years ago.

He dipped his head in greeting.

'Miss Marchant is coming with us,' Khaled said. 'Take her to the car. I'll be there in five minutes.'

If Rais was surprised by that announcement he didn't show it. He simply waited for Lily to get to her feet and politely stood aside to allow her to walk out of the suite.

At a private side entrance a car waited, its rear door held open by the guard she'd encountered earlier. The heavy thud as it closed, trapping her inside, felt so ominous it took her three fumbling attempts to fasten her seat belt.

Minutes later Khaled joined her. Now in a grey suit and blue shirt, he looked composed and ridiculously handsome, and in with him had come that scent of citrus and spice.

As it swirled around her an odd excitement fluttered low in her belly. She edged closer to the door, to ease that unsettling sensation and to put more space between her and the figure beside her. She'd thought the car impressively large, but now Khaled had climbed in it seemed filled with him.

As they pulled away she cast him a sidelong glance. He was checking messages on his phone. In the darkness its glow cast eerie shadows across those impossible cheekbones. Lily knew it was a trick of the light, but where before he'd appeared stern, now he had that infamous air of melancholy about him.

Maybe there was still a chance to reason with him.

'Perhaps we could come to a compromise?' she said.

No response.

'I admit hiding in your rooms doesn't look good. I'm actually quite embarrassed about it.'

A thumb scrolled upwards, scanning new messages.

'If I can go home tonight, I promise I'll meet you wherever you want in London tomorrow.'

Now he looked up. 'London?'

'You said you have business in the capital,' she said haltingly. Something in his expression had set alarm bells ringing.

'I have. But I meant the capital of my country.'

'Your country?' It was barely a whisper.

'After the stunt you pulled, did you think I'd simply let you go? Whilst your faithless stepbrother remains at large? No, if he wants to gain your freedom he'll give himself up. Until he does, I'm keeping you close. And as I'm going home you, Miss Marchant, are coming with me. To Nabhan.'

CHAPTER TWO

IF A MAN could be made to combust from a mere look then Lily Marchant was doing her damnedest to send him up in flames. From her seat on the opposite side of the cabin, as far from him as it was possible to get on a Gulfstream V, she glowered at him.

The mood he was in, Khaled could have glared right back. They'd almost missed their flight slot because of her nonsense back at the house. She'd had every opportunity to confess, and yet insisted on dragging out that ridiculous charade.

A lost bona fide guest? Did she imagine he was a complete idiot? Perhaps she did—her duplicitous stepbrother apparently had.

Khaled's rage welled up at the reminder of Nate Marchant's duplicity. His closest friend, whom he'd elevated to director of his new charity because of his ability to schmooze millions from the wealthy. He'd never imagined the man would help himself to those millions.

The excuses he'd had to make tonight to cover for his absence…

But beneath the rage lay true hurt: the cold shock of betrayal by a friend who'd become like a brother to him.

A flutter of movement drew his attention back across the aisle. They'd hit air turbulence and Lily fingers had convulsed around the armrest. Had she'd never flown before?

'This is perfectly normal,' he said kindly. 'We're quite safe.'

His reward was another fulminating glare.

Perhaps she was still smarting from the way she'd been manhandled aboard. Well, he'd make no apology for that. There'd been mere yards between the car and the jet, and still she'd managed to make a fuss. Yelping as a piece of grit dug into the soles of her bare feet, hopping about, making a show of trying to brush it away.

She'd demanded her shoes but, feeling vengeful, he'd ordered that they be disposed of, and he'd told her so, adding that they'd still be on her feet if she hadn't been intent on breaking and entering. When she'd sent him an evil look, as if he was the villain here, the last of his patience had evaporated and he'd hitched her beneath his arm like a piece of baggage and toted her the final few paces to the plane.

He'd have happily hauled her on board like that, too, even with the risk of paparazzi camped out nearby, but the steps had been too narrow. So he'd shifted his grip, swept his arms about her torso and pulled her back against his chest, her naked toes dangling.

As he'd carried her into the cabin she'd felt so slight, her curves more girl than woman. Except where the weight of her breasts had pressed against his arm.

Khaled tugged at his sleeve, still feeling that sweet, warm pressure. Irritated for allowing it even to register.

Frowning, he looked up, and their eyes clashed again. This time, before she turned away, he caught a flash of fear in her expression.

He felt a prickle of guilt. Why? He wasn't to blame for her predicament. Had she not broken into his rooms she'd be safely at home right now.

He massaged the bridge of his nose, eyeing the papers before him—documents he wanted to get through before they landed. At this point on a flight he'd normally be engrossed in work, but tonight his powers of concentration had deserted him—or, more accurately, been hijacked by the young woman sulking in her seat.

'Can I get you anything, sir?'

Stella, the flight attendant, stood beside him. A great favourite of his family, she'd served them since Khaled had been a boy.

She'd presumed on that level of familiarity tonight, admonishing him as he'd set Lily back on her feet inside the jet. To his annoyance, he'd actually blushed.

And now his appetite appeared to have gone the same way as his concentration. 'Nothing, thank you.'

'Then I'll attend to Miss Marchant. She's seems a little… discomforted.'

He watched Stella approach Lily, wishing it had been one of the other stewards on duty tonight. They'd never dare show any reaction to him bringing a woman on board.

But the problem wasn't really that Lily was female. Girlfriends had often joined him on flights. The difference was that they never travelled with him to Nabhan. Other destinations, yes. Wherever his duties took him. Just never to his home. He knew if they did it would be assumed he had serious intentions about the woman.

Always he was careful to keep such speculation to a minimum. Much good it did him. The media seized upon any titbit, real or otherwise, about the Sad Prince.

That blasted moniker—how he despised it, and the endless attention that went with it. Anyway, damn it all, he did smile sometimes. His mother even had a photo to prove it.

But right now he'd never felt less like smiling.

Speculation was rife that he was about to announce his engagement and press attention had intensified—which, in turn, increased the risk of the charity theft becoming public.

How his enemies would love that.

There'd be questions again about his decisions, his choice of friends, whispers about nepotism and corruption. And the loudest dissenter of all, disguised beneath the pretence of loyalty and concern for the country, would be George

Hyde-Wallace—his mother's seventy-four-year-old cousin, and Leader of the Council of Families. The Englishman who, in his thirties, had quit British Special Forces to take a post in Nabhan as bodyguard to the young King Bassam, and years later introduced his widowed employer to his beautiful cousin, gaining him the King's grateful patronage.

Intelligent, ambitious, with a genius for politics and a passion for all things Nabhani, he'd risen to a position of great influence in the country. He'd married into one of its senior families, and eventually become the only European ever to serve on the Council.

Hyde-Wallace had been elected leader by the other families a month after the King's first heart attack.

He'd been a thorn in Khaled's side ever since.

Having become related to the crown by marriage, he'd thought to control his young cousin. When he'd found that wouldn't be the case, he'd tried undermining him instead. Speaking against the Prince's reforms. Claiming they would destroy traditional Nabhani values.

But Hyde-Wallace didn't really care about tradition; he cared about power. Khaled's move towards greater democracy would strip that from him.

Many Nabhani people had made donations to the new charity, but the most substantial had come from Hyde-Wallace. If the theft were discovered he'd be sure to make capital out of it.

And all this when the six-month-long secret negotiations for his marriage were nearing conclusion.

The irony was that the match had been suggested by George. And, much as it irked Khaled to admit it, it was a sound proposition. The daughter of the King of Qaydar had been raised to the royal life, and would be equipped to deal with its demands. More importantly, with her would come much-needed access to water for the remote western reaches of Nabhan, with an agreement to build a new dam in the mountains straddling their shared border.

But the talks had been difficult. Stalled again and again

by the King of Qaydar demanding a curb on the Prince's re-forming policies. Khaled had quickly recognised that Hyde-Wallace had brokered the alliance to yoke his cousin to a conservative, backward-looking father-in-law.

Once the engagement was announced, no doubt the union would be spun into some great love affair.

As if. He would have no truck with sentiment.

While there was deliberately no one at present, Khaled had of course taken lovers. But those relationships had only ever been about mutual companionship and the sating of physical needs. Not long term and never sentimental. Messy, tangled emotions got in the way of the day job, and he wouldn't allow that. Because nothing was more important to him than duty.

How else was he to make amends for the loss of his brother?

Khaled picked up his papers, remembering previous occupants of the seat opposite him. How at this point in a flight they'd be sitting demurely, most likely working. Not disturbing his concentration. And certainly not flouncing away, as soon as the pilot had announced it was safe to do so, to sit as far from him as possible.

His eyes lifted again in Lily's direction, this time to see her chatting with Stella.

From beneath his lashes, Khaled studied her.

She wore a dress of dark green. A lucky choice. It disguised the grubby stains she'd acquired scrambling up the ivy outside his rooms. Yet the shade also complemented her ivory skin and set off the rich auburn tones of her up-swept hair.

Khaled snorted. Unkempt, more like. The style was in disarray, and if more evidence of her misspent evening were needed, one cheek sported smudges of dirt.

Now Lily was flicking through a magazine and getting comfortable, lifting her legs to tuck her bare feet beneath her. There was a flash of grimy soles.

And with that simple image Khaled was assaulted with

a rush of memories. Memories of a long-ago summer and a skinny girl, all red hair and freckles. Her feet black as a street urchin's as she clambered up trees or ran laughing through the gardens of her stepfather's estate. A girl with scraped knees, dirt on her face, and always grass stains on her clothes.

How long was it since he'd thought of her and how, for two weeks that summer, she'd brought him a measure of peace when he'd thought he'd never know peace again?

The summer they'd lost Faisal.

His bright, brilliant brother.

His reckless brother, they'd said.

Oh, if they but knew…

He closed his eyes and endured the familiar wave of guilt and loss. It never lessened, and why should it. After what he'd done.

He'd been sixteen. Lily seven.

And now…?

He did the maths.

Twenty-three.

Sixteen years older and little had changed. Still climbing, still barefoot, and still with scraped knees.

Khaled looked closer. A gash to her shin that he hadn't noticed before was oozing blood.

He called Stella over, issued instructions, and then, abandoning his work, crossed the cabin to slide into the space opposite Lily.

Her mouth twisted. 'If I'd wanted to talk to you I'd have stayed in my original seat.'

Her expression softened as Stella appeared at his shoulder, presenting him with a towel and placing a bowl of water and first aid provisions on the shelf beside them.

'Your shin is bleeding,' he explained, laying the towel over his lap and tipping disinfectant into the water. 'There's dirt in the wound, too. It'll get infected if we don't attend to it.'

He started rolling back his shirtsleeves.

'I don't need you to do it,' she said crossly. 'I can look after myself.'

She soaked the sponge Stella had left and bent forward to dab at the torn skin.

In that position, in that dress, it was hard for him to ignore the creamy swell of her breasts. He shouldn't be looking. He should be focusing on Lily the burglar, not Lily the woman. Better yet, he should imagine she was still that skinny schoolgirl he'd once known.

But she was not.

When she'd emerged from his dressing room he'd been surprised by the surge of heat as her big hazel eyes had lifted to his. He'd told himself it was the normal reaction of any red-blooded male finding an attractive young woman in his bedroom. He wasn't concerned. It meant nothing.

Except her floral perfume teased him. It had clung to his clothes after he'd carried her on board and now it invaded his senses again.

She rose to soak the sponge in fresh water. Her teeth worried at her bottom lip as she worked. Her full, sensuous lip of dusky pink...

Khaled cleared his throat. 'You're lucky that you only have a cut or two. You could have been badly injured on that damn fool climb,' he said.

She shrugged. 'It's just a few scratches. Anyway, Nate needed my help,' she answered, not looking at him.

She bent forward again. This time he sent his gaze to the safety of the carpet.

'What exactly has your stepbrother told you? And don't even think of lying. My patience is wearing thin.'

She looked up at him. 'That there's money missing from the charity fund and you believe Nate is responsible—which is crazy. You know him. He doesn't care about money.'

'That's because he's never been without it before. He lost everything when his father's fortunes collapsed. There was nothing left for either of you, I understand?'

'I don't see what it's got to do with you, but, no, there

was nothing. Even the house is to be sold. I moved out two days ago.'

Moved out? Did she have somewhere to go?

There was an unpleasant tightening in his chest. *Get a grip*, he thought, and responded sharply. 'It has everything to do with me if it becomes a motive for theft.'

'However bad it got, Nate would never steal.'

'There is compelling evidence that suggests otherwise.'

She shuffled forward to perch on the edge of her seat, checking for remaining scratches. Helplessly, Khaled's gaze travelled the length of her body from pale shoulder to slender ankle.

Hell.

'Have you considered that someone is trying to frame him? Or that actually it's you they're trying to hurt?'

He gave a wry, mirthless laugh. 'Lily, I'm a political leader introducing reform in a region that clings to its traditions. I have numerous enemies. That's why I'm careful to protect myself, and my interests, and why it's almost impossible that anyone other than Nate has the money.'

'*Almost* impossible, but not completely? Then I know Nate is innocent.'

'The transfer originated in his office.'

'Maybe his secretary did it.'

'Penny? Her alibi is solid. Plus, she's worked for the family for years. Even for my mother's cousin for a while. She's beyond reproach.'

Lily shifted again, this time checking the inside of her calf.

He gritted his teeth. He was *not*, he reminded himself, attracted to short, troublesome redheads, and he'd prove it.

He snatched the sponge from her hand. 'You're not being thorough enough. I'll do it.'

As his fingers touched the soft skin at the back of her knee a shot of pure energy raced straight to his groin. He masked his reaction by carefully checking each scrape for dirt and then reaching for tape and bandages. She'd gone very still, and when she spoke her voice was less certain than it had been.

'Then there is…is some other explanation. Are you even looking for anyone else?'

He gently pressed a lint pad against her skin and secured the edge with tape.

'Not yet. There would be no point.'

'Then you're letting the real culprit get away. You're a fool.'

He stuck on the last pieces of tape and lifted his fingers from her skin, disregarding how he instantly missed its warmth, concentrating instead on her impertinence.

'Says the woman who believed she could gate-crash a private party and not be discovered from the start?'

She watched him, a faint line creasing her brow. He saw the exact moment the penny dropped.

'You knew I was in your dressing room. Even before the phone call.'

'Did you imagine it would be that easy to enter my home? That a prince of Nabhan would be so little protected? Besides, you made so much noise the entire household would have known you were there.'

He didn't mention that her scent had lingered, too. That he'd picked up on the unfamiliar fragrance the moment he'd entered his suite. She made a hopeless burglar.

She ignored his last remark, clearly caught up in another idea altogether. 'You knew I was there and yet you…you…' She flushed—presumably at the memory of him undressing. She even had the audacity to sound indignant.

'You break into a man's private rooms and expect the social niceties to be observed? I'm on a strict schedule. I had to be ready to leave. I imagined that for decency's sake you would reveal yourself before, shall we say, I did.'

The fabric of her dress suddenly held deep fascination for her, and she plucked at the hem. 'Why did you allow me to break in?'

'I wanted to know what you were searching for.' He invested his voice with the full force of royal authority. 'And now would be a good time to tell me.'

She remained stubbornly silent.

'I know you were there for the laptop.'

She stared at him.

'Lily, you'd moved it to the table by the window. We have the folded bag you brought with you to carry it away in. Who brings a shopping bag to a party? We presume your stepbrother sent you to access something on the hard drive. What was it?'

Her chin came up.

'If Nate had wanted you to know that, he would have told you himself. Obviously he doesn't trust you, and neither do I.'

She was going to defy him? Again?

He was hit with several emotions at once: incredulity, anger, and a sudden, irrational urge to reach over and stop her impertinent little mouth with his own.

It was not good that she'd wound him up to that extent. Time to wrestle back control—in particular of his wayward hormones.

'In that case I think you should prepare yourself for a long stay in Nabhan.'

'How lovely,' she mocked. 'It's ages since I've had a holiday.'

'It won't, I assure you, be any kind of a holiday. That would suggest the freedom to come and go as you please. Which will not be permitted.'

'Why not just throw me in prison and have done with it?'

'Don't tempt me,' he muttered.

Then he took a breath. This was achieving nothing. He forced himself to calm down.

'Before we arrive in Nabhan I think we should set a few ground rules,' he said, as pleasantly as he could.

Lily eyed him suspiciously.

'Under the circumstances, it's hardly appropriate that you should meet any members of my family. So I've—'

'Might they be tainted by my criminal presence?'

Damn it—now she was interrupting him. 'Whilst you have a point,' he snapped back, 'you know that's not what I meant. This is not a social visit. I thought perhaps, both for your sake and Nate's, you would appreciate as much discretion as possible.'

She opened her mouth to reply, but then closed it again, perhaps recognising the sense in keeping this whole sorry affair quiet.

'I've arranged for you to stay in an apartment in Nabhan city. It's on the waterfront and has its own staff. You'll be quite comfortable.'

'You could have shown this level of concern before you dragged me halfway round the world,' she said.

'And you should remember your trip would have been unnecessary had you stayed away from my home or if you'd told me where Nate is. You'll be free to go as soon as you tell me what I want to know or he comes forward.'

'So I'm being kidnapped? Surely even a prince can't just take a woman against her will.'

His temper flared again.

'*Habiba*, trust me—if I were to "take" you, not only would you be willing, but you'd be begging me for more.'

Her jaw fell open. As well it might. What had possessed him to say something so outrageously inappropriate? He needed to end this conversation.

He stood abruptly, rolling down his shirtsleeves.

As if that was going to dignify his last remark.

'It's late and we still have several hours before we land. I have work to complete,' he said, staring down his nose at her, trying to regain some authority before he went back to his seat. 'I suggest you try and get some rest.'

And before she could throw another impertinence at him he turned away.

CHAPTER THREE

THE LIGHTS WERE DIMMED. Rais and his team dozed at the rear of the plane. This was the smallest of the royal jets, with no bedroom. Khaled never needed one. He mostly worked during a flight. But in the last ten minutes he'd read the same page a dozen times. Nothing had sunk in. His gaze kept travelling back to where Lily was stretched out on her seat.

Miraculously, she'd done as she was told.

Stella had reclined the seat and converted it into a bed. Now his additional passenger was curled beneath a cashmere blanket, asleep. Her head rested on a plump pillow, but the throw had slipped from her shoulders.

Khaled went to her. He gently tucked the blanket back in place. She murmured and snuggled further beneath its warmth.

He was filled again with the strangest emotions. An odd mix of anger and protectiveness—and something else he felt it wise to ignore.

There were purple shadows beneath her eyes. How many late nights had she endured recently?

Before his death last month, she'd acted as housekeeper to her stepfather. They hadn't been close. Edward Marchant had viewed the young Lily as an encumbrance, and the older version as cheap labour.

Had she known the extent of his financial difficulties? Had it been a surprise when, essentially, she'd lost her job and home in one day?

In the decade since they'd last met, how had she fared? Because her stepbrother was a close friend of the royal family, Khaled's people would have performed regular background checks on her as a matter of course, but nothing had ever been brought to his notice.

Long dark lashes swept low over pale cheekbones where those smudges of dirt still sat. Her ruined hairstyle even sported a withered ivy leaf. Khaled moved to pluck it clear and found his fingers tangled in silky tresses. They lingered, gently twining one loose curl.

Lily Marchant...

In all kinds of trouble, not really of her own making.

What was it her stepbrother needed so badly that he was prepared to expose her to danger?

There was a sound from the galley. Stella was watching him.

He straightened, felt his cheeks heat. 'Please find Miss Marchant another blanket. It's cool in here,' he ordered, retreating to the safer territory of his own seat.

He snatched up his discarded work, determined to finally make headway.

His efforts were fruitless. Lily held all his attention.

She was in her twenties now, but beneath all her bravado there were traces of that lonely little girl with the heartbreaking air of vulnerability he remembered from that winter...the second and only other time they'd met.

She'd been thirteen—one year younger than his sisters were now and far too young to lose her mother.

Once a feted actress, Niamh had been thirty-three when she'd succumbed to her alcohol addiction. The more romantic version was that it had been the weariness of a broken heart that simply wouldn't heal. Lily's father—dead over a decade by then—had, they said, been mourned to distraction by his beautiful widow.

Lord Rupert Hastings had been a world class eventer, but when a terrible fall had left his spine fused with pins and metal plates he'd been told to retire, or risk death. He'd ignored all pleas to quit, even those of his wife, who had begged him on behalf of their young daughter.

The inevitable had happened.

Niamh's second marriage, so soon after the accident that had ended her first, had been a disaster.

Widower Edward Marchant, who'd inherited his wealth from Nate's mother, had thought he'd married the perfect trophy wife. A famous actress with the added cachet of a connection to a titled family. Once he'd discovered she'd been disowned by her former in-laws and was little more than a heartbroken creature, he'd neglected her, leaving her to seek solace, then oblivion, in a vodka bottle.

When Niamh had died so suddenly Nate, abroad and unable to get home in time, had begged Khaled to go to Lily on his behalf.

'You know she and my father aren't close, and she still talks about you all the time. You're in England at the moment. Be her big brother for a few hours?'

Khaled had remembered the little girl with the kind heart and sunny smile. In all conscience he'd known he couldn't leave her alone on such a day.

His people had worked miracles, carving a few hours from his packed schedule, but even they hadn't conjured up enough time for him to attend the funeral itself. For which, to his lasting shame, he'd been grateful.

It would have been too vivid a reminder of a similar day, six years previously.

The day they'd buried Faisal…

In the cabin, Lily stirred in her sleep. The dim light caught in her hair, a wave of red-gold against the white of the pillow.

His work forgotten, Khaled recalled the girl he'd found that day in her stepfather's house. Alone. Ignored by everyone at the wake. Hiding in a cloakroom, her face buried in the line of coats.

She'd jerked upright when the door had opened. Someone had tried to smarten her up in a neat black coat, and to tame that riot of auburn hair by squashing a black beret firmly on her head. It had only made her look paler. More out of place. More lost.

His heart had gone out to her.

She'd blinked at him in confusion, then flung herself at his chest, sobbing as if her heart were breaking. He'd pulled her close, wrapping his arms around her, murmuring soft words in Arabic—words she wouldn't understand, and yet they'd seemed to soothe her as the racking sobs had subsided.

Later, they'd sat together in her mother's neglected rose garden and he'd asked her where she'd go now.

She'd looked up at him, puzzled. 'I'll stay here, of course.'

Her stepfather had become her legal guardian. Her mother had even changed Lily's surname when she'd married him. If Edward Marchant had been hoping her father's aristocratic family would claim her he was to be disappointed.

They'd cut all ties when their younger son Rupert had, in their opinion, married beneath him. They were an ancient family, and proud—too proud to accept a mere actress as their daughter-in-law, however celebrated. And at their head was the most intransigent of them all, the Duke, who had steadfastly refused to recognise his own grandchild.

'The only one who's ever pleased to see me is Nate,' she'd told him. 'He's my family now.'

'But who will look after you?' he'd asked. 'Nate's hardly ever home.'

'I'll look after myself. Like I've always done,' she'd said, adding hurriedly, when she saw his shocked expression, 'And there's Mrs Stone.'

He'd remembered the housekeeper from his last visit. Sour-faced and ill-tempered. Hardly the embodiment of maternal tenderness.

'I'll have clean clothes. I'll be fed. She'll get me to school on time.'

There'd been a dismissive shrug, as if to say that was enough.

Enough? For a parentless child?

It had been a dire prospect, and when he'd left that day he'd wanted to scoop her up and take her with him.

'I can't arrive at the airport looking like this.'

The voice of the adult Lily cut through Khaled's reverie. She stood barefoot in the aisle, fiddling with the torn hem of her dress. Outside the sky was bright with sunshine. They were less than half an hour from landing.

'I look like I've been partying all night.'

The tender feelings evaporated. The girl might have evoked his compassion. Not the woman. They'd been forced together because of her attempted burglary. But she had a point. He wanted a low-key arrival.

A white dress shirt was retrieved from his luggage, and Stella leant her a pair of leather sandals.

The shirt swamped her. It fell almost to her knees and her hands were lost in the sleeves. But once she'd rolled them back, and knotted the shirttails at her waist, she looked more presentable. She'd tidied her hair, removed the dirt from her cheeks. It would do.

Besides, they'd disembark far from the public terminals of the airport, and his team would spirit her away to the anonymous apartment. Few people would see her. Fewer still would know that she was here as his 'guest'. Essentially as a hostage to her stepbrother's betrayal.

For now, Nate's stepsister sat quietly in her seat, looking anywhere but at him.

Good.

Judging by his inconvenient reaction to her over the last few hours, it would be wise to put some distance between them. He'd be free of her company in about thirty minutes, and while he waited for Nate to be caught, and the money returned, there would be no need for further contact between them. This disturbing episode could be forgotten.

He relaxed, picked up the report he'd been trying to read throughout the flight, and was finally rewarded by the return of his errant concentration.

In front of the airport's private terminal a dozen men in sharp grey suits and mirrored sunglasses stood in strict formation around a motorcade of five cars. At its centre were two shiny black limousines with darkened windows. Their royal pennants fluttered in the breeze.

Khaled swore.

Not the anonymous four-by-fours he'd ordered.

'A change of plan, Miss Marchant.'

'Oh? I hope it's inconvenient for you,' she said tartly, from the other side of the plane.

'I'm afraid it will be inconvenient for us both,' he said, as he watched a woman step from one of the cars.

He knew in that instant that his plan to discreetly install Lily in the waterfront apartment was foiled. For out there waited the one person who would always happily interfere in his life—without doubt precisely why she was here now. Though why had she chosen to meet what was supposed to be a routine arrival?

Stella bustled past, gathering blankets and pillows to stow away. She saw his suspicious look. Blinked at him. This time it was she who blushed as she disappeared to the rear of the plane.

Of course. The family favourite had called ahead.

For the first time ever he'd brought a woman with him to Nabhan, and the figure out there, with her romantic notions, would be gleefully jumping to all the wrong conclusions.

He looked to the heavens. Was he to be beset with meddlesome females?

Lily dropped into the seat opposite his. She peered at the scene on the Tarmac for a moment. Looked more closely. Then blenched.

'Is that who I think it is?'

'Yes.' He sighed, getting to his feet. 'Unfortunately it's exactly who you think it is.'

He smoothed his shirt and donned his jacket, glancing down at Lily, who was still staring nervously at the welcome party outside.

'I suggest you prepare yourself and remember what I told you. Because, as you've realised, you're about to meet the Queen of Nabhan.'

And worse, he thought, running a hand through his hair in vexation as he headed for the exit, much worse than that, they were both about to encounter the force of nature that was his mother.

CHAPTER FOUR

LILY TUGGED NERVOUSLY at Khaled's oversized shirt. Was she really about to be introduced to a queen? While dressed like a charity case herself?

She wrapped steadying fingers around the handrail and stepped from the plane straight into a wall of heat. A pool of sweat bloomed in the small of her back.

Khaled, looking annoyingly cool, had reached his mother and bent to kiss her cheek. Even as he straightened, Lily saw the other woman watching her approach.

Dressed in a lilac linen dress, with a matching jacket draped casually about her shoulders, the Queen was even more beautiful in person than in her photographs.

The marriage of England's 'It' girl, Eleanor Wallace, to the widowed King of Nabhan had been the romance of the age. She'd been eighteen, he twelve years her senior, when they'd been introduced and fallen head over heels in love. Her family had objected to the match, arguing she was too young to take on the role of consort to a foreign king…too young to be stepmother to his three-year-old son.

Eleanor hadn't agreed.

Within two months they'd been wed. Ten months later little Faisal had gained a half-brother with the arrival of Khaled. Three decades on and she'd made an art form of bending people to her will.

Such was the nature of the creature awaiting Lily has she arrived at Khaled's side.

'Mother, allow me to introduce Lily Marchant. Lily, this is Her Majesty the Queen of Nabhan, my mother.'

'Please, call me Eleanor,' she said, raising Lily up from her curtsy. 'And there's no need for that, my dear. We're not big on ceremony here. I'm only sorry it's taken you so long to visit us. The girls in particular will be thrilled to meet you.'

'Nate suggested they holiday together in Nabhan,' Khaled explained. 'As he couldn't join her straight away I offered to bring Lily with me, so she wouldn't have to travel alone.'

'That was thoughtful of you, darling,' Eleanor said, watching Khaled's bags being carried from the plane.

Lily's were conspicuous by their absence.

'Miss Marchant's luggage has met with an accident,' he said. 'Her hotel had a problem with its sprinkler system.'

'How unfortunate.' Eleanor glanced at the plasters on Lily's shin. It was obvious she didn't believe the story.

'Mother…' Khaled's eyes were grey flint '… I hadn't expected to see you this morning.'

'I found myself with a few spare hours.' She flashed him a dazzling smile. 'So I thought it would be a nice surprise if I came to meet you.'

Khaled remained unmoved. 'I see. And the cars I requested?'

'Oh, I sent them away, dear. I presumed you would be coming to the palace with your guest.'

A muscle ticked in Khaled's jaw. 'Miss Marchant won't be staying at the palace. I've offered her and Nate the use of the waterfront penthouse. One of the cars was to take her there.'

'At the new harbour development? What a lovely idea. It's so close to the old city and it makes a wonderful base to explore from. You'll love it there, Miss Marchant.'

At that, Khaled appeared to relax.

Which was the moment Eleanor made her move, stepping between them and taking Lily's arm.

'But I won't hear of you staying alone while you wait for your stepbrother,' she said, leading her away.

Lily could almost taste the anger pouring off Khaled. They might have just met, but she decided she liked Eleanor already.

As they climbed into the limo Khaled moved to join them.

'No, darling,' said the Queen. 'You take the other car. You must have calls to make, and Lily and I will only disturb you with all our girl-talk. We'll see you back at the palace.'

Before he could protest, Eleanor's door had closed and the car was pulling away. Leaving her son standing on the Tarmac, entirely out manoeuvred.

Lily glanced back to see him, with an expression like thunder, stalking towards the remaining limo as the security team scattered to clamber into theirs.

'Oh, dear,' said Eleanor, with a mischievous glint in her eyes. 'Does he look much put out?'

Lily nodded.

'Well, it does a man good to be thwarted once in a while. Khaled is far too used to getting his own way. Though not with you, I think?' She sent Lily a disconcertingly knowing look. 'I doubt it was just my turning up unannounced that got him in such a temper.'

'Well, he's… We're…' Recalling Khaled's warning not to divulge any information, Lily fell silent.

'Don't worry. I won't pry,' Eleanor said, patting Lily's hand. 'But if he's been high-handed you mustn't let it bother you. Under that gruff exterior he's actually a kind and thoughtful man. He puts everyone else's comfort first. Everything he does is for his family and his country. Since his father's illness he's worked so hard…'

Eleanor's voice trailed away sadly.

There was truth, then, in the stories of Khaled's punishing schedule since the King had suffered a series of heart attacks.

The cars had cleared the airport now, and joined a broad

modern highway. Desert stretched away to far-off mountains in the west, and to the east was sparkling turquoise ocean. The motorcade sped north, towards the modern glass towers and the redbrick old town of Nabhan City.

Eleanor chatted…pointing out landmarks, putting Lily at her ease.

They'd reached the bustling suburbs. Men in long white robes sat drinking coffee outside roadside cafés, while women in vibrant headscarves gossiped on street corners. A group of schoolchildren ran along the pavement, waving at the cars and their royal occupants. Lily even spied a camel sitting sedately in the rear of a flatbed truck, travelling south.

All around her lay a new landscape, far removed from the sleepy green countryside she'd grown up in, and despite her worries for Nate she felt excitement ripple through her.

'It's beautiful, isn't it?' Eleanor said. 'I still remember how I felt the first time I encountered all this. We arrived late afternoon and came along this very road. The sun was setting beyond the mountains. I'd never seen anything so affecting.' She gave a wistful sigh. 'There's something about Nabhan that gets under one's skin. Of course, it helps that the men here are as sexy as hell.'

She chuckled at Lily's startled expression.

'Forgive me. I was remembering how Khaled's father looked, sitting right where you are now. Bassam was quite something… But then you've seen the son. I'm sure you can imagine.'

Again there was that penetrating look.

Lily turned away to hide her blush. Yes, the son was spectacular—but she'd rather not dwell on that, or the physical effect he seemed to be having on her.

Their car slowed and passed through gates flanked by saluting soldiers. The motorcade swept past them and up a wide drive, climbing through an avenue of soaring date palms. Then came the palace. Built of pale rose sandstone, the sprawling two storey Family Wing and the adjoining

Royal Court buildings still managed to convey the sense of a family home.

Lily felt welcome the moment she set foot inside the cool entrance hall. A grand curved staircase led to a first-floor landing, while beneath her feet the white marble floor shone like glass, with a perfect reflection of the high domed ceiling above and the vast chandelier that hung there.

'Khaled's grandfather built the palace and he was fond of putting on a show,' Eleanor said, following the direction of Lily's gaze. 'But this hallway is rather beautiful. I know I'm truly home when I step into it.'

Lily stared in awe.

'What did you expect, Miss Marchant?' a deep voice drawled behind her. 'Tents? Huts built of earth?'

Khaled's car had arrived. Unfortunately his mood hadn't improved during the journey.

'Of course not,' she retorted. 'Nate has told me how beautiful your home is, but his descriptions haven't come close to the real thing.'

'Khaled!'

A delighted yell came from the top of the stairs as a blur of denim-clad coltish limbs and streaming ebony hair slid down the banister and launched itself at him.

'Amal, *habiba*.' He caught the slender girl and placed a kiss to the top of her head. 'Have you been good while I've been away? How are your studies progressing?'

Amal groaned. 'Why do you never ask about anything interesting—like, maybe, who's coming to Daddy's anniversary party?'

Then Amal saw Lily, and her eyes widened in surprise.

Khaled disentangled himself and set his sister in front of him. 'Please forgive the informal arrival, Miss Marchant, and allow me to introduce Amal—one of my baby sisters.'

Amal rolled her eyes. 'We're fourteen—and I'm the elder by ten minutes.'

On the landing above, a second figure appeared.

'Hanan, get down here!' Amal said in an excited stage whisper. 'Khaled's brought an actual girl home.'

Eleanor muffled an un-regal snort behind her hand.

Her brother scolded Amal for her unseemly behaviour. It didn't dampen the twins' excitement.

After giving her big brother a hug, Hanan asked, blushing, 'Are you Nate's Lily?'

Ah… It looked as if her stepbrother had a young admirer.

Khaled called both girls to his side, producing a book for each from his pocket. He drew their attention to something he'd marked on one, and three dark heads bent over the pages.

'Since they were babies, whenever he returns from a trip Khaled always has something for the girls,' Eleanor said.

Memories of her stepbrother's homecomings came to mind. He was the only person who'd ever been pleased to see her, seeking her out the moment he arrived and gathering her up in a bear hug.

Where was he now? Lily's throat tightened. Moisture prickled behind her eyes.

At that moment Khaled's gaze lifted to hers. Now he was surrounded by his family, the grey flint had melted into a beguiling tenderness. It reached out, embracing her, too, soothing her moment of distress.

He held her gaze and the air became thick.

Time slowed.

The twins, his mother, the staff around them…all faded to shadows hovering at the edge of a dream.

She saw only him.

The glint of the chandelier lights in his ebony hair. The high slash of his cheekbones. The firm, full lips and that molten silver gaze, pinning her to the spot.

A strange yearning tugged at her womb and his nostrils flared like a big predator, catching her scent. On a broken breath Lily's hand fluttered upwards and settled across her heart. She didn't know if it was a defensive gesture or a way to control its wild pounding.

Khaled's brow knotted. Away went the tenderness, back came the flint.

'Mother,' he said sharply, 'Lily is tired. Perhaps she could be shown to whatever guest room I'm sure you've organised? Now, if you'll excuse me, I have work to attend to.'

'Of course. But, darling, you've been travelling all night, and I know you won't have rested. Won't you take a little time off and join us for coffee?'

'No, I'm afraid I can't.'

Eleanor sighed sadly as she watched her son disappear along the corridor linking the Family Wing to the Royal Court, while Lily wondered what had just happened. One minute he'd been chatting with his family, and the next it had been as if that burning look had consumed everything around them and they were the only two creatures left on the planet...

'We love our big brother to bits, Miss Marchant,' Amal said, 'but I think we should warn you he can be a totally grumpy workaholic.'

Lily attempted an answering smile.

'You do look tired, my dear,' Eleanor said. 'Why don't we show you to your rooms, where you can rest?'

The twins led the way up the staircase to a veranda with ornate metal balconies. In the courtyard below there were lush plantings and fountains tumbling into tiled pools. Lily even caught the chattering of birds as they swooped between the trees.

'They used to keep caged songbirds here, but Bassam had them released,' said Eleanor. 'They must have liked it here, because they stayed.'

Lily was enchanted by it all. 'It's beautiful.'

'You should see it at night, when the lanterns are lit,' Hanan said, with a stunning smile.

She shared her brother's fine-boned features, and it was only a small step to imagine how he might look, should he choose to smile at her, too.

That brief heated look notwithstanding, since walking

into his suite last night he'd been nothing but stern. Ever the
Sad Prince, even here, in the heart of his family. Weighed
down with cares, perhaps, or still tortured by the tragedy
that had changed the course of his life.

Lily's heart softened at the memory of the teenage boy
she'd first known. She could only guess at the responsibilities heaped upon the man now.

'I think you'll enjoy this suite.'

His mother had paused at a set of doors. Lily swiftly untangled her thoughts.

'It's the most comfortable we have, and the views are
wonderful,' Eleanor said, ushering Lily into a stunning set
of rooms.

Cream sofas scattered with silk cushions and side tables
of intricately carved rosewood sat before arched windows
that led to a balcony with a view of the sea. To her right,
in a second room, a vast bed stood dressed in ivory linen,
piled with downy pillows.

Eleanor placed a hand to Lily's cheek. 'We'll leave you
so that you can rest. A servant will come later, to help you
find your way around, but for now take as long as you need.'

She gathered up her girls, and in a flurry of goodbyes
they were gone.

Lily took a breath.

It would be too easy to be seduced by all this. Eleanor
had been so kind, and the twins had obviously been excited to meet her.

And then there was the Crown Prince himself, and the
impact of that searing look.

Not ready to explore the reasons for that, she explored
her suite instead.

The bedroom alone would swallow her entire flat back
home.

Another floor length window led to the balcony. Lily
pushed it open and stepped outside.

Eleanor hadn't exaggerated. The views were beautiful.
Below there were more lavish gardens, and beyond a clus-

ter of sand dunes and a beach of ivory sand that ran down
to the sea.

Lily inhaled a breath of clean salt air laced with the warm
spicy scent she'd noticed when she'd first stepped from the
plane. Was even the air itself seductive in Nabhan?

A yawn erupted from somewhere.

How little sleep she'd had in the last few weeks since her
stepfather's death, with the hurried sale and clearing of the
house. Was it really less than a day since she'd deposited
her possessions in her new shared flat? Mere hours since
she'd hidden in Khaled's dressing room?

It wouldn't hurt to rest a little. Then, later, she'd figure
out how to help Nate.

She lay down on the bed, sank into blissful comfort and,
lulled by the distant wash of waves on the shore, closed
her eyes.

Her last thoughts were of a sad teenage boy who'd become a sad beautiful man. A man with a haunted expression but such gentle hands.

Mercifully, before she could torture herself further, Lily
was asleep.

Lily woke with a start, confused by the unfamiliar surroundings and the lingering images of a dream she hadn't
had in years.

She'd dreamt of Khaled.

Not the man he was now, but the grieving sixteen-year-
old she'd first met that summer in her stepfather's house.

She'd been nearly eight, and would have proudly shared
that fact with anyone interested enough to ask. No one ever
had.

But one day that summer the household had been even
more uninterested than usual, with the staff in a complete
flurry. A school friend of her stepbrother had arrived suddenly and mysteriously, and nobody would answer her questions except to say he was 'Prince Khaled' and not to be
disturbed.

'A prince?' she'd asked breathlessly. 'Like in Cinderella?'

'Never you mind,' they'd said.

She hadn't minded. Quite the opposite. She'd been thrilled that there was someone in the house even remotely close to her own age. None of her friends lived nearby. Nate was away on a school expedition. Her mother kept to her rooms. Even her stepfather, who mostly ignored her anyway, was abroad on business.

But more than that, there was a real, live *prince* in her house.

There'd been a man seated by the library door. With his deeply tanned skin and bald head he'd seemed rather intimidating, but then he'd smiled, said his name was Rais, and asked if she'd come to meet her guest.

Amazed that someone thought her important enough to meet the visitor, she'd forgotten to be nervous and nodded.

'Well, then,' he'd said, opening the door for her, 'you'd better go in.'

The room had been flooded with sunlight. Dust motes from ancient books danced in the beams that hit the floor. It had taken a moment for her eyes to adjust, to see the tall figure standing in the shadows beyond the window.

He'd been dressed in a black suit and tie. A neatly folded handkerchief had peeked from his breast pocket. A man's attire, though he'd really been still a boy. His dark hair, cut short at the sides, had been luxuriant on top and tumbled over his forehead. Thick ebony brows had sat above deep-set eyes of a startling pale grey. His long straight nose and chiselled cheekbones had lent him an aristocratic air.

He had been the handsome young prince from any of her favourite fairy tales come stunningly to life, and quite simply the most beautiful thing she'd ever seen. Right there, Lily had lost her heart.

She'd drawn nearer and greeted him.

As he'd swung towards her his expression had shocked her and, being so young, and unused to company, she'd said the first thing that came to mind. 'Why are you so sad?'

The teenager, wrestling with a raw grief he'd hardly been able to comprehend, had replied just as honestly. 'Because my brother died.'

The moment the words had left his mouth he'd been over-come. She'd instinctively wanted to help this boy, and had gone to clasp his hand in her own. She had remembered the one thing that her own stepbrother loved, and had used it to try to divert him.

'Do you like horses?'

The Prince, too distressed to speak, had given a nod.

'Nate has three. We could go and see them if you'd like?'

He hadn't known how brave she was being even to men-tion them. They terrified her. Her father had died when he'd been thrown from his horse.

'Yes,' he'd said. His grip had tightened on her hand as if clutching a lifeline. 'I'd like that a lot…'

Lily sat up and swung her legs over the side of the bed.

No, that bewildered boy was nothing like the man he'd become. He was not even like the man who, six years later, had been so kind to her at her mother's funeral—who'd found her sobbing in a cloakroom, pulled her close and al-lowed her to weep all over him.

The man now was harder, colder. More remote.

So how—when she recognised that, and when life had taught her to rely only on herself—had she let that moment in the hallway blur the edges? Imagined being in his arms again while he fended off the world and all its pain for her.

The man had a kingdom to rule, and an entire people to protect. What time would he have for the likes of her?

Through the window, she saw the sky was almost dark. She'd slept all day. She'd been more exhausted than she'd realised. Not only last night, but the preceding weeks had taken their toll.

In the sitting room a servant was moving about. As prom-ised, the Queen had sent someone to help their new guest.

A bath had been drawn, and when Lily emerged fresh clothing had been laid out. The embroidered linen tunic and slim trousers were comfortable and cool, even matching Stella's sandals. Her damp hair was dried and styled to fall in burnished curls down her back.

'His Highness asked that you be brought to him once you had risen,' the servant said.

Bathed and dressed, ready to be taken to the Prince?

Lily's heart thumped with an entirely inappropriate anticipation as she was led through airy corridors and quadrangles open to the skies where the verdant green of clipped box softened stark slate pools.

They'd left the Family Wing and entered the Royal Court—a large complex with all the private offices, public reception rooms and staff areas required for a modern working royal family. Staff hurried past, intent on their evening duties. They bowed to Lily, politely concealing their curiosity. Mostly.

Several times she caught looks that lingered longer than necessary. Perhaps their prince bringing home 'an actual girl' was a surprise to the palace staff, too. They couldn't know that it was the intervention of his mother that had brought her here…that her son had intended she be secreted away from public view and from him.

She refused to feel a moment's disappointment about that.

Up ahead stood a pair of imposing doors, flanked by two of the palace security team. Across the threshold waited Rais and a sumptuous salon. Stately gilt-edged sofas and chairs were arranged around the perimeter. A vast Persian rug covered the floor. And on the walls hung a series of elaborately framed mirrors.

This must be Khaled's *majlis*, or public reception room.

As Rais showed her to a seat she considered who else had visited here. Prime ministers, presidents, other royals… Since Khaled had taken on his father's role, probably all of them.

From beyond a second set of doors the murmur of voices reached her. One had a deliciously deep rumble. The voices grew louder as the doors opened. She took a deep breath.

She must remember she was here for Nate. There was nothing delicious about it.

Then Khaled walked in and every good intention deserted her. Dressed head to toe in black, his hair tousled as if he'd just run a hand through it, he was utterly, bone-meltingly beautiful.

He crossed the floor in a few easy strides. 'Lily, I trust you are rested and feeling refreshed?'

'I am, thank you.'

She sounded breathless. She was. That face. That *voice*.

She shifted position, sitting back on the sofa—only to find her feet dangling in mid-air. She quickly tipped her sandals off. They landed on the carpet with a soft plop as she folded her legs beneath her.

A royal brow lifted. Perhaps it was inappropriate to be so casual in these surroundings, but right now she didn't care. She couldn't let him see how he'd affected her just by crossing a room with his elegant, loose-limbed stride.

It didn't help that she knew exactly how he looked beneath his clothes. Only a narrow stretch of body between waist and thigh was a mystery. Her gaze lingered there before she looked away, horrified that she was actually mentally undressing the man.

Khaled settled in the seat opposite. 'Your room is satisfactory?'

'Yes, thank you. The suite is lovely.' Being angry at her situation was one thing—being ungracious quite another. And at least he was trying to be civil. 'The view from the balcony is fabulous.'

Khaled looked puzzled. 'The view?'

'The gardens and the beach?'

His eyes narrowed. 'You are in the guest suite in the Family Wing?'

'Your mother said it was the most comfortable.'

'She's correct, it is. But those rooms are reserved for particular friends of the family—which, under the circumstances, I'm sure you would agree you're not.'

So the polite veneer hadn't lasted long. Gone, too, were all traces of the passionate interlude from that morning. The Stern Prince was definitely back.

She lifted her chin. 'Should I ask to be moved, then?'

'No, it would cause too many awkward questions. You will have to remain there for the time being.'

'And how long will that be? You can't just keep me here. I have a life to start in London. A new flat...a job.'

'I understood you were unemployed at present.'

He wasn't asking a question. It was a statement of fact. She'd been lying about the job and he knew it.

'For what it's worth, I'm sorry—at least for that part of your predicament.'

She was surprised to hear genuine compassion.

'I'm not completely heartless, Lily.'

'All evidence to the contrary...'

His jaw tightened. 'You break into my rooms, search my possessions, and you accuse me of behaving badly?'

'I wouldn't have been there at all if you hadn't believed the worst of someone you should trust. Nate isn't capable of betraying you.'

'And you,' he said sharply, 'are fooling yourself. He's left you alone to deal with this. You are only here because of his dishonesty.'

'No. I am only here because he had to ask me for help. He should have been able to come to you, his oldest friend. But you've sunk so low as to abandon him.'

Khaled's face hardened. 'Let me make things perfectly clear for you. You are here because I want it and you will stay here as long as I wish. As you have pointed out, your stepbrother and I are old friends, and for that reason alone I haven't yet involved the authorities. But one way or another Nate will be caught. Until then you will be staying in Nabhan, and while you are here you will obey me.'

'Obey you?' Lily shot to her feet. 'I will not. You have no power over me.'

She headed for the exit, determined to leave, only to find an apologetic but nevertheless unmoving Rais in her way.

'As you see,' that annoyingly cool voice said from behind her, 'you will remain here until I decide you may leave—and that includes right now. Sit down.'

By the door stood a marble-topped table bearing a small bronze of a Roman warrior. His lips were pulled back in a snarl and his arm was raised, brandishing a lethal-looking sword, ready to mete out damage to anyone in his way. Had it not been so finely wrought, and probably valuable, Lily might have scooped it up and launched it at Khaled's pompous head.

But, having no choice she returned to her seat, dropping into it as petulant as a scolded teenager.

Khaled calmly brushed an invisible speck from his trousers. 'My family are expecting us to join them for dinner. They believe you're here to explore Nabhan with your stepbrother. I've told them Nate has been delayed on charity business but will be joining you soon. Remember, they also think you arrived without luggage because it was ruined when the sprinkler system malfunctioned at your hotel.'

'You mother didn't believe that nonsense for a second.'

A muscle ticked in his jaw. 'Then it's your job to convince her it's true.'

'I won't do it.' She sprang from her seat again, faced him with her hands fisted at her hips. '*You* invented that ridiculous story. *You* convince her it's true.'

She stalked away to wait at the door. It would have been a most satisfying finale to their conversation had she not forgotten her sandals.

Khaled rose from his seat and bent to gather them up. He strolled over to her, placing them in her hands. 'At least they're a better fit than the shoes you tried to steal from me.'

She stared ahead, ignoring his jibe.

He caught her chin in his hand, turning her face to him. 'I will remind you, Lily, of the precarious position you are in, and I absolutely will not allow you to upset my family or compromise my integrity in any way.'

Despising herself for the way his touch sent shivers through her, she snapped back. 'You should have thought of that before you kidnapped me.'

She was gratified to see a flicker of alarm in the depths of those clear, grey eyes.

He released her. 'There is still the option to involve the authorities,' he said, his voice silky and menacing. 'We have police cells in Nabhan every bit as accommodating as those in England. I suggest you keep that in mind.'

And he nodded for Rais to open the door and let them pass.

CHAPTER FIVE

'GOOD MORNING,' SAID the solitary occupant of the breakfast room. 'You must be Miss Marchant.'

Lily had been directed here by a servant. She'd hoped to find the twins or the Queen. Even the King himself. They'd made feel her welcome last night. Unlike the scowling, monosyllabic Prince, who'd brooded in a corner for pretty much the duration of the evening.

There'd been no repeat of that heated moment in the hall yesterday, and she'd almost convinced herself she'd imagined the whole thing.

'Forgive me,' the stranger said, smiling, 'but as the family is elsewhere I'm obliged to introduce myself. I hope you will excuse the lapse in manners?'

His manners appeared to be as impeccable as the immaculate grey *dishdasha* and white head-covering he wore.

'I'm George Hyde-Wallace,' he said, inclining his head, 'cousin to the Queen and her children and Leader of the Council of Families.'

Lily knew of him. Who didn't? The passionate Arabist who, four decades ago, had settled in the region, embraced all things Nabhani and risen to the top of its society. Weather-beaten, sinewy and straight-backed, there was a restless energy about him that belied his seventy-four years.

'I'm delighted to meet the person who has so captivated the twins. They would talk of nothing else this morning.'

He smiled again, though it didn't quite reach his eyes.

Instead they were watchful, assessing. Lily had the curious feeling that George Hyde-Wallace had been waiting for her.

She offered a restrained smile of her own. 'I'm pleased to meet you.' She stretched out her hand. Did she imagine the pause before he took it? Perhaps, because now he'd clasped it firmly in both his own.

She glanced at the coffee cup and newspaper next to his seat. 'I was told I might find the family here. I'm sorry if I disturbed you.'

Dark eyes swept her from head to toe. 'Think nothing of it. If only all interruptions were as charming. But I regret the family have already breakfasted. However, I am here.' He squeezed her fingers once before letting go at last. 'And I am failing in my duty as stand-in host. Have you eaten? Please…' he indicated the seat next to his '…join me.'

He called the servant, ordered breakfast for her, then waited politely for Lily to sit before seating himself.

'I understand you are here to explore Nabhan. Have you decided where you'll begin?'

Of course not. As Khaled had so graphically informed her, this was no holiday. How did she answer?

'I'm fascinated by the country's history.'

'Excellent. Well, we have extraordinary treasures here. Dating back millennia. And, conveniently, I happen to know the Minister of Antiquities. I'd be happy to organise a private tour of our National Museum.'

George's gaze was intense. His attentions equally so. Lily was grateful for the jug of fruit juice that arrived at that moment. She busied herself with pouring a glass.

'Once your stepbrother has arrived, of course,' he said. 'Is he expected soon? The family seemed a little vague on the matter.'

His expression was bland. The question felt anything but.

'I think so. Nate heads off around the world so often it's hard to keep up.' She hoped she sounded convincing.

'Ah, yes. The intrepid Nathaniel Marchant.'

For 'intrepid' she could infer any number of insults, judging by the man's tone.

'It's a shame he's not here with you,' he continued. 'Of course in the meantime you have the protection of the Crown Prince himself.'

And what on earth did that mean?

She was saved from this increasingly disconcerting conversation as a breakfast tray was set down beside her.

'Bon appétit,' George said, smiling, and returned to his newspaper, leaving her to eat in peace.

The tray held a paprika-spiced omelette, served with plump tomatoes. There were diminutive chapattis, the size of her palm, and an engraved silver pot of sweet, cardamom-scented tea.

She'd taken her last sip when a servant approached. Khaled wished to speak with her.

She glanced at her companion, about to make her apologies, but he was already on his feet.

'Don't worry about me, my dear Miss Marchant. You must not keep His Highness waiting. I'm sure we'll see each other again soon. In fact I'll make sure of it. But for now, goodbye.'

This morning there was no waiting in the *majlis*. Lily was taken directly into Khaled's private office.

He was behind his desk, on the phone, speaking in Arabic. He glanced at her, nodded once, then continued his conversation.

It was left to his aide to offer a more polite welcome. 'His Highness will be a moment, Miss Marchant. I am Sabir, his secretary. May I bring you some refreshments while you wait?'

Lily declined, but for this man who had at least shown some manners she offered up her best smile. Blushing, Sabir departed to his own workstation in an anteroom.

Khaled's frowning gaze watched his secretary's hasty retreat, then swung back to her, glaring, as if she'd deliberately discomfited his staff.

She stared right back, one brow raised, until he returned to his call.

Free to look about her now, Lily was surprised to see none of the grandeur of the *majlis*. The room was merely businesslike. She would have expected something that spoke of Khaled's status, but apart from a long, leather sofa and a sideboard set back against the wall, there was only an austere wooden desk and two chairs facing it, one of which she occupied.

No antique furniture, no fancy artwork—barely any individual touches at all except for a framed picture on his desk. She couldn't see the subject. His parents, perhaps? His sisters? Or...she bit her lip at the comical idea...a favourite horse?

By far the most striking feature of the room was the wall behind Khaled's desk. Lined from floor to ceiling with books. Hundreds of them. In English, Arabic, French, and on every imaginable subject. A cursory glance took in volumes on history, economics, engineering. There were political biographies and classical works from ancient Greek and Roman authors, and those were just the English titles she understood. All his? She was awed by the hours of reading those shelves represented and the fierce intellect of their owner.

Tucked away at the far end of the last shelf, and quite different from the rest, sat a small group of slim leather bound volumes. She peered closer, trying to make out their titles, but became aware of a sudden stillness from the figure on the other side of the desk.

Khaled was listening to his caller, but she knew from his frown that the look of censure was meant for her. What? Was she supposed to stare meekly at her feet until he deigned to speak to her?

He swivelled his chair away, laying his free hand flat along the desktop as he continued his conversation. The sleeves of his close-fitting white shirt were rolled up, revealing muscled forearms covered in fine dark hair. The solid links of the gold watch clasped about his wrist enhanced the lean strength of his hands. Strong hands that she knew could be so gentle.

Lily absently twirled a lock of her hair, remembering how he'd tended to the cuts on her leg. Remembering the warmth of his palm wrapped about her calf, the glide of his fingers as they secured the bandages to her shin. What if he'd gone higher? Over her knee…along her thigh—?

'Good morning.'

She jumped. The phone call had ended while she'd been busy fantasising about him. Furious with herself—she didn't even *like* him—she lifted her chin and offered a frosty, 'Hello.'

His expression was equally cool. 'I'm returning some of the possessions you lost the other night,' he said, beckoning to Sabir.

On the desk, the secretary placed the beaded evening clutch that she'd last seen hurtling into the rose bed beneath Khaled's balcony. Remarkably, it looked none the worse for its adventure. No scuffs, no dirt. She opened it. No phone or anything else of real use either.

'If you were wondering, you've had no messages or calls from your stepbrother,' Khaled told her. 'Neither has he responded to any we've tried to send or make to him.'

'I was supposed to message him when I left the party. He'll have worked out I'm with you. He won't get in touch. He'll know you'll try to trace him. But I should call my flatmates. They'll be worried.'

'They've already been reassured that you're safe. They were most impressed that you're a guest of the Nabhani royal family.'

'They wouldn't be if they knew the truth,' she muttered, rummaging through the remaining contents of the bag.

Her wallet was still there, though her bankcards were missing. All that was left was the folded tote she'd planned to use for Nate's laptop, an expired train ticket, and the money she'd kept for her taxi home the evening of the charity event.

No phone. No cards and a pitiful amount of cash.

Khaled wasn't taking any chances.

'I was wondering what you will do when you return to England?'

She glanced up. The question had thrown her.

'Look for work,' she said. 'I need to support myself as soon as possible.'

'I see. Perhaps it's a little indelicate to ask, but how much money do you have?'

'Enough savings to cover two months' rent and living expenses. Three if I'm careful.' Where was he going with this?

'Three months? That's all?'

He sounded appalled. It wasn't her fault she hadn't been able to save much. Edward Marchant's fortunes had been ailing for years—so, too, had the allowance he'd begrudgingly paid her.

'And after that?'

'I guess I'm on the street if I don't find a job,' she replied tartly. How was this any of his business?

'What about the provision your parents made for you in their wills? They both had personal wealth.'

'Whatever money there was, my mother signed over to Edward Marchant.'

'All of it?'

'My dad left everything to my mum. I guess he thought she'd take care of me.'

His snort told her what he thought of that decision. 'So your mother's poor judgement means your inheritance is lost?'

He seemed so angry. A secret, silly part of her was thrilled that he might be genuinely concerned for her. Who'd ever cared enough to get angry on her behalf before?

'Like your stepbrother's.'

Okay, not concern. Accusation.

She swallowed down her disappointment. 'So now I'm guilty, too, because I need money?'

'No, I think you've been duped. Nate's laptop has been thoroughly checked. There's nothing on it to prove his innocence. In fact, quite the opposite. It proves he personally transferred ten million pounds from the charity funds into a private account.'

'Ten *million*?'

Khaled stared at her. 'I gather he didn't share that detail with you. It's about the same sum his father squandered. Perhaps your stepbrother was simply replacing his lost inheritance.'

'You can't honestly believe Nate would do something so out of character—and for money? He'd never expected to have an inheritance, and he didn't want it. He wanted to make his own way. You know he and his father didn't get on.'

'Yet all the evidence points to him. He disappeared at exactly the same time as the money.'

'But you've been friends for years. Is that really the man you know?' She fixed him with an expectant look. 'What does your gut tell you? Do you really, truly believe Nate could steal anything?'

That tell-tale muscle ticked in his jaw as he gazed back at her. Then he exhaled heavily, as if a deep tension had left him. 'It is, as you say, out of character.'

She scooted to the edge of her seat. 'So, what are we going to do about it?'

He raised a brow. '"We"?'

'You think I'd sit and do nothing when Nate needs help?'

She jumped up and began to pace. She didn't see his gaze follow her, darkening as the morning sun gilded her hair into a curtain of fire.

'It's about his schedule. Did someone hack into his diary? They seemed to know exactly where he'd be. You said the theft happened while Nate was using his bathroom.'

'I said nothing of the kind.'

She waved a hand vaguely in his direction. 'Must have been Nate who told me that.'

'Did he, now? What else did he tell you?' He sounded suspicious again.

She turned on him. 'For heaven's sake. You've just admitted it can't be him, so start looking for other solutions. Think of a way to help him.'

He didn't answer. Instead that intense grey gaze studied her. As if sizing her up. She forced herself not to look away, even though an annoying heat began spreading across her cheeks.

'Actually,' he said eventually, 'there is a way you can help.'

Lily let out a breath. 'Excellent. What can I do?'

He stood and ambled round his desk towards her. 'If Nate truly is innocent, the longer we can keep the theft quiet the more time we'll have to find out who really did it. So we need a distraction. A smokescreen, if you will. That's something you can help provide.'

He'd stopped a pace in front of her. Close enough for her to truly appreciate the breadth of his muscled chest under that snug white shirt.

She forced her gaze back up to his face. 'I… I can?'

'Yes. And we must also consider that my mother's showy greeting at the airport and your presence in the palace means that people will have certain expectations.'

She frowned. 'What expectations?'

'That I have serious intentions about you.'

'Isn't that a bit over the top? This isn't Regency England.'

'No, it's Nabhan, and it's a proud Islamic nation. Modest and conservative. Society here is very traditional. As Crown Prince I must, of course, be seen to respect those traditions.'

'And what does that mean, exactly?'

'It means we get engaged.'

Holy…*what*? She couldn't have been more shocked if he'd suggested she strip naked and do cartwheels through the palace.

'How would…?' She swallowed, hard. 'How would our being engaged help Nate?'

'Think about it. If the real culprit is attempting to ruin your stepbrother, or to drive a wedge into our friendship, proclaiming you as my future consort and him my future brother-in-law would show they have failed.'

He'd spoken at least two full sentences, but Lily's attention snagged on only one word.

Consort.

Said in that sexy rumble of his, it started a reel of X-rated images playing through her imagination. It didn't help that he was standing so close. The heat of his body made her fingers flex, as if they wanted to splay out across his torso and get toasty in all that warmth.

She scrunched them into fists at her sides. 'Why would anyone believe you've chosen me, a nobody, when you've had your pick of countless high-profile women? You've famously left a trail of broken hearts all over the globe.'

A brow rose at her less than flattering description of him. 'Because you are unlike anyone I have been associated with before. A well-born girl of limited experience.'

'Limited—'

'A virgin.'

Lily gaped at him. 'That's a big assumption to make. Anyway…' she folded her arms across her breasts '…you're wrong.'

Liar.

She'd never trusted anyone enough to do *that* with them. Everyone in her past who should have loved her had let her down. She wouldn't risk being hurt again. She only trusted herself now.

His eyes had followed her defensive move. 'I see. You have some experience. Then what's making you so nervous?'

'I'm… I'm not.'

'But I only have to look here…' He laid two fingers across the pulse beating furiously at the base of her neck, then lightly brushed the line of her collarbone to the hollow at the base of her throat. 'You have a very revealing blush.'

She swayed towards him, snared by those grey eyes.

Then, all matter-of-fact, he lifted his fingers clear. 'You do know it wouldn't be real?'

Her gaze refocused. 'No—I mean, yes…of course.' She clumsily tucked a lock of hair behind her ear. 'I know that.'

'And we don't actually have to make an announcement. A suggestion that we're serious will be enough.'

She pulled herself together. 'Who else will know it's a pretence?'

'Apart from us? My father, Rais and Sabir.'

No mention of the Queen.

'You'd lie to your mother about this?'

'If we want a quiet life, yes. If she knows we're pretending she'll do everything she can to make it real. The moment she heard you were on that plane my mother began concocting romantic plans for us. I assume you understand they are her plans? Not mine.'

She didn't want there to be any plans either. So that was good. Wasn't it?

'However, I have asked her to take you shopping, to buy you a new wardrobe for your stay.'

'You organised all that before consulting me? I don't want it. I buy my own clothes, and right now I'm fine.'

His gaze swept her linen tunic and trousers. 'No, you're not. It would be inappropriate for my prospective fiancée to be parading around in borrowed clothes…' he glanced at her feet '…and stolen shoes?'

She was still wearing Stella's sandals. 'They're also *borrowed*,' she reminded him, 'and I can't afford to buy new clothes.'

He looked at her as if she was an idiot. Of course he would be paying for them.

'I'm looking for Lily. Is she with my son?' Eleanor's voice floated in from the anteroom.

'Right,' Khaled murmured, 'time to practise looking like you're madly in love with me.'

'I'm mad, all right,' she answered, just as Eleanor walked in.

Khaled hesitated just long enough before jumping away from her, to appear as if they'd been caught embracing. Lily glowered at him.

'I'm sorry if I'm interrupting.' The Queen didn't look sorry. She looked thrilled that there might have been something to interrupt. 'I'm here to take Lily shopping, as instructed, but I can come back later if you're in the middle of something?'

'Only your son being a tyrant again,' Lily muttered.

He shot her a quelling glance.

In a grey sheath dress, Eleanor looked elegant and cool. The exact opposite of how Lily was feeling. How had this man got her so worked up so quickly?

She had to fight back. 'I'll manage with some T-shirts and a skirt or two.'

Perfectly adequate for a fake fiancée.

'My dear, fashion is my one vice,' Eleanor said. 'Allow me the fun of helping you chose a wardrobe for your stay.'

'By the way, I've decided to join you,' Khaled announced, ignoring Sabir's startled expression. 'Whatever was planned for this morning can be rearranged.'

Eleanor's eyes danced. 'But, my heart, you despise shopping.'

'Not at all—in fact, it will be a pleasure.'

From where Sabir stood, frantically reviewing the diary, came an incredulous snort which, too late, he tried to disguise as a cough. Horrified by this dreadful slip in etiquette, he made his apologies and fled to the anteroom.

Eleanor was leaving, but as Lily followed her arm was caught and Khaled bent low to speak in her ear.

'Remember, you'll be dignified and restrained, as would befit my fiancée, and you'll curb your insolence while you're with my mother.'

'It won't be hard to be nice around Eleanor. I actually like her.'

'Then that should make it easier for you to convince her we're serious about each other.'

'How I am supposed to do that? I can hardly bear to look at you.'

They'd reached the cars. Not limos today, but a line of four-by-fours.

'Improvise,' he said sweetly, placing a hand on her back and giving her a shove towards his mother's car.

'Oh, don't you start,' she muttered, dredging up a smile and walking towards the Queen. 'Nate said that, too, and look where it got me.'

CHAPTER SIX

HIS MOTHER WAS RIGHT. He did loathe shopping. But her interference yesterday had forced a change of plan. This was him regrouping and turning events to his advantage.

The Qaydari King was dragging his feet on the terms Khaled wanted. He'd lay odds on the man changing stance when a potential new bride appeared on the scene.

As for the missing charity funds, he admitted Lily might be right about her stepbrother's innocence. Resolve that issue, too, and she could return home. An outcome he'd have been fine with until that revelation about how little stood between her and destitution.

He'd been appalled to discover she was so vulnerable, and had dealt with it in the only way available to him: by getting angry. Of course it was none of his concern, but somehow the moment he'd hauled Lily on that plane she'd become his…his…

His.

No, damn it, not that. Never that.

What he meant was his *responsibility.*

That moment in the hall yesterday had meant nothing. The sight of her tear-filled eyes had moved him—that was all.

The ache in his groin almost made a liar of him, but he knew that for what it was: abstinence. He'd been celibate since beginning negotiations for his marriage. It had nothing to do with the specific female now on the other side of the dressing room curtain.

So what if she'd been interestingly flustered earlier, which had made him wonder, despite her claims, if any man had touched her? His blood had leapt at the thought, but he'd quickly mastered that. All that should concern him was ramping up the rumour mill. If his plans worked there'd be a rash of photos across the media in the next few hours. The sole purpose of his presence here.

In the meantime, he resigned himself to a dull hour or two of shopping. Provided he made some appreciative noises here and there, his contribution would barely be needed.

He picked up a newspaper from the pile laid out for him and applied himself to the first article of interest.

Ten minutes later the curtains swished back.

He politely lifted his head.

And all the air left his body in one breath.

An actual physical punch to the gut couldn't have had more impact.

The sea-green silk dress was simple enough: cowl-necked, cap-sleeved, cut to the knee. But it flowed in sinuous, loving lines over breast, hip, thigh. Despite the plaster and healing grazes to her shin, Lily looked...

With a flourish, Eleanor gathered up all that glorious auburn hair and caught it with a clasp at the nape of Lily's long pale neck.

Beautiful.

The assistant produced matching heels, urging Lily to slip them on. Now there was also the arch of an instep and taut, shapely calves to contend with.

Eleanor twirled her fingers in the air, encouraging Lily to execute a spin.

'Charming. Absolutely charming.' She turned to Khaled. 'Don't you agree, darling?'

Where, he thought, slightly panicked, had those enticing curves come from? She'd felt almost girl-like when he'd lifted her aboard the plane.

'Indeed,' he muttered, mourning the loss of the linen tunic and Stella's flat sandals.

Lily was studying her reflection in the mirrors, as if she couldn't quite believe the transformation a simple dress had achieved.

She wasn't the only one.

He was still staring when the curtain closed again.

Then a clothes rail was wheeled into the room and left beside him.

Khaled exhaled slowly.

Lingerie. Lots of it. In a heart-stopping selection of silk and lace, and in every colour from virginal white to sex siren's scarlet.

Somewhere a door opened, and a gust of air dislodged a pink lace thong from its hanger. Downwards it went, to land close to his left foot. It lay there, delicate, distracting, an utterly feminine contrast to the robust dark tan leather of his shoe.

He slid his foot away, resumed his reading.

But the pale pink lace refused to be ignored.

Khaled's gaze drifted from the newspaper.

Creamy seed pearls had been stitched in a heart shape across the lace at the front. A bow graced the back, designed to sit just above the swell of a shapely bottom. But it was all so insubstantial it would fit easily in his closed fist.

His fingers tightened, feeling not the newspaper but the softness of lace, the pearly nub of a lustrous bead.

From beside him came a soft cough. An assistant had returned to the rail and, her lips pressed tight together, was watching him.

A grown man. Infamously stern. Leader of his people.

Transfixed by a silly scrap of lace.

He made a great show of adjusting his newspaper, and to his relief the rail, plus offending panties, disappeared behind the curtain.

Unfortunately the respite lasted only moments.

'You must try this pink lace bustier,' he heard the assistant say. 'It gives a wonderful shape. And there's a matching thong. The bows and pearls are so pretty. It's a popular set for honeymoons.' There was a conspiratorial chuckle. 'I'm told it brings bridegrooms to their knees.'

The newspaper was forgotten.

Concealed by nothing more than a fall of fabric, Lily and those curves were feet away, trying on man-slaying lingerie.

A message arrived on his phone from Rais.

They're here.

Thank God. He wasn't sure how much more of this he could take.

He typed his response.

Expect us in five minutes.

Time to action the next part of his plan.

He dumped the newspaper, banished all thoughts of Lily in pink lace, and beckoned an assistant over.

'I'd like to see the green dress again. With the heels. Her hair up. Neater this time. Maybe a little make-up.'

The assistant disappeared behind the curtain to deliver his instructions. He heard a murmured discussion, one voice louder and increasingly indignant. But the Crown Prince had asked and, no matter what the objections, those assistants would deliver exactly what he wanted.

Minutes later the curtain was drawn back to reveal their handiwork: Lily in the green dress and heels. Glaring at him, hands fisted at her hips.

'Well, do I come up to scratch?'

Perfectly.

Except for the angry stance and mutinous look. They

wouldn't suit his purposes at all. It was time to bring back the softly flustered woman from earlier.

Khaled stood and began strolling towards her.

Lily watched as Khaled came closer, all smouldering masculine intent. Seconds ago she'd been in a snit. Now she couldn't remember why. By the time he reached her she was boneless and unresisting, letting him gather her hand and lift it to his lips.

'*Habiba*, you are beautiful,' he purred.

Beautiful? Her breath fluttered out. Dear Lord, she'd sighed. She'd actually just sighed.

He dipped his head. He was going to kiss her. She shivered as warm lips brushed the tender skin of her ear. A delicious, scintillating caress.

But not a kiss.

He was whispering to her.

'Something has come up. Follow my lead.' Louder, for the benefit of the others, he said, 'Mother, ladies, our apologies. An urgent matter needs our attention and we must go.'

Okay. It was part of the act.

'Can I leave you to gather everything Miss Marchant will need for her stay? You have her sizes?' The assistants nodded vigorously. 'And please send a selection of everything you think appropriate.' He turned to gaze adoringly at her. 'Don't stint.'

As if they would. They were staring at him as if he were a god come down to earth, imagining all their commission.

His long fingers curled through hers, warm, strong and wonderfully comforting—drat the man. And then he set off for the private lift they'd arrived in.

Focus, Lily.

He'd said something had come up. Perhaps there was news on Nate?

The lift doors closed. 'What's so…?' Where had that husky note come from? She tried again. 'What's so urgent that we needed to leave?'

'This.' He gathered her close and pressed his mouth to hers.

She should have pushed him away—there was no audience here—but his mouth slanted over hers in a kiss so tantalisingly gentle she leant in. He began a delicate exploration of her jaw, her throat, and found a tender spot beneath her ear, teasing it with a slow swirl of his tongue.

Her fingers sank into his biceps.

When he nudged a thigh between her legs she instinctively rubbed against it, seeking contact where she needed it most.

'Come,' he said.

Yes, oh, yes...

Wait…no. What?

He was walking. He meant she should go with him. He was leaving the lift.

She teetered in her new heels and he drew her protectively against his side. Together, eyes locked, they crossed the foyer and stepped outside into the now familiar intense heat and something else—something new.

With the dazzle of sunshine came camera flashes. A cacophony of voices. Crowding figures.

'Your Highness? Sir? When's the wedding?'

'Lily? Has he bought you a ring yet? When did you know it was love?'

She blinked as the lights exploded, over and over. With a jolt she realised he'd walked them into a press pack—and he knew enough about those for it not to be an accident.

Beside her Khaled purred his answer, poised, prepared. 'I have no comment at this time,' he said, guiding her towards a waiting limo, its door held open by Rais.

A limo? What had happened to the four-by-fours they'd arrived in? And the security team that materialised around them had doubled in size from earlier.

He'd set the whole thing up. They even had her name.

She came to her senses as fury replaced all that melting distraction.

She'd been played.

If he thought he could whisper a compliment, ply her with kisses and she'd go just along with this charade, he was in for a shock.

She swivelled in Khaled's arms and aimed herself at the nearest reporter. 'Actually, I'm sorry to say there won't be an announcement any time soon.' Every microphone strained towards her. 'His Highness is a great believer in tradition, so I know he would never propose without formally asking permission of my stepbrother.'

'And where is he, ma'am? Will he be arriving soon?'

'He's so busy I have trouble keeping up with his time-table. But, Your Highness…' Lily batted her eyelashes at him '…he's your most loyal friend. I'm sure you'll know where Nate is.'

All faces turned eagerly in Khaled's direction.

The little madam. She'd pay for that.

'He'll be joining us soon,' he said, propelling her forward in earnest now. Time to get her into the car before she did any more damage.

She was halfway in when some buffoon shouted, 'Are you going to say yes, Lily?'

Her head popped up. Tempting as it was to manhandle her back in, he knew it would make too much of a scene. He was forced to grant her the last word.

'I'm not sure. There's wealth and status in his favour, but I've also been reliably informed that he's a bit of a grumpy workaholic. So, you know, guys, it's gonna be a tough decision…'

Hell.

To the sound of laughter and a barrage of new questions Khaled bundled her onto the back seat and climbed in after her. She scooted to the far side, folded her arms, then stuck her nose in the air, all puffed up like an indignant chicken. If he hadn't been so angry he might have laughed.

'Congratulations. Far from keeping Nate under the radar,

you've now encouraged every reporter from here to Buenos Aires to hunt him down.'

'Perhaps if you'd told me what to say before you walked me into *that*—' she flung a hand back in the direction of the dispersing journalists '—I might have reacted differently.'

'All you had to do was walk beside me and pretend you're in love. Why was that so difficult? I also said "dignified and restrained". Are you forgetting our agreement already?'

'Funny, that. You say agreement... I say blackmail. But what's a small semantic difference between friends? Anyway, you told me to improvise, so I did. And while we're on the subject of that little farce, don't ever kiss me like that again.'

'I was also improvising. I needed your compliance. It seemed the quickest way to get it,' he said, settling back and stretching out his legs.

He saw her gaze flicker over them, lingering where his flexed thigh strained against the fabric of his trousers. He waited until her eyes lifted back to his. He raised a brow. She flushed at being caught ogling, but her nose went higher.

'Well, don't do it again. I didn't like it.'

He did laugh at that bald lie. 'Yes, you did. A man doesn't...what was it?...break hearts all over the globe without knowing when he's pleasing a woman.'

Awareness flared in her eyes, as if she were imagining how he might please her again, but her mouth compressed into an angry line.

'I doubt you'd know how to please a woman if you were presented with detailed diagrams and precise written instructions.'

'Really?' he said, oddly insulted. 'Care to test that theory?'

The instant she uttered that stupid remark Lily knew she'd made a mistake. Khaled loomed closer, grasping her chin, his stormy gaze fixed on her mouth.

She pushed at his chest. 'I don't think we—'

He kissed her.

Whatever words she'd been about to say, even the thought that had prompted them, disintegrated under the hot, hard press of his mouth. The entrancing gentleness was gone. Now there was just heat and anger.

She knew he was punishing her disobedience, but her traitorous body didn't care. It craved more of him…his kisses, his touch. It wanted to be *pleased*.

A big hand spanned her ribcage, pulling her close. When his thumb brushed the sensitive underside of her breast Lily moaned and opened her mouth beneath his, inviting him to feast.

He accepted the offer.

With a growl, he hauled her onto his lap, his hands roaming free. One drifted down her thigh, over her knee, then retraced its path. The hem of her silk dress was riding up with the steady glide of his fingers. Then they disappeared beneath the fabric altogether and slid between her thighs.

His touch was incendiary. Building the heated throb of desire that had started the night he'd brought her here. She whimpered, restless and edgy, and shamelessly spread her legs wider for him.

When a finger slipped inside her knickers, to slide into the wet heat between her legs, he muffled her gasp with a kiss, his tongue exploring her mouth with the same stunning intimacy his fingers were employing elsewhere.

Now his lips went to her neck, his nose brushing along her jaw to that sweet spot behind her ear, and Lily's head fell back.

Her world shrank to this: Khaled's cheek against her hair, his deep voice murmuring hot, delicious demands—'Yes, let go…show me…'—and the wicked rhythm of his fingers.

Her body answered his every demand, reacting in ways she'd never known it could, climbing higher and higher. Almost overwhelmed, Lily clamped an arm about his neck, hovering taut, suspended.

'Please…' she begged, mindless with need, not truly knowing what it was she pleaded for.

Until he pressed his thumb against her…just so.

'Come for me,' he ordered—and, oh, God, her body obeyed him, shattering in panting, moaning ecstasy. She sobbed into his shoulder, clinging to him, riding out an orgasm so intense only the anchor of his solid bulk kept her from flying into pieces.

Slowly she came to, her heart rate slowed and her breath steadied. Khaled traced soothing circles across her spine and murmured to her in Arabic. As though all his English had deserted him.

Lily lifted her head and warily met his gaze. The grey eyes glinted with a strange emotion that looked incredibly like wonder. She sighed as he pressed a kiss to her lips, so sweetly tender it reached into all the lonely, abandoned places in her soul.

Like the day all those years ago when, her mother gone, she'd hidden in that cloakroom so alone and lost. He'd spoken to her in Arabic then, too. Held her as she cried. Been there for her when she'd needed him.

What pleasure had he taken just now? None. It had all been about her. *Her* pleasure, *her* needs.

Those empty spaces that craved love and belonging, that she'd thought permanently sealed up, had been filled with warmth and, more dangerous still, hope.

The world turned and Lily trembled, nearly believing…

On a whoosh of air, the car door opened. Out on the palace forecourt the servant looked astonished to find the Prince's guest not in her own seat, but draped all over the Prince himself.

And with crashing hurt she remembered.

This wasn't real.

That tender kiss, that dazzled look. They were lies. Like the rest of it. All done to gain the thing he wanted. Her compliance.

She unclenched her fingers, dismayed to find she'd crushed one side of his collar and torn two shirt buttons loose. There was even a small bite mark in the curve where his neck and shoulder met.

Khaled was speaking to her, stroking her, trying to re-assure her, but she batted his hands away, scrambling from his lap to land in an undignified heap at the feet of the star-tled servant.

Before he could help her up she'd shot to her feet and raced up the steps into the palace, about to bolt for her rooms. But they'd arrived at an unfamiliar entrance and she had no idea which direction to take.

Those few seconds of indecision allowed Khaled to catch up. His arms went round her. She tried to squirm free.

'*Habiba*, shh… It's all right.'

But she felt too damn used to be calmed by him. 'I don't want you touching me.'

He flinched. 'You were telling me something different in the car.'

'And you took full advantage of that, didn't you?'

Her cheeks burned in humiliation, but he was right. Even now her whole body hummed from being held by him. She shoved at him, trying to escape. She might as well have tried to move a mountain. He'd braced every muscle to hold her still.

'Behave. You're supposed to want me in public. Not just when we're alone together. So you're going to take my hand and trot along beside me like the adoring girlfriend I need you to be.'

She glared up at him, but read the warning in those grey eyes. She'd do as she was told if she wanted to help her stepbrother.

Nate, she thought, offering up her hand, hating the siz-zle of energy as Khaled's fingers closed around it, *what's happening to me?*

The staff they met gaped at him as he strode by, hand in hand with a woman. With her flushed cheeks, swollen lips, she looked ravished, undone. Khaled gritted his teeth, hating that they could see her like this.

Mine, a possessive voice nagged him. *Not for their appreciation.*

Sabir greeted them as they crossed the threshold of his office. 'Good afternoon, Your Highness, Miss Marchant. I see the shopping trip was successful. Your dress is most becoming.'

'Thanks, Sabir. His Highness chose it,' said Lily, sending Khaled a filthy look. 'Then he had me dolled up and paraded in front of the press.'

'Yes, the…ah…the pictures are circulating already. Excuse me, Miss Marchant, but His Highness has a call waiting. Sir, you'll want to take this straight away.'

Lily tugged her hand free, quickly moving from him to stand at the window, her arms wrapped about her waist. The protective gesture nipped at his conscience.

Not taking his eyes off her Khaled reached for the receiver. 'Azir.'

Expecting to hear the Qaydari ambassador, requesting an urgent meeting, he was stunned when instead came an entirely different but deeply familiar voice.

'Is that the grumpy workaholic? This is your loyal friend speaking.'

Khaled spun away from Lily to hide his shock at hearing Nate Marchant.

'You've got a nerve, ringing like this,' he said, switching to Arabic. Nate had travelled extensively in the Middle East and was fluent. 'Where are you—and where the hell is the charity money?'

'How should I know? I didn't take it.'

'Then why does all the evidence point to you?'

'Because someone went to a lot of trouble to set me up. But never mind that now. I'm checking on Lily. Is she with you in the palace? Is she okay?'

Khaled glanced at her. 'Yes.'

It was an honest enough answer to the first question.

The accurate response to the second was up for debate. She looked vulnerable and brittle and lost.

She swung round to face him. 'You're busy,' she said, 'and I'd like to freshen up.'

'No, wait.' He couldn't let her go like that.

But she'd whisked out of his reach. Though she paused at the door. 'The flowers are a nice touch, by the way.' She gestured at a bowl of roses on his desk. 'They soften you up a bit—and, let's be honest, you could do with it.'

The blooms had appeared during their visit to the store. Most certainly placed there by order of his mother and precisely for that reason, no doubt. But he didn't need softening up. He just needed people to do what they were told. Not elaborate or interfere. Or damn well improvise at the wrong moments.

'What was that about flowers?' Nate asked. 'Hang on, was that Lily?'

'Yeah.'

'Out of your depth already?'

Khaled bristled. 'Certainly not.'

He was the Crown Prince. He'd been de facto King for seven years, shouldering the responsibility of the entire nation. Little fazed him now, and certainly not a mere slip of a girl. He was not, nor ever would be, out of his depth.

'So if you've been set up who's behind it?'

'You have to ask? He hates that we're friends. He hates your reforms. He's engineered a way to get rid of me and discredit you at the same time.'

'Impossible. He wouldn't dare.'

'Yes, he would. Discredit you and you'll lose the support of the Council. He'll put a stop to every one of your reforms. You're telling me you really hadn't considered it?'

Khaled dropped to the sofa. 'The implications are so bad I didn't want to face it.'

'If the theft becomes public and you can't get any evidence against him you'll have to. Parading Lily around as your girlfriend is genius, though,' Nate continued. 'Even if news gets out, who's going care? It'll buy us some time.'

'That was the idea,' Khaled said.

'She's agreed to it all?'

He ran a hand across his brow. 'She isn't being as obliging as I'd hoped.'

Nate chuckled. 'Yeah, I saw the footage outside the store. By the way, how did you catch her in the first place?'

'My rooms. She climbed the ivy and broke in via the balcony.'

Nate whistled. 'That's a ballsy move. And you expect a girl like that to meekly trot after you, pretending she's in love?'

She hadn't been so averse to him in the car.

The roses caught his eye. His mother wanted a great romance for him. Most decidedly he didn't. It would get in the way. But did that mean there couldn't be passion? He wondered if the Qaydari Princess would be as thrillingly responsive as Lily had. He pushed that thought aside. That wasn't important. Their union wasn't about his pleasure.

'Sabir,' he called, 'take these flowers away.'

'I'll put them on my desk, sir.'

'You will not. You'll stick them somewhere out in the corridor, where my mother can see them. The same with any more she tries to put in here. For whatever reason.'

'Of course, sir. No flowers. Under any circumstance.'

Nate's disembodied voice came again, sounding amused. 'Having a tantrum over a few flowers? Like I said, mate, you're out of your depth.'

'Where the hell *are* you?' Khaled snapped, irritated by the other man's enjoyment.

'Doesn't matter right now. I have friends doing some digging. I'll get back to you. Keep Lily safe, won't you? Until we know exactly what's going on.'

'Of course. Isn't that why you sent her on that wild goose chase in the first place? So I'd bring her here?'

'She'd have been determined to help in some way otherwise, so that's what I hoped you do once I'd realised you thought I'd stolen from you. What the hell, mate? What was going on in your head?'

Khaled grimaced, feeling guilty for the first time. 'In my defence, if someone has set you up, they've made a damn good job of it.'

'*If?*' Nate shouted, and cut the connection.

Khaled tossed the phone aside. Why did the Marchants think they could ride roughshod over him?

He crossed to the window where Lily had been. His fingers drifted to the sore spot on his neck. If her claim to be experienced was true he had a low opinion of her lovers. Whoever they were, they'd obviously been selfish bastards, seeing to their own pleasure and ignoring hers. Because that had been the first time a man had given her an orgasm. He'd bet his life on it.

Was that why she'd looked so shocked? As if the world had just shifted beneath her feet and she had no idea how to deal with it?

He wanted to do it again—but next time he wanted them both naked and to be buried to the hilt inside her when she came apart.

He ran his palm down his face.

There would be no repeat. It would only complicate matters.

He put it from his mind.

He had more important things to worry about.

Back in her sitting room, Lily was feeling just as conflicted. Thinking she was either about to burst into tears or sprint from her room, run towards the beach and never stop. She just couldn't quash the idea that something momentous had happened.

Which was ridiculous.

All she'd done was make out with a man in the back of a car. People did that sort of thing all the time.

Except in this case the man was a prince, the car a bulletproof limo, and it had felt like so much more than just making out. More as if she'd handed over an essential part of herself.

Why had she let Khaled touch her like that? When she knew everything he'd done that morning had been to manipulate her? He'd said so himself. He was simply gaining her 'compliance'. Not only had she fallen for it—she'd practically flung herself at him.

She started moving, heading for the bathroom. She had to get back to being in control, safe. She'd start by getting out of this silk dress. It rode up far too easily beneath a man's fingers...

She unzipped it and shoved it from her shoulders. She snatched up a face cloth and scrubbed at the make-up they'd applied at the store. Dragged the pins from her hair and yanked the style loose.

Then she saw her reflection in the bathroom mirror.

Wild eyes, swollen lips, hair tumbling in disarray about her naked shoulders. Who *was* this wanton?

Through the fall of her hair she glimpsed her bed, and conjured an image of Khaled lying there. Naked. Stretched out over her. Deep inside her.

Lily snapped her thighs together. That was never going to happen. She wouldn't allow it.

She turned her back to the mirror. Not wanting to see that woman any more. Not wanting to be her.

Her hands were shaking as she finished stripping everything off, including her tell-tale damp knickers. Those she shoved straight into the laundry bin, slamming down the lid on the evidence of what she'd been doing.

She'd come apart in Khaled's arms. So overwhelmed by her body's reaction she'd bitten his neck. Her eyes squeezed shut against the excoriating embarrassment and the shameless thought that quickly followed.

Could another man deliver her to such abandon?

Lily sank her face into her hands as an ancient feminine instinct whispered back. *No, just him. Always and for ever, just him.*

In the shower, she cranked the water to scalding hot and scrubbed at her skin, washing away the feel of his hands, the scent of his skin, attempting to expunge every trace of him.

When her skin was pink and her fingertips shrivelled to walnuts she gave up, dried herself and tugged on a bathrobe. The black lace knickers she'd arrived in that first night, now freshly laundered, were tucked away in a drawer. She pulled them on. They might only be simple lacy pants, but they were from her regular life, and right now they felt as substantial as armour.

And what of Nate in all this? Pretending to be Khaled's girlfriend was all about helping her stepbrother. To help him, would she steel herself to do it?

Yes.

But there'd be no more kissing or touching. And absolutely no repeat of the incident in the car. She'd resist, whatever Khaled did.

There was a knock at the door.

The knot of excitement in her belly wasn't a good start. But surely it wouldn't be him.

Out on the veranda stood Eleanor. Behind her was a seamstress and three palace maids, each with a dress rail loaded with boxes and garment bags bearing the department store logo.

'Khaled said you'd come to lie down for a while. If you're still tired we can come back later, but all the goodies from the store have arrived.' Eleanor smiled hopefully. 'I thought you might like an afternoon of trying things on.'

Some retail therapy? The perfect diversion.

'Actually...' Lily reached for the Queen and practically dragged her in. 'Now is great.'

CHAPTER SEVEN

AFTER CHECKING IN with his mother, and hearing that Lily had spent the afternoon happily trying on everything that had been delivered from the store, Khaled felt his earlier unease dissipate.

She had looked, Eleanor told him, 'stunning', 'gorgeous', and 'perfect'. When she'd added, in rapturous tones, that she'd been the very image of a modern princess, he'd decided it was time to change the subject. Lying to his mother about Lily's presence in Nabhan was necessary. He'd no desire to completely rub her nose in it.

Keeping away from Lily this evening seemed expedient, too. 'I won't be there at dinner,' he'd told his mother. 'I have work to do.'

Always. He made sure of it.

For once Eleanor hadn't tried to dissuade him.

Instead, she'd sent in the big guns.

The King had walked into his rooms just after dark, asking why his son wouldn't be joining them, brushing aside Khaled's protests and declaring that if the Crown Prince failed to take at least occasional time off he'd also be having heart attacks.

He'd slapped his son jovially on the back, but Khaled had seen the flicker of pain in his father's eyes. It never sat well with the King that he could shoulder so few of his responsibilities, and that his son was being forced to deal with them in his stead.

If it eased his father's sense of guilt, he'd give up a few hours. Guilt, Khaled understood. It was the thing that drove him.

Now, an hour after everyone else, he climbed the stairs to the rooftop restaurant. He saw her at once. Standing alone at the edge of the terrace, looking out over of the old city. The hem of her dress fluttered in the evening breeze. Her hair fell in loose waves down her back.

She looked like a girl, he thought, with an ache in his chest, and yet not. She was a woman, and everything they'd done in the car that afternoon only confirmed it.

No matter. There'd be no repeat of that.

Something caught her eye in the street below and she smiled a sweet, sad smile.

The ache deepened.

Then, on the other side of the terrace, unaware of Khaled's arrival, a man rose to his feet, his gaze fixed on Lily.

George Hyde-Wallace.

It took seconds. And done before he even knew he meant to do it. But suddenly Khaled was at her side and the other man was sinking back down, forgotten, into the shadows.

When Eleanor had said they'd be dining at a favourite restaurant in the old city, Lily had expected some grand establishment. Not this magical roof garden dotted with brass lanterns, where the royal party reclined on rugs and cushions, serving themselves from copper platters, with the restaurant owner and his family sitting amongst them and everyone gossiping like old friends.

Lily watched it all with a quiet, bittersweet delight. So this was how it felt to have family…to belong.

Her gaze roamed again over the cluster of groups. Only one man was missing.

Khaled had been noticeable by his absence when the whole family—even George and an off-duty Rais—had piled into the fleet of cars waiting on the palace forecourt.

She'd chided herself for the stab of disappointment. After today's incidents, surely the less she saw of him the better.

Needing a moment to herself, she'd risen from the cushions and moved to the edge of the terrace. In the street below a couple emerged from one of the homes. Their tiny daughter, her hands clasped safely in theirs, toddled between them. With a wistful smile Lily watched the doting parents guide the little girl safely across the street.

Had there'd ever been a moment when her parents had walked with her like that? Keeping her safe...the centre of their lives?

'My father claims that from this restaurant you can see the four corners of the world.'

Lily whirled round at the sound of Khaled's voice.

He stood a few paces away.

'It's a bold statement,' he continued, 'but I think he means the four corners of Nabhan. To him, of course, it's all the same thing.'

He was watching her with a warmth and intensity that rendered her quite speechless.

He stepped closer.

'Let me show you.' He stretched out his arm beside her shoulder, pointing to the open plain beyond the edge of the suburbs. 'To the north you can see the beginnings of the marshlands.' The moon had risen and its gleam was reflected in a distant patchwork of streams and tidal flats. 'It's recently been designated a conservation area. It has a rare and sadly endangered collection of flora and fauna. In fact, I've just launched a charity to support it...'

The corner of his mouth lifted in the ghost of a smile, and she knew he was teasing her. She'd come apart in his arms this afternoon and she'd vowed not to let him under her defences her again. But how was she supposed to resist this charm?

His hands settled on her shoulders. He turned her so she looked over the heads of the gathered party and across the flat rooftops of the old city to the harbour and the ocean beyond. That simple contact raced through her body. To places she'd really rather it didn't.

She focused hard on the view before her. In the marina the lights of luxury yachts and pleasure cruisers sparkled, while out at sea giant tankers rode at anchor.

'For centuries merchants sent their ships from here, loaded with frankincense and pearls and purebred Arabian horses,' he said. 'They went east to India and China. The trade made the city wealthy. Now those tankers provide a different source of wealth. No less vital to our people, but perhaps not as romantic.'

The sultry evening breeze, laden with the scent of spice and the salt tang of the ocean, tugged lightly at her dress. From a terrace nearby came the strains of a slow, sweet melody.

He turned her again, and the gap between them closed. She felt the solid wall of his chest against her back. 'And to the south?' she asked breathlessly.

'To the south is the Rub' al Khali...the Empty Quarter. Nothing for hundreds of miles but sand dunes, scorpions and the occasional Bedouin tribe. It's beautiful, but one of the harshest places on earth.'

She barely heard the words, conscious of his breath ruffling the top of her hair, of the heat of his body so close to her own. She fought to hide the way he was affecting her.

As he turned her again his hands slid down her arms in a light caress. She kept her own hands curled tightly by her sides. At least they had their backs to his family now.

He bent his head, his mouth level with her ear. 'Do you see that line of shadow on the horizon?'

Citrus and spice and that certain indefinable something that was just him swirled around her. She closed her eyes and breathed him in.

'Yes,' she whispered, in truth seeing nothing at all.

Every sensitive nerve-ending along her cheek and neck tingled with awareness. As if some elemental charge pulsed back and forth between them. She turned her head, her eyes flickering open, and Khaled met her gaze. The soft light had turned his grey eyes black, picked out all the haunting curves and lines of his face.

He was breathtaking.

Her lips parted and his gaze went unerringly there. His head dipped, angled as if he meant to kiss her. She tilted her face upwards.

From one of the groups behind them came a flurry of laughter. Abruptly Khaled released her. With a sharp intake of breath he stepped back.

'That dark line on the western horizon is the foothills of the Sakhr mountain range.' His voice had hardened. 'A ridge of almost impassable granite and schist that separates us from Qaydar, our nearest neighbour.'

Why had his expression become so desolate?

'I can see why your father makes his claim,' she said, smiling up at him, wanting to bring back his earlier teasing.

But there was no answering warmth. The shutters had slammed down.

He was staring at the mountains. The moonlight picked out forbidding summits and deep, fathomless wadis.

'I actually came over to talk to you about something else,' he said, his expression as distant as those far-off peaks. 'What you told me this morning has deeply concerned me. I had no idea you had so few resources to fall back on. I'd like to help you, if you'd permit me?'

'Thank you, but I'll manage by myself. I always have. I actually prefer it that way,' she said. Their stilted politeness felt so weird after what he'd done to her in the car this afternoon.

'Of course. I remember you look after yourself. You were adamant about that once.' There was that ghost of a smile again. 'But perhaps on this occasion you might accept the assistance of a friend who is concerned for you? If it helps, consider it a favour returned.'

Oh, how tempting to accept, to lean on him, to have all his strength in her corner...

'But I think you've already repaid that particular debt,' she said. 'You helped me once, too, remember?'

He inclined his head in agreement.

One of the staff approached with a tray of coffee and dates. For two.

Khaled glanced at his family, who all appeared to be deliberately looking anywhere but in his direction. With a sigh, he indicated the cushions nearby. The servant left the tray on a low table beside them and he waited for Lily to sink down, folding her feet beneath her, before pouring and offering her a cup.

Her fingers trembled as she took it. The acerbic Khaled, she realised, wasn't anywhere near as intimidating as the stern, quiet man opposite her now. Tonight, the male diners were all in traditional Nabhani dress, so perhaps it was the fault of the grey *dishdasha* he wore, the twist of the snowy white *ghutrah* about his head.

But he looked only slightly more stunning in traditional robes than in formal black tie. It was the man, and not the clothes that was so arresting.

'I presume you have so little money because you worked for your stepfather?' he asked. 'He couldn't pay you?'

Wrestling with the emotions unleashed by the last few minutes, Lily didn't reply at once, keeping her eyes fixed on the expanse of rug between them.

'Forgive me,' he added, 'perhaps I'm being impertinent?'

She shook her head. 'No, you're not. It's a valid question. The answer is no, not for the last few months. And it was never that much when he did pay me.'

'Then it puzzles me…what was it that kept you in that house once you were old enough to leave?'

She looked up at him. 'Because it was my home. At least the only one I've known. And it suited my purpose to stay. I studied at the local college and it was cheaper to live there than to move out.'

'But your stepfather insisted you work for him as a condition of your remaining there?'

'As housekeeper, you mean? Yes, but it didn't really feel like work. I loved that house,' she said. 'The old library, my mother's roses. Even the leaky roof and the crazy antique plumbing. Yes, sometimes things were difficult, and I often worried over how we'd get the house through another winter without money for repairs. But I got to see Nate when he came home for visits, and Edward had been my guardian and the only parent I ever had. I guess I hoped that one day he'd—' She stopped, shook her head. 'You don't want to hear about this.'

'Yes, I do.' He reached out, taking her hand in his. 'Tell me, please.'

She looked at their entwined fingers, then met his earnest gaze. 'I secretly hoped that one day he'd be like a real dad,' she said. 'You know…that he'd choose me first.'

'Choose you first?' he repeated, in a soul-stealing voice, and those little tendrils of hope came flooding back, curling around her heart.

'Everyone who should have loved me and looked out for me,' she whispered, 'they chose something else instead. My dad chose his career over his wife and daughter. My grandfather chose family pride over me. My mum… Well, you know how that turned out.'

She hadn't meant to share all that with him. But under that intense gaze and the slow caress of his thumb across her knuckles it had slipped out.

'So that's why you stayed with your stepfather?'

'Yes—though it made no difference. Edward couldn't have cared less. About me or my mum. Like my real father, I suppose. There's only one thing I know about him for certain. At the beginning at least, he loved Mum enough to defy my grandfather, make everything legal and get married. He must have cared then. I've clung to that.'

'Sir?' An aide had appeared and bent to whisper in Khaled's ear.

He listened, frowning. Then, with only a curt nod to her,

as if she'd being talking about nothing more significant than
the weather, he followed the aide from the terrace.

'That's the thing about royals,' said George, strolling
over. 'One never really has their full attention. Aisha will
understand, of course. Being royal herself.'

'Aisha?' Lily parroted, still stunned by the way Khaled
had simply left.

'It's actually a secret. But I don't want to see you getting
hurt, so I think you should know.' He sank to the cushions
beside her. 'Khaled is in negotiations for the hand in marriage of the eldest daughter of the Qaydari King. Our border with them sits in the middle of the Sakhr mountains. I
assume that's what His Highness was pointing out to you
before?'

She'd poured out all that stuff about wanting someone
to choose her first, stupidly thinking that Khaled genuinely
cared. When what he actually cared about was the woman he
was negotiating to marry—the woman he'd already chosen.

A stab of pain pierced her heart. Swift and sure. Lily
didn't like the Queen's cousin, but she was grateful to him.
He couldn't have told her about the Qaydari Princess at
a better time. It reminded her that none of this was real.
Khaled wouldn't ever really be there for her. Despite his
offer to help.

Nothing had changed.

She was no worse off than before.

So why did it feel as though a piece of her had just split
apart and fallen in two?

CHAPTER EIGHT

THE NEXT MORNING the photos were everywhere.

Photos of her gazing up at Khaled, all dreamy and besotted as they stepped from that store.

Of him holding her hand at the restaurant while she looked helplessly dazzled.

Pathetic.

Lily flung her phone across the bed. She'd fallen for his false charm twice in one day and now there were stupid photos to prove it.

When she thought he'd steered them to a quiet corner of the roof terrace so they could talk privately, he'd been manoeuvring her to the best spot for the long-lens cameras.

Had that almost-kiss been part of the act, too?

She groaned and flung up an arm to cover her eyes.

Why did she have to think about that?

Because now she knew exactly what it was like to be kissed by him. The passion he could elicit from her body.

Her belly tightened at the thought. She flung up the other arm and blotted out the world completely.

So what if he was a great kisser and good with his hands? Okay, *really* good with his hands. How dense would she be to give her heart to the most unavailable man on the planet? Another in a line of people who wouldn't put her needs before his.

Didn't she know from bitter experience what that could do to a person?

Lily recalled other mornings when she was still very young, when she'd climb into her mother's bed and cuddle in close. Her mother would tell her stories about the amazing places she'd filmed in, the handsome men she'd acted with. *'Though none so handsome as your daddy,'* she'd say, with a sad catch to her voice.

Then she'd sit Lily at her dressing table, take up a beautiful ebony brush with silver inlays and gently tease the knots and tangles from her daughter's hair, the same dark red as her own. Singing to her—nonsense songs to make her laugh and distract her from any painful tugs, though she'd rarely hurt her. Her mother's fingers had been nimble and soothing.

But then had come the days when Mummy had been 'too tired', or wouldn't wake up at all, and there'd be a sour smell to the room and empty bottles on the bedside table.

After that Lily had learned to do her own hair. Raking at the tangles with a cheap plastic brush the housekeeper had bought for her.

Needing someone who didn't care had cursed her mother to a life of despair before leaving her only child to fend for herself.

But that child had survived and learned the lesson well.

It didn't matter how Khaled's touch made her feel. There'd be nothing but heartbreak with him.

Flinging open the wardrobes to rediscover her new clothes made her feel better. Forty-eight hours ago she'd had one good dress to her name. Now, cleaned and mended, it hung there, looking decidedly drab next to all its new and glamorous sisters. Everything from day dresses to the most exquisite but revealing evening gown that Lily doubted she'd ever have the courage or the right occasion to wear.

But today was a dress-down day. She was spending time with the twins later.

Rummaging through the rest of the selection Eleanor had insisted she keep, she unearthed a white cotton peasant blouse and denim shorts with cute turn-ups. Spying a colourful scarf on a shelf, she snatched that up, too, knotting it at her throat. She might feel miserable, but she was damn well going to look cheery.

Finally, after slipping on some wedge-heeled sandals and admiring her new look in the mirror, she decided that if she could find more of those chapattis and that scented tea they'd served her yesterday, she'd be about ready to face her day.

In the breakfast room, Khaled was taking his morning coffee. He was hidden away in a nook near the window, scrolling through the news on a tablet, when Lily strolled in.

His instinctive surge of delight was followed by irritation. It was barely past seven. He'd planned on being safely in his office long before anyone else was up. In particular Lily.

Yesterday's photos were circulating, and the press was filled with nothing but the Sad Prince and his new girlfriend, which meant the story was driving itself. There was really no need for him to see Lily while they were in the palace. Last night's accord could continue, while his people and Nate searched for the evidence that would implicate Hyde-Wallace.

So why was he gazing at her?

Right now she stood there, surveying the breakfast buffet. He noted the shorts. Obviously from the new wardrobe the Queen had helped her acquire yesterday. A scarf was tied at her throat. Accessories, too? His mother had been thorough.

Khaled was still for a long moment. God, but she looked young. Young and fresh and heart-stoppingly pretty. Her hair was caught up loosely in a clasp that left tempting tendrils spilling over her shoulders. A man would only have to lift a hand and a single tug would set all those glorious locks tumbling free.

Khaled reached for his coffee, giving his fingers an alternative occupation. He took a sip as Lily stretched to gather an apple from the fruit bowl. Her blouse rode up, exposing a slender midriff of smooth ivory skin. His fingers tightened

as he remembered the petal-soft skin between her thighs…
how she'd come apart when he touched her there.

The cup clattered back into its saucer.

This was intolerable. He'd been determined to put yesterday's events into their proper perspective. Not relive the more enticing moments. He'd allowed himself to be drawn in, to care what happened to her. When she'd whispered how she'd wanted Edward Marchant, that feckless social climber, to be a father to her, he'd reached for her hand without thinking…

It was probably as well that he'd been called away. He shuddered to think what he might have ended up saying to her. A woman could not be allowed to have this kind of hold over him. It was entirely unacceptable.

Sabir entered, on his way to his regular breakfast rendezvous with the Prince. Time to get on with work for the day. But his secretary halted as Lily greeted him and now, his morning duties apparently forgotten, he was retrieving his wallet to share photos of his baby daughter.

Lily's mouth spread into that bright, enchanting smile of hers and Khaled's heart constricted. What man wouldn't be stopped in his tracks by that?

Two days she'd been here.

Two.

Was that all it took for a man's self-control to begin slipping away? Well, not this man. The attraction was an aberration. He'd master it.

Rais walked in and joined the pair by the buffet. After a moment he threw back his head, guffawing at something Lily said.

Khaled's mood worsened. Since when did his grizzled security chief guffaw? First Sabir…now Rais. Was every one of his team under her spell?

His sisters bounded in.

'Lily! Mummy's going to invite you to stay until Daddy's anniversary party.'

'Say yes. Please.'

No. Definitely not happening.

He spoke. 'Lily.'

The flash of surprise in those big hazel eyes was followed by a wariness he thought they'd got past last night and which, to his annoyance, pained him. As he drew closer he saw she looked pale and drawn, as if she hadn't slept well. That troubled him, too.

Damn it, he was putting a stop to this nonsense right now. 'A word, please.'

He pulled her from her little fan club, marched her out into the corridor and backed her into a quiet alcove, using those precious seconds to wrestle his libido under control.

'It appears you're about to be issued with an invitation to my father's anniversary party next month. You will decline.'

Lily shook free of his grasp. 'Can't you even say hello before you start ordering people about?'

'I didn't bring you out here to exchange pleasantries. We'll be ending our arrangement long before the party, and you will, of course, be returned home at once.'

Her expression brightened and she looked up at him with big, hopeful eyes. 'You think we're going to prove Nate's innocence soon?'

He'd barely given the man a moment's thought this morning, and now he was finding it hard to think at all while she gazed up at him like that.

'Perhaps. You'll need to be here for a few more days. You'll tell my mother you have a previous arrangement. A friend's engagement party, maybe.'

'How ironic.'

'And while you're here I'd prefer it if you didn't flirt with the staff. They have work to do, and you are creating too much of a distraction.'

For him, too. Right now it was those shorts and sandals. They were doing incredible things for her legs.

'Is that so?' she said, in a tone he didn't much care for. 'And here's me thinking I'm just being polite to people who have been kind to me.'

'That's not how it looked from where I was sitting.'

'You've been spying on me?'

He didn't answer that. He just stared down his nose at her. He didn't have to justify his behaviour to this woman. He was the Crown Prince. He did as he damn well pleased.

'Now I know why you've had to resort to blackmail to get a fiancée. You are absolutely without charm.'

Offended, he snapped back without thinking. 'I've had no shortage of women.'

'But a distinct lack of willing fiancées, apparently.'

'My previous partners had no interest in marriage to me.'

That had not come out the way he'd intended. And of course she instantly leapt on his mistake.

'Gosh, I can't imagine why...'

Now, quite frankly, her manner was insulting. No one dared speak to him this way. The tenuous grip on his temper began to slip. He planted a hand on the wall beside her head, shamelessly using the advantage of his height to tower over her.

'But, *habiba*,' he purred, 'I've had numerous thoroughly satisfied lovers.'

He was rewarded with that blush of hers, blooming over her neck and cheeks. But then she squared her shoulders.

'Good for you. I take it you went to their homes? It would be difficult bringing them here...as you're still living with your parents. Does Aisha mind that, by the way? Your other potential fiancée.'

How the hell did she know that? He disregarded the jibe about him still living at home. He was not like other men. This was not a regular home.

'I have meetings this morning, but we'll discuss that later.'

She lifted her chin. 'I may not be available.'

'I'd advise on making yourself available.'

'Or what?' she challenged. 'What can you do without revealing that I'm only here because you've lost millions of pounds and have absolutely no idea where it is?'

'Perhaps your beloved stepbrother would enlighten us?' he sneered, ignoring the niggling voice of conscience that told him he hadn't let her know Nate was safe.

She rolled her eyes. 'How many times? He doesn't have it. Which you should have known from the start. I've had pet hamsters with more sense than you.'

She was comparing him to a *rodent*?

Nate was forgotten. With a growl, up went the other hand, trapping her between his outstretched arms. 'Don't taunt me. You won't like the consequences.'

She rose to her toes and pushed her face into his. 'I don't like it *now*.'

Hell, she was arousing. Her sweet rosebud mouth was so close. He wanted to flatten her to the wall and ravish it until she melted against him.

'Sir?' Rais had emerged from the breakfast room.

'What?' Khaled snarled, not taking his eyes from Lily's.

'Perhaps you should take your conversation to a more suitable location?'

Yeah, his bed…with this woman sprawled naked beneath him, asking—no, *begging* for him to take her.

One of his sisters giggled. He dragged his gaze from Lily to see four people watching him: Rais disapproving, Sabir startled, and his sisters peering round their shoulders, looking gleeful.

Damn the palace and its lack of privacy—and damn the way this woman could rile him so easily.

He pushed away from the wall. 'This conversation is not over, and you will present yourself when sent for,' he said, spinning away, not giving Lily a chance to respond, and getting the hell out of there before he did something he might truly regret.

Sabir hurried after the Prince and Rais tactfully hustled the girls back into the breakfast room, leaving Lily alone. A small mercy.

She didn't know if she wanted to howl in mortification or pummel the wall in frustration.

Khaled was driving her crazy.

He'd crowded her—all hard, pumped-up Alpha male, trying to intimidate her. It had had the opposite effect. It had made her want to plaster herself against his chest, tell him to shut up and kiss her already.

This man who snapped at her one minute and the next looked as if he was about to ravish her. This man who was going to marry someone else.

Oh, God.

Lily buried her face in her hands. She didn't want to feel any of this.

'Madam?'

She snapped upright. One of the Queen's staff was hovering a few paces away.

'Excuse me but, if it is convenient, Her Majesty wonders if you will join her for coffee?'

Convenient? Jeez, this family's timing was something else. *Because here comes the invitation*, she thought. The one that she'd been ordered to decline.

With its ivory walls and carved rosewood shutters at the windows, the Queen's study was an oasis of calm after Lily's fraught start to the day. An elegant writing desk sat before a group of sumptuously upholstered sofas and armchairs, and on a low table in their midst, in a nod to the European origins of its owner, was a Wedgwood vase filled with blowsy English roses.

On a side table against one wall was a collection of framed photos—the kind of shots of family and friends to be found in the sitting room of any wife and mother.

Lily looked closer.

Although in this case the 'friends' were more likely to be found gracing the front pages of the morning newspapers or TV reports: they were famous faces in their own right.

What a potent reminder of how little she belonged in the Azir social circle.

Lily spun away—only to be confronted by the most arresting image of all.

On the opposite wall to the desk, in perfect view for whenever their mother raised her head, hung a large framed photo of the Queen's children.

It had been taken some years ago—the twins looked about six years old. They were on a tropical beach, the girls caught up in the arms of their big brother, each balanced on a hip. One brandished a prize for the camera: a great tangle of seaweed. The other was lost in a fit of giggles. But it was the image of Khaled that had stopped Lily in her tracks. An image the world would barely recognise. For there was no trace of the famously melancholy Sad Prince.

Chest liberally coated in patches of sand, ebony hair all tousled and wet, eyes brimming with mirth, he was *smiling*.

Lily just stared.

The man was already insanely handsome, but that smile took those stunning looks to another level.

It was dazzling. *He* was dazzling.

'It's quite a shot, isn't it?' said Eleanor, entering the room. 'Bassam took it. It was the summer before his first heart attack. Our last real family holiday. A friend owns an island in the Indian Ocean. We were there for a week and Khaled and the girls just stayed out on the beach all day. I've never seen him so relaxed—before or since.'

Lily flushed, embarrassed to be caught gawping. 'It's a lovely photo.'

The Queen's eyes glittered as she led her guest to the sofas, calling over the servant holding a tray of coffee and pastries.

'If he'd unleash that smile for the cameras once in a while all that Sad Prince nonsense would go away,' Eleanor said. 'But even as a child he was a sombre little thing, following his big brother around. From the moment Khaled could walk, all he wanted was to be with Faisal. That boy was so full of life. We all adored my stepson. But he and Khaled were particularly close. After the accident he became so stern. You were young yourself, but perhaps you remember his visit a little?'

She did. She remembered the boy standing so still and grave in a room filled with sunbeams.

'You helped him a great deal, you know,' his mother said. 'We thought you would. We imagined being with another child would be easier than being with adults, and we wanted to get him away from all the press attention.'

She poured coffee, handing Lily a cup.

'It was Nate's suggestion, wasn't it?'

'Yes, clever boy. His friendship with Khaled wasn't well known at the time, so the Marchant estate was the last place anyone would have looked. He said that, left to their own devices, his "Baby Sis" and Khaled would get along famously. How right he was.'

The glitter in the Queen's eye intensified. 'And it seems those childhood bonds of yours have become even stronger in adulthood.'

'It's early days, really,' Lily said into her coffee. 'We seem to be having a lot of arguments. Quite public ones.'

Eleanor chuckled. 'You mean the grumpy workaholic remark? That was priceless! I've never seen my son at such a loss for words before.'

'I maybe went a bit too far...'

'My dear, it was no less than he deserved. I've no doubt he engineered your visit, and all the nonsense around that shopping trip, to force your hand in some way. When he wants something he goes after it with a vengeance. But you must stand firm. We're thrilled he's brought you here, but don't be coerced into something you don't want.'

So Eleanor thought Khaled was resorting to underhand tactics to secure her hand? He was forcing her hand, all right, but not the way his mother thought.

'I do hope you give him a chance, though. My son is a good man and he deserves to be happy. I think you're just what he needs.'

Lily took a gulp of coffee.

'The twins have been good for him, of course,' Eleanor said. 'He was certainly less desolate once they arrived. When Khaled was born there were complications, and we were told I'd have no more babies. At the time it was devastating, but Bassam and I were grateful for the two boys. After losing Faisal, and seeing Khaled so altered by it, we decided to take some advice. Treatment had moved on, you see. And we were fortunate to be blessed with our girls.'

'The twins have helped him?' Lily asked, grateful for the change of subject.

'Yes, although nothing has stopped him from punishing himself. He works all the time. I think he was actually glad to take on his father's responsibilities. He wants to make amends.'

'Amends?' Lily asked, surprised. 'For what?'

Eleanor's eyes misted over as she looked up at the image of her first-born child. 'For being the wrong prince to survive.'

Lily stared again at the smiling man who strove every day for the good of others and yet believed he personally had no right to exist.

'The boys and their father had gone into the desert,' Eleanor said. 'They loved racing dune buggies. But that morning Faisal lost control of his. The poor boy. He was always a little wild...'

She trailed off, but then roused herself. 'But I didn't invite you here to get all maudlin. It's Bassam's anniversary party in a month, and I wondered if you'd consider staying with us until then. Khaled will be away in America briefly, and I know you might have plans to accompany him, but there would still be time for you to get to know the country. To see if you might like to stay permanently.'

Staying permanently wasn't an option. Lily knew that. But to stay for another month...? If she did, maybe she'd be able to help Nate? But would she emerge on the other side with her heart intact?

She was falling more and more for this place. For the

kindness of Eleanor and the welcome of the family. For the heat and endless sunshine.

And…for Khaled.

The tyrant who'd melted her heart.

Who would never really have time for her.

'Please say yes. We'd be delighted to have you,' Eleanor said.

If she agreed, Khaled would be furious. After his performance this morning she'd take some pleasure in that. So before she could talk herself out of it she heard herself say, 'I'd love to.'

Eleanor clapped her hands together. 'Wonderful. Perhaps Nate will arrive in time to join us? You know, Bassam and I were delighted when he took the job as director of the charity. He's already exceeded the initial targets. The biggest coup, of course, was recently getting all those millions from George. I never knew my cousin had any interest in conservation…'

Lily tried to hide her shock. George Hyde-Wallace had made a donation to the fund just before a chunk of it went missing? Something didn't sound right with that…

But doing anything with the information would have to wait. The girls had arrived for their promised morning by the pool.

CHAPTER NINE

SOME HOURS LATER, Khaled was reflecting on his morning. It wasn't the worst he'd ever had—but, hell, it was up there.

First that spat outside the breakfast room, which had left him ready to snap the head off anyone who crossed him—not the best of moods for his series of morning meetings.

He'd started with a delegation from the United Nations, finalising details for his speech to the General Assembly in New York later that month. Nothing in his career to date had been more important, nor had consumed his professional life so completely, yet no less than three times Sabir had had to prompt him when his attention had wandered.

He'd actually lost his train of thought completely when he'd imagined he'd heard Lily's quick, light step approaching, and the maid bringing refreshments for his UN visitors had quailed under the Prince's fierce glare and hastily retreated after serving the guests. He'd concocted a plausible apology and had it conveyed to the woman. It wasn't her fault she'd been mistaken for Lily. But when had he learned the sound of her footsteps—and, more importantly, why was he allowing it to matter?

The second meeting had been with the Qaydari ambassador, who'd changed his tune since the last time they'd met, and had arrived with a new set of proposals, finally granting the concessions Khaled had requested. A result—or so he'd thought.

Until the man had revealed the outrageous caveat.

If Nabhan would meet all costs for building the new dam and its associated infrastructure.

He'd barely stopped himself from telling the ambassador where he could stick his concessions. Parading Lily as his new lover hadn't softened the King's stance at all. If anything, he'd become more demanding. And Khaled had wondered, not for the first time, if he really wanted to align himself and his country with such a man.

His anger had still been simmering when the third set of guests had walked into his *majlis*. This time from the Marsh Bedouin, to discuss the conservation work for the marshlands they depended on, and the funds raised at the recent charity launch. Five men in blue *dishdasha* and red *shemaghs*. Six, if you counted the additional surprise delegate.

A 'delegate' bearing revelatory, almost incendiary information.

He was still processing the impact of what he'd been told, and just when he thought his day couldn't get any worse...

'I have to talk to you.'

Lily bounded into his office unannounced, all glossy hair and shapely legs. Still in those damn shorts.

Khaled scowled as he watched her drop, uninvited, into the seat opposite him. 'Were you never taught to knock before entering a room?'

'Your trained killer on the door was awfully sweet and let me through without batting an eyelid, so I assumed I was welcome.'

The man might not be on the door much longer...

'I remembered seeing him at your house in England, so we had a little catch-up. Do you know he's going to be a father for the first time in the New Year? Looks like at least one of your guards will be powdering something after all. A baby's bottom.' She giggled at her joke. 'They're having a girl. They're naming her Elnoor, after the Queen. Isn't that lovely? I said that if *we* had a girl we'd—'

He raised a staying hand. 'What exactly do you think you're doing?'

After the morning he'd had, if she said *improvising* he was going to smash something.

'Acting all happy and loved-up.' She looked puzzled. 'You said I was to be convincing. Asking about a member of staff's baby seems quite natural. We'd be planning babies, too, wouldn't we? If we were really getting engaged? But if you want me to be cool and distant let me know—though please stop changing your mind. I can't keep up with your contradictory instructions.'

A sound like someone choking back a laugh had her spinning towards the corner of the room and the robed figure standing there. She looked horrified that she'd chattered on while Khaled still had a guest.

Then the guest winked at her.

'Nate!'

Lily jumped to her feet and ran to her stepbrother, flinging herself into his waiting arms, bestowing her most dazzling smile on him.

Khaled ground his teeth. If she'd used that on the guard, no wonder he'd been so amenable.

'Hey, Baby Sis.'

'Where have you've been? What happened to you? Are you okay?'

She fired questions at him, patting his chest all the while, as if checking he was in one piece.

'I'm fine. I've been hiding with the Marsh Bedouin. They're good friends.'

Khaled watched the exchange and experienced a new and most unwelcome emotion. He was being ridiculous. Nate was her brother.

Stepbrother, an invidious little voice reminded him, and no blood relation.

He had to curb the impulse to march over there and haul her away from his friend.

Then his attention caught on what she was saying.

'So we can end this pretend relationship?'

'No!'

Stepbrother and sister turned as one to stare at him. Nate's eyes were glinting in unholy amusement at his emphatic response.

'I mean,' Khaled said, being careful to sound more measured this time, 'it's safer for Nate if we continue until we can prove who's behind the theft.'

'Plus, I've already given my consent,' Nate said.

Lily looked at him, aghast. 'You've done *what*? I don't need your consent.'

'That's not what you said to the press.' Nate grinned at her.

'That was a ruse. You know this whole thing isn't real. And in the eligibility stakes isn't he a bit out of my league.'

'You're the granddaughter of a duke.'

'Estranged granddaughter,' she reminded him.

Nate shrugged. 'Makes no difference. You have a legitimate aristocratic heritage going back generations. Much further back than his. There could be no objection to your marriage.'

'Except that he's a tyrant,' Lily muttered.

The tyrant lounged in his chair. Broad-shouldered, divinely handsome.

Even if their relationship were real she wouldn't marry him. His wife would be side-lined over and over in the name of royal duty. But in a dark, locked-away corner somewhere, a part of her still reached for him. For his heat and his strength and all the things he could make her feel.

His hand rested on the desk, fingers slowly drumming. She shivered. Those fingers were magic.

Their eyes clashed. His gleamed. He knew exactly what she'd been thinking.

'Is there a purpose to your visit?' he said.

Purpose…

What was it again? Oh, yes.

Big donation.

Queen's cousin.

Theft.

She sat up straighter. 'I think George Hyde-Wallace is behind the theft.'

'Yeah, we know,' said Nate bitterly. 'He's been boasting to one of his cronies that I'll soon be gone from Khaled's inner circle and that Khaled's going to have to start toeing the line or risk being ousted. And by "toeing the line" he means dropping all attempts at reforming the role of the Council of Families, which means George will maintain his hold on power. The traitorous bastard.'

'How do you know all this?' Lily asked.

'George believes he has the entire Council in his pocket. He's wrong,' Khaled said darkly.

'But it's all hearsay. We can't prove a thing,' Nate added. 'He's covered his tracks too well.'

'Then call his bluff to draw him out. Make a big deal of the Hyde-Wallace donation and start on the projects the money was raised for. If the funds are being used as intended, how can he cry foul without revealing that he knew something already.'

'You're missing the essential point,' Khaled said. 'The money is gone.'

'Only ten million—I'm sure you're good for it.'

'But if the theft becomes public it will look like I covered it up and Hyde-Wallace will discredit me anyway.'

'Then your plan needs the sanction of someone in the highest of places,' Lily said.

Khaled looked blank.

She rolled her eyes. 'Duh. Your father. Who would dare question the word of the King?'

'You know, that idea's got legs,' Nate said. 'Why didn't we come up with that yesterday?'

Lily's flush of pride was forgotten. 'What do you mean, yesterday?'

Nate frowned at Khaled. 'You didn't tell her we'd spoken?'

It was like a slap to her face. 'You were talking to my stepbrother yesterday and you didn't let me know last night, or at any point since? When you know how worried I've been?'

'I wasn't entirely convinced. I needed to check Nate's story,' Khaled said, not the least repentant.

She rounded on her stepbrother. 'Why are you even friends with this man? He hasn't an ounce of trust in his body.'

'I'm a prince. I don't have that luxury,' Khaled said.

'To be fair, Baby Sis,' Nate added, 'the evidence against me was pretty damning.'

'Don't you dare defend him. Do you know, while he's parading me around as his pretend fiancée, he's already promised himself to a foreign princess?'

She was ashamed now of her antics in front of the journalists. She'd meant to embarrass Khaled, not some poor woman who was apparently just as much a pawn in all this as she.

'There was no need for you to know that. It would have only complicated matters,' Khaled said coolly.

'Too right. I would have said no.' She glared at him. 'Dragging me halfway round the world... Using me as bait... You really are the lowest kind of man.'

His jaw tightened. 'I won't tolerate your insolence in here.'

'You don't have to. I'm leaving. Take care, Nate, and stay in touch.' She pecked him on the cheek.

'Where are you going?' Khaled demanded.

'I thought I might look at engagement rings.' She held out her left hand, waggling her naked ring finger. 'I'm thinking something brash and showy that's trying to look like a diamond but is actually fake. In other words, a big fat liar. Just like you.' Lily glared at him. 'Two fiancées at the same time? What a gallant way to treat women. Your mother and sisters must be so proud.'

Then she turned on her heel and headed for the door, leaving the handsome tyrant to stew.

CHAPTER TEN

THE BEACH THAT ran beside the palace looked much like any other stretch of Nabhani shoreline. Except for the soldiers patrolling the perimeter and the steel-grey gunboat skimming the waves in the near distance.

This stretch of perfect ivory sand was reserved for the sole use of the royal family and its guests.

After Lily had stomped into the family room the Queen had diplomatically suggested her current guest might appreciate some time to herself there, beyond the dunes, where she wouldn't be disturbed. In the late afternoon they benefitted from a cooling breeze, she'd told her, and in her opinion were rather restful.

Lily, too angry to be good company, had thought it an excellent suggestion. So now, in a bikini and a loose shirt, shaded by the brim of a sun hat, she sat beneath an umbrella in the lee of one of the larger dunes.

She still seethed about Khaled's lies, and how he'd hidden from her the fact that Nate was safe. And jealousy was gnawing away at her, too, and she hated herself for it. Somewhere out there a young woman waited, destined to be Khaled's bride, to share his bed, to know his touch.

Aisha might be in love with him. If her affections weren't returned, would she be doomed to a half-life, dwindling away, yearning for the attentions of a man who would never put her first? Because he was a world leader, with hard choices to make and little room for softness of the heart?

Except Lily remembered a day when he'd been more than kind to her...

After her mother's wake.

Khaled had been leaving, and as they'd crossed the hall on the way to his car he'd seen a pile of that day's newspapers on a table in plain view. Her mother's image had been splashed across every front page. In a rage he'd snatched them up and dumped every one of them in a wastebasket. Then he'd dropped to his haunches and begged her, on no account, to look at any of them. She'd promised him she wouldn't and put her arms about his neck.

'Good girl,' he'd said, and squeezed her tight.

But later, when the house had been quiet, she'd crept downstairs and taken those newspapers into the library. She'd read every one and cried in hurt and humiliation. They'd published the worst photographs, the most shaming stories. Stories she'd never heard before.

How her mother had been fired from her last film for turning up hours late and forgetting her lines. How she'd been thrown off a flight, blind drunk, foul-mouthed and fighting with the security staff who had been attempting to keep her and the other passengers safe.

And, worst of all, how she'd neglected her only child.

But nobody knew that once, before her husband had chosen his career over them, and broken her heart, she'd sat with her daughter in the mornings, softly singing to her and brushing and untangling her hair with deft, gentle fingers.

Lily had torn the papers to shreds and then run upstairs to her mother's room. The pills, the tumblers and the empty vodka bottles had all been cleared away. But on the dressing table had sat the ebony and silver hairbrush.

Lily had snatched it up, climbed into her mother's bed, and cried herself to sleep.

The next day Edward had left for London, and she'd gone to school and pretended that none of it mattered. Because hadn't she really lost her mother years ago?

She'd gone to her classes. Sat with friends at lunch.

Caught the school bus home to an empty house and eaten the meal the housekeeper had left for her. She'd tidied the kitchen, done her homework, then got herself ready for bed. Like she did any other day.

Pretending none of it mattered.

Except that tucked away in the bottom of her school bag, carefully wrapped in an old handkerchief, was the ebony hairbrush with silver inlays and long strands of deep red hair caught in its bristles.

Lily closed her eyes on those bitter memories. She should have listened to Khaled and never read those stories. He'd tried to protect her. He'd been kind.

A thundering sound reached her. Not from the sea. From behind her—from the dunes. She sat up. It was coming her way…and fast.

She scrambled to her feet and reached the path between the banks of sand just as a horse and rider galloped out of it.

The startled horse reared up, its thrashing hooves missing her head by inches. Lily lurched backwards, tripped on a piece of driftwood, and landed flat on her backside. In her panic, she scuttled backwards, staring in horror as the rider sawed at the reins, working to get the animal under control.

At last the horse was calmed. Its rider flung himself from the saddle. 'Lily, my God, are you hurt?'

Khaled.

Looking magnificent in white shirt, skin-tight riding breeches and long leather boots, his head swathed in a checked *shemagh*.

Grateful for the cover of her hat's brim, because one glimpse of him had sent heat to her cheeks, Lily struggled to her feet. 'I'm okay,' she spluttered.

Did he always have to look so gorgeous?

'What the hell do you think you were doing, running in front of a horse like that?'

Typical—the concern had lasted about a nanosecond and now he was angry at her.

'Enjoying some peace and quiet—until you came pounding up on that horrible beast. If I'd known anyone was riding out here I would never have come— Ow!'

She couldn't stop the yelp of pain as she placed her full weight on her left ankle.

'You are injured?' One hand arrived beneath her elbow, the other curled about her waist.

'It's nothing,' she protested, acutely aware of his touch through her flimsy shirt.

'Let me look at it.' He dropped to one knee beside her. 'Put your hand on my shoulder.'

He waited until she'd obeyed and leant her weight against him, before lifting her damaged foot.

There was the heady scent of fresh male sweat, and beneath her fingers Lily felt the shift of solid muscle as he worked. Yet he was infinitely gentle as he carefully manipulated the joint.

'I don't think it's serious, but the sooner we get some ice on that the better.' He rose up. 'I'll take you back with me.'

The allure of the man beside her was forgotten as Lily glanced at the black monster tossing its head. Her heart pounded as Khaled swept past her, scooped her few possessions into a neat pile on the lounger, then strode back to grasp the horse's reins.

'Really, I'll be fine. I'll take it slowly,' she said, trying her weight again and gasping at a fresh stab of pain.

'Don't be ridiculous. You can't even walk.'

In one swift move he was back in the saddle, with a ripple of muscle and power that had her heart racing faster still. He edged the horse closer.

'What about my things?' she asked, stalling. Anything to avoid getting on that animal.

'Someone will be sent for them.' He stretched out his hand.

'Won't the people on the boat out there have seen what's happened and send help?'

Khaled peered at the grey shape out on the waves. 'Not if they value their positions. The security teams don't set foot on this beach unless they perceive a genuine threat. They'll only approach at a sign from me.'

'Then couldn't you wave to them?'

He turned cool grey eyes on her. 'You want me to wave at a gunboat and scramble security for a twisted ankle? Besides, in the time it takes for a Jeep to get here we could be back in the palace. That ankle needs treatment. The quickest route is back through the dunes.'

The horse, getting impatient, pawed at the sand with a great hoof.

Seeing her shrink back, Khaled said, 'You've nothing to be afraid of. I'm the master here. He does as he's bid.'

And didn't that sound as much about her doing as she was told as the beast he sat upon?

But the animal was obeying him, and beyond her mistrust of it came a far more tangible sensation. Her ankle had started throbbing. Getting ice on it seemed appealing right now.

Steeling herself, Lily squeezed her eyes shut, stretched out a hand, and felt the ground fall away as she soared upwards.

It was the fear, Khaled decided. It had robbed him of his good sense. First the horror of watching Lily disappear beneath Mu'tazz's hooves, and then seeing her in pain.

His only thought had been to get her to a doctor. He just hadn't considered the implications of having her perched, practically naked, in his lap, and how good it would feel to hold her close. Or that she in turn would cling to him so fiercely out of a fear of her own, foisting upon him another inconvenient emotion: the urge to protect her.

Perhaps he should have hailed the gunboat. They'd have sent someone soon enough and he'd have avoided all this.

Because now Khaled realised his second mistake. Something he'd quite forgotten in his haste to get Lily back to the palace. Something that explained her reluctance to approach

Mu'tazz and why her hands were now desperately knotted in his shirtfront, her face hidden in his neck.

Too late, he remembered the fearless little girl who'd been afraid of only one thing—who'd always stayed safely behind fences whenever he'd taken her brother's mare out in the paddock. The girl whose father had died in a riding accident.

He felt her tremble and pulled her closer, cursing his inattention.

Horses. They terrified her.

Mu'tazz shifted his weight and a new shudder went through her.

'Please can we hurry?'

Her muffled plea came from deep in the folds of his *shemagh*.

He wanted to be angry with her. He'd abandoned work for the day because he'd been achieving precisely nothing. When she'd stormed out on him earlier he'd wanted to go after her, kiss her, touch her until she came apart for him again. Instead he'd come out here to ride, to the point of exhaustion if necessary—whatever it took to banish Lily Marchant from his mind.

But here she was, hurt, frightened, and he was to blame.

He gathered up the reins, folding her tighter against him. 'You're safe. I promise.'

The stallion began walking on command. Lily whimpered and shifted even closer. Her rump pressed into his groin, evoking memories of what had happened the last time she sat in his lap.

Khaled gritted his teeth. He needed something to distract them both.

'Did you know our fathers met?' he blurted.

He felt her start of surprise, but she didn't look up.

'Bassam knew my dad?' she asked.

'Met him,' he corrected. 'My father said it was only briefly. At a garden party in England. But you were with him at the time.'

The death grip on his shirtfront eased a fraction. 'I was?' She peeked up at him from beneath the brim of her hat. 'He's sure it was me?'

'He said that all the time they were speaking your father had a little girl with unforgettable red hair sitting on his shoulders.'

'"Unforgettable red hair"?' she grumbled. 'That sounds like me, all right.'

A wistful look clouded her eyes. It reached into his chest and closed tight about his heart.

'Perhaps that's where my memory of him comes from,' she said. 'I remember sitting on a man's shoulders. We were having fun. Apart from with Nate, it's one of the few times I ever felt like someone really wanted me around. But that can't really be true, can it? Because in the end he abandoned my mother and me to chase his career.'

Mu'tazz navigated a dip in the path and his riders swayed in the saddle. But that wasn't the reason for the tightening of the protective arm about Lily's waist, nor for the tender glance directed to the top of her head.

'Even though that's true, I still miss him, you know?'

'Yes, I do,' Khaled answered, reminded of his own loss, of the agony of having a beloved brother wrenched from him.

It was curious how being close to this girl eased that pain. Guilt nagged at him. He should have eased her anxieties over her stepbrother yesterday.

'It was wrong of me. Not telling you I'd spoken with Nate. I apologise.'

She looked up sharply. He allowed one corner of his mouth to lift.

Her eyes narrowed on him, but then she slumped back against his chest. 'I know what you're trying to do. You're trying to charm me so I forget to be cross with you.'

'What a dastardly and devious thing to do,' he said, and after a pause asked, 'Is it working?'

He heard a huff of irritation, but the trembling of her shoulders told him she was laughing.

'You know you're incorrigible?'

'That's actually a desirable skill in my line of work.'

She laughed again, then cautiously reached out to touch the horse's thick neck muscle. 'What's he called?'

'Mu'tazz.' On hearing his name, the stallion's ears twitched. 'And he's fond of neck-rubs.'

She scratched her fingers back and forth. 'Maybe he's not as frightening as I first thought.'

'Back there he was probably more terrified of you than you were of him.'

'I doubt that,' she said, but he noticed she was stroking the glossy black mane, slowly curling one strand over and over in her slender fingers. He looked elsewhere as need shimmered over his skin.

'Will you tell me something?' she asked.

Right now he'd gladly talk about anything. 'What do you want to know?'

'About Aisha. I mean, why her?'

'Because of who her father is. An alliance with Qaydar will have benefits for the people here.' Not that he was quite so certain of that any more.

'So what were you hoping to gain by pretending I'm your girlfriend?'

No harm in sharing that with her now, and he realised that he trusted her. 'Her father has been dragging his heels on certain details. I thought seeing you on my arm might prompt him back to the negotiating table.'

'And never mind if Aisha gets hurt?'

'It's not that kind of arrangement. Emotion doesn't come into it.'

'Spoken like the one with all the power. If she's going to be your wife, don't you think she'll want to be chosen first—you know…for her? Not because of the mountain range she happens to live by.'

'Aisha has been raised as a royal. She understands how these things work.'

She muttered something indistinct and fell silent.

Up ahead the entrance to the stable block came into view, and he felt an odd ripple of energy go through her. But those fingers still idly twirled in Mu'tazz's mane. He tried not to stare. He was *not* envious of his damn horse.

'I suppose now you've apologised to me,' she said, 'it's only fair that I should say I'm sorry, too. About how I've behaved in all this. I know you're in a difficult position, and that you really are trying to protect Nate.'

She looked at him, her hazel eyes genuinely contrite, and to his surprise she reached up and kissed his cheek. It was nothing more than a simple peck, but it set his pulse racing.

When her lashes lowered, and her gaze dropped to his lips, he couldn't prevent the hitch in his breathing. She touched her mouth to his. A brief buss of soft lips.

Like some breathless untried teenager he swallowed. She traced the movement of his throat with her fingertips and he shuddered as desire surged through him.

He pulled her close.

Too rough. She hissed in pain. The movement had wrenched her injured ankle.

'I'm sorry, I—'

'Shh, it's all right.'

She laid her palm tenderly against his jaw, as if it was he who needed soothing. Then her hand went higher, pushing the *shemagh* backwards so her fingers could tangle in his hair.

He groaned and, carefully this time, drew her nearer. The warm mounds of her breasts, the sharp peaks of her nipples pressed against his chest. The smell of her and the sea breeze mingled together, and he couldn't tell where one ended and the other began.

He gave himself up to the kiss...to her.

Slender fingers tightened around his skull, holding his face to hers, but nothing would have induced him to pull

away. He never wanted to come up for air again. He didn't
care about breathing. He needed this more.

A sound intruded nearby. Whatever it was, he'd ignore
it. This woman was all that mattered.

His hands spread possessively across her back.

Someone cleared his throat, and then again, louder.

On a growl of frustration, Khaled lifted his head. To discover they were in the centre of the stable courtyard, surrounded by goggling stable hands, and with them was Rais,
inscrutable as ever.

In the absence of any other command, Mu'tazz, had simply plodded home.

'The team on the boat called it in, sir. The doctor is waiting,' his security chief said, walking up to take Lily. 'If you
will permit me, Miss Marchant?'

She unwound her arms from Khaled's neck.

'Oops. Looks like we wandered into an audience and
you had no idea. Not nice, is it?' she whispered, and then
shifted to allow Rais to lift her down and carry her away.

His blood roaring, his heart racing, Khaled watched her
go. Leaving him how? Aroused. Conflicted. Out-played.

She'd used that sweet, giving mouth and delectable body
to distract him, to lure him back here and serve him up his
own medicine. The little madam. She'd probably claim she'd
been 'improvising'.

Suddenly, and much to the astonishment of the grooms,
he threw back his head and laughed. She constantly challenged his authority, tested his patience—but, by God, the
woman made him feel awake.

Climbing that ivy. Breaking into his rooms. Standing
up to him and fighting him every step of the way. She had
some nerve. And some loyalty. Believing absolutely in her
stepbrother and doing everything in her power to help him.

A woman like that would make a damn fine consort for
any man.

Khaled slid from the saddle, gave Mu'tazz an affection-
ate, if absent-minded pat, and handed the reins to a stable

lad. As he walked he considered the Qaydaris and their slippery negotiating. Would an alliance with them be more trouble than it was worth? Would he come to regret it? And did that change his options?

What if his marriage created no problems of that kind? What if, instead of Aisha, he took an English girl, with nothing to offer but an aristocratic lineage and the delight of her body?

Feeling energised, taking the stairs to his rooms three at a time, he began to wonder.

What if...?

Was it crazy?

What if he genuinely chose Lily Marchant to be his wife?

CHAPTER ELEVEN

TWENTY MINUTES LATER, towelling himself dry after a shower, Khaled decided he'd found the perfect solution to the question of his marriage.

Marry Lily and there'd be no awkward father-in-law to placate. No risk of poor chemistry between husband and wife. He was physically drawn to her, and that kiss they'd shared hadn't been all for show on her part. She'd get as much satisfaction from the marriage bed as he would.

She seemed unfazed by palace life. She'd even handled their encounter with the press. With guidance from his mother, he had no doubt she'd be able to manage the demands of being his princess.

Better still, his strange yearning, this inconvenient concern for her, would disappear. They were just the symptoms of sexual frustration. His focus and concentration would return and he would be able to get on with being the Crown Prince.

God knew, that was the least he owed to his father.

As ever, on the next breath, Faisal came to mind. What would he have advised?

With a clench of pain, he recognised the question was irrelevant. The advice would have been going the other way. His brother should have been choosing the next Crown Princess of Nabhan.

Brooding on that, when the phone rang he answered

automatically—and cursed himself when he recognised the caller.

'My apologies for disturbing you,' said George Hyde-Wallace, his tone, as always, hovering just on the wrong side of deferential. 'I understand Miss Marchant has been injured and I want to offer the assistance of my personal physician.'

Khaled bit his tongue. He knew for certain now that Hyde-Wallace was definitely plotting against him. And the endless impertinence of the man. As if the royal family didn't have access to the finest doctors already.

'It's merely a twisted ankle,' he said, waiting for the real purpose of this call.

'I'm relieved to hear it. Such a charming young woman. You seem to be growing rather fond of her yourself. Some are even suggesting you might propose to the girl—though of course sadly that's impossible. The Constitution forbids it.'

'The *Constitution*?'

'Lily Marchant is illegitimate.'

As a shock tactic, the statement was masterful. It rendered Khaled temporarily speechless.

Illegitimate? It couldn't be true. Her parents had been married. Famously so. It was what had cut them off from her father's family. But icy shards pricked along his spine. George was too careful to make a claim like that without evidence.

'And you know this how?' he said eventually, as casually as he could.

'I've always had my concerns about Nathaniel Marchant, so I had him and his stepsister investigated some time ago. For your protection, of course.'

Yeah, right.

'It turns out her parents' romantic beach wedding was merely a handfasting performed by an unlicensed celebrant. Certainly not legal in Nabhan. However, in light of your interest in the girl, I've taken the precaution of concealing what I've discovered from anyone else who bothers to look. For now.'

Khaled didn't miss that tagged-on veiled threat.

For only the second time in his life he experienced a feeling of utter impotency. There was nothing to be done if this were true, because George was right. The Constitution forbade such a marriage. The requirement has been built in to it to ensure peace amongst Nabhan's senior families. Both monarch and consort must be legitimate.

But George hadn't finished. 'It would be terrible if this information reached the press... I imagine it would destroy her. All those stories about her disgrace of a mother would resurface... There would be no chance of reconciliation with her grandfather... Apart from that stepbrother of hers, she would be completely alone.'

His thoughts landed with a ferocious determination. *She would not be alone. She would have me.*

But how? How could Khaled stand between her and harm when the best way to protect her from George's threats was to push her away.

'May I suggest a solution?' George drawled into the silence. 'Announce your engagement to the Qaydari Princess and the media will quickly shift their interest. Who would bother to search any further into Miss Marchant's background then? Her reputation would be safe.'

And George would have a powerful ally against Khaled's reforms in the shape of the conservative King of Qaydar.

'I'll leave you to ponder on that. Perhaps we could meet later, to discuss what you've decided? Shall we say before dinner this evening?'

Without waiting for a response, George ended the call.

First the theft. Now this. Hyde-Wallace was using whatever means he could to try and control Khaled.

As for Lily...

So be it. It was a passing infatuation anyway.

And that stab of anguish at the thought of letting her go? That would pass, too.

He'd make it appear that their affair had ended. Suggest they'd had a falling-out. A terminal one. But while the theft remained unresolved it would be safer if she stayed in Nabhan. He'd leave her in the palace with his family, say that she was staying on as a guest of his mother and sisters while he removed himself from the country.

He wasn't due in New York for another three weeks. But there was little in his diary before then that he couldn't just as easily do using New York or London as his base. It was almost a month before he'd need to return for his father's anniversary party. A month ought to do it.

He swept up the phone again, to instruct Sabir to make the arrangements.

He was leaving for Europe tonight.

'No bones broken, young lady. It's just a sprain and should mend in a few days.' The doctor gathered his bag, getting ready to leave Lily's suite. 'Alternate ice and heat to help with the swelling, and walk as much as you can, hmm? Use that if necessary.' He pointed to the crutch just delivered from the palace sick bay.

Lily wondered if he could have so easily prescribed something for her other symptoms. The racing heart, the breathlessness, the feeling that she was on the edge of a precipice and could just as easily fly as fall...

Why, *why* had she been so stupid as to kiss Khaled again? Because now she could think of nothing else. Her plan for revenge had seriously backfired.

She left the twins, who were busy organising ice packs and footstools for her neatly bandaged ankle, and hobbled to the bathroom, to change and wash away the grime from the beach.

When she re-emerged, she found Eleanor had arrived and Amal was excitedly recounting the details of her accident.

'Khaled brought her back on his horse.'

Eleanor's eyes glowed. 'On Mu'tazz? Oh, that is romantic.'

Eager to change the subject, Lily said, 'Hanan mentioned

you're having a beach barbecue tonight. That sounds lovely. I hope I can get there?'

'Don't worry—Khaled can carry you!' Hanan sniggered.

'If he joins us at all. Girls, why don't you go and invite him? You might be able to persuade him.' Eleanor's indulgent smile for her daughters became wistful. 'We know he'll work all evening otherwise.'

'I'll go,' Lily said, reaching for the crutch.

'Are you sure, dear? He'll be in his office. It's quite a walk.'

'The doctor said I should try to use the ankle.'

She took a few tentative steps. With the crutch it wasn't so hard. Either way, she needed to move.

She felt so restless. A thrilling image of Khaled carrying her to the beach had come too easily to mind. She knew precisely how it felt to be in arms, how easily he could lift her, the potent strength of him.

She stabbed the crutch down. Ridiculous to be salivating over how strong he was when she should be remembering the pertinent facts in all this. He'd used her to force another monarch back to the negotiating table so he could wring better terms from the man.

Even so, she was ashamed of how she'd behaved this afternoon. Playing the same trick on him he'd used on her didn't make things right. She needed to apologise.

But she'd badly overestimated how far she could walk. By the time she reached the office suites her ankle was in agony. It must have shown on her face. The guard on the door took pity on her, leading her straight into Khaled's office.

It was empty, though she was assured the Prince had only stepped out for a moment. On his desk sat an open laptop and a scatter of papers.

She sank into Khaled's chair, reaching down to rub her aching ankle, and found she was at eye level with the framed photo she'd noticed yesterday.

It was not of his parents or sisters, or Mu'tazz, but of

two young men. The older of the two, grinning broadly, had his arm slung across the other's shoulder. Both had the same luxuriant ebony hair and strong, determined chin. The younger had pale grey eyes.

Brothers.

Faisal and Khaled.

The grey-eyed boy was so like the teenager she'd first met she knew the photo must have been taken close to that time. He was still unsmiling, but there was no sadness there. She thought of the other image she'd seen today, and of the stunning smile this boy, as a man, would hardly use.

The sun had set and the room, lit only by the desk lamp, was wreathed in shadows. But from the farthest of the bookshelves behind her came a dull glimmer. It was the gold-lettered spines of the little collection she'd spied yesterday. Unable to resist, she hitched herself out of the chair, limped over and bent closer to study their titles.

The Adventures of Huckleberry Finn, Wind in the Willows, Treasure Island... Classic children's books. A dozen or so.

Even more curious now, she slipped two from the shelf and hobbled back to her seat. She angled one under the light and opened it to the first page, to find a neat handwritten dedication.

For Faisal on his tenth birthday.
With fondest love from Grandpa Wallace

The second book held a similar message, this time for Faisal's eleventh birthday.

The breath caught in her throat.

Amidst all the scholarly texts and professional journals, in an office devoid of any other personal touches, Khaled kept his brother's photo and his childhood books.

'You seem to have great trouble respecting my privacy.'

Lily jumped, snapping the book closed.

Khaled filled the doorway.

Awareness flooded through her, along with a sensitivity in her breasts and her thighs, as if her clothes had suddenly become too tight.

But in that same instant she recognised that she'd been intruding on something deeply personal to him and, ashamed of herself, babbled an apology. 'I'm so sorry. I was just looking at the books while I waited.'

He glanced to her hands and his face contorted. In four strides he reached her and wrenched the books from her fingers. He returned them to the shelf, then took up station by the window. Arms folded, legs planted wide, he stared into the blank darkness beyond.

She struggled to her feet. 'I didn't mean to pry,' she said to his back, 'but I've always loved old books and those are so beautiful.'

He ignored her explanation. 'What exactly are you here for?'

'I came to apologise.'

Over his shoulder, he stared at her. 'For which particular transgression? There have been so many.'

'The kiss…at the stable block.'

He shrugged. 'Why? We enjoyed it and we both know it meant nothing. But if it makes you feel better I accept your apology. Now, if you will excuse me, I have work to do.'

Confused by the change in him from just an hour ago, Lily stumbled on. 'But…but your mother hoped you'd join the family for dinner on the beach.'

He gave a dismissive snort. 'Please pass my apologies to my mother, but I've no time. I'm leaving for England in an hour.'

'England?'

'Yes.' He shot her an odd glance, loaded with a meaning she couldn't decipher. 'I know you've been invited to remain here until my father's anniversary party, and after reconsidering I think that could be useful. Until we can categorically prove your stepbrother's innocence, more speculation about us won't hurt.'

Why was he so angry? Just because of the books?

'You may go,' he said, and when she still didn't move he snapped, *'Now.'*

Shocked and hurt by that curt dismissal, Lily lashed out. 'To think I actually felt sorry for you because you keep your brother's things close by. But I'll save my sympathy for Aisha. She deserves it.' She grabbed the crutch and hobbled round the desk. Her ankle throbbed, but she just wanted to get out of there. 'How do you live with yourself?' she demanded. 'Don't you feel any guilt at all?'

There was a flash of movement by the window and she felt a new tension in the room, as if the air had become electrified. He moved towards her, halting so close she had to tip her head back to meet his glittering gaze.

'You dare speak to me of guilt?' All the shadows in the room seemed to coalesce around him. 'It's burned into my soul. It curses my very existence. But I keep Faisal's things close by in case I'm ever tempted to forget.'

'Because you survived and he didn't?' Lily whispered.

His beautiful mouth twisted into a cruel sneer. 'Oh, every damn psychologist my mother dragged me to said precisely that. They thought they knew the story. You all do,' he said bitterly.

'Your brother lost control of a dune buggy and there was an accident...'

'Ah, yes, that accident. Caused by my poor *reckless* brother. Everyone was so ready to blame him.' He grasped her shoulders, dragging her closer. 'But shall I tell you what really happened that day?'

When he closed his eyes he could still see it. At the base of the dune the wheels of the upturned buggy spinning wildly and Faisal, his head at a sickening angle, lying motionless in the sand.

He never had been able to remember how he'd got down

that slope. Days of dull pain in his left flank suggested that he'd pitched headlong at some point, but all he knew was that one minute he was at the top of the ridge and the next he was on his knees in the sand, staring into his brother's lifeless eyes.

How long had he knelt there, his mouth open in a yawning cavern of grief? Minutes? Hours? A lifetime of agony had been compressed into those moments.

At some point arms had enveloped him. Gently urged him to his feet. Turned him away from that broken body and held him.

His father. Comforting his only surviving son. An embrace he almost hadn't been able to bear, because in it had been the forgiveness he could never deserve.

'Faisal always won,' he told Lily. 'Whatever we did, he always won. It drove me crazy, and for once I wanted to prove I was better. If I'd known how sheer the drop was on the other side of that dune I would never have done it. But I pushed and I pushed, and I drove him too close to the edge. My father knew. I heard him say the words to Rais. It was to stay between the three of us. It was an accident. We'd say Faisal had been driving too fast. But it was a lie. A terrible lie. My brother wasn't reckless. He was fearless. Because of me, even that distinction was stolen from him. All this—' he threw a contemptuous glance around them '—is a sham. It should have been his. I stole his birthright and I didn't even have the guts to make my father tell the truth.'

He saw her gaze flicker through the room. Finally she was understanding the starkness of it. There was nothing that spoke of his status. It wasn't his to make his own.

'Every day I work to ease my father's burden. It's the only thing I can do. I know his grief for Faisal burns sharp in him and he never stops feeling his loss. But still I see him watching me, willing me to forgive myself. He doesn't know the torture that is. He's trying to pour life back into me when it's too late. I'm already dead inside.'

Lily gave a strange gasping sob.

Yes, here it comes, he thought in bitter triumph. *The revulsion, the loathing, the innocence dying in her gaze as she looks at me.*

Even though it struck at him like daggers, he embraced the pain of it, determined to drive home every last word, so she truly understood what kind of worthless creature stood before her.

He bared his teeth in a snarl. 'I killed him, Lily. I killed my brother. And guilt is the only thing I feel any more.'

Lily stared into his eyes and saw such torment in their depths she knew she was staring right into the dark and damaged soul of the Sad Prince.

Perhaps he'd meant to frighten or repulse her with his confession, but after glimpsing the despair behind the ice-cold facade she felt only the most profound compassion.

'Oh, Khaled,' she said softly. 'All these years... What a terrible burden you've had to bear. But you loved your brother. You didn't mean to hurt him. You don't deserve to be so unhappy.'

He gave a bark of ugly laughter. 'I deserve nothing less than the torment I've suffered every day since.'

'No, you don't.' Her hands unfurled and she pressed their warmth against his chest. His brow creased, his gaze dropping to where her fingers splayed across his shirt. 'It's time to forgive yourself. It's time you had peace,' she said.

His gaze flew back to hers and a violent shudder went through him. His fingers tightened, digging into her soft flesh. 'Lily, you've no concept of all the things I may not have.'

Then his mouth crashed down on hers.

The kiss was wild, not gentle. But she kissed him back, though her lips felt bruised and his grip on her shoulders was only just not painful.

He gave a low, agonised groan and crushed her hard against him. The crutch clattered to the floor as he lifted her from her feet. He carried her to the desk and laid her on it. Papers were scattered. His laptop landed on its side in the chair. The precious photo toppled.

Lily hardly noticed. Their kiss this afternoon had been nothing compared to this. That had been a summer breeze. This was a firestorm of need, obliterating her awareness of anything other than the heat and weight of him stretching over her.

She moaned at the dark pleasure of it and in frustration—because this wasn't enough. She wanted more.

They grappled with each other. Greedy lips and frenzied, groping hands wanting to touch everything, everywhere at once.

He hitched her skirt to her waist, his palms sliding along her bare thighs. She tugged his shirttails free, her fingers finding the warm, silken skin of his back. He sighed into her mouth and sent his hands on more discoveries of their own, reaching between them to pop the buttons of her dress.

His hand slipped beneath the fabric and closed about a lace-covered breast. Her hands flew upwards, fisting in the dark silk of his hair when he wrenched the lace aside and closed his mouth around a tightly budded nipple.

'I'm afraid His Highness is occupied at present. I'll tell him you wish to speak with him, sir.'

Sabir's raised voice came clearly, in English, from the *majlis*.

Khaled lurched away. He'd straightened his shirt and smoothed his disordered hair before she'd even gathered her wits enough to push herself upright. She shuffled her bottom off the edge of the desk and balanced awkwardly on her good leg. With trembling, clumsy fingers she tidied herself, righting her bra, refastening buttons, pushing her dress down.

Khaled set the desk to rights and then, taking her elbow, helped her towards the sofa. He retrieved the crutch, placing it within her reach, and made sure she was seated, with her face, her swollen lips and her flushed cheeks directed away from the door, before he summoned Sabir.

The secretary entered at once. Had he witnessed how they had been practically ravishing each other and retreated to the *majlis* to stand guard? Lily's face flamed.

'Hyde-Wallace?' said Khaled.

'Yes, sir.'

'Gone?'

'Yes, sir.'

A muscle pulsed in Khaled's jaw.

'I'll go now and find him.'

She stared up at him in disbelief. He couldn't confess what he had, kiss her like that, and then simply walk away.

But he avoided her eye and spoke to Sabir. 'Miss Marchant has wrenched her ankle again. I don't want her walking back to her suite unaided. Organise someone to help.'

'There's a wheelchair in the sick bay. I'll have it brought round,' Sabir said.

Once he'd disappeared to make the arrangements Khaled turned to her. He looked ravaged.

'Lily, what I just did was unforgivable.'

His regret rolled over her like a winter fog. She hugged herself, rubbing her shoulders to ward off the chill.

'I have hurt you?' He sounded appalled.

'No.' She swiftly dropped her hands into her lap. 'I'm fine.'

It was a lie. She wasn't fine. Her body raged at the loss of him. Her heart broke for the pain in him. And that voice of experience she'd just ignored completely berated her.

Give of yourself and see what happens. Rejection. Have you learned nothing?

'Lily...' He thrust a hand through his hair and stared at her helplessly. 'I'm sorry,' he said at last. Then spun away, striding unevenly from the room.

Sabir reappeared, quietly announcing that a servant was coming to help her back to her suite. Ever the consummate aide, he didn't press her for an answer, leaving her to her thoughts. Perhaps he understood as well as she just what had happened...

Khaled had confessed his darkest secret to her, but when she'd offered emotional comfort he'd rejected that, taking something entirely more basic. Then he'd fled in shame.

Did a girl need any more humiliating evidence of where she stood in his affections?

Lily closed her eyes and fought back the welling of scalding, bitter tears.

CHAPTER TWELVE

KHALED'S CAR ARRIVED at ten minutes after midnight, gliding through the palace gates with little ceremony. Today was the day of his father's anniversary party. In a few hours the preparations would make this entrance a bustling thorough-fare. For now, a routine snap to attention by the guards and a single aide stepping forward as the car drew to a halt was the extent of his welcome home.

Exactly as he'd ordered.

He wasn't ready to face his family.

Or the family friends starting to fill the guest suites.

Or the single occupant of the most comfortable guest suite of all.

It was almost a month since he'd absented himself from his home to keep Lily safe. Hoping, too, that physical dis-tance would lessen the craving he felt for her.

It had not.

Desire still burned like a fever in his blood. As fiery now as when he'd left her that evening, with the taste of her on his lips and the imprint of her hot little hands on his skin.

Every day, even though he'd plunged into work, his wak-ing moments had been dogged by thoughts of her, and when he'd slept—if he'd slept—she'd haunted his dreams, too. He'd woken sweating, frustrated, and more than once to embarrassingly sticky sheets after the dreams had felt viv-idly, erotically real.

Hot, too, was his shame, seething like a nest of vipers in his belly.

To have treated Lily as he had—a woman effectively under his protection—simply because she'd had the temerity to accuse him of feeling no guilt… How could she have known it was carved across his heart? Touching a wound so raw he'd lashed out, wanting to humble her. A female less than half his size, injured and in pain.

May God forgive him.

But even that wasn't the worst of it. That was not the memory that made his skin crawl with utter self-loathing. He'd saved that for the final tawdry act…the most shaming thing of all.

When he'd confessed his darkest secret she hadn't turned away in revulsion. She'd offered him compassion and comfort. And how had he responded? By almost ravishing her on his desk.

No matter that she'd been eager beneath him, her hands tugging at his clothes. He had known the risks, what might have happened if George had discovered them together. Thank goodness for Sabir's interruption—because even now… Hell, he wasn't sure he'd have stopped without it.

Yeah, searing, gut-wrenching shame.

They'd reached his office. The aide pointed out a number of files awaiting his attention. There was an hour's work there before he retired if he chose.

He ran a palm across his face. When had he last truly rested? Slept for more than a few hours at a time? Sometimes he felt it had been years. But heading to bed with the promise of another night of disturbing dreams did not appeal. He welcomed the prospect of a densely worded report to plough through. It might deaden the clamour in his head.

Dismissing the aide, Khaled fired up his laptop and reached for the first file.

An hour later he was down to the last two. An update on the missing charity funds and the continuing negotiations for the terms of his marriage.

No new evidence had been found to implicate George, and Khaled had done as Lily suggested. Made a noise about how the charity funds were being used, praising Hyde-Wallace for his loyalty and his concern for the Nabhani marshlands. For the time being George couldn't hint at malfeasance without arousing suspicions about how he'd gained that knowledge.

Won over by Khaled's successes in New York, the Council of Families had also rallied round. George was losing his leverage. Meaning he needed to be carefully watched. A cornered animal was dangerous and unpredictable.

As for his marriage? Khaled had told his team to get it done or they'd be looking for new employment. It had worked. He now had water rights on acceptable terms, though his prospective father-in-law continued to hinder reform in the region.

Khaled's hope lay in shape of the seventeen-year-old Crown Prince—a moderniser like himself. Eventually he'd hold the power in Qaydar, and in the meantime he'd be taking the boy's sister to be his wife.

Not the woman he truly desired.

Lily.

What would become of her? Would Nate be there for her? He was all she had.

The thought of her being alone in the world tightened a steel band around Khaled's chest.

He hadn't had George's claims investigated. He couldn't risk it. Word would get out.

His absence from the country had lessened press interest in his mother's guest, and they'd leave her alone completely once he announced his marriage plans. No one would dig any deeper, and Lily's fantasy about her parents could stay intact.

Either way, in less than thirty-six hours he was sending her home. He had no business concerning himself any further in her life.

He closed the laptop. He should try for some sleep. There

was another packed day ahead of him, and at the end of it his father's party.

The corridors were deserted as he made his way back to the Family Wing. Leaving him with the sensation of being the only human creature in the Royal Court.

Alone.

Despite the countless people around him, the life of a prince was a solitary one. Would his marriage remove this crushing loneliness? He imagined Aisha waiting for him in his bed. Then tortured himself by putting Lily there instead, her glorious hair spread across the pillow, her slender arms lifting in welcome as he eased into her.

He crossed the last quadrangle and arrived at the stairs to the first floor of the Family Wing. From across the courtyard he caught the flicker of the TV screen in the family room. His steps faltered.

It couldn't be…?

No. She'd be asleep. Safe in bed.

He ignored the disappointment that flared in his chest. It was becoming familiar and, like his other regrets, he'd learn to live with it. He'd have to.

At this hour it could only be his father. Since his heart attacks he often suffered bouts of insomnia. Perhaps he'd catch him watching re-runs of a melodramatic Nabhani soap. It had recently become the King's guilty addiction.

Feeling in profound need of his father's company, all at once Khaled changed direction, heading for the family room.

Sleep just wouldn't come. It had been difficult enough for the last four weeks, but tonight it was impossible.

The reason was due back at any moment.

Lily pulled a wrap over her silk camisole and shorts and slipped from her suite, meaning to seek fresher air out on the veranda, but somehow making her way to the family room.

She flopped down on the sofa in front of the TV. Watching something light-hearted might help. Stop her wasting time thinking about Khaled. Because his leaving the country to put thousands of miles between them had made it pretty clear how he felt about her.

His absence had also changed the nature of the press interest in her. There'd been some reports, dredging up stories of her mother's death, but she'd been carefully protected from the worst of it and their interest seemed to have moved on to Khaled's appearance in New York.

In a few hours she'd see him again.

The shiver of excitement hit instantly, but she tamped it down. She'd had nearly a month to practise controlling the stormy emotions the man unleashed in her. Plenty of time to think about how she'd conduct herself when they next met.

She'd decided she was going to be polite, but distant, as if nothing of any note had ever passed between them. She would attend Bassam's party and the next day ask, politely but firmly, to go home.

Being here, and being welcomed as part of this family, had been wonderful, but at some point she'd have to return to reality.

She wasn't a child any more, enchanted by fairy tales. Princes didn't sweep nameless girls off their feet and put their needs before everything else.

And she'd be fine—really, she would. She'd always looked after herself before. She could do it again.

The TV was tuned to the local news, in English. Before she could switch programmes there was an announcement of the next segment: a repeat of the Crown Prince's speech to the General Assembly of the United Nations.

Khaled's visit to New York had been a resounding success. Everyone in the palace—family and staff—had talked of little else for the last few days, but she'd not seen the speech before, pleading a headache when the family had gathered to watch the broadcast live, cravenly avoiding any coverage since. She hadn't wanted any reminders of the man.

She should change channels now, but her fingers stalled on the remote.

On screen, the General Assembly appeared. The great hall was full to capacity. Millions more would have watched around the world. Waiting to hear a speech from the enigmatic Crown Prince of Nabhan.

An expectant hush descended as all eyes fell on the heart of that iconic hall: the podium of green marble.

Lily lifted her legs and wrapped her arms tight about them as the camera zoomed in.

Khaled stepped up. His impeccable suit was a sharp dark navy. His tie ice-blue. The white shirt made a stark contrast to his olive skin and haunting grey eyes.

Lily dropped her chin to her knees, curling up tighter.

His deep voice filled the room. The time was now, he said, calling upon the help of the world to build equality and justice for his homeland and beyond. His voice was confident, his message clear. This was Khaled the consummate statesman.

In that darkened room, with only the TV for company as the rest of the palace slept, Lily watched its prince standing alone, winning over the world's most powerful assembly. All the time hiding the terrible burden he bore of guilt and grief. That he'd caused the death of his beloved brother.

She'd bickered with him and snapped at him and caused him endless trouble. She'd railed at him on Nate's behalf when, to Khaled, it must have felt like his most trusted friend had betrayed him. Making him even more alone.

And she hadn't seen it.

She hadn't understood a thing.

Lily's heart thudded once, twice in her chest, and then paused. A second later she shivered as it began beating in the same steady rhythm as before, though nothing, *nothing* would ever be the same again.

Because now she understood—finally, and with an awful clarity. Being polite and distant wasn't going to work.

There'd be no pushing her feelings aside. She'd been fooling herself.

She was already in love.

Completely, hopelessly in love with the Sad Prince.

His own voice greeted him as he approached the family room. Was his father listening to a repeat of his UN speech?

One of the carved double doors stood wide, spilling a glow across the marble floor ahead. The other cast delicate shifting patterns of light through the fretwork panels. They danced across the pale fabric of his shirt as he drew near.

Khaled halted in the shadows as it registered precisely who was listening to his speech. She sat transfixed, watching him deliver the performance of his life.

What was she thinking?

Presidents and prime ministers had called him after he'd left that podium. Pledging their support for his efforts to drive reform in the region. But the only opinion that mattered right now was that of this young woman.

Weeks and oceans of separation had made no difference.

Want slammed into him.

Khaled lifted a hand. His fingers brushed the door's fretwork, tracing the curve of her cheek, the tumble of auburn hair, the bare toes peeking out from beneath her robe.

How beautiful she was—and how forbidden to him.

One step forward and she would see him.

One step back and he could leave unnoticed.

He dropped his hand, and with a strength he hadn't known he possessed he took a step back.

But his shoe scraped against the floor...

There was someone beyond the fretwork of the door. The light from the TV cast patterns across his shirt. Definitely a man. And he was broad of shoulder and tall. Taller than anyone in the palace except Bassam.

But the King wouldn't hover just out of view. He'd come striding in with a breezy greeting, bemoaning her viewing choices, demanding she change channels, making her smile. More than once she'd kept him company in the early hours, watching old movies or re-runs of his favourite soap when neither of them could sleep.

The figure stayed motionless. Watching her.

Not the King. Though just as tall.

The son.

'Khaled…'

His name escaped her on a soft exhaled breath. As if her yearning heart had called directly to him. And now she was on her feet, turning towards that shadowy figure.

Love guided her fingers to loosen the knot on her wrap and let it slip from one shoulder. Cool air hit her sensitised skin. Her nipples peaked.

From the corridor came a long, harsh indrawn breath.

Emboldened, she let the wrap slide again, baring both shoulders.

There was a thud as something landed against the door. A set of fingers appeared, curled around its edge, as if a big body was braced against it.

She heard the faintest low groan. Then all was still.

Had he ever seen anything more lovely? Anything he'd wanted more?

How easy to cross the space between them, gather her up and just this once forget all the things he couldn't have, and didn't deserve, and lose himself in her sweetness?

But they would meet tomorrow publicly at the party, amidst George and his spies. For her safety, he needed her to behave as though she detested him.

He emerged from the shadows. Her expression drew him forward, step after helpless step, until he stood before her.

The light and welcome in her eyes was nearly his undoing. She lifted her hand, placed her palm against his cheek. On tiptoe, she stretched up to kiss his lips. 'Welcome home,' she said.

He fought the driving need to pull her against him and

take them both down onto the sofa. Instead he grasped her wrist and pulled her hand from his face.

'It is not your place to welcome me back. This is not your home. I only came to tell you I shall be making arrangements for you to leave straight after my father's party. Four weeks you've been here. You're on the verge of overstaying your welcome, don't you think?'

He didn't wait for her response. He knew the hurt in her big eyes would destroy him. And how could he explain why he'd rejected her without revealing what she was?

So he turned and walked away, raging with longing and regret, and melted into the darkness, wishing he'd never been there at all.

CHAPTER THIRTEEN

LILY PACED THE veranda outside her rooms, attempting to steady her nerves.

Her evening gown—a chartreuse silk-satin number, and the single most beautiful thing she'd ever worn—whispered across her toes as she walked. Her newly buffed and freshly painted toes.

That afternoon a cadre of hairdressers and beauticians had set up camp in her suite. From the top of her glossy chignon to the soles of her baby-soft feet she'd been primped and preened till she barely recognised the elegant creature they'd created. Even the seamstress had been on hand, to ensure her gown fitted to perfection—the gown Eleanor had insisted she buy the day Khaled had footed the bill.

She should tear it from her body. Go out there clothed in nothing but a bed sheet rather than parade herself wearing anything his money had bought.

But, oh, *this dress…*

From the swirling hem it rose upwards, its heavy silk lovingly skimming her figure and ending just above the swell of her breasts. A drape of fabric slanted from one shoulder to slide provocatively from the other, revealing impossibly tiny shoestring straps. Then came the truly daring part of the design. The dress plunged at the back, to bare her skin almost to the base of her spine.

She made a turn, shivering in excitement as the sultry

evening air drifted across her exposed back. She'd never felt so alluring, so utterly feminine.

Well, good.

Tonight she wanted to be a temptress, a goddess, a veritable man-slayer.

Tonight she wanted to be so desirable that a certain crown prince would be clawing the walls with frustration when he discovered she would never, ever allow him to touch her again. Not if he fell to his knees and begged.

Rejection twice over was enough for a girl to get the message. She wouldn't be risking it a third time.

She sashayed through another turn, shakier this time as she remembered just how it felt to be touched by him…as if a melancholy angel had come down and swept her to heaven.

How pitiful—remembering those moments amongst all the other ones, far less pleasant, when he'd been autocratic, a bully.

Oh, she hated him!

For believing Nate could be a thief.

For blowing hot and cold.

For kissing her with such passion that she'd glimpsed paradise even as he'd snatched it away again.

But she would not be like her mother and throw her heart beneath the feet of a man who didn't care. She would keep her head. She'd get through the next twelve hours and then she'd move on with her life.

With perfect timing, her escort for the evening arrived: a major in the British Army, on attachment to the Queen's staff as equerry. They'd met numerous times over the past weeks and got on well. Tonight he would be someone familiar in a daunting gathering, when the family would be occupied with their royal duties.

The Major took his role seriously, keeping her nerves at bay by recounting hilarious tales on their walk to the party. When the nerves threatened to bubble up as they arrived at the reception rooms he leant closer, telling such a terrible joke that she laughed out loud.

Which was how they made their entrance. An enchanting young woman in a gown of green silk, gliding down the stairs, laughing up into the eyes of her dashing escort.

Stiff with disapproval, Khaled watched Lily's arrival. How she clung to her companion, smiling up at him as if he were the moon and stars and every damn thing that lay between.

Jealousy roiled in his gut, so bitter and sharp he could taste it. He knew the Major, even liked the man, but at that moment he'd have happily smashed a fist into his face.

One word pounded over and over in his skull.

Mine.

It was that dress, shimmering over her body as she moved. It was enough to scramble any sensible thought he had.

Before she gained the bottom step and disappeared into the crowding guests she flicked a glance around the room. He waited, barely breathing, until she found him.

When she did, she held his gaze, then speared him with a look of such electrifying sensuality he stopped breathing altogether.

Then her lashes lowered and her expression soured, as if his very existence repulsed her. That hit him, no doubt as she'd intended, right where all the sexual promise had gathered.

Another mantra started in his head. *She's going home tomorrow.* He only had to navigate the next few hours, then he'd never have to see Lily Marchant again.

The French Ambassador was speaking to him. Khaled plastered on an interested expression and set himself to being sociable.

For an hour he circulated, keeping a precise distance from her. It wasn't hard. He just looked for a group of fawning males—because, invariably, she was right in the middle of one. When she moved, he moved.

His ploy worked well enough, until fate threw an elderly relative in his way. The old man was so obviously thrilled to have the Prince's attention that Khaled lingered longer than he ought to have done. Too late, he became aware of a subtle shift around him, of heads turning, conversations pausing.

He looked up and the reason for their interest became clear.

For there Lily stood. Beautiful. Bristling with hostility.

'Good evening, Your Highness,' she said, sinking into an over-deep curtsy.

He marvelled at how she made such a respectful gesture practically drip disdain.

She rose up, haughty as an empress. Her proud chin lifted. Her neck long. He wanted to press his mouth to it and taste every inch.

'A wonderful party…is it not, *sir*?'

More contempt. For 'sir' he heard *Something unpleasant that lurks beneath a rock.* Aware they were surrounded by dozens of avid observers, not least of whom was Hyde-Wallace, he tried to keep the conversation pleasant.

'I'm glad you're enjoying—'

'The French Ambassador was just saying how glorious everything looks tonight,' she said brightly. 'We agreed the florists have excelled themselves.'

'I think my mother—'

'Though of course it's their job. Oh, look. There's his wife! I really must ask where she found that fabulous gown.'

She spun away without so much as a by-your-leave, dragging her escort with her. She didn't give a damn about that woman's gown. She'd moved in exactly the opposite direction.

Over her head, the equerry sent him a pained look, part apology, part sympathy.

Khaled was left to seethe. She'd snubbed him in every way possible. Breaking protocol by speaking to him before he'd addressed her, interrupting him, and then walking away instead of waiting politely for him to move off first.

And as he wrestled with which impertinence to be most offended by she presented him with the final insult: a view of her departing back.

His mouth went dry. From that angle it was as if the dazzling dress had vanished and there was nothing but delicate spine and endless bare flesh. A male guest leant in to hear something she'd said, placing his hand just where the fabric ended and her naked skin began.

Anger, jealousy and desire churned into a lethal cocktail, and a menacing, barely human sound rumbled up from Khaled's chest.

Eleanor arrived beside him. 'I know you two aren't an item any more,' she said. 'But I do hope you haven't said something to upset Lily?'

'*Me* upset *her*?' It took every atom of self-control he possessed to not tell his beloved, interfering mother to go to hell.

'I wouldn't want her evening spoiled. She's been magnificent tonight. Everyone's talking about her.' Eleanor's gaze rested on Lily. 'Watching her work the room, you'd think she was born to it.'

Khaled snorted. 'It's only one night. Doing it day after day is the real test.'

'Oh, I suspect Lily is a natural. She's charming everyone.'

'Not quite everyone,' he muttered. 'I'm sorry, but I'm required elsewhere. I'm expecting a call. I've made my apologies to Father.'

Her face fell. 'But you've already worked so many hours today.' She placed a hand on his arm. 'Perhaps you could come back later for the firework display? It's supposed to be particularly dramatic this year.'

Not if he could help it. He'd had his fill of drama for one evening.

An hour later, his call concluded, he sat alone in a darkened anteroom. Sprawled on a sofa, head thrown back, he was quietly fuming.

It had been a failed conversation and it was his fault. He'd been distracted and short-tempered when he should have been conciliatory and diplomatic. He hadn't been able to focus. All he'd been able to think of was Lily in that stunning dress. Surrounded by men feasting their unworthy eyes on her, probably having the same lascivious thoughts he was. He couldn't stand it.

He heard the finale of the evening getting under way in the parade ground. Every year local schoolchildren laid on a musical extravaganza for the King. Massed drums, pipers and scores of dancers performed traditional Nabhani songs. Afterwards fireworks would be set off from barges in the bay, for everyone across the city to enjoy. Guests and staff alike would be crowding into every vantage point, leaving most of the palace deserted.

Thank God for that, at least. He was in no mood for company.

A light step fell in the doorway.

He lifted his head to see a figure slipping into the room. In a shaft of lamplight from the courtyard he caught a flash of green silk and an expanse of pale skin.

Beneath his breath, he cursed.

Unaware she had an audience, Lily bent to slip off her shoes, groaning as her bare soles made contact with the marble tiles. There was such an erotic quality to the sound Khaled's entire body tightened.

The drumming from the parade ground grew more thunderous, with the pipes picking up in a mesmerising melody, and—heaven help him—she began swaying her luscious behind in time with the rhythm. Her hands joined in, floating upwards. Her spine arched, her head fell back, and she abandoned herself to a sensuous dance that reignited every forbidden fantasy he'd had about this woman.

Another step sounded outside. A heavy tread. Male.

His gaze snapped to the doorway.

She was meeting someone. Right under his nose.

Not in this lifetime.

Blind jealousy propelled Khaled to his feet and across the room before his rational mind had time to stop him.

A hand across her mouth stifled the scream before Lily could make it. An arm lifted her clean off her feet as she was swept backwards to the rear exit of the room.

She struggled—until a growled, 'Be still!' identified her captor and her fear became righteous anger instead.

She'd slipped away from the party to have a few minutes in which she could stop smiling and pretending that her heart wasn't breaking.

Now the very cause of her misery was right here, hauling her about like a piece of baggage.

Khaled dumped her back on her feet, manacled her wrist with his fingers and set off down the deserted corridor, towing her behind him.

She yanked at her trapped arm. 'Let go of me!'

'No.'

His scowling gaze fixed forward, his robes billowing around him as he walked, he looked every inch the desert prince: proud, vital, and maddeningly handsome.

Lily's heart skipped a beat.

She was weak, weak, *weak*—wanting him even while he was behaving like a tyrant.

At the party she'd searched for him as subtly as she could. Her heart squeezing when she'd spotted his imposing figure, spectacular in his robes, but not by so much as a flicker of recognition had he acknowledged her. It was pride and hurt that had made her send him that smouldering look. When she'd seen desire flare in his eyes she'd deliberately looked away, hoping she'd left him burning with need.

She'd wanted to shake that cool façade.

Then she'd wanted to forget him entirely.

'I'm not going anywhere with you.' She stopped dead.

Without missing a step he carried on, dragging her with him. She only just kept her feet.

Through empty corridors they went. Across courtyards echoing to the thunder of fireworks as the display began. Past placid pools reflecting the starbursts overhead. Into the Family Wing he marched her, then up the stairs, and along the veranda, with its romantic lanterns and vista of lush trees below. He ignored it all, only stopping when they arrived at her suite. He pulled her inside it, kicking the door shut behind them, before finally throwing her arm from him in disgust.

Lily rubbed at her wrist while he prowled back and forth, his furious stare fixed on her bedroom, where the lamps were lit and the bed turned down ready for her return.

'So what have I done this time?' she snapped.

He turned towards her.

'You flaunt yourself all evening. Treat me with blatant disrespect. And then dare ask how you have transgressed?'

Flaunt herself? She'd quit the party to get *away* from male attention.

She stamped her foot in frustration. There was a soft slapping sound. She'd left her shoes behind.

He snorted. 'Bare feet, green dress, bad behaviour. All we need now is something for you to steal and we'll be back where we started.'

She glared at him. 'You're despicable.'

'I'm merely stating facts.'

'Facts? The facts are that I did nothing but try to be pleasant to your father's guests. I smiled. I chatted. I attempted to be charming. You should try it sometimes. It'd be a big improvement on how you normally conduct yourself.'

That landed a blow.

His cheekbones flared red. 'You'll curb that insolent tongue—or, so help me, I will take you across my knee.'

'You could try,' she flung back at him.

'Do not challenge me.' He took a step closer.

'Then don't threaten me.' She stepped nearer, too.

His eyes, diamond-hard, glittered down on her. 'Have a care,' he cautioned, 'and remember who you're speaking to.'

'Oh, I'm sorry.' She dipped into her second mocking curtsy of the night. 'God forbid that anyone should point out when you're behaving badly, Your High and Mightiness.'

He moved lightning-fast, grabbing her waist, hauling her against him. 'Damn it. You will show me some respect.'

'I'll do that when you behave in a manner that earns it,' she snapped.

His eyes flashed. He was breathing hard. His whole body vibrated with anger.

'Woman,' he growled, 'this time you go too far.'

And his mouth crashed down on hers.

Oh, no. He was not going to drag her about, accuse her of being a shameless flirt, and then expect to kiss her into submission.

She struggled against him and the onslaught of his lips. 'No! You didn't want me last night. Now I don't want you.'

He lifted his head, shot a tormented glance at her bed. When he looked back his expression was one of raw need.

'Lily…' he groaned. 'For the love of God. Kiss me.'

That plea was her undoing. That and the hunger in his eyes, practically eating her alive.

He wasn't trying to punish her. He wanted her.

Everything soft and feminine in her responded. Her own need burst into life inside her. Her breasts ached. Her nipples peaked. Between her legs she was damp.

Realisation dawned. Last night he'd rejected her not because he didn't want her, but because he wouldn't allow himself to have her, to be happy.

Her hands lifted, ripping the *thurgal* and the white *ghutrah* from his head. She plunged her fingers into his hair. His mouth covered hers again, then moved lower, along her throat, her collarbone. Licking, nipping, teasing, right to the swell of her breast.

In ecstasy, she arched against him. Her dress slipped to her waist. He'd lowered the zip. When? How? She'd felt nothing but the blazing delight of his mouth and fingers moving over her skin.

The stunning dress fell from her hips to pool at their feet. He lifted her clear, his mouth back on hers. Her naked breasts, belly, thighs…all were crushed against him.

A small, quiet voice urged caution, but it was too late. She was lost to reason. She let him carry her to the bed. Tumble them both onto it.

Desperate to touch him, she pushed the gauzy black *bisht*

off his shoulders and began wrestling with the buttons of his *dishdasha*. He simply dragged everything over his head, flinging it all to the floor in a wild tangle. He disposed of his shoes and underwear, then stretched out over her.

He was stunning. Golden-skinned, exquisitely muscled…

Lily blinked.

Big.

The glide of his hands distracted her, slipping beneath her behind, lifting her clear of the bed so he could ease her knickers down her legs. He tossed them aside.

Panting in little staccato breaths, she squirmed as his hot gaze roved her naked body.

'Beautiful,' he breathed, sliding a hand to her thigh, lifting it, opening her up to him.

With a flex of his hips he pushed into her.

Lily cried out.

It hurt.

She was shocked at how much.

Startled understanding flared in his eyes. He knew now that she had lied about her experience.

He began easing back.

'No, don't stop…make love to me… Khaled, please.' The words tumbled out as she lifted her hips, offering herself to him, dragging his head down to hers, kissing him over and over.

'Not like this. I'll hurt you,' he said roughly against her mouth.

'I don't care.'

'But I do.' He captured a hand and planted a kiss in her palm. '*Habiba*, hush. I'm not going anywhere. But we're going to take this slowly.'

He swept a tangle of hair from her brow and placed his lips there instead, then over her eyes, across her cheek, soothing her, calming her. He found the tender spot beneath her ear and sucked softly. She shuddered as lust surged through her.

His head went lower and his mouth fastened on her

breast, taking a nipple between his teeth. He bit down and
Lily moaned.

Warm hands floated along her flank, over her belly then
one slid between her thighs.

A gentle exploration at first. Delicate, enticing.

Not enough. She moved against him. A finger slid inside her, then a second, moving gently back and forth until
she was slick and juicy and grinding shamelessly into the
heel of his hand.

Suddenly his fingers were gone, and in one swift movement he was inside her.

The sharp pain stole her breath, but he held absolutely
still, giving her time to adjust to his body inside hers.

'Okay?'

The look of tender concern melted her heart. She nodded.

He withdrew, then eased himself back into her. And
waited.

The tightly corded muscles of his neck told her what this
restraint was costing him. But the ache had lessened and
the feeling of fullness was…good.

He thrust again. Deeper.

The ache was giving way to a new raft of sensations.

Little tremors racked her as he increased the pace. Waves
of pleasure that ebbed and flowed and built higher with
every pass of his body inside hers. His hands caressed her,
held her, guided her. And his mouth…oh, the glory of his
mouth. Against her own, at her neck, on her breasts. She
whimpered and sighed and moaned as he took her higher
and higher.

She sensed him losing control and loved it. Loved watching his face twist in sweet anguish as pleasure ripped
through him, too. Loved how his movements became more
urgent, how his fingers curled through hers and clung on.
And the storm in his eyes as he held her gaze sent her heart
soaring.

All the pain of rejection became meaningless, sunk beneath the wondrous knowledge that she'd brought him to

this. To the soul-wrenching groan and the spurt of heat low in her belly as he poured himself into her.

And that was when bright, blinding pleasure overtook her.

On a long, keening cry, Lily threw back her head and convulsed around him.

Khaled lay there, shaken, his heart thundering wildly in his chest. He'd never been like that before at the end. So out of control.

'*Habiba?*' He raised his head. 'I'm sorry. Did I hurt you?'

She brushed her knuckles across his cheek. 'It's okay. I'm good.'

He leant into that caress, felt her forgiveness pouring balm over this new guilt, and deep inside a fissure appeared in that older knot of self-loathing.

She began wriggling, squirming to get out from beneath him. He lifted himself up. Let her push him on to his back. Then she knelt beside him, staring at his torso and his sex as if she wanted to devour him. He'd let her.

She moved over him, her glorious hair trailing like silk over his shoulder. She pressed her lips to his collarbone, across his sternum, then took a tight nipple between her teeth.

He groaned. She kissed the little hurt she'd made and sent him the smile of a courtesan.

His fists clenched in the sheets.

This was pure madness.

Wrong to have dragged her back to this room.

Even worse to stay. He should leave now. But he could no more do that than tell his heart to cease beating.

She went lower, over his abdomen, using her lips and her tongue to explore each ridge of muscle with tormenting thoroughness. Finally, with a hum of pleasure, she took him into her mouth, tasting them both with a sweep of her tongue that sent his hands into her hair.

Her eyes held his as she worked him. Learning how to

please him. Teasing him, testing him. Driving him to the edge of sanity. He stopped her before he lost the power to control anything. She sent him that smile again and, as if she'd been savouring a feast, licked her lips.

The minx.

Well, two could play at that game.

He rolled on top of her, pinning her down, kissing her breasts, nuzzling the soft flesh, lapping at each distended nipple. Excited by her moans of pleasure, he kissed lower and lower, to the curls between her thighs.

She was honey-sweet. Like nothing he'd ever tasted. He couldn't get enough. He kissed, he licked, he suckled the little bud at the very heart of her.

She bucked and writhed but he held her down with a hand splayed across her belly. Watching her come apart, hearing her broken little cries, was the most erotic thing he'd ever witnessed. Oh, how he wanted this woman.

He rose to his knees, grasped her hips and shoved into her, groaning as the last of her orgasm pulsed around him.

She'd been a virgin. He should be more gentle. But he couldn't. He'd never known such abandon.

A wild joy leapt in his chest. *Mine*, he thought, fiercely. *Truly mine.* Something pure and good. Completely untainted by years of self-loathing.

That new fissure cracked wider.

He thrust again, and Lily arched beneath him on a long sigh of bliss. With a smile—a dazzling sunshine smile she'd never gifted him before—she placed her hand on his chest, over his heart, and lifted her hips. Giving herself to him so completely he felt that cold, unyielding part of him finally shatter into pieces and knew he was changed for ever.

Love, he thought, half dazed. *It's love. I love her.*

Trembling now, he lay over her, crushing her into the mattress, desperate to imprint himself on every inch of her. His sweat bathed her body, his seed was in her mouth and in her womb, but it wasn't enough. He wanted to be the very air she breathed. He wanted to be lodged indelibly in her heart. He wanted her as changed as he was.

'Lily…' he breathed. Like a vow.

Then he sealed her lips with his and set about seducing her all over again.

Her hands dug into his buttocks, pulling him in closer. Her hips rose up to meet his. 'More,' she moaned, urging him on.

And all finesse forgotten, pumping hard and fast, he answered that siren call. Utterly lost in her.

CHAPTER FOURTEEN

THE STEADY *THUMP-THUMP* against her ear was soothing. Khaled's heartbeat, and the slow fall and rise of his chest as he slept, was not what woke her. That was the far-off whir of a helicopter, ferrying away the last of the party guests.

The noise disappeared into the night and Lily nestled closer. Khaled's arms enclosed her, his chin rested on top of her head. Whatever came next could wait until tomorrow. For now, she was cocooned in happiness.

She pressed her lips to his chest, laid her cheek on that same spot, and drifted back to sleep.

When she woke again the noise was closer. This time from outside her rooms. Someone was at the door.

She stirred in Khaled's arms, about to wake him.

'It's all right. I hear it.' He pushed up to an elbow as another knock sounded, more urgent.

'Put on your wrap,' he whispered, 'and go and see who it is.'

In the sitting room, she scooped up his *ghutrah* and black *agal* and tucked them away from view. Her discarded dress she laid neatly over the sofa, as if removed when she undressed herself, not stripped away by the hands of a lover.

She was no fool. The Prince being found in her rooms would be scandalous.

She ran her hands through her tangled hair, tightened her wrap, then cracked open the door.

On the other side, his expression grave, stood Sabir.

'Miss Marchant, forgive me. I must urgently find His Highness.'

Should she to lie to his secretary? 'He's… He's…'

'Here.'

Khaled emerged from the bedroom, almost dressed, pulling on the gauzy black *bisht*, his face just as shadowed. 'What is it?'

The secretary entered the suite, quietly closing the door behind him.

'Sir, it's your father. He collapsed in his rooms twenty minutes ago.'

Lily gasped, her face lifting to Khaled's.

A muscle flexed in his jaw. 'How bad is it?'

'The doctors don't know yet, sir. He's being helicoptered to hospital. The Queen is with him.'

The noise Lily had heard. Not the departure of happy guests but Bassam, that kind, wonderful man, being rushed to Emergency.

'Your mother asks that you follow with the Princesses,' Sabir said.

Eleanor was gathering the family. She must fear the worst. Lily's heart ached for them. And for the man beside her most of all, with that terrible new fear in his eyes.

'How can I help?' She laid a hand on his arm. 'Shall I come with you? I could be with the girls?'

'No, it wouldn't be appropriate.' He dismissed her offer without a glance, but then, on a shuddering breath, snatched her close, kissing her brow, softening the blow. 'But thank you for your kindness. Stay here. I'll send someone to you later. There are things between us to discuss.'

He offered only that cryptic comment. So she pressed her hands to his chest, giving comfort in the only way she could.

Until he was gone, striding away, and Sabir, with a bow, closed the door after them.

It was three in the morning—hours before the palace would be up—but going back to sleep would be impossible.

Lily perched on her bed and slid a hand into the tangle
of sheets. Still warm from their bodies. Hers melted at the
memory of what they'd done together, how he'd unravelled
for her.

There are things between us to discuss.

A stunning notion had her on her feet, pacing the room.
Was she seriously imagining Khaled might propose to her?
How wrong to be thinking of her own happiness when Bas-
sam might be fighting for his life. But she couldn't help it.
Last night had changed everything.

Khaled kept everyone at a distance. Even his family.
He'd woven a near impenetrable barrier about himself. But
when he'd sunk into her that final time there had been such
a fragile joy in his eyes she'd known he'd surrendered an
essential piece of himself to her.

For now, she'd wait as asked, and pray that Bassam would
recover.

She showered, dressed, set her suite to rights. A servant
normally did this, but today she resorted to housekeeper
mode, needing to be busy.

She found a TV documentary about the Nabhani coast-
line. Two hours passed during which she stared at a screen
filled with dolphins and whale sharks and took in almost
nothing.

The sky lightened and early-morning sunshine poured
in through her windows, filling the room with a brightness
and hope she desperately clung to. A teary-eyed servant arrived with a breakfast tray, but no news.

The palace staff were waiting. Like her.

She nibbled on fruit, sipped tea, but had no real appetite.
She was too worried for Khaled, desperate to be with him,
to comfort him, support him.

Beneath a cushion she spied his neatly folded *ghutrah*.
She drew it out and lifted it to her cheek, inhaling its beloved hint of citrus and spice.

She must have dozed, because suddenly she was jerking
upright as the phone in her suite rang.

'I see the Prince hasn't given you up.'

Waking from dreams of Khaled, the unexpected voice confused her.

'Excuse me?'

'Don't bother denying it,' said George Hyde-Wallace. 'I know he spent the night rutting in your bed. But you should know he can't marry you.'

She fought off the remnants of sleep.

'As Leader of the Council of Families, when I see our future king being beguiled by an unsuitable woman, I must act.'

Unsuitable? That woke her up. 'I'm the granddaughter of a duke.'

'Biological granddaughter only, I'm afraid. Your father didn't bother to check that his wedding was legal. He wasn't married in the eyes of the law, which makes you illegitimate—and so barred from ever being our Queen. In short, you are entirely ineligible.'

Shock silenced her. That cherished image of her father, the fact that he'd loved her mother enough to whisk her away to a tropical beach for their ceremony. Was even that a lie?

'Imagine the scandal,' George drawled. 'The great name of Azir being linked with a woman of questionable birth. There would be a constitutional crisis. It might even destroy the monarchy. But you can prevent that if you do as I say.'

She wanted to denounce him for the scheming traitor he was, but she had to think of Khaled and his family.

'What do you want me to do?'

'The King may not last the day, and by nightfall your lover might be our new monarch.'

Oh, Bassam. Lily squeezed her eyes shut against the sting of tears.

'There must be no hint of scandal…of anything that might throw a shadow on the Prince taking the throne. If you leave now, I'll make sure what I've discovered never reaches the press. A car will be on the palace forecourt in ten minutes to take you to the airport. You have a seat booked on the next flight to London. Be on it.'

Whatever rosy future she'd hoped for, she knew she had to walk away and spare the royal family the trauma of a scandal. Even if that meant never seeing Khaled again.

Somehow keeping the heartbreak out of her voice, she said, 'Okay, I'll do it.'

'A wise decision. Let's just say a foreign national getting caught up in all this would be…inconvenient.'

There was no chance for her to ask what that meant. George had cut the connection.

Numb with shock, Lily replaced the receiver, then realised she still held Khaled's *ghutrah*, crushed in her other hand. The once crisp white cotton was crumpled and soiled. Now it was no better than a rag.

No longer fit for a prince.

She had only ten minutes before that car arrived, and she was grateful. Less time to dwell on what she'd just learned. She focused instead on preparing to leave.

She was already dressed in jeans and a T-shirt. While Khaled had been in the States her bank card had been returned, and her passport delivered from London. She tucked them into her back pocket now. She grabbed a sweater for the plane, a jacket for travelling through London, and she was ready.

Everything else she left. Including the dress she'd first arrived in. She'd never wear it again. The memories would be too painful. Even the clothes now on her back she'd donate to a women's refuge. She wanted no reminders of her time here.

She sat down to pen a note to Eleanor, thanking her for all her kindness and explaining why she'd had to leave so suddenly. Something about it being too uncomfortable for her now Khaled was home again and wanting to give the family space while the King was ill…

It wasn't entirely untrue.

She looked up at the knock on her door. Time to leave already? Her stomach twisted.

But it was Sabir, and all other thoughts fled as she took in the secretary's anxious expression.

'No, madam, please do not upset yourself,' Sabir quickly reassured her. 'His Majesty is still poorly but doing better than expected. The doctors think he over-exerted himself at the party. He danced with the schoolchildren…' He gave a small smile. 'He did not want to disappoint them. It's a tradition that he does so every year.'

She slumped in relief. 'Is the family still with him?'

'Yes, madam.'

'And the Prince?' she asked tentatively. 'How is he?'

'He is naturally much relieved.' Sabir suddenly looked discomforted. 'But he has sent me to talk to you. May I come in?'

There are things between us to discuss.

Whatever they were made little difference now. Even if Khaled had been thinking of proposing to her she couldn't accept.

Lily walked back to the sofas and sat down, gesturing to the one opposite hers. He followed her and sank down, looking deeply troubled. Nothing like the normally calm Sabir.

'His Highness has first asked me to convey to you the extremely high regard in which he holds you,' he began. 'How in the short time since you have been reacquainted you have come to mean a great deal to him.' He paused, his hands working nervously around the leather binder he carried. 'But he regrets that he is unable to make you any formal offer. Instead he has an alternative arrangement.'

A 'formal offer' being a proposal of marriage? Here she was, about to make the grand gesture and sacrifice her happiness to keep him safe, and he wasn't about to offer his hand anyway.

The last of Lily's hopes withered around her.

'A private jet is standing by to take you to Greece,' Sabir said. 'His Highness has a villa on an island there which from now on will be permanently at your disposal. He will join you when he can, though at the moment he can't say when that will be. In the longer term, should you wish it, a property may be organised elsewhere, providing it is discreet and within easy distance of his usual travel routes. It cannot, of course, be in Nabhan.'

Sabir opened the binder and withdrew a sheet of paper, placing it on the coffee table between them.

'In addition to the property, this is the sum that will be settled on you per annum.'

She tried to make sense of the astonishing figure. More each year than she could hope to earn in a lifetime.

'He was most insistent that I make it clear you will want for nothing ever again.'

Except her self-respect.

Beyond Sabir, the door to her bedroom stood open—the room where Khaled had made love to her as if she were precious to him. Say yes and she'd see him, touch him, be held by him again. If there was no marriage who'd care that she was illegitimate? George's threats had become meaningless.

For a heartbreaking few seconds she actually considered it. Sacrificing everything to take the life he offered her.

But what life? a stark voice asked her.

Because she knew exactly what his offer meant.

Never again would she hold her head up and walk through the palace, sit with Eleanor and the twins in her sunny sitting room or keep Bassam company in the wee small hours when neither of them could sleep.

As for seeing Khaled... It would be like last night. Snatched moments, secret assignations. A life lived in the shadows. Never would she be publicly acknowledged, but everyone would know what she was, and behind her back they would call her by that name.

Mistress.

Or, worse.

Because she'd be complicit in making Khaled an

adulterer, his new wife cheated on from the start. That poor woman...

And where would she truly be in his list of priorities? After his wife, after his family, after his country? He wasn't even choosing her second, and when he tired of her, and the difficulties of conducting such a relationship, what then? There'd be a pay-off—generous, no doubt—but she would be permanently dropped from his life. To do what? With the only skills on her CV earned while lying on her back?

She was her mother's daughter after all. Giving her heart to a man only to discover she wasn't that important to him. Because if she were Khaled would never have offered something that served his needs entirely at the expense of hers.

There had been no surrender last night. At least not from him. He'd just been sampling the wares to see if they would suit his purpose. Taking her to bed with no thought of the consequences for her.

Consequences? Lily's stomach flipped. They hadn't used any kind of protection. She hadn't given it a moment's thought. Her hand went reflexively to her belly.

'And if...if there were any children?'

Sabir looked even more uncomfortable.

'Sadly, they could not be publicly recognised, but they would know their father.'

No, they would not. She would not be a party to that. Hiding sweet, blameless babies away like dirty little secrets. No matter how much she loved their father.

She buried her face in her hands as a wave of something like grief tore through her. Was this how her mother had felt? Was it this agony that had made her give up on life and drink herself to death?

But she was not her mother. She was stronger. She could survive on her own and she was definitely worth more than a life lived skulking in secret.

She'd decline Khaled's shameful offer because Lily Marchant was done with being second-best.

She lifted her head. 'The flight to Greece—can it be re-arranged to take me home to London, instead?'

Sabir's expression brightened. 'Yes, Miss Marchant. It can.'

'And how soon can I leave?'

'As soon as you wish it.' He stood, purposeful and efficient Sabir again. 'I'll make the arrangements at once.'

'You won't get into trouble?'

He sent her a rueful look. 'You must let me worry about that, madam.' He was at the door when he turned back to her. 'This recent offer notwithstanding, His Highness is a good man.'

She gazed up at him. 'I'm going to miss you, Sabir.'

'And I shall miss you, and how the Prince has been with you here.'

Her mouth lifted in a small, sad smile. 'Impossible, you mean?'

'No, madam. Alive. More alive than I have ever seen him.'

A lump of raw anguish knotted her throat. 'Look after him for me, won't you?' she whispered.

Nonsensical though that was, Sabir, bless him, answered as if it mattered. 'Always. You have my word on it.'

With that he gave her a low bow that she'd only ever seen him use with the King and Queen. The highest mark of respect he could bestow upon her. And that little kindness helped bolster her resolve more than he knew, because as he left, taking with him her last link to his master, and her world turned empty and grey, she almost ran after him, to tell him she'd changed her mind. But that bow reminded her that to some she was worthy of respect. Worthy of more than a life lived as man's plaything. However exalted the man himself might be.

Khaled's royal head gear still sat on the sofa beside her. The crumpled white cloth and the roped circlet taunted her. To think a few hours ago she'd imagined their owner might be about to make her his princess! What planet had she been living on?

She stood, leaving them where they lay. They were meaningless to her now.

George's promised car would be waiting.

Let it. She was leaving anyway. What did it matter how? He had spies who'd informed him that she and Khaled had been together last night. Let him find out she'd left in the same underhand way.

She wandered to the window, to gaze one last time at the dazzling view—another thing she knew would haunt her dreams in the years to come—and to wait for Sabir's call.

It took her a few seconds to register that the soldiers patrolling the dunes today were much closer than usual. Almost in the palace grounds. Several of them were moving together and crouched low. That wasn't normal either. Was this an exercise?

Icy fingers crawled along at Lily's spine. The men were masked, their weapons raised.

What had George said? A foreign national getting caught up in this would be inconvenient? Was this what he'd meant? Was he launching an attack on the palace itself?

The security in this part of the Family Wing was minimal, to allow everyone their privacy. If they'd already got past the perimeter guards, how easily might those men below reach the Royal Court itself?

In the next breath, Lily was sprinting along the veranda. She had to warn Sabir and the rest of the staff.

At the entrance lobby, she skidded to a halt. Two of the men were already inside, creeping from the direction of the garden. Behind them was a third figure, taller, leaner, but as intimidating as the mercenaries, in head-to-toe black combat gear. He pulled off his mask as he saw her.

George Hyde-Wallace was brazen enough to join the attack himself.

'Still here?' he said. 'How tiresome you Marchants are. Always getting in the way.'

His thugs aimed their weapons at her chest. Lily froze, trying to control her terror and *think*.

'If only he'd given you up and married Aisha, as I wanted. You'd have been spared this.' He stalked towards her. 'Too late now. Your fate is tied to his.'

The rattle of gunfire sounded from the Royal Court. Lily's heart almost stopped.

'Yes. You're witnessing a coup,' George said, almost casually. 'At this moment my men are at the hospital, removing your lover and his family from power. In the next hour they'll be on a flight out and heading into exile.'

Exile. Not execution. It was a sliver of hope amidst the horror. Khaled might survive this.

'You'd betray the family and the country that have given you everything?' she said. 'You're disgusting.'

George lashed out so fast there was no time to flinch. The back of his hand smashed into her cheek and sent her sprawling sideways. Her head caught on a side table as she went down. Pain exploded in her temple…the coppery tang of blood spilled over her lips.

He grabbed her shoulders and hauled her to her knees, pushing his face into hers. 'And you are nothing but a common harlot,' he snarled.

Through the agony in her jaw, the near-paralysing fear and the raw ache in her heart, she summoned what courage she had to lift her head and face him. 'Better a harlot than a filthy traitor.'

He flung her from him as if she was something foul he'd been obliged to touch. 'I wonder how the Prince could bear to entangle himself with you. Being aware of the stain you would be on his family.'

A new anguish tore at her. Khaled knew about her parents…?

'Oh, didn't I mention it?' George said with a reptilian smile. 'I told him before he left for America. Why do you think he departed so suddenly?'

Because he'd discovered she was only good enough to warm his bed and hadn't even cared enough to explain why.

Lily's heart cracked wide open.

There was a shout from behind them and a lone figure appeared at the entrance to the Royal Court.

A man supposed to be on his way to a life of exile.

But instead there he stood, like an avenging angel. More beautiful than she'd ever seen him and never more out of reach.

'Azir…' George hissed, and a lifetime of loathing was crammed into that name.

'As you see,' Khaled said.

His ice-cold gaze raked the scene: Lily crumpled on the floor, bloody and bruised, George towering over her.

'Your plot has failed and you're finished—but touch the woman again and you'll die where you stand.'

George's face turned puce and veins bulged in his forehead. In a flash of movement he whipped a revolver from his belt, hauled Lily upwards, and jammed the gun into her bruised temple.

'You want the whore?' he said, clamping his other hand around her throat. 'Well, come and get her.'

His two mercenaries drew in beside him. Like George, they were using Lily's body as cover.

'It's over, man,' Khaled said quietly. 'You've nowhere to go. Think of your wife. Think of your sons.'

George stepped back, dragging Lily with him. 'My sons? They were too afraid to be a part of this. What use are they to me now?'

Khaled matched his every step. Talking all the while as Rais and his men fanned out, cutting off any escape route.

'Your sons aren't here because they're ashamed of you and what you've become. They're the ones who called to warn me of your attack.'

There was a low, menacing growl from the man beside her. She wanted to scream at Khaled to stop. Stop baiting him. But the fingers wrapped around her throat had tightened. All she could do was watch in horror as Khaled came closer.

Then her hip glanced off another side table. She remembered there was a vase of flowers on it. She stretched out, groping for it. Her fingers found the rim and she heaved it upwards, aiming at George's head. It was only a glancing blow, but the drench of cold water and the falling stems covering them both loosened his grip just enough for her to wrench free.

She had split seconds while George pushed sodden hair from his eyes. She couldn't hope to wrestle his gun away or to disarm his two guards. She had one thing. The protection of her body.

Praying that her shaking legs would support her, Lily took off. Aiming straight for Khaled.

He bellowed at her to get down. When she was two paces out he sidestepped, moving to snatch her to safety behind him.

No.

She launched herself straight at his chest.

Their eyes locked. In his was such a hollowed-out terror she almost believed he cared for her. But not enough to put her needs first, to be honest with her and let her go.

Her heart shattered all over again just as two pistol shots sounded behind her.

Something slammed into her back. Hard. The extra momentum was enough to send Khaled flailing backwards, and her body went down with him.

There was the rattle of automatic weapons, and strangled cries as booted feet pounded by.

Urgent hands turned her onto her side, pressed against her back. A voice yelled her name over and over, begging her to stay with him.

Stay with him?

'Why? You don't really want me,' she said out loud…or perhaps not. It was getting harder to breathe and, though she tried, she couldn't keep her eyes open.

George must have hit her harder than she'd thought. Her mouth was filling with blood and everything else was blurred, coming from further and further away.

At last only one thing punctured the gathering gloom: an unearthly, inhuman roar sounding next to her, like an animal in unspeakable pain.

Then there was nothing but the quiet and the dark and Lily, unbearably weary and sad, gave herself up to it.

CHAPTER FIFTEEN

THERE WAS A drift of voices. Lily tried to focus. Was she awake or dreaming? It was so hard to tell.

'Sir, you cannot remain in this room all the time. The patient is in my care and I must insist you leave.'

A woman was speaking. There was an indefinable accent to her English, but no mistaking the determined tone.

'Come on, mate. It's been nearly three days.'

This from a man, gently cajoling.

'The Sister is right. It won't hurt to step out for a while.'

'I will not.'

The third voice—also male, but not in the least conciliatory—sent a ripple of unease through Lily. Who was he that she should be afraid of him?

'I have to be here when she wakes.'

Now he sounded desperate.

'I have to be, Nate.'

Nate.

Her head felt stuffed with cotton wool, her body equally feeble, but Lily summoned what strength she had and forced her eyelids open.

Three figures swam into view.

Nate was here. Whoever that other man was, she was safe.

Perhaps she'd given voice to that fervent wish.

Three heads swivelled in her direction.

'Baby Sis? Oh, thank God.'

Nate reached her side and took her hand. The woman, a nurse in spotless scrubs, bustled towards her, smiling kindly. The third figure, the owner of that disturbing voice, came closer, too, but Lily instinctively shrank back. A bolt of pain shot through her right side.

'Where am I?' Her voice was a scrape of air in her throat.

'You're in the Prince Faisal Hospital. You were injured, but you're safe now,' Nate said, squeezing her hand.

The nurse fussed around her, checking tubes and charts.

'Injured?'

'There was an attack on the palace,' the stranger said. That voice... It was so achingly familiar... Who *was* he?

The memory hovered, just out of reach.

She'd been running. To warn someone.

Her gaze focused on Nate.

'Sabir? The staff?'

It wasn't Nate who answered.

'They're all safe, *habiba*.'

Sweetheart.

Fragments of memory formed.

There had been a night. A magical night when, out of love, she'd given herself to a man. She glanced at him. *This man.* He'd called her sweetheart. His big body had moved over her, inside her, coaxing her to the heights of ecstasy and she'd given him everything she was.

But what had she been worth to him? The position of mistress. Good enough to warm his bed. But nothing more.

Second-best.

The hurt and humiliation came flooding back.

She tugged her stepbrother closer. 'I don't want him here.'

Khaled flinched as if he'd been struck. 'Lily, let me explain.'

Frowning, the Sister planted herself firmly between him and her patient. He turned ashen, as if he couldn't quite believe what was happening.

'Come, now,' said Nate. 'I know he can be a difficult bugger, but does he really deserve to be sent out, hmm?'

Lily tightened her grip on his hand. *'Please.'*

Nate searched her face and finally, exhaling heavily, turned to the other man. 'I'm sorry, mate, but perhaps you'd better give us a moment.'

At first it looked as if Khaled would refuse. The muscles in his jaw working, he stared at Nate. But then, with a last anguished look at Lily, he spun away and left the room.

She crumpled in relief.

'Baby Sis, what the hell's going on?'

'Oh, Nate,' she wailed, 'I've been such a fool.'

The requested 'moment' stretched into four long, tortuous days. Days when Khaled thought he might actually lose his mind.

He'd barely kept it together during those terrible hours after the shooting, in the agonising wait while Lily was in surgery to remove two bullets. She'd taken one to the shoulder; another had collapsed her lung. Later, while she lay unconscious, he'd sat with her, holding her hand, willing her to come back to him.

But this waiting was a whole new level of torment.

She was recovering well, her doctors said. She was young and strong and responding to treatment as they would wish. There would be no lasting damage.

Physically.

Her state of mind was another matter. After what she'd been through that would take longer to be restored. His Highness would need to be patient.

Patient? He was practically wearing a hole in the floor outside her room.

Lily was being cared for in the same private wing of the hospital where his father was recuperating. After refusing point-blank to leave, Khaled had been given an adjacent guest suite, complete with office facilities. But he was barely in it. Sleep was fleeting. Neither could he work. Nothing held his focus.

Right now, all he cared about in the world was on the other side of that closed door.

And refusing to have anything to do with him.

Could he blame her? Hadn't he done the same as all those who'd gone before? Put her needs second to his with that shameful offer he could hardly bear to think of now.

The truth was, he'd panicked. With his father perhaps on his deathbed, and his enemies closing in, a dynastic marriage had seemed his only option. And taking Lily as his mistress had seemed the only way to keep her in his life.

What did he have now?

In his most desolate moments, may God forgive him, he'd been glad they'd been so careless as to make love without protection. She'd be irrevocably bound to him if she carried his child.

After being told she did not, he'd felt as if she were slipping even further away. As lost to him as if she'd died at his feet on the palace floor. Like Faisal. Gone for good.

How was he to bear it?

Nate remained the only visitor she'd see. He'd dashed from the marshes as soon as he'd heard Lily had been injured. Hours later had come news about the theft. The real culprit was unmasked. Had confessed, actually.

Lily had been right all along. The secretary was responsible. Penny had been secretly in love with George since she'd worked for him years earlier, and the bastard had played on that, persuading her to do his dirty work.

After the attempted coup, Penny had come to her senses and walked into a police station to confess all.

She'd done it for love, she'd said. The same reason Lily had thrown herself between a prince and his would-be assassin. Even though she'd believed her love wasn't reciprocated.

'You don't really want me.'

Those barely whispered words as she'd lain bleeding in his arms had been a lance through his heart. Would he ever get the chance to put things right?

For now, he'd done everything it was in his power to do.

All that was left to him was to watch the back and forth of her medical staff—and wait.

On the afternoon of the fourth day the doctors pronounced her to be progressing well enough to go home and continue her convalescence there.

Home? Khaled thought, slumped in a chair. Where was that to be?

'Khaled, mate.'

He looked up. Nate stood beside him.

'She wants to see you.'

He was out of his seat and halfway to her room before a firm hand to his shoulder stopped him.

'Wait. I need to say something. I know you love her. I've never seen you like this before. And I'm pretty sure she feels the same way. But whatever you did, I don't think she's forgiven you yet. If you can persuade her otherwise, you have my blessing. But I give you fair warning: hurt her again and I'll shoot you myself.'

He wouldn't argue with that. When the time came, would he demand anything less of those courting Amal or Hanan?

The last hurdle was the Sister, standing sentinel on the threshold, watching his approach with undisguised disapproval. 'We're right outside if she needs us,' she warned him, before reluctantly letting him pass and closing the door behind him.

The afternoon sun glinted towards him, gilding two armchairs set by the window. In one of them, dressed in a satin robe, her hair falling loose about her shoulders, a blanket over her knees against the chill of the air conditioning, Lily sat watching him.

She was porcelain-pale, except where faint bruising still marred her jaw and temple. Her right arm was cradled in a sling. His heart clenched tight. God, how close he'd come to losing her completely.

'Hello,' she said, sending him a watery smile.

It was a slug to the gut. She'd been crying and he knew it was his fault.

'Hello,' he answered, unable to move or remember any of the heartfelt speeches he'd planned to give.

'I'm sorry about the other day,' she said.

'You had every right to kick me out. I understand completely.'

'You do?'

'I offered you a role in my life that was shameful. You think I put you second.'

She chewed on her lip and her free hand plucked at the blanket. Yeah, that was exactly what she'd been thinking.

At last his legs propelled him forward. The Sister had placed the empty chair at least six feet from her precious patient. Well, to hell with that. He dragged it closer, so that when he sat his splayed knees encompassed hers.

She promptly shrank back.

To hell with that, too.

He leant forward, his elbows propped on his knees, and reached for her good hand, gently loosening its grip on the blanket and folding it in both his own.

'How are you?' he asked.

She blinked at him with big owl eyes. 'Getting better, thank you.' She studied their clasped hands. 'Nate said you've been here all the time.'

'I have.'

She peered up at him from beneath her lashes. 'There was no need. You shouldn't feel guilty for what happened.'

'After what you've been through because of me? I don't think I'll ever stop feeling guilty.'

In a small voice she said, 'I thought he was going to kill you. I was so scared.'

The bile rose in his throat. What she'd endured because of him...

'But you prevented it,' he said, squeezing her hand.

'Are you safe now? From the Hyde-Wallaces, I mean?'

'Yes. George's sons don't share his ambitions. Just as well.' His voice gained a menacing edge. 'I'd have crushed them all for what he did to you.'

She shuddered.

He'd frightened her.

He changed the subject. 'The doctors tell me you can leave tomorrow.'

She nodded, keeping her eyes downcast. 'They've arranged therapy for me in London, and a serviced apartment to convalesce in until I'm fit enough to go home.'

He didn't tell her that those arrangements had been made at his order and his expense. Even the 'apartment', which in reality was a penthouse in a luxurious Chelsea development, with every conceivable comfort and convenience she could need and medical staff on call, even though he hoped none of them would be needed.

'That's good,' he said. 'But I may have another option for you to consider.'

She tensed.

'No,' he swiftly reassured her. 'Not that.'

She watched him, wary and fey, as if she might slip from his grasp and dissolve on the slightest breeze.

Instinctively he drew her hand closer. This time she didn't resist.

Now, he thought, *ask her now.*

He took a steadying breath. 'I should begin by saying I don't deserve you. Certainly not after the way I've treated you, and not after what you've gone through because of me. But I have a question to ask. Though I must insist you don't give me your answer tonight. I want you to think of the consequences of saying yes. If that's what you decide. You may say no, of course, and that would be okay, too. Well, obviously not for me...'

Her pale brow creased in confusion.

Not surprising. Had a man ever made such a hash of proposing?

'What I mean is...' He paused, took another breath. 'Lily, will you marry me?'

She gave the tiniest gasp, but her fingers within his remained motionless. That didn't seem good. What if Nate had misjudged her feelings? What if she really couldn't forgive him?

He blundered on. 'I know I have no right to ask you. It's a selfish act. God knows, it's not an easy life. I should let you go.'

But then, oh, then his heart leapt. He felt her fingers move against his.

'What if you're what I want?' she said.

He raised his eyes to hers. Pale grey to determined hazel. And he dared to hope. But she had to understand that often her life would be hard.

'Perhaps what you want isn't good for you?' he said.

'I think it's for me to be the judge of that, don't you?'

Inside, he gave a crow of triumph. There she was. His fierce Lily.

'I know that you'll be good for me. Your stepbrother has already threatened violence if I don't take care of you, but it seems to be the other way round. You keep saving me,' he said. 'That summer, when I arrived in England, I wasn't sure how I was going to get through the next hour, let alone the rest of my life. But you…' He slid his thumb back and forth across her knuckles. 'A little kid, with a big heart, you showed me there was a way.'

She was watching him intently now. Waiting for more. For the words he knew she wanted—no, *needed* to hear. But after all that had happened how did he say them? The words he'd never said out loud before.

How did he tell he loved her?

He looked at their entwined fingers, his large hands engulfing her small one, which somehow looked perfect together.

'Marry her,' his father had said. His parting advice before being discharged from the hospital that morning.

'And inflict this life on her?' Khaled had replied.

The King had laughed. 'I thought the same thing about your mother. But she thrived on it. Lily reminds me of her. The same strength and courage.'

'She told me I should forgive myself.'

'A wise woman. You should listen to her.'

He'd nearly lost his father twice now, and still he'd never told him, never said...

'I'm sorry, Papa. I never meant to hurt Faisal.' His voice had cracked. 'He was my brother.'

'Oh, my boy, my boy,' his father had said, gathering him up. 'I've always known that. *Always*. But you would never let me close enough to tell you. We've worried for you so, your mother and I. But Lily's brought you back to us. So marry her. She'll make you happy.' He'd chuckled. 'And she'll drive you crazy, and challenge you in ways that no one else can.'

Hadn't she already done that? Forcing him to see his frailties and errors. Loving him in spite of it. Making him stronger.

Quietly, almost to himself, Khaled said now, 'My father is right. My mother understood from the start. I just never knew this was how it could be.'

Faisal was gone. Nothing could alter that. But to live a half-life as penance was an insult to his memory. This was the debt he owed his brother and his father: to live the best life he could.

It was time to forgive himself and embrace all that life had to offer.

To embrace love.

He raised his head, looked into the eyes of this incredible woman and felt a seismic shift, a sense of absolute rightness. Suddenly the words were easy.

'I'm yours,' he said, simply. 'I've been yours since the day you first put your hand in mine and led me out of that library. Perhaps I didn't know it then, but I know it now. I love you, Lily. Whatever stupid, dishonourable offer I made in the past, don't let that blind you to the truth. I'm in love with you, and I will be to my last breath.'

Whatever reaction he'd expected, it wasn't the one he got.

She dissolved into tears—great, heaving sobs that shook her whole body.

Completely flummoxed, he did the only thing he could think of. He carefully scooped her up and placed her in his lap.

She clung to his shirt as the tears rolled on. 'I'm sorry. I never used to be such a crier, but these days I can't seem to stop.'

He dug a handkerchief from his pocket and presented it to her. 'These are happy tears, though, aren't they?'

The relief, when she nodded, was indescribable.

She blew her nose, then said uncertainly, 'You really want me?'

'*Habiba*, I've been out of mind these past few days, because I thought you'd kicked me out of your life for good.'

'I was just scared,' she whispered.

'Me, too.'

'You were?'

She looked up at him. The violence of her ordeal was still reflected in the bruises to her skin and the shadows in her eyes, but to him she'd never been lovelier.

'Petrified. I knew I was in trouble from the moment you stepped out of that dressing room.'

She gave a weepy chuckle. 'I knew the minute you took your shirt off.'

'Shameless!' he said in mock outrage, pulling her close again, with her head on his shoulder, her hand on his chest.

She sighed in contentment and his heart swelled. But there was more for her to know—more pain he'd have moved mountains to spare her if he could.

'There is something else...'

She hid her face in his neck. 'If it's about my parents' marriage, I already know. George told me.'

Khaled said nothing, just pressed his cheek to her hair, lending her his strength, his love.

'It's okay,' she said. 'They cared for each other in their own way. Maybe not enough, and maybe too much. But that was their life. Not mine. I won't let it determine how I live any more.' She stroked the fabric of his shirt. 'But what happens to us if the truth comes out?'

'My lawyers may have found a loophole in the Constitution that we can use. As you're not Nabhani, they can argue that the constitutional rule doesn't apply. And if it comes out, and the people really can't accept it, then I'll step down in favour of Amal.'

She stared up at him. 'You'd give up the throne for me?'

'In a heartbeat. We'd live as private citizens—though I'd support Amal from the sidelines, of course.'

'And how is Aisha about all this?'

'Relieved to be spared marriage to me. She wants a different future for herself. Her father is furious, and refusing all contact with me, but I have great hopes for the Crown Prince. He's only seventeen, but growing in confidence. He's a reformer like me.'

'You'll be cultivating his friendship, then? He'll help with those water rights you need?'

'Yes, ma'am,' Khaled said, rewarding his newest advisor with a kiss.

And then they talked. About nothing of great importance. His favourite food. Her favourite films. Books they'd both read. Simple, homely things, but so important to heal them both.

Finally he spoke of Faisal. And for the first time in years he spoke of him without pain. Sharing the memories he had of him. Marvelling again at how Lily had the power to bring him such peace.

They spoke until the sun disappeared and the stars came out and Lily's head began to nod against him. Then he called for the nurses, saw her put to bed, and at last took his leave.

The day outside was blisteringly hot. Lily indulged in a moment's sympathy for the news teams Khaled said were camped out below.

'Whatever you decide,' he'd told her last night, 'I promise I'll always try to protect you from their intrusion.'

Curled up in his arms, with the strong beat of his heart against her cheek, she'd believed him. She'd never felt so safe, so cherished.

That had been just before he'd left. He'd been serious about her taking time to consider his proposal.

'But I can tell you now—' she'd said.

He'd pressed a finger to her lips. 'No. You must think about it and tell me tomorrow.'

Then, with a sweet, lingering kiss, he'd gone. Leaving the hospital for the first time since they'd both entered it over a week ago.

It had taken her all of ten seconds to decide. Whatever her life as a royal consort might hold, once she knew he loved her—he *loved* her—she'd had no doubts.

And today she was going back to the palace—going home, to be with Khaled.

'Good morning, *habiba*.'

The thought of him had conjured the man in the flesh. She heard his soft tread as he crossed the room behind her.

His lips brushed her hair. 'Did you sleep well?' he asked.

She nestled into his shoulder, reaching round to capture a hand and draw it about her waist. His returned caress was gentle, careful of her healing shoulder, of her arm still in its sling.

'Yes,' she replied, actually answering a different question entirely.

'Oh? Was there nothing you had to think about?'

'Yes, but it was all rather pleasant.'

'Pleasant? Might I allow myself to be encouraged by that?'

He'd moved the heavy fall of her hair aside so he could press kisses behind her ear. She shuddered in delight, tipping her head to give him greater access. 'Yes, I think perhaps you might.'

A ripple of tension left his body. He hadn't been sure of her answer, then.

'You look practically edible in this dress,' he murmured against her skin.

It was the one she'd tried that day at the store. She'd requested it be sent from the palace. Along with one or two other items.

'How am I going to keep my hands off you?'

Before she could ask why he saw the need to, he tipped her face up to his with his fingertips.

'But I'll allow myself this,' he said, slanting his mouth across hers in a kiss so filled with the promise of everything to come that Lily swooned against him.

The next instant he lifted his head. The Sister had entered, with a hospital porter pushing a wheelchair.

Lily frowned at it. 'I don't need that. I'm perfectly capable of walking.'

'Your Highness, Miss Marchant is still recovering, and under no circumstances should she walk out of the hospital.'

'For once, madam, you and I agree,' he said, and swept Lily up in his arms.

She squeaked in protest.

'I know. You can take care of yourself,' Khaled said as he bore her away. 'But will you please learn to accept my help sometimes, woman?'

'Yes,' she said, smiling. 'I will.' And she reached out a hand to trail it through the black silk of his hair. How she loved his hair, and the joy of being able to touch him.

He stepped into the lift. 'I've heard you say yes to me several times this morning, and I think I know what you're really saying.'

She gazed beatifically up at him,

'Don't distract me,' he scolded, 'I have something more to say. My parents and sisters are waiting at home for you. And Nate, too. The press, inevitably, are waiting outside. But I want you to know you can still say no. I've put you through so much. I'm asking you to give up so much. Are you sure I'm what you want?' he asked.

He was looking so uncertain she took his face tenderly

in her hands, wanting to banish all his fears. She'd fight dragons for this man.

'You may be a grumpy workaholic, and in my experience far too bossy and autocratic...' His expression clouded over. 'But I'm yours,' she added quickly. 'I've been yours since the very first moment I saw you in my stepfather's library. I knew it then. I've always known it. I'm in love with you and I will be to my last breath. So, yes, I couldn't be more sure.'

They'd arrived at the foyer. As he crossed to the exit his expression softened. The anxiety faded and the most delicious crinkles formed at the corners of his eyes. Another step and the doors to the entrance were swept wide, revealing them at last to the banks of photographers and waiting news crews.

And as the massed cameras went crazy, suddenly there it was. More dazzling, more breathtaking than any photograph. Because the whole force of it was focused on her alone.

A smile.

The smile.

His smile.

Oh, wow. She'd happily devote entire weeks of her life trying to coax that from him again.

He halted on the steps.

'Ladies and gentlemen, allow me to officially present Miss Lily Marchant.' His smile widened as he gazed down at her. 'Who has just done me the great honour of consenting to be my wife.'

Bombarded with congratulations and questions, Lily obliged the cameras and reporters with a few waves and smiles of her own until they were moved back by Rais and his team and Khaled, still beaming, strode through it all, carrying his precious burden to the waiting limo.

'Well, that was an experience.' Lily laughed, as the car pulled away.

'Are you okay?'

Khaled was mindful that this was her first time outside the hospital since the attack, and only her second experience of a press pack. Though she'd handled it with aplomb...

He narrowed his eyes on her. 'Did you actually just pose for them?'

She twinkled at him. 'My mother was an actress. It must be in my genes.'

'Lily, the truth about your parents' marriage may still come out. It may not all be easy from here.'

She stopped his explanation with a kiss.

'I know,' she answered. 'But as long as I have you I'll get through it.

She'd slid closer, and her fingers were in his hair again.

Damn, that felt good. But he'd done some hard thinking last night. He'd treated her shamefully from start to finish and he'd vowed to make it up to her. They'd be married soon, but before then he'd woo her properly—and that started with a little restraint on his part.

He captured her hand, kissed it, then placed it firmly back in her lap.

'I thought we could marry at the end of next month. In five weeks. Until then you'll be staying in the waterfront penthouse. We'll go on dates, and I'll visit, of course, but only when Nate or my mother is present to chaperon.'

There. Boundaries clearly established.

'Dates? I see...' she said demurely—which, he'd realise later, should have made him deeply suspicious.

She tapped at the window. 'No one can see us in here, can they?'

'What? No, the glass is one-way,' he answered, distracted by her meek acceptance of his plans.

'And they can't hear us?'

'Only the driver and front seat passenger when you use that intercom button.'

She pressed it.

'Rais?'

'Yes, madam?'

'His Highness would like to take the scenic route home. The one that takes…ooh…let's say about half an hour.'

'The thirty-minute scenic route?' Khaled heard the suppressed laughter of his security chief. 'Of course, madam.'

She lifted her finger from the button.

'Oh, dear. Looks like we're stuck in here for a while, and without a chaperon.' She walked her fingers up his thigh. 'I guess we're just going to have to improvise.'

'Lily.' He caught her wrist. 'We won't be doing any *improvising* until after we're married.'

She actually pouted at him. It was adorable. How was he going to keep his hands off her for five minutes, never mind five weeks?

'Well, that doesn't quite work for me,' she said, watching him with lambent eyes. 'Perhaps I can change your mind?'

His heart stuttered as she did a little shimmy, hitching her dress up her thighs. He caught a flash of her panties.

Tiny. Pink. With pearls and a bow.

The Bridegroom-Slayer.

He was done for.

She straddled his lap.

'What about your injuries?' he said, desperately searching for something to firm up his resolve whilst a certain part of his anatomy was enthusiastically firming up all on its own.

'This hand works fine.' She waggled the free one at him, then demonstrated how fine it was by unbuttoning his shirt and exposing his chest to her hungry gaze.

As her fingers dropped lower, found his fly and freed him, he tried to say *Stop*, but it came out more as a strangled, *'Ohh…'*

'Now,' she said, squeezing her hand around him, 'about these five weeks of abstinence…'

His head fell back as he moaned his pleasure. 'But I was going to woo you properly.'

'What if I prefer being wooed improperly? Don't you think this is much nicer?'

She lifted herself up, pushing the thong to one side before sinking back down and taking him inside her.

He was panting now. 'What is it with you and the back seat of limos?'

'It's not the car.' She feathered kisses along his jaw. 'It's the man. He's as sexy as hell. Now, stop talking and make love to me.'

'I'll never be fully in control of anything again, will I?' he groaned, finally surrendering and lifting his hips to thrust into her.

'Perhaps not,' she answered a little breathlessly, 'but imagine all the fun you're going to have.'

Apart from her bare thighs and rucked-up hem, her dress and hair were otherwise pristinely in place. He, however, was a mess. His shirt and trousers were half off, and his hair was probably sticking out in all directions. He suspected she'd step from this car a little flushed, but otherwise as neat as a pin. Whereas he, even after he'd tidied himself, would look exactly what he was: seduced and thoroughly ravished.

My God, he thought, *this woman.*

And a bubble of laughter and happiness rose up, exploding like a starburst inside him. He was smiling as she bent her head to kiss him.

'See,' she said. 'You're enjoying yourself already.'

The scenic route back to the palace was, indeed, spectacularly scenic, and the limousine, travelling at an unusually sedate pace, gave the occupants of the back seat every opportunity to enjoy the view.

But neither noticed any of it.

Lily and her very *happy* prince were otherwise occupied. Improvising all the ways she could make him smile. Again and again and again…

* * * * *

COMING SOON!

MILLS & BOON

Coming next month

BOUND BY HER RIVAL'S BABY
Maya Blake

A breeze washed over Amelie and she shivered.

Within one moment and the next, Atu was shrugging off his shirt.

"W-what are you doing?" she blurted as he came towards her.

Another mirthless twist of his lips. "You may deem me an enemy but I don't want you catching cold and falling ill. Or worse."

She aimed a glare his way. "Not until I've signed on whatever dotted line you're determined to foist on me, you mean?"

That look of fury returned. This time accompanied by a flash of disappointment. As if he had the right to such a lofty emotion where she was concerned. She wanted, no *needed* to refuse this small offer of comfort.

Return to her room and come up with a definite plan that removed him from her life for good.

So why was she drawing the flaps of his shirt closer? Her fingers clinging to the warm cotton as if she'd never let it go?

She must have a made a sound at the back of her throat because his head swung to hers, his eyes holding hers for an age before he exhaled harshly.

His lips firmed and for a long stretch he didn't speak. "You need to accept that I'm the best bet you have right now. There's no use fighting. I'm going to win eventually. How soon depends entirely on you."

The implacable conclusion sent icy shivers coursing

through her. In that moment she regretted every moment of weakness. Regretted feeling bad for invoking that hint of disappointment in his eyes.

She had nothing to be ashamed of. Not when vanquishing her and her family was his sole, true purpose.

She snatched his shirt from her shoulders, crushing her body's instant insistence on its warmth as she tossed it back to him. "You should know by now that threats don't faze me. We're still here, still standing after all you and your family have done. So go ahead, do your worst."

Held head high, she whirled away. She only made it three steps before he captured her wrist. She spun around, intent on pushing him away.

But that ruthlessness was coupled with something else. Something hot and blazing and all-consuming in his eyes.

She belatedly read it as lust before he was tugging her closer, wrapping one hand around her waist and the other in her hair. "This stubborn determination is admirable. Hell, I'd go so far as to say it's a turn on because God knows I admire strong, wilful women," he muttered, his lips a hairsbreadth from hers, "but fiery passion will only get you so far."

"And what are you going to do about it?" she taunted a little too breathlessly. Every cell in her body traitorously strained towards him, yearning for things she knew she shouldn't want, but desperately needed anyway.

He froze, then a strangling sound leaving his throat, he slammed his lips on hers.

He kissed her like he was starved for it. *For her.*

Continue reading
BOUND BY HER RIVAL'S BABY
Maya Blake

Available next month
www.millsandboon.co.uk

LET'S TALK
Romance

For exclusive extracts, competitions
and special offers, find us online:

- facebook.com/millsandboon
- @MillsandBoon
- @MillsandBoonUK

Get in touch on 01413 063232

For all the latest titles coming soon, visit
millsandboon.co.uk/nextmonth

MILLS & BOON
MEDICAL
Pulse-Racing Passion

Set your pulse racing with dedicated, delectable doctors in the high-pressure world of medicine, where emotions run high and passion, comfort and love are the best medicine.

Eight Medical stories published every month, find them all at:

millsandboon.co.uk